Snow Sisters

Also by Carol Lovekin and available from Honno

Ghostbird

Snow
Sisters

by

Carol Lovekin

HONNO MODERN FICTION

First published by Honno Press

'Ailsa Craig', Heol y Cawl, Dinas Powys, Wales, CF64 4AH

1 2 3 4 5 6 7 8 9 10

A catalogue record for this book is available from the British Library.
Published with the financial support of the Welsh Books Council.

ISBN 978-1-909983-70-0 (paperback)
ISBN 978-909983-71-7 (ebook)

Cover design: G Preston
Cover image: © Shutterstock, Inc
Text design: Elaine Sharples
Printed in Great Britain by Gomer Press

For
Janet Thomas
Mentor

"Sometimes it snows in April"

~ Prince

Part One

My name is Angharad and I am not mad.

My heart is made of fragments: of bindweed and despair; thinner than skin and bloodless and my story is as old as the moon. It is one of love and death, as are the stories most women tell. These two things make up the fabric of our lives, although I do not speak of romantic love. I refer to the kind that ought to provide a child with protection and in the end can destroy her.

The birds saw everything.

Unconcerned in their courtship and quarrelling, what they witnessed meant less than nothing. And yet, years later, their offspring still circle; continue to observe this place, and my unfinished story. High in the branches of trees, wild crows perch, rooks shout; sparrows flutter, brown and gregarious. And above the house gulls drift like litter.

However it may have looked, regardless of how the story has since been told, the birds knew what happened was no fault of mine.

My impressions are little more than a nod to memory. As a record of the truth they may be ambiguous. I may struggle to write them down. No matter. They must suffice until I am braver.

It wasn't that I was mad; it was what they did to me that made me that way.

Present

Memory is prompted in many ways.

Mine is triggered by the gulls, exultant; crying and skimming the high chimneys of the house like white gliders. It is April and the lilac is out. Gull House is famous for its lilac.

The scent is mesmeric. I inhale it, half expecting Allegra to appear, a swathe of blossom across her arm, cigarette smoke and the smell of turpentine trailing behind her. Languid and dazzling, bangles tinkling; the latest barbed comment loitering behind a raised eyebrow. My mother's beauty was so startling it stopped people in their tracks. They stared at her and forgot how to speak. Not that it mattered. She soon filled in the gaps.

She had been an artists' model and then, an artist. She had the look of a stylish gypsy, what with the beads and floating frocks, the ever-present pack of tarot cards. She read them daily, for herself, regardless of the fact she barely understood what the images meant. Allegra made the world to fit her view of it and the spiritual world could take it or leave it. She hurled herself at life and when life fought back, my mother threw a tantrum.

I have returned to my grandmother's house. (We called her Nain – the old Welsh name.) Her given name was Mared and she told us she was a witch; told us the sweet things she did for us were good spells and the only kind that counted.

Preferring to walk up to the house, I've left my car on the road. Out on the narrow lane it's easy to miss the entrance. Elegant iron gates open onto a short, steep drive bounded by feral shrubs.

Gull House is made from weathered stone the colour of

storms, oak beams remembering where they once grew. It tilts into wild, sea-born winds and as children it was easy to believe, on a stormy night the wind might lift the whole thing and blow it away.

'No chance,' Nain told us. 'It's made of sturdy stuff this house; it'll take more than a bit of wind to shift it.'

It is a place of nooks and crannies (or as Nain insisted, 'crooks and nannies') with unexpected deep cupboards large enough to hide two little girls. And it seemed to us to possess a sense of the past redolent with the murmurs of people from other lives.

It's a tall Victorian house and approaching it people are taken aback, expecting grander proportions. Instead it's neat, secluded and undemanding. To the left, nearest the road, a small tower assumes a space that isn't there – a decorative affectation straight out of childhood legend and housing only a single room with an attic space above it.

Meredith called it Rapunzel's tower.

The gable end faces the garden, overlooking where it turns in on itself, and disappears towards the wood. Across the stone walls, gnarled branches of wisteria hang in twisted blue ropes. The wisteria has been here as long as the house.

Nain said the Victorians called it the clinging tree. 'Long before though, in Japan, where it originated, it symbolised unrequited love and they named it the Wisteria Maiden.'

She called the one in her blue garden her wistful tree and it wasn't until I was older that I understood the significance.

Nain is dead now and so is Allegra, too young, her cracked heart finally breaking like glass carelessly handled. Gull House is mine: mine and my sister's. Meredith too is gone, although as far as I know she's still alive. The last time I wrote, to an address in Greece, it was to tell her about Nain's death. (The last time I saw her, asked what would bring her back, she'd answered, 'The kind of magic we used to believe in.')

My sister never doubted the presence of magic and when she

was five years old she told me she could grow flowers from her fingertips. Her solemn conviction was such, I half believed her.

There is no longer any magic here and I'm not sure there ever was. We were barely in our teens the year we left, the year it happened. And Meredith, my vivid sister, with her genius for being unlike other people, had possessed an imagination uninhibited enough to conjure any manner of fanciful notions. She said the house whispered secrets to her though try as I might I could never quite believe in a sentient building.

Other than the gulls and a sigh of breeze through the grass there are no other sounds and, as far as I can tell, no ghosts. There is something missing though and I realise it's the other birds – the sparrows and chaffinches, the curious rooks. I'm standing in a broad and birdless silence, and it is as if I'm being watched.

The sky is feathered with light, and a vague whiff of the sea filters through the air. Dark stretches of woodland as dense as legend still form a backdrop to the house – the shadows more solid than the trees casting them. They merge in a seamless, interlocking frieze.

In my bag is a packet of sandwiches and a bunch of keys I haven't set eyes on for twenty-one years. I have fretted about coming back, still raw in the aftermath of my beloved grandmother's recent death. Torn between my longing to return to Wales and nervous about what I might find, how it might shape any decision I make about the house.

Carla says I have to do what my heart tells me.

'Stay safe,' she said before I left, tracing the long line of my cheek with her finger.

We are slender, we Pryce women. We have cheekbones, and collarbones curving like bows under our pale skin, and we don't look strong enough to lift a log. It's a false impression. My sister and I discovered we could do almost anything we wanted.

And we have hair; an excess of it: wilful, red haloed hair you wouldn't be surprised to find a family of robins nesting in.

'Come back, Verity,' Carla said, 'and tell me all about it.'

I kissed her and told her not to worry. There's nothing for me there, I insisted; there will be nothing to tell.

Meredith would no doubt have had it otherwise. She believed in ghosts, even though, before it happened, she swore she'd never seen one.

One

Meredith Pryce was exactly the kind of child who might be seduced by notions of a ghost.

It came as no surprise to Verity when her sister decided she was being haunted. Earlier, before Allegra was up, Meredith had announced she was bored, and Verity knew her sister was dangerous when she was bored.

'Find something to do.'

'There isn't anything *to* do,' Meredith said. 'We live in the back of beyond. It's nineteen seventy-nine and we're relics. We may as well be living a hundred years ago. Why doesn't anything spectacular happen to us? Why don't we ever go places?' She frowned. 'It's ... unpardonable.'

Verity looked up and pressed her lips together. Meredith regularly dotted her sentences with precocious words. There would be a pause before she produced her newest discovery and while Verity admired her sister's confidence, she couldn't always resist the urge to mock. It wasn't unkindness; Verity was good-natured and generous but her flamboyant younger sister could make her presence known simply by entering a room. Verity relied on small victories.

'Don't laugh, it isn't funny.' Meredith swung her legs back and forth against the leg of the chair. 'We never go anywhere, we don't *do* anything.'

'It could be worse; we could be going to school.'

If only...

Verity suppressed the words. The idea of school terrified her sister.

Only slightly mollified, Meredith agreed. 'I suppose.'

Verity wasn't in the mood for Meredith. 'Stop kicking the chair, you'll break it. And your breakfast's getting cold.'

Inside, Gull House was as scaled down as its exterior, squeezed into the space it occupied. Hints of the past clung like the cobwebs in the corners. The kitchen was warm and crowded, the windows steamed up and the scent of yesterday's ashes lay in the iron grate. A tarnished copper warming pan hung on the stone fireplace. In front of the range huddled two low-slung, dilapidated cane chairs draped with rugs. From a wooden rack, tights and socks and blouses trailed like tired bunting. Dirty plates, an opened packet of biscuits, pencils, exercise books and an overflowing ashtray littered the table.

Meredith slapped her spoon against the despised porridge. 'Stupid chair's probably got woodworm anyway. Everything in this house is falling to pieces. And why don't you ever answer me properly?'

'Why don't you ask sensible questions?'

Why do you pretend to be contemptuous of everything when wild horses wouldn't drag you from Gull House?

'We go places,' Verity said. 'We go to the pictures.'

'We go to the pictures if Allegra decides to give us the cash.'

'We go to the beach.'

'Well, get us.' Slap, slap went the spoon. 'Boring.'

'The beach isn't boring.'

Meredith kicked the chair again, frowning at the bowl.

'Please, Meredith, don't make a fuss. There's no other food in the house and until I can persuade Allegra to go shopping it's the only thing on offer. Those daft chickens have only laid three eggs in a week.'

'It's revolting. I'd rather starve. And don't call my chickens daft. You know Legbars are superior and choosy about when they lay.' Meredith flung her hair over her shoulder: hair like her mother's – an out of control firework, so red it made her skin look white.

8

Her face was sharp and knowing. One moment her grey eyes were dark as puddles, the next as brilliant as diamonds and flecked with danger.

The force of Meredith's anger could shatter windows.

'I'm sorry,' Verity said. She was wary around anger. 'Do your best.'

'I'll leave it if you don't mind.'

The door from the hall opened and Allegra swept in, swathed in smoke and a fringed, cream shawl splashed with great scarlet poppies worn over a thin dressing gown.

'My God, it's colder than a day in Bangor.' She rattled around making coffee. 'What the hell is that?' Poking in the porridge saucepan, she grimaced.

'There's no food,' Verity said. 'Someone needs to go shopping.'

'Later, I promise.' Allegra wound her hair into a knot, fixing it with a pencil she picked out of the clutter on the table.

Allegra Pryce was a woman without a shred of self-awareness, and a contradiction: one minute dismissive and terse, the next full of extravagant laughing praise and admiration. When her work was going well, she would lavish attention on the girls; the other version of her was to be avoided. Her unedited enthusiasms, and her evaluation of her daughters, ruled their lives. Meredith was her darling. With Verity her compliments nearly always came out as criticisms and, no matter how she smiled when she paid them, her words could hurt. Nothing was ever her fault and both girls were regularly treated to silence, which, when directed at Verity, could go on for days, particularly if she'd pointed out a flaw in her mother.

'And what are you up to this morning, my sweet baby brat?' she said, setting down her coffee and sidling close to Meredith.

'Nothing, my irritatingly predictable parent.'

Allegra raised her eyebrows. 'Darling, no one can be up to nothing. There's no such thing.' She pulled her tobacco pouch and a box of matches from the pocket of her dressing gown. Pushing a collection of bangles up her arms she worked a pile of tobacco along a brown cigarette paper and rolled it up. It left a trail and she pinched it off, tucked it into the pouch, lit the cigarette, and inhaled, let out the smoke in a thin stream. A strand of tobacco caught on her lip and she picked it off with a practised gesture.

'You *reek*.' Meredith moved her head and wrinkled her nose.

'Sorry, darling.' Allegra coughed, waved the cigarette behind her shoulder. 'If you're bored, go and feed the chickens. You love doing that.'

'I've already fed them. I always feed them.'

'I know; you're such a good girl.'

Meredith batted away the compliment as if it were a bothersome fly. 'There's nothing to eat.'

'You can go shopping with Verity. She said she'd go.'

'No, I didn't.'

'Oh, do what you like, boring people.' Meredith threw a wide-eyed look across the table. 'Since there's no such thing as nothing, I'm off in search of something.'

Before either Verity or her mother could come up with a suitable reply, Meredith disappeared, letting the door slam behind her.

'Honestly. She's impossible.' Allegra leaned back in her chair. 'Whatever does that mean?'

Verity said she had no idea. 'And I don't care. I can't ever remember being that annoying.' She picked up Meredith's bowl, scraped the remains of porridge into the chicken feed pail and dumped it on top of a pile of unwashed dishes on the draining board. 'Or such a show-off.'

'She's just expressing herself. You should try it,' Allegra said. 'You take after him of course.'

If Verity was surprised by this sidewayss mention of her father, she gave no indication. It was as if Idris had never existed. There were no remnants of his life, no pictures or keepsakes (unless you counted the pearl ring Allegra wore on her little finger). Anything that might serve as a clue was missing. Allegra, who must have memories, rationed them, dishing out clues like rare treats.

Or occasional punishments.

Neither Verity nor Meredith cared enough to pursue the matter of their father. Even their grandmother, who didn't have a bad word to say about anyone, couldn't make him sound worth missing. ('A well-meaning rogue who vanished into thin air.')

Meredith declared this was stupid. If the air people were supposed to vanish into was thin, you'd be able to see them.

Verity ran water into the sink. 'Why can't you do the shopping, Mam? You're supposed to be the parent.'

'Oh, please, don't be bourgeois, Verity. How old are you?'

Lately, her mother's dislike had developed an edge, as if Verity had been elevated to a new level of contempt.

'You know perfectly well how old I am and if you don't, I'm not helping you out.'

'Sixteen; and quite old enough to have gained some empathy.'

Verity could hardly believe her ears.

Allegra drained her coffee. She slid a black velvet bag out of her other pocket. 'And being unkind about your little sister doesn't show you in a good light either. Jealousy's such an unattractive look.'

'I'm still only fifteen.' Verity refrained from saying she wasn't jealous of Meredith. It was an old argument she was unlikely to win. 'And she's not so little either. We're practically twins.'

At times, the seventeen months between Verity and her sister could feel like joyful minutes passing too quickly. At others they stretched, weighing her down with a guilty resentment.

Allegra rolled her eyes, puffed smoke and gave another cough, cleared her chest and the sound of it made Verity frown.

'Have you got a cold coming? Or is it too many fags?'

Allegra didn't reply. She removed a pack of tarot cards from the velvet bag, gave it a quick shuffle and turned one over. They were thin and worn at the edges.

11

'See?' Resting the cigarette on the lip of the overflowing ashtray, she nodded. 'The Hanged Man.'

Verity thought he looked ridiculous in his bright red tights with his leg tucked up, his bland, upside-down face and yellow hair sticking out like straw. She never asked for an interpretation of the cards knowing she wouldn't have long to wait for one.

'Sacrifice!' Allegra smiled broadly. 'The cards don't lie.'

These cards don't have a choice.

Allegra carried on. 'You could quite easily pick up some things for me. I have work to do, and you don't. '

'How do you know I don't have work to do?' Verity began sorting dirty plates and mugs. 'I need to go to the library for a start.'

'In which case, what's the problem? It's on your way.'

'It's the principle. And shouldn't you be setting us some work? We haven't done any maths for weeks.'

'Oh, maths. No one needs maths, not these days.' Allegra dismissed arithmetic with a wave.

'Everyone needs maths.'

Allegra had stopped listening. 'It'll be bloody freezing in the conservatory. I hope there's some paraffin for the heater. God, it's cold.' She pulled the shawl closer to her body. 'It ought to be warming up by now, it's April for heaven's sake.'

Verity squeezed washing-up liquid into the water. 'It snowed in April the year Meredith was born. Nain said so.'

'A freak of nature.'

'Well, it feels like snow to me.'

'Nonsense,' Allegra said, gathering the cards and slipping them into her pocket. 'Don't be ridiculous.'

Verity wasn't so sure. She had a nose for the weather and made the most of what she – and probably her mother – viewed as her only accomplishment.

My mother had a cultivated, evasive eye which could, in a moment, become critical.

Nowhere in my description of her will you find a woman you will warm to. It is not my intention. I do not want you to love her. She was a woman who kept her counsel and who occasionally showed flashes of malice rendering her cold and unapproachable. In contrast, my father was a brash, egotistical man who began talking as he entered a room giving no one else a chance to order their thoughts or conjure a contradiction.

Mama began many of her sentences with a question which tended to confuse me since the answer was invariably self evident.

'Aren't you resting?'

(Clearly not, since I am standing in front of you.)

'Haven't you finished yet?'

I would glance at my sewing, sense the implicit rebuke, and apologise.

Caught reading, she would ask if I was doing 'that' again, and before I could answer, inform me I was ruining both my eyes and my chances.

What chances these might be I was at a loss to understand.

And I had a brother. As befitted a son, he was sent away to school. There was, my father stated, no profit in educating a girl, as if I were an entry in one of his bank ledgers.

Two years older than me, my brother had been a cruel, sly child. Once, when I was seven, I found him in the garden, home from school and bored, deliberately picking the wing off a butterfly.

'Please,' I begged, 'leave the poor thing alone.'

Held fast in his hand, the dying butterfly twitched.

My brother grinned and with a slow precise movement, tightened his finger and thumb on the other wing.

'No!' I ran at him and he dodged, grinned, and, running his tongue over his lips, pulled off the remaining wing.

'It's all yours,' he said as he flicked the tiny, mutilated body in my direction.

When I told my mother she said I was making a fuss, to ignore the ways of boys, and reminded me that no one liked a tattle-tale.

As he grew older, my brother turned into a bully, arrogance making both his face and his intentions as ugly as they were clear. By the time I was seventeen, I had grown to fear him with his eyes that saw everything and understood nothing.

This is no bedtime story, little girl. Do you have courage enough for both of us?

Two

Some days are too beautiful to be real.

The sky turns to silver and you know anything could happen. Verity decided to pretend the day was out of a storybook, she could mark the page and keep it for later. It was so cold she could barely breathe.

Her mother was right – it was far too cold for April.

My mother is always right.

For once she didn't mind. Maybe it would snow after all.

The Pryce sisters' favourite book was *The Lion, the Witch and the Wardrobe*, and they knew it by heart. They were so fond of it they had a copy each. Snow was their favourite thing in the entire world and they loved it the way they loved their grandmother's stories about it.

Mared could remember snow on Christmas day when she was a girl.

'You should have seen it in nineteen twenty-seven,' she told them. 'Up by my friend Jenni Lloyd's farm you couldn't see the tops of the fence posts. Gethin and I were playing there and we had to stay over three nights. We built a snow house in Jenni's mam's garden.'

Verity and Meredith said it sounded like heaven.

'Well, yes, it's not all fun and games though. Not for the farmers. In forty-seven, when your mam was little, the snow was deep enough to bury sheep. It was still thick on the hills in March.'

She told them about the Big Freeze, the year Verity was born.

'Your mother carried you right the way through that snow. It was so bad it made the news. Then, before Christmas, a blizzard blew in and the drifts were twenty-foot high. They said in town the sea froze. Lasted months that snow did.'

Mared said she thought Verity must have been able to sense it from the womb. 'And then it snowed in April the year Meredith was born. It's no wonder the pair of you are obsessed with the stuff.'

Verity eyed the sky, willing it to snow, wanting it to make everything clean and new. She thought about the list in her pocket. If Mared still lived with them she would understand about the shopping. She wasn't afraid to challenge Allegra. And she understood how annoying Meredith could be, even if she refused to take sides.

'Sister love matters,' she told them. 'You have to look out for each other.'

Once Meredith was born, Verity was relegated by her mother from 'pleasant little thing' to the odd one. It made no difference. From the moment their eyes met, Verity loved her sister with all her heart and there was no jealousy, however hard Allegra had tried to cultivate it.

'Meredith is so pretty,' she insisted.

'The prettiest baby ever,' Verity agreed, quick as you like. 'Far prettier than I am.'

Whenever she said things like this, she had an impression of confusion, as if she had found her mother out in some act she was slightly ashamed of.

By the age of nine months, Meredith could talk. (She could soon say whole sentences and from then on said the first thing that came into her mouth, which for the rest of her life would get her into no end of trouble.)

'Pretty *and* clever!' declared Allegra.

Out on the lane, Verity coasted to a stop. She leaned on the handlebars afraid she might cry.

It isn't that children don't understand adult feelings or motives. They understand them only too well. It's because children don't have the words they're powerless.

I want my mother to be superior to us, the way mothers are supposed to be.

There were times Verity felt contempt for Allegra with her clichés and her silly tarot cards, her ability to be in a room and yet absent, hovering on the edges of conversations like a vaguely interested passer-by.

And I want my grandmother to come back.

When Mared left Gull House, Verity had been eleven. Like Meredith she was frightened by the idea of London, the word itself rounded with a threatening kind of purpose. In the intervening years, they'd visited only twice, Allegra complaining each time that she had better things to do.

Better than what, the sisters had wondered.

Neither of them thought much of London. It was too vast, too frantic and clamorous, as if it wanted to devour them.

London took her beloved grandmother and though she understood Mared had to look after her brother, whose dementia made him too vulnerable to live alone, Verity was bereft.

Allegra's response to her mother's defection had been outrage. She saw no difference between this and her husband abandoning her.

'Everyone deserts me,' she wailed.

She isolated herself, declared Mared a traitor and the few friends she had managed to make soon gave up on her. From time to time she found herself drawn to unsuitable men. (Any suitable ones soon ran a mile.) Allegra dared men to let her down and sooner or later they did.

Verity thought her mother, with the over-stated cool more suited to a teenager, probably missed Mared more than she would admit. Mared left and it was as if the clouds blowing across the sky stilled. When the wind picked up again, like Verity and her sister, the clouds had lost their way.

17

Hooking her foot underneath the pedal she set off again. She rode along the path, the thin river on one side, the flat grey sea on the other, the wheels of the bicycle ticking, her scarf flying. Pale colours surrounded her: a light-saturated sky – the sea tinged with milky blue. Gulls, the white of them as bright as clouds, followed her for a while before turning back to their own territory.

The tyres rumbled over stones and tufts of grass. As she left the path, the wheels bounced, hit the tarmac and the rumble became a swish. She pedalled over a bridge, past rows of houses, tall and ice cream coloured. Buildings reeled by: hotels, a dry-cleaners, a chemist, along the promenade, past the pier stretching out to the ocean collecting seaweed and barnacles. She cycled up a narrow street, pushing hard, her breath coming in short gasps.

The library was an elegant building and ought to have been on the seafront, preening alongside the grand hotels. Instead, it was squashed between two tall houses and somehow diminished. A steep gable reached above stone walls dressed with sandstone; sturdy wooden doors opened onto a lobby, the walls lined with glazed green tiles. Stairs led up to a reference department. The public area on the ground floor set an example by holding its breath, hushing the occupants into silence.

Verity was never without a book; she could walk and read, and never once trip up. She favoured folk tales, quirky novels laced with legend and old magic. For a rational child, her choices might have appeared odd. Her life was odd; the unreality of these made-up stories was the perfect antidote.

Lifting her books out of the bicycle basket Verity went inside. Warmth enfolded her and she took a long breath of contentment. She was at home in the library and could stay as long she liked. If she was quiet and didn't bother anyone, no one bothered her. Naturally self-conscious and reflective, Verity found the library a kind place, expecting nothing more of her than that she appreciated what it had to offer. Nobody cared about any troubles she might have because nobody was aware of them.

'Hello, Verity.' Miss Jenkins, tall, thin and clever, regarded Verity with a mixture of affection and preoccupation. Her deep-set eyes reminded Verity of the bluebells in her grandmother's garden. 'How are you?'

'I'm well, thanks, Miss Jenkins.' Verity placed her books on the counter.

'Excellent. No fines. Good girl.'

Verity never accumulated fines.

Miss Jenkins sighed. 'No Mr Tallis today. I've hardly had a moment. I'm sure he can't help having a cold, but it's most inconvenient.'

Verity walked through the hushed room, running her eyes along the serried banks of books. From the high windows light fell in dusty bands. Someone coughed, another whispered – loud in the silence – and was instantly shushed.

Libraries are full of coughers. No wonder Mr Tallis has a cold. It's a miracle we don't all have one.

'Have you read this?' Miss Jenkins came up behind her. 'Third part of her Arthurian Saga? Mary Stewart. You like her, don't you?'

'Oh, yes, I do.' Verity ran her finger over the cover. 'I've read the other ones.'

'I thought so. I kept it for you. You're lucky, it came in today; you'll be the first to borrow it.'

With little money available for books, a newly published library copy was the next best thing. As Miss Jenkins date-stamped the pristine paper inside the cover, Verity experienced a thrill of pleasure.

'Thank you so much,' she said, a grin breaking out on her face.

'It's always a pleasure to encourage a serious reader, Verity.' Miss Jenkins smiled back. 'You should consider librarianship, you know. You could do a lot worse.'

I already have.

It was a secret she wasn't ready to share. She couldn't be sure Miss Jenkins might not let it slip to Allegra. The less her mother knew about her ambitions, the better.

'I will.'

Tucking the book into her shopping bag, Verity walked out into the chilly afternoon. She freewheeled down the hill and, drawing to a halt outside a small grocery shop, propped her bicycle against the wall.

'Butter. Three tins of beans and the tea. Bacon, eggs, strawberry jam. Large bloomer. Milk.' The woman behind the counter smiled. 'That it, lovely?'

'Tobacco and cigarette papers please, Mrs Trahaearn.'

'Right you are.'

Verity swallowed, and her skin flamed. 'And…'

'It's all right, *cariad*. I'll tuck it under the rest.'

Verity watched as Mrs Trahaearn slipped the bottle of gin under the bread, packed the rest of the groceries into the shopping bag.

'Can you put it on her account, please?'

Mrs Trahaearn hesitated and Verity felt her blush deepen.

'Just this once, dear, but if you could ask your mam to pop by and settle the outstanding, I'd appreciate it.'

Verity nodded. Mrs Trahaearn dropped a couple of packets of Spangles into the bag. 'For you and your sister.'

'You don't have to.'

'I know.' Mrs Trahaearn winked.

Verity managed a smiled and thanked her. 'Meredith will be pleased as well.'

'You take care, *cariad*.'

Verity loaded the shopping into the basket. Above her, the town gulls screeched. As she cycled back along the path the sound followed her until, like an extended soundtrack, the house gulls took over and welcomed her home.

Three

Standing in the hall, Verity's voice echoed up a wide staircase covered with a wine-red carpet held in place by brass stair rods.

'Meri?'

To one side of the front door stood a hat stand and on the other, a Chinese umbrella holder. Light from the window above struck one of several mirrors. Mared was fond of mirrors; of the way they played with light, making spaces look bigger and brighter. Allegra simply loved her reflection, repeated to infinity. She couldn't pass a mirror without looking at herself.

A long-case clock stood to attention next to a door leading into the tower room. It had fallen silent years before, the key lost and time stopped in the teatime past. A semi-circular table stood against the wall, piled with unopened envelopes, spare gloves, a sprig of dead leaves and neglect. Dull and finger-marked, her grandmother's old telephone sat like a black frog.

Nain will be horrified when she sees the state of this place.

Her grandmother had met her husband in London: two wartime Welsh exiles, a nurse and a doctor keeping their longing for home at bay while they waited out the war. When they married, Dylan was happy for them to make their life in Mared's childhood home. Escaping to Wales for a brief honeymoon, his love for Gull House began the day he carried his new bride over the threshold.

Now that's what you call a proper romance.

Calling her sister's name again, Verity listened to the house creaking around her. She thought she heard a noise coming from the unused tower room – a soft thud and then silence.

21

In the kitchen, she unpacked the shopping, cut some slices of bread and buttered them, placed them on a plate. She lined the packets of Spangles next to it, like cutlery, and unscrewed the lid on the fresh pot of jam.

Meredith burst through the door smelling of dust and mischief.

'You will never, *ever* guess what I found, not in a million years.' Her eyes were glittering ice stars. Ignoring the buttered bread and sweets, with a reverence still managing to be a flourish, she placed a wooden box on the table. Painted on the lid were faded pink flowers surrounded by a washed-out turquoise border, tiny touches of gold paint still visible. 'Behold and be blown away!'

Verity stared. 'Where on earth did you find that?'

'In the attic.' Meredith grinned in triumph. As if it were a casket of precious gems, she stroked her fingers across the lid of the box.

'Are you crazy, Meri? Which attic? I thought they were locked.'

'Not the one above Rapunzel's tower. There's no lock. You just pull down the ladder.'

'You know how dangerous it is up there.' Verity was appalled. 'That's why Nain warned us to stay out. The floors aren't safe.'

'Rubbish. So long as you step on the joists it's fine.'

'What do you mean? Have you been up there before?'

'Loads of times.'

'I don't believe you.'

'Well, I have. Don't freak.' Meredith gave a mock shiver. 'It's a bit creepy, mind, dust and *billions* of spiders. Rats too, probably.' She pulled a face and grinned again. 'And there's one of those dressmakers' dummy things up there too, without a head. I thought it was a ghost at first, except everyone knows you can't actually see ghosts.'

'How many times?' Verity tried to control her annoyance. 'How many times have you been up in the attic?'

'Oh give over, Verity. I was bored and you did tell me to find something to do.' Meredith placed her hands on the wooden box.

'It was under a dustsheet, in an old wooden trunk with a pile of moth-eaten clothes.' She hooked a finger under the catch. 'Look.'

With another, slower flourish she opened the lid revealing a sewing box lined with faded paper the colour of a robin's egg. In the top lay a shallow tray divided into compartments with a silk pin-cushion in the centre. In each of the sections lay a collection of sewing aids: a tarnished silver thimble, ivory-handled tools; a cloth measuring tape in a case hand-embroidered with flowers, and a pair of scissors with mother-of-pearl handles.

Meredith lifted out the tray and underneath Verity saw reels of faded thread, another tape measure in an ornate brass barrel, scraps of lace, trails of ribbon and a felt needle case. Cards of cloth buttons, black metal hooks and eyes dotted with rust marks; small skeins of embroidery silk and wool in neat, washed-out bundles.

Running her finger over a piece of cream lace as delicate as a snowflake, Verity swallowed. The hairs on her arm stood on end. 'Oh my days, Meredith, this is amazing.'

'I know.' Meredith reached deeper into the box and like a conjurer pulling a rabbit from a hat, produced half a dozen little red flannel hearts in various stages of construction, some stuffed with kapok, each one showing tiny, immaculate stitches. 'Aren't they incredible? When I picked them up, they made me go all shivery.'

Although the flannel was faded it was still possible to sense the vibrancy of the original colour. The little hearts lay in Meredith's cupped hands like old-fashioned Christmas tree decorations.

'And wait until you see this.' Meredith laid the hearts to one side and lifted out a folded piece of cloth. Before she opened it, she gazed at her sister with a look of such seriousness Verity's heart skipped a beat.

'It's her.'

'Her?'

'The mad girl.'

'Meredith, what on earth are you talking about?'

'The girl Nain told us about, the one who lived here. You remember.'

In a moment of recollection, Verity did.

Once upon a time, they say a sad, mad girl lived in this house…

Nain had told them the story as if it were a memory, although she said no one knew for certain if it was true. Her mother had told her – and everyone knew Dilys hadn't been the full shilling, God rest her soul.

'It's a bit unkind to call the poor thing mad though,' she'd said. 'In those days, well, things were different. Dreadful, really. People had a peculiar attitude to anyone they decided didn't fit in, or were troublesome or a bit *twp*. It wasn't uncommon to send them to asylums.'

As Meredith unfolded the fabric, a picture emerged – a pattern of cross-stitched images: a tiny house, a cat and a row of birds each one perfectly rendered in a meticulous hand. Below them, the letters of the alphabet in a neat line, followed by the numbers: zero to ten.

'See,' Meredith whispered, 'it's her name.'

Beneath the pictures and the letters and numbers, Verity gazed at the words, equally beautifully worked in faded wool and intersected by crosses: Angharad Elen Lewis X Age 9 Years X 1870.

I was not, it was agreed, a pretty girl.

There was a wideness to my eyes that made people uncomfortable. I had uneven teeth and flat, brown hair resisting the tightest of curling rags; a girl who ripped her gowns and lost her gloves, whose bonnets slipped and revealed too much of her disobedient hair.

As a child, I slept badly and this too was viewed as a flaw. When I was five, Cook suggested fresh air. Against her better judgement, Mama agreed. One full moon night the first moths appeared: fluttering against the lampshades scattering silver dust from their wings. I was enchanted by them and straight away began to settle. Neither my mother nor the maid had any idea why, in the morning, they sometimes found moths in my bed.

Learning to sleep was simply one of a list of things expected of me. My life was ordered by wretched rules concerning gloves and hemlines and hair, decorum and a mantra of manners.

And not asking to go to school.

My duties were plain and prescribed, my enjoyments inconsequential. The linen handkerchiefs my mother insisted I hem bored me witless and set my eyes squinting. My sewing rarely came up to her exacting standards. And when she discovered the flannel hearts I'd started fashioning, her eyes stopped their darting and alighted on me and the air in the room fell still.

Frippery she called them and forbade me to continue. I enjoyed making them – they were bright and cheerful, like a robin's breast and as comforting. If I held them close to my own heart, I could hear my blood and know I was alive.

I sewed the hated handkerchiefs in public, and my hearts in secret.

Four

'Do you think we ought to tell someone?'

Meredith was horrified. 'Are you crazy?'

'What if it's valuable?'

'What if it is? I don't care. It's not like I'd want to sell it.' Meredith was adamant and already establishing ownership of the box. 'We can't tell anyone. It's a secret, Verity, it has to be. Allegra will take it off me. Or she'll make it a massive *thing* and it won't be mine anymore. She does that, you know she does.' Her gaze became beseeching. 'She can't bear to be left out.'

Verity couldn't argue with that. Allegra intruded, not like a normal parent, checking to see if homework was done or did they want her to read a story or brush their hair. What she wanted was their secrets, so she didn't feel left out and could make them about her.

Verity sighed. 'All right, although we ought to tell Nain, it's still her house. And if you're right about it belonging to…'

'Of course I am. It's her *name*. God, Verity, don't be so feeble.'

'Don't call me that.' Verity had the strangest feeling she was out of her depth.

Meredith snapped back. 'You're jealous because you didn't find it.'

'All right, all right; don't let's fight. I just think it might be important.'

Meredith picked up one of the flannel hearts and held it in her hand. 'Of course it's important.' She swallowed. 'See? Look at my arm?' The pale hairs on her skin stood on end.

'I was meant to find it. It's a sign.'

Verity stared at her sister. 'Don't, Meredith.'

'Don't what? How do you know? And even if it's only an old sewing box, I found it and I don't want you to tell anyone, including Nain.' Her mouth pursed. 'It's – non-negotiable.'

Verity had no problem with secrets, but she wasn't sure she wanted to encourage Meredith in what was beginning to sound like one of her obsessions.

'Promise me, Verity.' Meredith was looking mutinous. 'You can't say anything.'

'All right, I won't.'

'Oh, you're the best sister ever.' Meredith clapped her hands together like a child half her age. 'Shall we have a proper look?' She began emptying the box, examining each item in detail. 'Be careful mind. I want everything to go back in order.' She picked up a square of yellowed lawn. 'Look at those stitches. Is it a handkerchief? How could you see to make stitches so small? And imagine having to sew hankies?'

'Imagine having to sew, full stop.'

'Do you think she went to school?' Meredith fingered one of the flannel hearts again. 'Or did she sit in her room all day, making these. Maybe they kept her locked in the tower.'

Verity smiled. 'I doubt it. She might have had a governess though. Girls did in those days.'

'And that's why she went mad.'

'Don't be soft.'

'Well, I would; having some rumpled old spinster teaching me Latin.' Meredith arched her eyebrows, adopted a *faux* accent. 'Or how to play the pianoforte, my dear.'

'Idiot. A girl in the 1870s wouldn't have learned Latin.'

'Why not?'

'Most of them weren't that well-educated.'

'A bit like us then.'

Verity nodded. 'Exactly like us.' She ran her finger across the embroidered sampler. 'Don't you sometimes wish we could go to school?'

'No way! I'd rather have a governess. You could escape from one of those. School would be horrendous and I never want to go.' Meredith refolded the handkerchief. 'It would be a nightmare. Allegra wouldn't buy us the right clothes for one thing; we'd be freaks and no one would speak to us.'

'Doesn't it bother you that we don't know anything? We're quite ignorant, you know.'

'No, we aren't. We know loads of stuff. Well, I do.'

Verity didn't believe they knew anything. 'Speak for yourself. Most of the time, I feel like a total idiot.'

'Silly, you're clever as anything.' Meredith began folding the sampler. 'Nain always says you're the smart one.'

'Well, if I am, it's down to her. She's the one who made sure we learned to read and write and do our sums, not Allegra.'

'I know.' Meredith tucked the sampler into the box. 'You can't ever suggest it though, Verity.' She paused. 'School isn't only about the clothes.'

Verity said nothing. She understood her sister's ambivalence mirrored her own, in that it was about the scrutiny of her peers. Unlike her sister, Verity knew she would find a way to cope with school because secretly it was what she longed for. Meredith's fear ran deeper. Singular and quirky, she inhabited a world largely of her own making – one she instinctively knew might make her the subject of ridicule and mockery.

'You promised.'

'I didn't, actually.' Verity raised her hands. 'Oh, don't worry; I shan't say anything but we can't go on like this forever, Meri. We'll grow up completely thick and unemployed.'

Meredith began putting the contents of the sewing box away. 'I don't want a job. I'm going to be a writer.'

'That's a job, ninny. And you need to be able to spell.'

'No you don't. You write it down and people check it for you. It's called editing.'

Laughing, Verity found a mixing bowl, took a bag of flour from a cupboard and dumped it on the table. 'Okay, you win. No school.'

'Right answer,' Meredith said. 'We'll grow up illiterate and take rich lovers so it won't matter.'

Verity reached for the measuring scales. 'I shan't. I'd rather die. I'm never getting married either.'

'Well, as I shan't fall in love, that's both of us on the shelf.'

'How do you know you won't fall in love?'

'Because nobody with a brain cell believes that true love's kiss rubbish?'

'I thought you loved fairytales.'

'That's you.'

'No, I prefer myths.'

'You're such a pedant, Verity. And yes, I do like fairytales; so long as they don't have dopey princes in them.'

'Yes, it's always the princes who mess things up.' Verity wasn't overly romantic, even so she did think if the kiss came from the right person it could turn out to be perfect.

'I'm going to put this in my room.' Meredith closed the lid on the sewing box, picked it up and hugged it to her chest. 'I'm going to take care of it. And take care of her.'

'It could be nothing.'

'It's something, Verity. I know it is.' She held the box tenderly. 'And don't forget – no telling.'

Verity reached for the blue eggs. 'Okay, I told you, I promise. About all of it. Go on, then come back and help me make a cake. At least it's one thing we're good at.'

'And then I'll let you take me to the beach.'

'Well, aren't I the lucky one.'

Meredith's eyes sparkled. 'If you keep my secret, I'll stay on the beach until the sun goes down.'

Five

There they are.

From the window of her untidy bedroom, Allegra could see them, trailing along the beach. It would have been Verity's idea; dragging her sister out in the freezing cold.

Over the years a path had been worn through the grass. It led from the edge of the garden where a great fallen oak tree the girls called the lookout lay, sloped down the field to a wooden stile and a ledge marking the beginning of the beach. A grey cliff reached toward the shore. As a child, Allegra had been afraid of it: her mother told her it was a dragon and the idea gave her nightmares.

She's still ruining my sleep, always nagging me about something, as if I'm incapable of looking after her precious house.

Gull House oppressed Allegra; her mother's unspoken assertion that she remained its mistress irked.

All she cares about is this dump, and her brother. If she loves me like she says, it's not the way Pa loved me.

When her father died, Allegra had been distraught. She was seventeen and too young to deal with the death of a man she adored, and who adored her back.

It was the first abandonment but not the last.

Two years later, when Idris came on the scene, Allegra fell hopelessly in love. Idris was a loner and she, lonely.

He was shy at first and it had been endearing. They met in a clichéd moment you couldn't make up, in a record shop in town. She was listening to Ketty Lester singing *Love Letters* and when he asked her why, she said why not and he laughed and called her a romantic.

His eyes were as blue as the sky and her insides twisted as if they'd come undone. Quickly inseparable they wandered along the cliffs, across the beach below Gull House where they wrote love notes to one another in the sand.

She had wanted to be married in church. Idris wasn't a churchgoer; he said it would be hypocritical. It was the one and only time he won an argument with her. As a protest, she decided to get married in red. Everyone who knew her said it was a terrible idea. Red was for danger and debt and martyrdom; it tempted fate and tasted of rust and blood. Allegra was headstrong, and furious at being thwarted. And in any case, she knew better.

Ignoring the warnings, she stitched her wedding gown at night by candlelight. In the shadowy light the silk appeared darker and she sewed her tiny secret stitches, not noticing when she pricked her finger or the blood as it turned into invisible stains. On her wedding day the sun shone bright as hope. Allegra's hair and dress glittered like fire and rubies and people found themselves digging out their sunglasses.

There was no honeymoon; nothing memorable to mark the day, only a blood red dress and a pearl ring so small it didn't fit.

She hadn't thought she minded.

Twisting the ring round her little finger, she tasted old tears on the back of her throat.

You left because my love was too much for you. Because you weren't man enough.

From time to time a different man would cross her path and be invited in. Allegra would decide to give love another chance, until love let her down again.

Men were cowards and all the same.

Rolling a cigarette she struck a match and focused on the rock face – saw it for what it was – full of the kind of colours only an artist could see: gold, rust and sparkling quartz; slate grey and purple.

Art's real. It's the only thing I need.

Today the sea was full of colour too – steely blue threaded with bands of amethyst – storm colours more suited to winter.

It crossed her mind Verity might be right about the snow. Allegra disliked snow. She wanted to be warm and rarely was; she was too thin.

She couldn't help wishing her elder daughter wasn't so prosaic.

They're obsessed with it. Every year the same: when's it going to snow?

Pulling her shawl closer, she shivered. Watching the girls, heads bent close, whispering like little birds, Allegra felt left out of whatever conspiracy they were surely conjuring. Cigarette smoke trailed from her mouth and she stroked her neck, her breath dry in her throat, and coughed.

It isn't normal. Daughters are supposed to tell their mother everything.

She watched the way Verity walked across the pebbles, her head tilted, the way his used to, and an old scar bruised the edge of her heart.

Allegra didn't understand Verity one bit. She had expected a firstborn daughter to look like her, admire her and want to share clothes and secrets. Verity looked too much like Idris, and when Meredith was born – the image of Allegra – she wondered if a trick had been played on her. From the beginning, Verity claimed her sister. At night, if Meredith had a bad dream and woke up, she ran along the landing to her sister's bedroom and crawled in beside her. Allegra experienced a jealousy that burned and left blisters on her heart. The following morning Meredith would always tell her mother about the bad dream; Allegra would stroke her hair and try not to mind it was Verity who had dried her tears.

Verity ought to tell me when Meredith has nightmares: send her sister to me.

Although she rarely said so in words, Allegra sensed Verity questioned her about everything. Her blue eyes sometimes held scornful lights. The scent of Verity was sharp as lemons; dusty as old feathers and dried-up roses. Once she saw which of her daughters smiled the most and admired her – the one who smelled of honey and stars – Allegra transferred her expectations from her eldest to her youngest in the blink of an eye.

She stubbed out her cigarette; cleared her throat and turned from the window.

I am afraid of the sea.

It wasn't always that way.

Occasionally a maid would be instructed to take me (and my brother if he was at home) to the beach. These outings were an escape from Mama and her constant supervision. At one end of the beach the cliff unfolded in a rippling curve, a great primordial creature reminding me of a dinosaur or a dragon.

I loved the rough, salty wind coming off the ocean, sand blowing in my hair and clothes. The noise of the sea excited me. I admired the birds too, the waders with their orange heads dipping in and out of the rock pools.

My brother informed me they were oystercatchers and set about chasing them. When I protested, he laughed, took himself off in search of other victims – other birds to frighten and small creatures he could torture.

The first time I ventured down to the beach by myself I was eight. My brother was nowhere to be seen; my mother was unwell and had taken to her bed. It was the maid's day off. For a few precious hours, I found myself unsupervised.

It was a brooding day and had I been older I might have shown more sense. From the edge of the garden where an oak tree grew, I could see the tide was out, see the oystercatchers stepping daintily at the edge of the shore. The beach belonged to them and as I scrambled across the shingle to the sand, for a while it was as if it belonged to me too.

After twenty minutes the sky clouded over and without warning, a storm blew in from the sea. I fled the beach as fast as my legs would allow. As I ran up the field, out of breath and struggling, the clouds darkened and rolled over me. Rain streaked down, sounding like tiny stones on my head. Drenched in an instant, I blundered up to the garden, a sense of dread overcoming me.

Turning for the house, my hair flat against my head, my unease deepened. Darts of apprehension stabbed at me, a black-winged bird at the back of my mind. At the side of the house, the trees marking the periphery of the garden were all at once starkly black and made of midnight.

'Where have you been?'

He stepped from between the trees, barely touched by the rain now soaking me to my skin. At ten years old, my brother was already arrogant and unpleasant.

'Playing truant, my sly sister? I saw you down on the beach.'

'I wasn't doing anything wrong.'

He smiled his snake-eyed smile. 'The sea isn't for sly little girls. If you aren't careful, it will scoop you up and drown you. Sea monsters will drag you to the bottom of the ocean and feast on your scrawny body until your bones are all that's left.'

Seeing my terror, it fired his enthusiasm for taunting me.

'Sly things should have a care they don't get eaten,' he said before striding away through the lashing rain.

From that day I feared the sea and refused to go to the beach again. In my dreams it began to speak to me, filling my head with foreboding. I would wake in the middle of the night from dreams of sea monsters and drowning.

Six

In spring, the sky was a space so big Verity thought it must stretch all the way to heaven.

When she wondered what might lie on the other side of the hills, she tried not to think about why it made her feel so restless.

Other than going to London a few times, the Pryce sisters had hardly been anywhere. Allegra had taken them to north Wales once. It was a disaster. Meredith came down with chickenpox and Allegra swore she would never take them on holiday again.

The sheltered nature of their lives made little impression on Meredith who, in spite of her insistence that nothing exciting ever happened to them, had no real ambition to go anywhere else. Neither of them were the sort of girls who needed other people. They were wild and rare and when they were alone together, their voices sounded like snow falling.

Until recently, it had seemed enough.

Verity watched her sister scampering across the pebbles toward the rock dragon. Meredith negotiated the stones like a hare, barely faltering.

From the first time they'd heard Mared tell the story, they'd been enchanted by the idea this was the spot where the last dragon in Wales had died. The cliff was her body, Nain said. The submerged end her head and as she died, her tears turned to pebbles.

Meredith came to a stop. 'Verity!'

'In a minute.' Verity huddled on the shingle by a rock pool, her hands wrapped inside the sleeves of her jumper. The mirror-glinting water shivered as a chilly breeze blew across it.

Meredith turned and ran back, leaping and calling. She reached Verity again, panting for breath and pulled on her sister's arm. 'Please, Verity, come to the dragon with me.'

'You go. And don't be too long. I'm cold. This was a bad idea.'

'For someone who's supposed to love the beach, you're a bit of a disappointment, you know. I only suggested it to please you.'

'I know you did and it was really nice of you, only it's absolutely freezing, even for me.'

'Do you think it's going to snow?'

'I do and then I don't. It's April, it's spring already...'

'I know but it snowed when I was born. It would be brilliant!' Meredith's eyes shone. 'I'm desperate for snow, aren't you?'

'I'm desperate not to be cold.'

Meredith put her arm around Verity's shoulder, rubbing her back. 'I'll warm you up and then we'll go back.'

Huddled together, they gazed at the sea, the swish of it at the lip of the shore. Above them, a perfect mackerel sky spread like a great scaly fish.

'Sky-fishing,' Meredith said. 'It is beautiful here. I can see why you love it so much.'

A boat appeared on the horizon, a flash of a distant sail.

Meredith shaded her eyes. 'Where does the sea end?'

'Ireland.'

'Imagine if you were in a boat and you went on forever, not getting anywhere. Just rowed and rowed in your little boat.'

Verity shivered. 'Or swam.'

They were forbidden to go into the sea. The undertow was dangerous and Allegra made sure they stayed out of the water. As a result, they hadn't learned to swim. Meredith didn't want to – she was scared of water. Verity quite liked the idea of becoming a selkie, like the ones she read about in stories: women who had to shed their skins to live on the land but who were forever bound to the ocean.

Meredith picked up a shell, turned it over, dropped it in the rock pool. 'I do love the beach; I just love the wood more, which is perfect. We each have a special place.'

'And Nain's blue garden is for both of us.'

'Nain's garden is only for us.'

'Yes.' Verity rubbed her hands together. 'Have you noticed, the waves sound like the wind through the trees in the wood? And when we're in the wood, it's the other way round?'

Meredith said she hadn't and tilted her head to one side. 'Oh yes, so it does.' She pointed. 'Look at the oystercatchers. Aren't they sweet?'

The tide was on the turn; the line of the sea where it broke against the sand a frill of greenish-grey. Verity watched the birds at the shoreline searching for whelks and limpets. Further out only the line of the horizon showed where the sea began. The water and the reflected sky shimmered from the outside edges making the whole of it transparent, the sea-light constantly changing and elusive.

Verity supposed it was what attracted her mother, made her want to paint it.

Meredith dragged Verity to her feet. 'Okay. You win. It's freezing. Let's go.'

As the dark enfolded the house and the moon rose, the moths came, drawn to the glow of Meredith's determined heart, her luminescent hair. Fast asleep in a restless dream she heard a sound that may have been a song and could have been the whisper of a ghost. Moths fluttered against her skin and the air became as thin as spider web.

In the morning, when she woke up, she threw back the bedclothes and found a moth caught in a fold of the sheet.

'Hello, my pretty, what are you doing in my bed?'

Cupping the fragile creature in her hands she padded across the floor to the window, reached out and watched as it flew away on tissue-paper wings.

Seven

Verity lingered in her bedroom, reading.

In the room across the landing she heard her mother moving about, agitated, opening drawers; now and then swearing.

What frame of mind would she be in today? Allegra's moods were as mercurial as her love. Her mother's belittling of her was something Verity had become accustomed to. She wasn't desperate to have her small achievements acknowledged, only puzzled as to why they so rarely were. She suspected it had something to do with her father, who had broken her mother's heart. The space he left behind was dark and ragged. Now and then Verity thought her mother's sorrow meant she couldn't help fill that space with the daughter who looked like him.

She crossed her fingers.

Here's hoping. When she isn't depressed or we haven't aggravated her, she forgets even my faults.

'My girls,' Allegra would say, as if she had won her daughters, like prizes.

Then we're perfect.

Meredith burst into the bedroom.

'Don't bother knocking or anything.'

'Oh, don't be so grand.' Meredith plonked herself down on Verity's bed. 'Waking up is usually a right pain, only today I've had the most dazzling idea. You'll love it.'

No I won't. I'll hate it. Your eyes look like Catherine wheels.

'You know what I said yesterday, about wanting to be a writer. Well, I'm going to start practising. I mean, you're right; you can't just *be* a writer. You have to begin somewhere and learn the ropes. It's my plan to stop us having to get married. I'll write books and make a fortune and we can live here forever and not have to look for husbands.'

She looked so pleased, Verity couldn't help herself. 'You're mad as a bat, Meri, but I love you.'

'I know you do. And you'll love me more when I tell you my plan. Why don't we both write something? Ghost stories, so I can write about the mad girl and you can write whatever you like. We can compare notes and you can help me improve.'

Verity's heart sank. 'You're kidding, yes?'

'Unlikely. I never kid about anything.'

You are the best and cleverest fibber I know.

'I don't want to be a writer, I'm happy being a reader.'

'That's your problem, Verity. Allegra's right. You have no ambition.'

You have no ambition, darling. Look at Meredith and take a leaf out of her book. You need to make a bit of an effort, doesn't she, Meredith?

Stung, Verity said, 'You don't know what I want and neither does she.'

Meredith's eyes shone with excitement. 'Yes, I do. You want to be happy. We both do so listen, it'll be brilliant: a competition to spur me on, mostly to find out if I'm any good at it.'

'You'll be fine on your own.'

'You won't fob me off like that, Verity Pryce. I need you to be involved. You said it was a crisis.'

'I said nothing of the sort.'

'You said we were ignorant and stupid and we'd have to find husbands.'

'No, you said that.'

'Oh, what does it matter who said what? The point is there's no way I'm letting either of us get married!' She rolled onto her stomach. 'You're really good at spelling and you know about grammar and that kind of thing.'

40

'You read all the time; you know as much as I do.' Verity shoved Meredith away.

'No I don't. I never take any notice of those over-doing words.'

'Doing words, you idiot; they're called verbs.'

Meredith made a rude noise. 'You've read Enid Blyton; you know exactly what I'm talking about.'

In spite of herself, Verity laughed out loud. 'You are the most ridiculous, irritating, clever sister ever. Now, get off my bed!'

'So you will?'

'It's a crazy idea. I don't want to write some dull story about ghosts.'

As if Verity hadn't spoken, Meredith carried on. 'I'm going to write about her – Angharad – the mad girl. Only what if she wasn't? Remember what Nain said? It wasn't nice to call her mad because no one knew the truth.'

'That's the whole point, surely. We don't know anything about her.'

'Who says we have to? We can guess and make it up.' Meredith grinned. 'How do you think real writers do it? They use their imagination.'

'I'm getting bored now, Meri. And you're being a pest.'

'There's no need to be nasty.' Meredith picked at the quilt. 'In any case, it's educational. I thought you'd approve.'

Laying her book to one side, Verity slid out of bed. 'I'm going to get dressed now, so can you please get out of my room?'

'Now who's the boring one? You're boring and bourgeois.'

'And you sound like her.'

'She doesn't mean it.'

'Yes, she does.' Verity opened a drawer in her dressing table. 'She means every word. It doesn't matter. Now please, Meredith, leave me alone while I get dressed.'

Verity fished in the scummy water for the last bits of cutlery.

Meredith, her head on her arms, lolled on the table.

'Please, Verity, can we? Go on, it'll be a laugh.' Her voice was muffled against the wool of her cardigan sleeve. 'We can regale each another with deathless prose.'

'Idiot.'

'I'm not though. Remember what Nain told us? If we close our eyes we can be whoever we want.'

'And you reckon that's all it takes to be a writer?'

'It's a start.'

'It doesn't work like that.'

'It might.'

Verity felt her grasp on the argument slipping away.

'I still don't see why you can't write a story by yourself,' she said. 'You already know far more words than I've heard of.'

'It'll be no fun on my own.'

As the water spiralled down the plughole, Verity turned to face her sister. 'If I agree, will you promise to let me phone Nain and tell her about the sewing box? After all, it is her house and her things. It's about respect.'

'All right. Yes.' Meredith answered with the kind of swift response Verity knew meant that at a later date she could deny knowledge of any such agreement.

'If you mean it,' Meredith said, 'then you're on. And you tell Nain to swear she won't tell Allegra.'

'Okay. Only I get to write whatever comes into my head.'

'Yes, so long as it's a ghost story.'

'Deal.'

In the middle of the night, needing the lavatory, Verity paused outside her sister's bedroom. From the other side of the door she heard murmuring.

Is she talking to herself? Talking in her sleep?

It wouldn't be the first time.

The murmur stopped and not even a cobweb stirred. Shadows shifted throughout the house. Verity returned to her room and as she fell asleep they billowed and furled like no one was watching.

Gull House was a dismal place.

Throughout the rooms, the light was obstructed, swallowed by heavy curtains. The air was weighed down by the scent of polish and diligence. Looking glasses created tricks of light: distorted reflections. Under the high ceilings, formidable furniture and vast paintings dominated the rooms. Huge plants in bulbous china pots graced the drawing room and tasselled cushions the size of pillows lay piled on window-seats where no one sat. In gloomy bedrooms sat canopied beds as big as boats. My father's study, in the tower room, housed an ornate desk taking up most of the space.

And, overlaying it all, the faint smell of cigars; a hint of spoiled food, the result of a cook with few skills and less imagination. My mother's fragrance, lily-of-the-valley, always struck me as stale too; it had a touch of death about it.

Ghosts of course, can't smell anything…

Mama wore sombre clothes and was never seen without her jet earrings, as if she were in perpetual mourning for some dead relative. The tap of her heels on the wooden floors, alternating with a cat-like pad as they crossed a rug, announced her presence in the same way my father's brash pronouncements proclaimed his.

It was the secretive tread I feared … my brother's furtive footfall.

Are you brave enough?

It wasn't hard to anger him. A petulant child, my brother looked for reasons to be provoked. Most of the time, I struggled to recall what it was I had said to anger him, only that I had and must bear his taunts and pinches, and worse. He was tall and despite a wiry frame deceptively strong. He had large hands like the fat, skinned paws of an animal. They might break a pheasant's neck at a stroke and crack the shells of walnuts as if they were made of porcelain.

He would endeavour to deliberately trip me so I fell painfully against the furniture. Outside, he would barge into me causing me to stumble and land on the gravel. He would pretend to help me up, clasping my wrists so hard he left bruises on my skin.

I once overheard Cook saying to one of the maids it was no wonder *the young master wasn't popular; what with his lies to the mistress and his sneaking around behind her back. When the maid said she'd heard worse, my skin turned to gooseflesh. I turned away, reluctant to know what could possibly be more terrible.*

Knowing I wasn't the only one affected by my brother's unpleasantness was small comfort.

Present

The elegant door, its blue salt-worn to grey, still takes my breath away.

It's a thing of beauty, this door, and even with the paint peeling, the shape of it remains insanely lovely. It sits in the stone façade of the house like a picture my mother might have painted. At the top, set into the ornately curved frame, is a small window adorned with stained glass flowers. The curve continues out to the side and in it more small sections of glinting glass sit like jewels.

The steps leading up to the door are bowed and worn, the result of countless feet stepping on the stone. Toadflax creeps down the edges, green and purple lace. The shapeless expanse of old gravel is overgrown with dandelions and chickweed, distorted into something no longer cared for. Around me the garden stands forlorn, given over to thistles and molehills and shabby weeds. I try and recall where the chicken house used to be and can't. Nain had a fondness for Cream Legbars: friendly, lazy hens that laid blue eggs.

A thrush calls from a tree, and I am ridiculously pleased. Although it's as invisible as the ghosts I no longer believe in, the sound comforts me. Listening hard I try to conjure Meredith's voice again and for a moment I almost do. And I can see her, waving to me, disappearing into the trees, her laughter lingering on the air, daring me to follow.

From the time she could walk my sister spent as much time as possible out of doors. Birds followed her and at dusk foxes waited on the edge of the garden, enticing her into the wood.

You can think more than one thing about a person in the same second and each will be true. Meredith was a pest and a kindness and an angel. She was fearless then too. Until Allegra made us leave Gull House she was unafraid of anything.

It may be shabbier now – the house isn't without its charm. It isn't that it's falling down – Nain was right – it would take a hurricane to dislodge it. Time has simply softened the edges, changed the brilliance of the original, muted it the way Allegra did with paint when she swirled her brushes in a jar of water, making the colours merge.

On the edge of the terrace, a series of steps lead down to the garden. I sit and lift my face to the pale sun, lean back on my hands. My finger catches on something hard. It's a stubbed-out cigarette, a filter-tipped one. Frowning, I pick it up. It smells disgusting; strong and fresh. It's half-smoked, as if someone has been disturbed and abandoned it.

I tell myself it can only be the caretaker.

For several years, Nain has employed a man to keep an eye on the place, see to necessary repairs, tidy the garden, look out for damp patches and slates falling from the roof, a jackdaw nesting in a chimney. Eying the wilderness it's obvious to me that, whoever he is, he's clearly reneged on the latter task. And leaving half-smoked cigarettes lying around is a bit of a cheek. I dig in my bag for a tissue, wrap the offending butt and stuff it in my pocket. The idea the caretaker might be taking advantage irritates me.

Above me, gulls drift against the sky and I hear my mother, almost smell her – her perfume mixed with the sweet scent of burning liquorice and for some absurd reason, I want to cry.

I am motionless, uncertain what to do.

The keys in my bag mock me. I touch them again and my fingers move as if by their own volition. I now wish myself anywhere other than here. The cigarette butt has unnerved me. The idea someone might have been here, by arrangement or not, makes me uncomfortable.

Was he still around?

Perhaps it wasn't the caretaker at all. The house has been empty for a long time. Tramps and vagrants could easily have found their way here. My heart patters against my ribs. I try and work out how long it's been since Nain visited. The last years were hard for her and following Allegra's death she shrank before my eyes. My vibrant, marvellous grandmother became a shadow.

She used to telephone him from time to time – the caretaker.

'Remind me to call him, *cariad*. I'm worried about the pipes.'

And I remember now – the last time was not long before Allegra died. Mared wouldn't have had the *hwyl* for it since.

I try and recall the caretaker's name. Huw somebody? Hywel? I can't remember. His telephone number is in my iPhone under 'Caretaker'. My mind is racing, trying to piece things together. I don't want to look at the house; a sudden confusion takes me unawares. I can hear Meredith saying everything was falling apart; how irritated it had made me, how I told her not to be disrespectful.

These are Nain's things, Meri. They matter.

I can see my sister as if she is in front of me: Meredith, her incandescent eyes wide and considering, as if she doubted everything and had no choice but to challenge even me, answering, *Things don't matter, Verity. They're not the house. It's only the house that matters.*

The gulls wheel and swoop, crying and seeing the world.

For a moment the air suspends the sound of them and the waves as they break on the shore below. 'This is our castle and no one can scale the ramparts,' Meredith used to say.

Her voice is distant and as far away as she is.

Eight

Meredith's bedroom was a clothes-strewn, book-scattered space.

It overlooked the ocean, and she could lie in bed and watch the moon.

Lying back against the pillow, she hugged a grey velvet rabbit.

Meredith had no words to describe how she might be hearing the voice of a ghost.

She knew the difference between daydreams and the ones that came to her as she slept.

Do you have the courage…?

'Courage for what?'

The voice came again, an echo, as if it was a memory, only Meredith didn't recognise it.

Could it be Angharad's? Was it possible to recall a dead person's memory? Meredith was headstrong and unruly. Her world was made up of infinite possibility and reckless promises, of light pouring through an open window urging her towards the day's adventure. Life presented itself exclusively to her and she grabbed it with both her unworldly hands. She was made from air and impulse and she hung a fishing net outside her bedroom window to catch falling stars.

'Then we can wish on them,' she told her sister.

Meredith's imagination had wings; it could fly and frequently did. She wasn't taken in by mundane fairy tales with their castles and princes and wicked spells; she preferred more benevolent landscapes where girls really did have wings and it was possible to talk to trees, where things were fair and kind. If the land of the

Fae existed, in Meredith's version unkindness was the worst of sins, trickery and disloyalty out of the question.

She refused to learn how to tell the time because she said if she needed to know it, she could ask someone. She told little lies all the time and unlike most people, remembered them. As a result, she was rarely found out.

Allegra called it charming and, needing an ally, made a favourite of her youngest child. Knowing this didn't mean Meredith colluded. Her mother wasn't always nice to Verity and Meredith didn't know why. She adored Allegra, she didn't always trust her.

She certainly didn't trust her with this new secret.

Do I trust Verity enough to tell her about the voice in my dreams?

'Can you hear anything, Nelly?' The benign face of the rabbit fell against Meredith's arm. Through the window, light from the moon picked out the gold paint on the lid of the sewing box. Swinging her legs over the edge of the bed, Meredith lifted it onto her lap. Her hand shook, knocking against the box, almost toppling it to the floor.

Running her hand across the lid, she opened it, lifted out the tray. Underneath, the flannel hearts lay in a bundle and she was reminded of tiny animals. Taking one out, she laid the tip of her finger on it. A shiver ran through her.

The birds know…

Was Angharad a trick? She didn't think so. The box was too real, too present. Could a girl from a hundred years ago really come back from the dead to haunt someone? And would she pick a child?

'Why would she choose me, Nelly?'

Was the voice she thought she was hearing real or part of a dream?

I have been waiting for someone to hear me…

People who die before their time can't rest.

Had she read this somewhere? It sounded wise. Perhaps her grandmother had said it.

'If you want me to, I'll try and hear you.' A whisper was all she could manage.

As Meredith placed the heart in the palm of her hand, a voice like a sliver of lost wind echoed in her head.

If I held them close to my heart, I could hear my blood and know I was alive ... I sewed my hearts in secret...

'I'll try.' She still spoke softly, afraid of being overheard.

The walls of Gull House were thick but she knew that ever since she had been a baby, in the middle of the night, her sister listened out for her. And her mother wasn't above listening at doors.

Mothers cannot be trusted...

A latticework made of moon-shadow branches and moths on their way to find her, decorated the bedroom wall. She strained to hear more. The voice was gone and the only thing she heard was the rustling of wisteria against the windowpane. She fell asleep, and then she woke again, confused and cold, with no idea if a minute or an entire night had passed, or if what she had heard was dream or reality.

A moth came in through the open window. It was transparent and light as a feather, its wings moving in a blur. Meredith reached out her hand and to her delight the moth landed on her finger.

'You're back.'

Nine

Early the following morning, Meredith came into Verity's bedroom, insisting on getting into bed with her.

'I'm cold. My room's like the north pole.'

'Don't be silly, it's a lovely day.' Verity wasn't sure how true this was. In spite of a sliver of sunlight at the window, the temperature was still unseasonably low.

Meredith's feet were icy. She had dark patches under her eyes.

'You look a bit tired,' she said, keeping her voice non committal.

'I've been awake *all* night. And now I'm cold and my room's absolutely freezing.' Meredith rubbed her hands over her arms. 'It's creepy cold, not like when it snows. It smells of weeds and dead things and I don't like it.'

'You're making it up.'

'No, I'm not.'

'Well, you're imagining it.'

'Perhaps I am. I'm supposed to.'

'What do you mean?'

'Verity, can I trust you?'

'You know you can'

Meredith let out a long breath. 'It's the story. It's inside me trying to get out.'

Verity felt her sister's cold feet against her calves and sighed. 'Of course it is.'

'Don't make fun of me, Verity, not after you said I could trust you.'

Something in her sister's voice struck Verity as out of kilter.

Meredith's bruised eyes were huge, the irises the colour of winter fog.

'Are you okay?'

'I don't know. I think it's her, the ghost. She's talking to me.'

Verity bit back a retort.

'She said she needs to be remembered.'

'You dreamt this?'

Meredith nodded.

I thought you said you'd been awake all night.

'I know what you're thinking,' Meredith said. 'It wasn't totally like a dream. It was like I was between a dream and a real place; as if she was there in the room and in my dreams at the same time.'

'Did you see her?'

'I told you, Verity, you can't see ghosts.'

'And yet you know she's talking to you?'

'I can't explain it. I know something weird's going on and she's trying to tell me what happened to her. She wants me to know.'

'Is it like being haunted?' As soon as she said this, Verity regretted it.

'No.' Meredith bit her lip. 'I feel *visited.*'

Verity swallowed. 'Aren't you frightened?'

'I don't know. I don't think so.'

I am.

Shivers of alarm ran down Verity's back. She was nearly sixteen and she was as scared as a child of five.

As if nothing had happened, Meredith was smiling again.

'It'll be okay, Verity,' she said. 'The cold's probably because it actually is going to snow and it'll be the best thing ever.' She leaned her head on her sister's shoulder. 'Angharad will explain and you wait, my story's going to be a million times better than yours and one day I'll be famous.' She snuggled down under the covers. 'You'd better make an effort if you want to keep up.'

A day or two later, with nothing more than a title, Verity knew she was in trouble.

'You aren't even trying.' Meredith scowled across the kitchen table. Her hand gripped a crumpled notebook and she pointed at a piece of paper on the table. 'What kind of a title is, "Behind You?" '

Verity made a face. 'A joke?'

'For once, why can't you take me seriously?'

'Because it's stupid.'

Meredith glared at her. 'You promised.'

'No, I didn't.'

'You won't say I'm stupid when I tell you mine.'

'Let's have a look then.' Verity reached across the table, only before she could grab her sister's notebook, Meredith snatched it up.

'What?'

'You can't. It's…'

Verity narrowed her eyes. 'You haven't written anything either, have you?'

Meredith's look turned fierce and she held the notebook against her chest.

'Let's see then.'

The black circles under Meredith's eyes darkened. Verity didn't care enough to enquire anymore about lack of sleep or nightmares about ghosts. She was tired of Meredith's nonsense.

'You don't understand,' Meredith said, and her voice dropped to a whisper. 'It's not the kind of story I can write down. Not in actual words. I've tried, Verity but she wants me to listen.'

'I'm right then. You haven't written anything. So why are you giving me a hard time?'

'It's not my story. I told you, it's hers.'

Exasperated now, Verity shouted. 'Why do you do this? You're always trying to draw attention to yourself. You're as bad as Mam.' She threw up her hands. 'I'm done. Sod your stupid story. I've got better things to do.'

'Like what?'

'For one thing, some school work. Just because Allegra doesn't believe education matters, I do. Because she thinks you're some kind of miracle child who's going to somehow make a success of her life by doing absolutely nothing, doesn't mean I have to join in. I want to make something of mine. Not end up like some thicko pretending to be a writer.'

'I don't care about that any more, I...'

'Oh, leave me alone, Meredith, go and be crazy somewhere else.'

'Well if you won't help me, I'm taking back what I said about telling Nain. Don't you dare tell her about the sewing box.'

'Like I care about your tatty old box.' Verity walked to the kitchen door and opened it.

The sky reached down, grey and pale.

It looked as if it might snow.

There is a feeling of rejection in the ritual favouritism feeding sibling rivalry.

What threat had I ever been? How were my desires for an education subservient to my brother's?

I did nothing wrong yet I was made to sit indoors, denied access to all but the most boring books and told the world was no place for me. My father's conviction was that the female brain was inferior. To educate me beyond my capacity would be a waste of money. He despised my cleverness insisting it was a vanity, unbecoming and unnatural. When I protested, he told me I ought to mind my tongue lest it cut me.

Contemptuous of my desire he said all I needed to learn I could acquire from my lessons with a dour governess who came to the house a few mornings a week. The rest I could learn from my mother and a kitchen maid. Young ladies from respectable families should be content to settle for suitable marriages. The only things required were a little learning embellished with a few decorative and domestic talents.

I was surrounded by indifferent silence, unremarked unless it was to criticise some perceived fault. Then I was noticed, with attentive eyes and thin mouths offering only rebuke.

Restless and frustrated, I wandered in the garden, feeding the birds. They were the only living creatures I had any affinity with. Robins ate out of my hands and chattering sparrows vied for crumbs. Even the bold, beady-eyed rooks didn't appear to mind me. They cocked their gleaming heads on one side as I passed as if they listened to my thoughts.

And haughty as ash-coloured galleons, the gulls swept across the sky and I saluted them.

The birds saw everything…

Ten

The Pryce sisters knew that outside the bounds of Gull House another more modern world existed.

Their days were a mixture of the carefree and the kind of isolation normally associated with children of a previous era. Although they were curious, they were fearful too.

In spite of her anxiety at their ignorance, and her secret desire to go to school, Verity still had reservations. If she were contemptuous of her mother's half-hearted efforts to educate them, like her sister, she was equally afraid of being exposed to a classroom of her peers who might ridicule their eccentric lifestyle. It was the early days of the home-schooling model; contact with the authorities was minimal.

Studious by nature, Verity tried to keep up. The problem being she was unsure what she was supposed to be keeping up with. Frowning at a page of sums, she laid down her pencil.

In the hall, the telephone rang and she ran to answer it.

Nain!

Discovering she was right only added to her delight.

'Hello, my darling.'

'Are you coming to visit?'

'Indeed I am, *cariad*.'

'When?'

'Don't I get a hello?'

Verity laughed, greeted her grandmother and repeated her question. She hadn't seen her for months and could barely contain her excitement.

It was Mared's turn to laugh. 'Slow down, child, take a breath! How are you? How's your sister?'

'Irritating.'

'Now then, that'll do. Sisters shouldn't fight,' Mared said. 'I never had one; you're lucky, don't you forget it.'

'I know. I love her to bits, Nain, it's only sometimes…'

'Sometimes you wish you could wave a magic wand and make her disappear.'

'Is that bad?'

It was Mared's turn to laugh. 'Maybe we can make a small spell – for special occasions. Turn her into a bird; make her fly away for a few hours.'

'I wish you could.'

'And how do you know I can't?'

Verity squeezed her eyes shut, searched her mind for her grandmother's face and found it. Her skin, soft and traced with a net of lines, so fine unless Verity was close enough to kiss her she couldn't see them. And her eyes, the colour of summer mist.

'I know you can.'

'That's better.'

Mared described the world as if it were a place of wonder. She cast a spell over everything; taught the girls about plants and flowers and how to walk as softly as cats. When they were little and she still lived with them, they sat with Mared in her blue garden under the moon counting stars. They had learned how to catch bird songs in their dreams, and she taught them how to laugh at themselves.

Mared Pryce was a little bit witchy, and the most sensible woman Verity had ever met.

'When are you coming and how long are you staying for?'

'The day after tomorrow, and I'm sorry, lovely, only for one night.'

'Can't you stay longer?'

'You know I can't. Polly can do one night. Anymore and it isn't fair. Gethin gets agitated and even more confused when I'm not around.'

Polly was Nain's neighbour and friend, as kind as could be but Gethin's dementia made him unpredictable.

'I'll set off at first light. Short and sweet is better than nothing, *cariad*.'

When Verity told her, Meredith's happiness bubbled over.

'It's the best thing ever.'

'Well, I hope she isn't expecting the fatted calf,' Allegra said. 'I don't have time to cook.'

'Mam, you never cook.' Meredith patted her mother's arm. They were sitting on the steps overlooking the garden. Verity lay at the bottom, her legs stretched along the stone. 'Nain will bring things, she always does.'

'She'll fuss and moan and tell me off.'

'She doesn't moan,' Verity said. 'Don't be horrid.'

Allegra gave a short sigh, as if a long one was too much bother.

'It doesn't matter, Mam,' Meredith said. 'Nain will be too happy to see you to be bothered by anything else.'

'Why are you always so sweet to me?'

'I'm not. I say terrible things behind your back, but I love you and I love Nain and I love Verity, so can we all be nice?'

'Don't gang up on me, okay?' Allegra looked at Verity. 'I know what you and Mared are like when you get together. I can't stand secrets.'

You are a secret.

Verity sometimes thought she knew less about her mother than her sister did about maths. On the outside, Allegra was an open book. It was the inside of her Verity couldn't fathom.

Meredith leaned into her mother. 'Do you want to go for a walk?'

'Where to?'

'The wood.'

'Why would I want to go to the wood?'

'It'll be fun.' Meredith reached for her mother's hands.

58

'No,' Allegra said and pulled away. 'I don't like the wood. It's dark; I don't know why you find it so fascinating.'

The Pryce sisters knew the wood the way they knew their own names. Mared told them it was descended from wildwood and remembered wolves and flint and hundred-year-old fox trails.

'When you were a baby,' Allegra said, 'I carried you to the edge of the trees in a sling. You would reach out, wanting to touch the leaves.'

'Green's still my favourite colour.'

'Yes.'

Verity kept her eyes averted. She knew her mother found the wood oppressive. Once Meredith had been able to walk, Allegra had delegated. It had been Verity who trailed in Meredith's wake, listening as she insisted the wood was home to not only the birds and animals but to a race of invisible people Nain called the Other.

And now she wants me to believe in ghosts.

Verity pushed the thought away. It was a whim and if she wasn't encouraged, Meredith would soon forget about it.

Meredith smiled at her mother, took her hands and this time, Allegra didn't resist. Behind them, the light through the trees was muted, the air smelled of ramsons and fungi.

'Come on, you'll love it.'

You really want her to go with you don't you?

Verity felt Meredith's need like a compulsion. As if a walk in the wood might somehow take the edge off her mother's mood and cheer her up.

'Do you believe in magic, Mam?' Meredith asked.

'Magic is a concept, darling.' Allegra smoothed the skirt of her frock over her knees, reclaimed her hands; folded them onto her lap.

'Everything's a concept to you. I don't even know what that means.' Meredith shifted along the step. 'And don't tell me, I don't care.' She shrugged and smiled, softening the edge of her words. 'Nain believes in magic.'

'Oh, Mared still believes in bloody fairies.'

'Yes, she does, only not the kind in storybooks. They're older and Other and we have to respect them.'

Allegra stared at her daughter. 'You do say the most extraordinary things, Meredith.'

'It's true.'

'Darling, your grandmother's a crazy old woman; she tried to fill my head with her fairy nonsense and scared the living daylights out of me. Take no notice of her.'

'I take notice of everything Nain says.' Meredith left a space. 'She isn't crazy, she's ... discerning.'

Allegra shook her head and smiled. 'What are you like?'

Watching as Meredith set off for the wood, Verity knew not to follow. For all her frivolity and wildness, it wasn't only her sister's choice of words that marked her out; it was the way that what she said sounded less like an observation and more like a truth.

I feel visited...

Eleven

Verity and Meredith didn't know how old their grandmother was; she wouldn't tell them and it was impossible to guess.

'I'm as old as my hair and as young as my heart.'

Mared arrived in her maroon Morris Minor, laden with food and books, new frocks and pretty cardigans for the girls. After a picnic lunch, she did the rounds of the house, checking and noticing and asked Verity to make a pot of tea.

'While your mother's pretending she's not avoiding me,' she said, 'and your sister's wherever she is, let's you and me sit out on the terrace and have a natter.'

'Still not going to proper school then?'

Verity nibbled gingerbread. 'No, we're not sure we want to.'

I'm sure I do…

'You're far too clever not to go to school, Verity.'

Verity thought about what Meredith had said about clothes and grabbed the tangent.

'We love the frocks, Nain.'

'Do you? I wasn't sure. You wear jeans or shorts all the time.'

'I know I do; a frock's nice when it's hot.'

'That's what I thought.'

'And the cardigans are gorgeous – thank you. You're so clever.' Verity fingered the soft blue wool, played with the seed pearl buttons.

'Sewing and knitting keep me from going mad, *cariad*, while I'm sitting listening to Gethin rambling on. God love him, he's in a world of his own.'

'Is it awful?'

'Good heavens no! He's my brother. Why would it be awful?' She poured milk into cups. 'I went through it with my mam, so it's not like I'm a stranger to it.' She smiled and her eyes sparkled. 'I could perhaps wish he'd been keener on Wales than London, mind. There's no accounting for taste, I suppose, and he was ambitious from the beginning was Gethin.'

'Do you think he remembers anything about when he was a detective?'

'Not a thing, *cariad*. Now and then perhaps – when one of his pals from the Met drops by.'

'It must be terrible to forget your own life.'

'At least he had a good one. He was a decent copper, was your great-uncle Gethin.' Mared stirred the tea. 'Now, does Meredith like her bits and pieces?'

'Of course she does.' Verity reached for a cardigan, abandoned in a deck chair, the sweet green of it like spring leaves. 'I know she's careless; she doesn't mean to be.'

'Your sister's a law unto herself, like her mother.' Mared winked. 'Meredith's a good girl, you both are.' She poured herself a cup of tea. 'Now, are you going to tell me what's going on with Allegra or do I have to guess?'

'It's no different from what it always is.' Verity fidgeted. 'Sometimes I think she hates me.'

'Don't be silly. It's a horrid word and I don't want you using it about your mam. Allegra's a lot of things, but she's not evil. And it's only evil people who hate.'

'So why is she mean? She's always angry, especially with me. It's like however hard I try I can never please her.'

Mared sipped her tea. Verity could see her reflection in her grandmother's glasses.

'I know it looks like that. She's not angry with you, lovely, she's angry with herself.'

'How come?'

'People who believe they're the centre of their own world usually are.' Mared sighed. 'I blame myself. Most of it's my fault.'

'How do you work that out?'

'Well, for a start, your grandfather carried her everywhere; until she was a great big girl perfectly capable of walking by herself. And I did too, like an idiot.'

'Why?'

'Now, there's a question. Your mother was spoiled rotten.'

Verity couldn't imagine her sensible grandmother spoiling anyone.

'Her father started it. Besotted he was; indulged her at every turn and she lapped it up. His little princess, he called her. Bit of a cliché.' Her smile turned to a wry twist. 'For a sensible doctor, he was blind when it came to that child.'

'Was she really that bad?'

'Yes. She'd wail for her own way and when she didn't get it, oh, the tantrums. And he gave in, the silly old fool. I tell you, your mother flounced her way through life.'

'She still does.'

'I know, *cariad*. There's something inside her; a rage I tried to ignore because it was an outlandish notion for a mother to have about her own child.' Mared took off her glasses and began cleaning them on the hem of her skirt. Her voice faltered and she closed her eyes for a moment. 'It was a mistake: mothers ought to look deep and ask questions – butt in and take charge.'

Verity wasn't quite sure what her grandmother meant.

'Her tantrums frightened me. I tried, nothing worked. I'd watch her sleeping – because it was the only time she looked like a proper little girl – and be afraid for her. I couldn't see inside her, couldn't find the rage so I didn't know how to heal it.'

'You make me feel sorry for her.'

'Yes, not too sorry though. Eh? Denying you an education is criminal.'

'Even if I wanted to go to school, and I'm not saying I do, she'd never agree,' Verity said. 'Allegra does things her way. No one stands a chance.'

'Yes, and that's what I mean. Your grandfather was as much use as a chocolate chicken. He couldn't care less when she didn't learn her lessons and got sent home from school so many times it was hardly worth her going. And he left me to deal with it. He was a hypocritical idealist. Said he believed in votes for women and in the next breath, education was wasted on girls; all they did was get married and have children.'

'At least that bit turned out to be true.'

'Yes, but I ought to have stood up to him, *bach*, stopped pandering to her much sooner. If she'd had a proper education then, maybe you'd be getting one now.'

'We're all right, Nain, we do okay. The education people sent a whole lot of new stuff – maths and history, English and all sorts. I like the English.' Verity grinned. 'And we have you, at the end of the phone. You're clever – you know loads of things.'

'That's as maybe. You need to look to the future, Verity. You've got a brain on you; it would be a sin to waste it.'

'I'll try not to.' She swallowed; determined not to cry.

Mared took Verity's hand, unwound her fingers and placed a small white stone with a hole in the middle on her palm. 'I found it in my blue garden this morning. That hole was made by a falling star.' She winked.

'Nain…'

'You better believe it, *cariad*. My garden magic's the best you'll ever know.'

'I'll save it for a special occasion then.' Verity smiled and slipped the stone into the pocket of her jeans.

Since Mared's arrival, Allegra had drifted round the house like an irascible ghost. Each time they crossed paths they crossed words.

Hovering on the landing, Meredith heard them in the hall.

'There's nothing to see, the house is fine.'

Mared gave a dismissive snort. 'It's filthy.'

Allegra sighed and huffed. 'You're as bourgeois as Verity. I—'

'Allegra, don't. Please don't criticise my grandchildren in front of me. It's insensitive and unnecessary.' Mared glared. 'And calling your own daughter by a fancy French epithet doesn't impress me one bit. It makes no sense and it's rude. She's a little girl, not a class convention.'

'She's difficult and argumentative. You don't know what it's like—'

'Oh, don't start. I know what I see and I'm telling you, you've had a downer on that child since she was a *dwt*. You ought to be ashamed of yourself. She's sweet and kind and what's more she's clever.'

'You don't see her when she's trying to get her sister to side against me.'

Meredith held her breath.

Verity doesn't do that.

'Sides?' Mared let out a spit of air. 'Enough, Allegra. You're a grown woman and you make it sound like a conspiracy.'

Meredith peered over the bannister. Her mother was making for the front door.

'That's it, walk away when someone calls you out.' Although Mared's voice was controlled there was an edge to it and Allegra stopped, her hand poised on the door knob. 'Those girls love you, Allegra. Verity may not like you very much, and frankly who can blame her? You need to get a grip and sort this out before you drive them both away.'

Allegra snatched open the door. 'And you need to mind your own, Mam. I'm not a child, you can't tell me what to do.'

'There you go again, making it about you.' Mared lifted a hand, her index finger poised like a pencil. 'And so long as you live in my house, rent free, I can do as I like. It's a pity I didn't do it years ago.'

'Typical.'

'There's ways of doing things; simple rules, Allegra. You have responsibilities.'

As Allegra slammed the door, Mared's shoulders slumped.

Meredith exhaled.

So why don't you come back and make her see them?

Mared's rules had come laced with love and Meredith knew it. When she left it was as if she took those rules with her. Allegra, who couldn't discipline herself, left the girls to it.

I'll stay here until you come back, Nain. Don't worry – she doesn't mean it and however badly she behaves, I'll never leave Gull House. I'll wait until you come back and then we can stay forever.

Later that evening, when Mared said she'd decided not to leave first thing and she would stay until the following afternoon, Allegra raised her eyebrows.

'Don't make yourself late on my account.'

'Your account's overdrawn, lady; I want some more time with the girls.'

Twelve

Verity caught Meredith coming out of her bedroom.

'There's still time to ask Nain about Angharad.'

'No.' Meredith was adamant. 'I meant what I said. Swear you won't, Verity. If Allegra gets a hint of it, she'll want to see the sewing box and I'm not giving it up.'

Verity shrugged and agreed. 'Okay, only if you really want to find out—'

'You promised. Swearing is promising and if you break your word—'

'I didn't, actually. Don't worry though, I won't say anything.'

Meredith turned away. 'You'd better not.'

Expecting their grandmother to be preparing to leave, the girls were over the moon when they found her in the kitchen, still in her dressing-gown and making breakfast.

Mared dished up creamy porridge.

'Lush,' Meredith said. 'No lumps.'

'That's more like it,' Verity said.

Mared grinned. 'It's an art, is porridge.'

Hovering by the back door, Allegra rolled a cigarette and said she had things to do.

'You go ahead, *cariad*.' Mared ran water into the saucepan. 'We'll be fine.'

'And then you'll leave. Same as you always do.'

'Don't start, Allegra, you know how I'm fixed.'

'Ah, yes, the saintly Gethin.'

Verity's spoon stopped halfway to her mouth.

Don't make a scene, Mam, please.

Mared said nothing, and Allegra made a noise somewhere between a sigh and a snort.

'Why do I bother,' she said. 'Go ahead, I don't need you, I don't need anyone.'

'Allegra…'

The door shuddered in its frame.

'Did she talk to our father like that?' Meredith said. 'Is it why he left?'

Their father's lack of curiosity about them meant the Pryce sisters rarely discussed him. An absence isn't a story.

'Or did he just die?'

Verity was shocked. 'Don't be disrespectful, Meri.'

'Why? I don't really care and it's not against the law to ask is it?'

'No, it isn't.' Mared filled the kettle and flicked the switch. 'And it's time you knew.' For once, Mared was cross enough with her daughter to stick her nose in. 'Your father was a well-meaning man, only not right for your mam. Her dad hadn't long passed when they met; she was in a right state.'

'You must have been sadder,' Meredith said.

'Grief isn't a competition, *bach*, and I had my work at the hospital. Your mam had nothing to distract her.'

'What did he do?' Meredith scraped her bowl clean. 'For a job?'

Mared scooped up the bowl and rinsed it. She moved round the room easily, rearranging the things Allegra insisted on changing. It was a game they played.

'He was poet, or so he said. A charming rogue who didn't have a proper job until Verity was born and then it was only on the farms.'

'Is that why he went, because he couldn't get a job as a poet?'

Mared laughed. 'You have to be good at it to get a job writing poems for a living.'

'So he wrote rubbish ones?'

'I never read any of them, *cariad*. I wouldn't imagine so. As far as I could see, he didn't sit still long enough to write his name. Always out, Idris was – over the hills and far away.'

From her.

Verity felt her grandmother's eyes on her.

'And so he left.' Meredith said. 'Well, I still don't care.'

'Best way, sweetheart. Best way.'

Meredith said she was going to pick lilac for her grandmother to take home.

'Ah, you're an angel. I do love my lilac and it'll cheer Gethin up – he likes the perfume.'

Meredith planted a kiss on her grandmother's cheek and disappeared into the garden.

'Did he have another woman?' Verity's curiosity was getting the better of her.

'What makes you say that? No, of course he didn't. He wasn't entirely without principle; it was more a need to be anywhere your mother wasn't.'

'And not because of us?'

'No, *cariad*, not at all.'

Verity wasn't convinced. Her father was as remote from her as the moon. It was unlikely he'd ever cared about them. If he had, he'd have stayed.

'Do I really look like him?'

If Mared was taken aback she hid it well. 'What makes you ask?'

'It's an easy enough question, Nain.'

Mared stopped what she was doing. 'All right then, you do, a bit. You have his eyes and some of his mannerisms: a way of moving your head when you're preoccupied.'

'Is that why she doesn't like me, because I remind her of him?'

'Your mother loves you, Verity.'

Verity understood her grandmother didn't want her to know

heartbreak; she wanted to protect both her granddaughters for as long as she could.

'That's not what I asked. You can love someone and hate the sight of them. I'm not a baby, Nain. And I'm not stupid.'

'I know,' Mared said. 'You're sharp as a knife and I'm not going to lie to you. Maybe you do remind her of Idris, but I don't think it's as simple as like or dislike or even love. Your mother's damaged and there are times I could throttle her for the way she is around you. But it isn't as personal as it must seem.'

Verity nodded. 'I believe you. Honestly, Nain, I do.' She crossed her fingers and hoped her grandmother believed her, and if she found her out in the lie, would be able to forgive her.

'He loved you too, *cariad*, believe me.'

Verity managed a smile.

'He came back,' Mared said, 'because he was in thrall to her – mad about her – and because he loved you both. I'm certain of that.' Mared paused and smiled. 'I didn't mind him; I told her, don't push him away, he has the makings of a good father.'

'Only she didn't listen.'

'No. Allegra doesn't do listening and Idris, well, he was too young – only a year older than her – and far too selfish.' Mared began moving things again: a couple of Toby jugs from the top shelf of the dresser to a lower one.

'Your mother was very demanding and Idris wasn't the kind of man to put up with emotional games. But if you ask me, after Meredith was born, it was post-natal depression too. We didn't go in for it much – not in my day. I reckon that's what it was though, so try not to judge her. Not long after Meredith's birth, he disappeared again and this time, I'm afraid it was for good.'

'And that was that.'

'Yes.' Mared sighed. 'The thing is, if he'd stayed for you and your sister, he'd probably have killed your mother.'

'But if he loved her—'

70

'Love,' Mared said, stroking Verity's hair, 'isn't as necessary to a man's happiness as it is to a woman's.'

I wasn't supposed to go into the walled garden, except under my mother's strict supervision.

As a small child I loved spending time there; sitting under the boughs of a fragrant wisteria, reading and listening to the birds. I fed them cake crumbs, imagined them listening to me. Eventually Mama would send the latest maid to find me, and if my hair was awry or my gown stained with grass, I would find myself chastised.

Even compliant children occasionally rebel and I adored this secret garden. As often as I dared, I sneaked off and hid myself away. There were niches in the walls holding little stone statues of cherubs and animals: a hare, a cat and several birds. It was formal and largely tended by my mother. A man came once a week from a neighbouring village to deal with the heavy work.

In the centre stood a sculpted lavender bush and radiating from this were four brick paths lined with low box hedges marking plots filled with herbs and lovely flowers: dainty pinks and London Pride and tall columbine. Stone troughs containing more lavender stood at the four corners; along the walls graceful ferns and grasses grew in orderly clumps. The borders were filled with stately delphiniums, hollyhocks and lupins, none of them allowed to defy my mother's idea of perfection.

Against one of the walls grew an espaliered plum tree: my mother's pride and joy. Its tiny fruits were ideal food for birds, which my mother did her best to scare away. The branches stretched like elongated fingers as if it was alive in a way beyond the simple existence of a tree. It looked trapped by the wires holding it and I longed to cut it loose.

Like me, nothing in the garden was permitted to break free or roam.

As I became older and learned my mother's routine by heart whenever I could, I slipped away to read my book or enjoy the birds.

It was a serene place, magical and protecting, as if a spell lay across it – perhaps the reason my brother never once found me there.

Thirteen

Enclosed behind brick walls, it was always twilight in the blue garden.

The scents were strong in high summer, and everything grew untamed and tall. It left a pure blue taste on the tongue and a sense of being touched by old magic. To Verity and Meredith it was enchanted: once inside they felt invisible and might well have been. Allegra certainly never found them there.

'Bring a rug, Meredith,' Mared said that evening. 'And Verity, you light a lantern.'

Since they were little girls, Mared had encouraged them to make small rituals in her garden. 'Welcome the new moon, listen to the full and bid the dark sleep well.'

She told them the moon was female the way the sun was male.

'Ritual is mostly a matter of showing up,' she said. 'Leave offerings and light candles. You can make your plans at new moon, watch them grow and by the time the dark moon comes around, chances are they'll be sorted.'

Meredith liked the dark moon, Verity preferred the new. She liked the idea of plans, even though right then the only one she had was pretty vague. She peered through the trees. There was no sign of the moon and she asked her grandmother which phase it was in.

Mared always knew.

'It's waning, *cariad*, soon be dark.'

'If you can't see it, how can you tell?'

'The moon is the ebb and flow of your life. She's your blood. You'll learn how to do it.'

Surrounded by tall grass and wild flowers, light from the candle lantern made the shadows come alive.

'Like ghosts,' Verity said.

Meredith caught her breath and Verity knew she was willing her not to say anything about the sewing box.

'Don't be silly,' Meredith said. 'Everyone knows you can't see ghosts.'

'You reckon?' In the flickering light, Mared's face looked older and wise.

'Tell us the story,' Meredith said, 'the one about how you made the garden.'

'Not the one about the snow child?'

'No, I want to hear how the garden started. Was it a new moon?'

'I can't remember; it was definitely a dark one when I sneaked back to that chapel.'

It started with a single blue poppy.

One day in 1940, honeymooning in Wales for a precious weekend, Mared Pryce had gone to town in search of something special to cook for her new husband. Passing a chapel, she noticed a blue poppy growing between the cracks in the pavement.

'In the middle of the day in summer the town's full of people. I wasn't daft enough to pull up a plant outside a chapel and risk the disapproval of whatever god-bothering flower arrangers might be on duty.'

'But you went back.' Meredith snuggled in, knowing what came next.

'I certainly did, *cariad*; under cover of darkness.'

'Like a spy!'

'Like a thief in the night!'

She took the poppy without a second thought. There wasn't the slightest trace of fear in her; Mared, a veteran of wartime London, hadn't been afraid of anything and, other than losing her faculties, she still wasn't.

'In any case, who would have missed it? Sooner or later someone would have trampled it to death; why wouldn't I save it?'

She planted it in the abandoned garden.

'What with two wars and one thing and another, it had been forgotten. I remembered the garden when I was a child, all overgrown like a jungle. When I got married and came back for good, it seemed like a nice idea to set it to rights.'

She'd cleared the space, cutting back, unearthing the remains of brick paths, broken stone troughs, monster ferns strangled by ivy and the dead leavings of an espaliered fruit tree she couldn't identify.

'And you pulled the ivy off the wall and found the hare.'

'Shush, Meri – let Nain tell it her way.'

'I pulled the ivy off the walls and discovered the gaps, the remains of the stone animals and the birds, little bits of cherubs like broken babies. The only piece that had survived intact was the hare.'

'The house must have been empty for a long time…'

Meredith interrupted. 'That's not part of the story, Verity.'

'I know – it's still interesting.'

'Yes, it is.' Mared nodded. 'When my grandfather bought the house, back in the olden days,' she said with a laugh, 'it had been empty for a very long time. No one ever stayed, too isolated I suppose. And people said it was haunted. He didn't believe any of that of course: he restored the place and here we are.'

'Was he rich?' Meredith said, determined they wouldn't pursue hauntings.

'Oh, there was money all right. Our family were what was known as trade – bankers – not influential, not so small they hadn't made a bob or two.' She pushed her glasses up her nose. 'We're not rich mind, and never were. We're comfortable. It makes a difference and makes us fortunate.'

'It doesn't feel that way.' Verity picked a closed-up daisy, tried to open the petals.

'The bills get paid and there's food on the table. That's what counts.'

Meredith had had enough of bankers and money. 'Go on with the story, Nain.'

Mared explained how the wind scattered the poppy seeds across the garden. And as if by magic, in spring the bluebells appeared, holding the space for the poppies which, year by year, spread in a sweet blue unwinding.

By heart, Meredith recited a list of flowers – the other blue ones her grandmother had planted. 'Lavender, lupins, cornflowers, scabious; campanula, forget-me-not and agapanthus.'

'Very good, *cariad*, well remembered.' Mared laughed. 'I rescued several woody lilacs too; cut them back and…'

'Sang to them until they flowered!'

'And they drenched the garden in perfume so the Fae knew exactly where to come.'

Verity listened to her grandmother's voice as if for the first time. Even the interruptions didn't spoil the story.

'They're still here,' Meredith said. 'I can hear them.'

Her grandmother stroked her hair and nodded.

The candle burned low as the garden faded to an illusion.

Verity hugged her grandmother so hard, Mared gasped.

'You'll hug the breath out of me, child.'

They stood on the gravel path by the car.

Unable to speak, Verity swallowed and forced herself not to cry. She made way for Meredith, clamouring for her own hug.

'It'll be all right, Nain,' Meredith said, making no attempt to hide her tears. 'I'll look after Verity.'

'You'll look after each other, the way I taught you.' Mared spread her arms and waved them both in. 'Come on now, big *cwtch*, no tears, only smiles.'

She turned her head to the eggshell blue door, the invitation clear.

Allegra, arms folded, leaned against the frame.

Mared spoke over her granddaughters' heads. 'Everything will be fine, my lovelies. I'm no more than a phone call away and before you know it, I'll be back.'

Allegra offered a hint of a nod. 'Drive safely, Mam.'

'I will, *cariad*, I always do. You look after yourself.'

Fourteen

Meredith's was the smallest bedroom, a youngest child's room.

Angharad's room?

She sensed it must have been.

Turning on the bedside lamp she looked at the red flannel heart in her hand. Once again, a shiver ran through her. The sensation was becoming familiar and almost welcome.

The voice settled in her mind: a storyteller's whisper.

I was surrounded by indifferent silence...

Meredith imagined she heard crying. She pinched her arm until it hurt and knowing she was awake, decided the only possibility had to be a ghost.

I was denied any hope...

However hard she tried to clear her head the words remained: sentences made from sorrow and spite.

You will not warm to my mother ... I do not want you to love her ... mothers are cruel and cannot be trusted...

Snuggling under the covers, the single heart held to her chest, she tried to imagine someone hiding the sewing box in an attic, abandoning it as if it no longer mattered.

Was it a clue? Would Angharad have put her own sewing box in a dusty old trunk? And if she hadn't, who had and why? If this had been Angharad Elin Lewis's bedroom, could anything else of her have been left behind?

Other than Nelly, her grey velvet rabbit, the thing Meredith loved best in the world was Nain's doll's house. It was old and her grandmother, Meredith decided, must have been an exceptionally well-behaved little girl to have been given a doll's house as beautiful as this one. Like Gull House, it wasn't damaged, only faded; made from materials that had lasted.

Meredith half-wished they'd asked Nain about Angharad after all.

'It could have been tricky though, Nelly – she might have told Mam about the sewing box.'

Meredith was determined her mother wouldn't find out about any of it. She tried to think back, to when they were little; remember what her grandmother had told them about Angharad. It wasn't much: a girl who had lived here a century ago and who people said was mad.

It sounded like the dark ages.

'This,' she said to Nelly, holding up the red heart, 'is a magic heart, from the olden days.'

Nelly stared her blank bunny stare.

'Do you want to hear a story?' She tucked the rabbit into the crook of her arm. 'Once upon a time, when girls went mad and people locked them up…'

Meredith's heart lurched and in an instant she knew the crucial questions.

If Angharad really had been locked away, what could possibly have made a girl go so crazy her parents would think it was a good idea to shut her up in an asylum?

'And how do I find out if it's true?'

She glanced at the sewing box. If they had got rid of her, it would explain why it had ended up in the attic. 'I definitely need to look for clues, Nelly.'

She recalled the whispered voice. Was this a ghost's bedroom: the ghost of a girl who had gone insane? Worse than this, Meredith found herself wondering about a flesh-and-blood girl hearing voices.

Suppose Verity's right and it is in my head? Suppose I'm the crazy one?

Like Angharad, who ended up being locked away in an asylum?

The word hung in the air like a threat. Meredith wasn't sure what kind of a place an asylum might have been. A hospital she supposed, for lunatics. Hugging Nelly closer, she padded across the floor to where her fishing-net hung outside the window.

Meredith made her best wish. 'Star bright, star light, let Angharad talk to me tonight.' For good measure, she added, 'Clearly, please, so I can hear everything she says.'

As she gazed out into the night, a shooting star made a run for it. On such a night it wasn't hard to believe your wishes might come true.

The moths began to dance in the wisteria and Meredith pushed open the window as far as it would go.

'Here's my wish,' she whispered. 'Take it and fly it up to the stars.'

Back in bed she left the lamp on and her eyes open.

If I'm not scared and if I can stay awake, maybe I'll hear her.

She pushed her face into the pillow, pinched the soft skin on her inner arm.

'I'll try, I promise. You can tell me.'

Her eyes drooped and she pinched herself again, only it wasn't enough to keep her from sleep. Her dreams were full of murmurs and dark corners she couldn't see into. In the early hours she woke again, unsure if she was scared or curious.

'I'm trying my best, Angharad. I'm sorry I fell asleep.'

When did a dream become a nightmare? And when did a nightmare become reality?

Am I being haunted or am I mad, like they said she was?

Her eyes fluttered open and as they did, Meredith felt a touch of ice-cold air on her face. It wasn't a moth and her skin crawled. She drew the bedclothes over her chin, her eyes scanning the shadows on the walls.

Don't be silly – everyone knows you can't see them.

Some ghosts were so quiet you could be forgiven for missing them.

Meredith had small ears and excellent hearing. Ghosts, she thought, were made of yearning and illusion. They were invisible. Real ghosts, Meredith believed, didn't show themselves, and what you thought you saw was what they left behind: the aftermath of the chaos that might have existed in their human lives. If you listened, you might perhaps sense a breath of longing.

It took a special kind of person to see a ghost.

The shape in the corner of her bedroom was lighter than shadow. It trembled and though she was lying down, Meredith thought she might faint.

It isn't real, it can't be. Everyone knows…

Meredith Pryce believed in ghosts with every bone in her body. When Angharad Elin Lewis' ghost had begun talking to her, she'd known, behind the murmuring lay a real voice.

Mine is a story as old as the moon…

And now, however hard she wanted to deny it, she could see her.

…a girl who ripped her gowns and lost her gloves…

Present

Backing away from the crumbling steps, I'm still uncertain about going inside.

Any house, left empty for more than twenty years, is sure to have suffered from the erosion of time. It isn't that though, it's the air of melancholy I'm unprepared for. A house you spent the first sixteen years of your life in imprints on your heart. You have a memory and it isn't meant to change. When it does, what was beloved can be diminished.

Rounding the edge of the building, I halt in my tracks.

Close to the wall, a vast gunnera has taken root threatening to undermine the foundations of the house. Behind it, half hidden and jutting from the wall, the semi-circular, once elegant iron-framed conservatory – never in the best state of repair – is now covered in a green patina. Russian ivy creeps across the roof. Beneath an ornate porch, the rusting door stands slightly ajar. Through the filthy panes of glass, the shadow of more vegetation looms.

There is a wild flapping as a bird hurtles through the gap in the door. Instinctively, I raise my hand. The bird knows its business and in a moment is gone.

Behind me, rain begins to fall, the fine horizontal kind that soaks through to a person's skin and leaves them shivering.

How very Welsh.

A shiver of breeze changes direction, a cast feather rises in the air, caught in the thin rain. I run my fingers over the conservatory door-frame, the layers of paint, repeated to a thickness almost holding the thing together. My hand touches a rusty patch.

I hear my mother's considered critique of her work (and her contrived criticism of me.) Again, I sense her; her disdainful smile, cleverly disguising her monstrous personality.

'Goodness, how clever of you. A *librarian*!' Her emphasis had made it sound like an insult.

My heart speeds up a little. I pause, listen, press the flat of my fingers to my breastbone as if to reassure my heart there is no longer anything to be belittled by.

I step inside.

At the back, hidden behind a wall of green, a smaller door leads to a room off the kitchen, an old scullery with a crock sink we called the glory hole. We stored our boots there, cans of paraffin, brooms and buckets, Allegra's easels and painting paraphernalia.

The door is open and I frown, knowing it ought to be locked. The key is missing. I think about passing tramps again – the glory hole leads into the kitchen and the rest of the house.

Could Nain have left it open?

The idea is ridiculous; my grandmother hadn't ever left a door unlocked or, unless someone was here, windows open either. I take hold of the handle meaning to close the door and notice a groove where the bottom of the frame has dragged over the ground.

It's fresh: a clean curve in the soil.

Someone has definitely been here. I reach into my bag, find my phone and search for the caretaker's number. I dial it and watch as it fades.

No signal.

Who knew?

Using my weight, I push the door, force it closed. Maybe the key is in the house. Or it's on the bunch in my bag. I'll check later, before I leave.

My thoughts are opening other doors and I brace myself against a rush of memories. I see Allegra and her ubiquitous hair, standing back from her easel, paintbrush poised. In my travel-crumpled clothes, my mother stands in her casual finery – splashed with paint and still managing to appear implausibly stylish.

An accumulation of verdigris on the glass creates the illusion of being underwater. I catch my breath and for a second I do see her: my mother in her absurd clothes, a child of the fifties enamoured of the twenties, addicted to gin and love and the conviction no one understood her.

I don't like myself when I'm unkind. It is Carla who is the kind one. In the face of Allegra's extravagant and embarrassing response to our relationship Carla had been simply amused. 'She means well.'

My mother never meant well.

Carla tells me I'm a good person. She tells everyone. It isn't true. After twenty years, she still hasn't found the nasty part of me and I don't want her to.

Looking around, I hold my breath.

Allegra's ghost isn't here. And even if she is a ghost, she's drifting on the ether, dressed to the nines, still insisting school is a waste of time, art is the answer to everything and if only I bucked up my ideas, I might make something of my life and be as clever as my sister.

Fifteen

Verity woke before daybreak, disturbed by a crash.

In the kitchen, Allegra was kneeling on the floor, rattling coals in the grate, her hair awry, a smudge of soot on the perfect skin of her cheek.

The coal scuttle lay on its side. A half-empty bottle of gin stood next to it.

'Damn the bloody thing; why won't it light?' She jabbed a poker at the embers with one hand, waved an empty glass in the other. 'I can't bear this cold.'

'Here, let me.' Verity righted the coal scuttle. 'What are you doing up at this hour anyway?'

'Couldn't sleep.' Allegra reached for the gin, sloshed a measure into the glass. 'You know how it is. I never sleep.'

Verity didn't. She slept like a log and in any case, her mother's claim was absurd. Allegra regularly made up for her late nights by sleeping until noon.

Leaning into the grate, Verity screwed up some newspaper and fed it to the embers. It caught and a few sparks flew out. She batted them away. Flames leapt up, she added twigs, a few pieces of kindling, held a sheet of newspaper across the opening to draw the fire. 'There we are.' Before the newspaper caught, she snatched it away, folded it and put it in the basket, settled back into one of the cane chairs.

Allegra carried on as if Verity wasn't there. 'This is no way to live. I wasn't meant for this kind of life.' She swallowed some gin. 'Why did she stay here?'

Verity knew her mother was talking about Nain. 'You know why. When they fell in love, Taid wanted to come back to Wales

84

the same as she did. If they both loved the house, why wouldn't they live here when they got married?'

Allegra poured more gin, banged the bottle down on the floor. 'It was selfish. To make me live here.'

'You make us live here.'

'That's different and you know it. You and Meredith like living here.'

'I thought you did. At least, there isn't any reason for you not to. Not really.'

Allegra gave a pinched smile. 'You think you know me, Verity but you don't. And you don't know how hard it is for me – trying to keep body and soul together.'

It's easy come, easy go though, isn't it? Nain always bails us out.

Verity kept this disloyalty to herself.

Were it not for Mared – the banker's daughter – Allegra and her children would be impoverished. Her personal income was erratic. During the tourist season, her watercolours sold fairly well. They hung in a shop with a tiny gallery, run by an arty couple with aspirations Allegra pretended to be impressed by. She helped out in the shop and although the proceeds from her canvases ran through her spendthrift fingers as easily as the water off her paint brushes, somehow they managed.

'You need to be more organised, that's all.' Verity watched the flames glowing through the iron bars, felt the heat on the palms of her hands.

Allegra rolled a cigarette. 'Oh, please. You sound like him.'

'Him?'

'Idris. He thought he knew me.'

Verity turned and looked at her mother. 'You don't talk about him much, do you?'

'Why would I? He left me. He was cruel.'

'I thought you loved him.'

'You're too young to understand.' Allegra took the other chair, cradled the glass.

'I didn't know him; how can I understand?'

'You're too young to understand about love.' Allegra sipped her gin. 'He adored my work you know. Idris wanted me to go to London and show there; then I fell pregnant with you.'

'Say what you mean why don't you?'

'There you go again, Verity, trying to be clever, taking it personally. It's not all about you. You have no idea what my life's been like, bringing up two children on my own.'

'Mam, get real. Until a few years ago you had Nain to help out.'

Once again, Allegra continued talking as if Verity hadn't spoken, as if what she said had no value.

'Love's complicated – especially when both people are artists.' She paused, a faraway look on her face. 'He was a poet, you know. It mattered.'

'And what about us; didn't we matter?'

Allegra looked pained. 'How can you say such a thing? I live for you girls.'

'That's not what I meant.'

Her mother ignored her. 'Everything I've ever done has been for you and your sister. I've sacrificed my talent and my youth to bring you up. If I'd gone to London things would have been very different. It's another world. City people appreciate art.'

The fire was settling. Verity added coal, filled the big kettle and set it on the hotplate, cut some bread, put it in the toaster. 'Do you want some?'

When Allegra didn't answer, Verity turned round. Her mother was staring at her, one arm over the back of the chair, her eyes filled with unshed tears.

'Don't.'

'You can be very cruel sometimes, Verity.' Allegra dumped her empty glass on the floor.

'Mam, please don't; it isn't true. You think if you cry it'll make me care, as if that's what it takes. I already care; I just don't buy the fake tears or the fantasy I'm against you.' The toast popped up and she buttered it, slapped it on a plate. 'Here, you need to eat something.'

Allegra waved away the plate and Verity shrugged.

'I'm not against you,' she said, nibbling the toast. 'I want it to be fair.'

Allegra had a habit of holding two fingers to her temple, as if her head hurt or she was struggling to recall something. It was an affectation and she did it now, cigarette smoke trailing through her hair, and Verity struggled not to say something really unkind.

The tears overflowed, ran down Allegra's cheeks like old pearls.

'You are though.' Sniffing, she dropped the cigarette butt into the empty glass. 'Against me. You don't try to understand. Not like Meredith.'

This was more than Verity could bear. 'Meredith does as she's told. She'll do anything to be in your good books because she thinks you're amazing and she wants us all to be happy. Do you really know what Meredith feels? What either of us feel? You haven't a clue? Why can't you be real?'

Allegra folded her arms across her body as if she was in pain.

'What? What's wrong now?'

Allegra's normally flawless face was patched with blotches; yesterday's smeared mascara making her look like a clown.

'You're saying I'm a fake? What I do isn't real?' She delivered the words as if they were a personal affront. Fumbling in her pocket, she pulled out her tarot cards.

'Oh, please.' Verity almost laughed. 'Go on then, consult the oracle. See what the cards have to say. May as well, seeing as how you haven't got a clue.' She fixed her mother with a glare, daring her to respond.

Allegra stared back, her face still, the tears stopped in their tracks. She inhaled several times and her nostrils flared. When she spoke, she hissed. 'How dare you speak to me like that? How did you get to be so selfish?'

'If I'm selfish, then what does that make you? The only person your ever think about is yourself.' Verity held back her own tears, stared at the toast crumbs. 'I wish you'd gone to London when Nain did and left us here so we could have a half-normal life.'

Allegra swept up the cards and shoved them into her pocket. Her eyes glittered.

'Well,' she said, 'you know what they say: better be careful what you wish for.'

Verity put her plate on the draining board and opened the back door. She could smell the sea and the scent of lilac drifting on the gathering light.

'Now where are you going?'

'Nowhere.'

As she walked across the sloping lawn to her grandmother's garden, she thought about wishes: how some were good and others hopeless: the kind that, however hard you longed for them to work, would never come true.

Sixteen

In the morning, Meredith's hair was decorated with dusty-winged moths.

Delighted, she shook her hair and they fluttered up.

'Thank you, my lovelies' she said, 'now off you go.' She waved her arms, herded the moths to the window and watched as they disappeared.

The voice from her dream hovered in the back of her mind. Pushing it away, Meredith thought perhaps she should try and forget about ghosts and focus on her made-up story.

Maybe Verity's right, and it is all in my head.

The echo of half-formed whispers insisted otherwise.

She put on the new frock her grandmother had made for her. The material was pale green scattered with daisies, with a full skirt and when she twirled it floated as light as a moth.

Standing in the hall behind the half-open kitchen door, she heard Verity talking to Allegra.

'I picked some more lilac; shall I arrange it for you?'

'Well you can try.' Her mother's voice had an edge to it. 'Very nice, although I'm not sure how successful you'll be. It's not like you have a natural aptitude for flower arranging is it, darling?' She laughed as she said the words.

Meredith frowned.

Why is she always so mean to Verity?

She watched her sister fling the flowers onto the table, find a jug and fill it with water.

'Do it yourself then.' Verity banged the jug down.

Water splashed over Allegra's sketchpad and she snatched it away. 'For God's sake, Verity!'

Meredith guessed this was the tail end of an earlier argument. Coming into the room she saw the empty gin bottle on the table. Her mother's face was grey with fatigue.

Hung-over, I bet.

Allegra scrutinised three tarot cards, placed in a line on the table.

'Pages,' she said. 'Goodness, two of them: pentacles and cups.'

Glancing at the cards Meredith said, 'Get the fancy gear. And why's he got a fish in his tankard?'

'It's a cup, darling.'

'Looks more like that old tin coffee pot of yours.'

'Don't be silly. The tarot's—'

'Gobbledegook?'

'That's not very nice, is it? The page of cups is sensitive and creative, like you – you're a Pisces…'

'I know I am, so what?'

'If you'd let me explain, you'd understand.' Allegra paused. 'Two pages – you see? They represent children and news.' She gave a nervous cough. 'I hope you two won't go talking about me behind my back.'

'Why would we do that?' Meredith kept her voice neutral.

'I'm joking, you goose.' Allegra stared at the cards. 'But pages… I'm only saying.' She patted the chair next to her. 'You look gorgeous in your new frock. That shade of green really suits you.'

Meredith ignored her. 'Pentacle boy looks a bit more normal. Is he creative too?'

'Not particularly. He represents earth.'

'Which means he must be very clever indeed because it's Verity's sign; she's a Virgo.'

Meredith watched her sister out of the corner of her eye.

Trust me…

'Meri, it doesn't matter…'

Meredith tapped the last card. 'What about this one?' Her eyes shone like stars in the rain.

'The Six of Wands.'

'Meaning?'

'Success, my angel. Success after conflict!'

Seeing her sister wince, Meredith said, 'Or you could wave the wands and make some kindness?' Propping her elbow on the table, she caught her chin in her hand. 'You could make a lot of kindness with six magic wands.' She pushed the card across the table, regarded her mother with her star eyes and the air in the room held its breath. 'If you wanted to.'

The words tasted sharp on her tongue. Bitter as pepper and she let them swirl around her mouth. Reaching for the sprigs of lilac, she began placing them in the jug.

'It's pretty,' she said. 'It was kind of Verity to get it for you, wasn't it?'

Meredith knew more than her mother guessed, and as if she sensed it Allegra swept the cards into the velvet bag and made for the back door. As she turned, her eyes narrowed and she let them rest on her youngest daughter's face. 'You're such a puzzle sometimes, baby.' She opened the door. 'I'm off to the conservatory. See what the muse has in store for me.'

Meredith said nothing. She shifted closer to Verity and the tang of pepper was warm on her tongue.

Seventeen

'You have to wonder,' Meredith said, 'what must have happened to make Angharad so unhappy.'

Verity held her book closer until her nose was touching it, let out an exaggerated sigh. 'Meredith, please? I'm reading.' Her legs stretched along the cushions on the window seat. Out on the terrace sparrows pecked in the gaps between the paving stones. It was cold and her breath misted the window.

The sitting room was spacious and in spite of a shabby veneer, still elegant. A pretty chandelier hung from a central rose, crystal lustres hanging in looped ropes. The walls were lined with books and pictures, a small grandfather clock, this one keeping time.

Meredith's eyes were wide with challenge. 'I know. I'm making conversation.'

'I don't want to talk about it. There's no point.'

'Why? Because she was mad?'

'Don't be silly.'

'I'm not. She was an outsider, Verity. People don't see outsiders.'

'What do you mean?'

'They said she was mad. She wasn't though, she wasn't old enough. Going mad takes time.'

'You're obsessed.'

'She was mad, only she wasn't, and that's the point. There's a difference between being mad and being driven mad.'

'You don't have to make things up to get my attention.'

'Get your attention? Oh for goodness sake – listen to yourself. They locked her up! It doesn't get much crazier than that.' Meredith's face froze. There was anger in what she left out: a glittering chaos.

'You don't know that.'

'I do – I feel it. No wonder she went mad.'

'You have to stop this, Meri.' Verity tried not to shout. 'It isn't real.'

'It is though. Don't you see? Before, she didn't know how to come back and now, somehow she does.'

'It doesn't make sense is all I'm saying.'

'I can hear how sad she is.' Meredith carried on as if Verity hadn't spoken. 'Although I still can't make out every word.'

Verity stared fixedly at her book.

'All right,' Meredith said. 'If you don't want to talk about Angharad, can we talk about our stories? Like we agreed? Or are you reneging on your promise?'

'Oh, stop showing off, Meri. And do I have to put up a notice to get you to leave me alone?'

Clearly she did. Meredith rattled on and Verity knew her sister wouldn't give up until she had her full attention.

'I know you don't believe me, Verity, I don't care. I know she's real.' Meredith pushed her sister's legs off the window seat. 'It's very, very cold in my room now, a sure sign of a ghost.'

Irritated, Verity snapped back. 'No. It's a sign we're in for an unusually cold spell, and April's acting strangely.' She rubbed the windowpane with her fingers. 'It still might snow.'

'Well, that too.'

If Verity thought she'd distracted her sister, she was mistaken.

Meredith leaned against the window frame, her notebook clutched in her hand. 'What if I told you, I've started writing mine down now only with an element of surprise?' She flicked through the pages and Verity caught a glimpse of scribbles.

'I'd say well done, and now can I get on with my book?'

'Verity, listen. I'm sort of managing to actually write a story, only because it's mixed up with hers, it's difficult.'

'Meredith, what are you talking about?'

Ignoring her, Meredith demanded to know if Verity had written any more of her own story.

'You are kidding? You didn't think I was actually going to do it did you? I told you, it's a stupid idea.'

Meredith's face fell. 'Sometimes, Verity Pryce, I suspect you actually hate me.'

'Oh, stop it; I do not hate you. You do my head in, that's all. And even if I did hate you, can you blame me? I told you I didn't want anything to do with your ridiculous scheme only you never listen. You're just like Allegra. Honest to goodness, sometimes it's like I'm completely invisible in this house!'

Meredith sniffed.

'And don't you dare start crying.'

'I wasn't going to. I'm sorry. You aren't invisible. And I'm sorry Mam's so mean to you.'

'Do we have to talk about her?'

'All right, I've said I'm sorry. Can't I at least tell you what I've managed to write?'

Verity set her book aside. 'If I say yes, will you leave me alone?'

'Yes.'

'Go on then.'

'Do you mean it?'

Outside, the sparrows flew up in a busy mob.

'Yes.' Verity felt a shiver run through her.

Her sister flicked the pages of the crumpled notebook. 'Actually, there's not a lot. It's too muddled. The thing is *she's* trying to tell me *her* story.'

'Who is?'

Meredith growled and slapped a hand against her head. 'Why do you have to be so obtuse?'

Verity couldn't help herself. She laughed out loud. 'Where on earth do you get these impossible words from?'

'Crossword puzzle.' Meredith grinned. 'Allegra's started doing them in some magazine, the easy ones with the answers in the back. And then I looked it up in the dictionary. It means dense.'

Still trying not to laugh, Verity said, yes, she knew what it meant and if Meredith wanted to tell her about the mad girl, she was all ears.

'I don't want to call her that anymore. Nain's right, it's horrible,' Meredith said. 'And I agree with her. Angharad was terribly sad and angry because something bad happened to her and she wants to tell me what it was.'

'Oh, Meredith, you don't really believe that, do you?'

Meredith folded her arms across her chest. 'See, I knew you wouldn't believe me.'

'How could a dead girl be talking to you? This is just you, being you. You're always making stuff up.'

'And you're a complete idiot.' Meredith flicked her hand at Verity's book, caught the edge and it fell to the floor, landing upside-down. 'You don't know anything.'

'You little bitch!'

'If I'm a bitch then you're a cow; a nasty, stupid, fat cow.'

Furious, Verity lashed out and slapped her sister's hand. 'That's for ruining my book!'

Meredith shrieked. 'You do hate me.' She broke into sobs and instantly, Verity tried to pull her into an embrace.

'I'm sorry, Meri, I didn't mean it.' Meredith struggled. Verity wouldn't let her go. 'Well, I did, about the book – I'm sorry I slapped you.' She felt her sister slump, took hold of her hand. 'Here, let me see.'

And Meredith did and it wasn't as bad as it looked or, Verity suspected, felt.

'I'm sorry, truly, I am,' Verity said stroking her sister's hand, 'only you can't do things like that. It's a library book.'

'Be all right if it wasn't then?'

Verity drew Meredith closer. 'No, it's never all right to mistreat a book.'

'And it's never all right to not believe me either.'

'And it's never all right to call me a nasty fat cow.'

'I'm sorry too. I didn't mean it.'

'I know. All right, I'll listen. Shall we go for a walk? Get out of here for a bit?'

'Can we go to the ruin?'

'If you like.'

'Not the beach?'

'Not the beach.'

'It's not that I don't like the beach.'

'I know,' Verity said.

You want to feel safe and you've always been a bit scared of the water.

'We'll go to the beach next time.'

I was rarely allowed out alone and must always have a chaperone to protect me from imagined influences, occasionally a housemaid, more often the despised governess who accompanied me on dull walks through the lanes.

Other than the walled garden my only sanctuary was the wood. I employed a level of stealth to fashion my small freedoms, telling Mama I needed specimens for my botany lessons or some quiet time to learn the set poetry which I must have by heart.

The wood was silent and concealing.

One day I came across a stone dwelling – some sort of gamekeeper's hut, abandoned for years, the last man let go by my grandfather. A low door hung off its hinges and threadbare leaves as old as the year skittered across the earth floor. When I first came across it, it was a squalid place; a single room with a small fireplace in which soot and the remains of a rooks nest lay. Although several tiles were missing from the roof, and when it rained they leaked, the walls were largely intact.

Over time I made the place habitable. I stole a tinderbox from the kitchen and learned to make fire. From the pantry I helped myself to a cup, a dish, a pan and a knife. I filched bread and apples, the occasional egg and slice of cake. Later, I smuggled an old blanket out of the house. I took a few of my favourite books too and in the quiet of my retreat, snatched an hour here and there where I could be alone and at peace.

No one ever found me.

The hut was my sanctuary and I believed myself protected there. The woodland creatures began to trust me. I made friends with a fox and the birds began to eat out of my hand.

Eighteen

Had Verity not been patient, the earlier argument with her sister might well have continued into the evening.

Meredith was quite capable of extending even the briefest of rows into hours of sulking resentment.

'If you don't like me, there's no one else. Only Nain.'

'Oh, Meri, of course I like you.'

'Liking and loving isn't the same thing.'

I don't think it's as simple as like or dislike or even love... Your mother is damaged...

'You think I don't love you? We all love you. And Mam adores you.'

Meredith strode ahead of her sister. 'It's still not the same.' She walked by the hen house, waving and calling to the chickens, past the fruit cage, making for the trees.

Behind Gull House the wood stretched for miles. They'd played in it their whole lives and no one had dissuaded them from exploring.

'You mind yourselves,' was all Mared ever said. 'And don't eat anything you aren't sure of.'

They created a secret path – complex and winding, a mystery to the uninitiated and deliberately so – they looked upon it as their personal right of way. Small signposts marked the way: a hummock, a fallen branch; a lump of stone thrown up in the past.

'Second stone on the right,' Meredith said, as they walked in, 'and straight on 'til morning.'

Peter Pan was one of her favourite stories. (It wasn't only boys who ended up lost.)

Once, years before, they had ventured to the other side of the wood and found a view of the hills, the sky like a magic carpet unrolling into the faraway. It looked to them like another country. They didn't go again. Deep in the wood they knew they belonged and it was enough.

It was still cold. Far too cold for April although the sun shone brightly, catching on the moist new green creating an illusion of otherworld magic.

Meredith always came prepared. On their way out she'd raided the pantry, found some cake; sneaked a couple of biscuits. She left the cake in the cleft of a thin twisted oak, taking the biscuits to the ruined hut.

'The Other are everywhere,' she said, her voice suitably solemn. 'Nain says they aren't the same as garden fairies. They're more important, so better safe than sorry and always bring a gift.'

If the stories Nain conjured for them were straightforward, Meredith imagined tales of a very different kind, perfect for the deep dark wood. She invented creatures with names: a good witch called Mrs Belladonna and her animal children: a fox called Roux, a hedgehog named Pin. Birds sang to Mrs Belladonna as she attended to her children and her chores.

'There are bad spirits too,' Meredith insisted. 'Their leader is Stinky Minky, he has eyes made from holly berries and he ties up his boots with deadly nightshade roots.'

They walked in single file, the path as narrow as a rabbit trail, until they emerged at a small clearing. What had once been some sort of gamekeeper's bolthole was no more than a shell, a ruin of moss-covered stones, the remaining walls barely supporting a rotted doorframe and skeleton chimney. Inside, several ash trees had taken root in the rubble.

'Do you suppose Angharad ever came here?' Meredith pushed aside a curtain of ivy obscuring the doorway.

'She lived in the house; she might have found her way here.'

'And if she was lonely and had no friends, she would have

wanted somewhere for herself.' Meredith crumbled the biscuits and sprinkled them on the stone hearth. 'Perhaps she pretended to give parties, with musicians, and her guests danced the night away.' She turned and took hold of Verity's hand. 'Are you sure you aren't still cross with me?'

'I'm sure.'

'And you don't think I'm making it up; about the ghost?'

Verity smiled. 'I'm not sure about that. You'll have to convince me, and make a good job of it too.' She patted the mossy stone of the broken wall. 'So come on then, tell me about your ghost.'

Verity wasn't particularly brave, neither was she a coward. She wasn't afraid of the wood although she knew it would be a mistake to venture into it in the middle of the night, or during a storm. Wary and respectful of foxes, she guessed that, like the birds, they were clever and smart and understood things humans had no inkling of. She was practical to her core. Although she half-believed in fairies, and that the moths Meredith told her about soothed her sister's dreams, what she had never believed in was ghosts.

Sitting on the ruined wall with the afternoon shadows gathering, listening to Meredith, she discovered she was frightened.

'I trust my heart far more than my head,' Meredith said, her voice full of wonder. 'I do believe what Nain told me about the Other but the stuff I make up about fairy creatures is for fun.' She took a deep breath. 'This is different. It's tragic. It comes in waves, like she's putting the words in my head and I try and remember and write them down, only I can't keep up.' She hadn't taken her eyes off her sister. 'Do you want me to tell you what she's said so far?'

Verity didn't.

Except I'm beginning to have a sneaking feeling it might be true.

She knew when her sister was lying. This wasn't one of those times.

'Have you actually seen anything?' The trees rustled and Verity shivered and it wasn't only because it was far too cold for April.

Meredith picked at the moss on the wall. 'People always want to know if you've seen a ghost when the question is, have you heard one.'

'Well, have you?'

'Yes, Verity. That's what I've been trying to tell you.'

Nineteen

Back at the house, Meredith dragged Verity up to her bedroom.

'Can't you feel it? How cold it is? It's really, really freezing.'

It was; even for Verity, who hardly ever felt the cold. 'And you honestly believe it's because of a ghost?'

'Yes, I do.'

'And yet you say you can't see her?' Verity stood by the open window, watching the mist settle on the sea not wanting her sister to see how anxious she was. Meredith's infatuations, normally a pain, were beginning to seriously concern her. Fantastical though Angharad's story sounded, a whisper at the back of her mind told Verity it was true, and that a ghost was talking to her sister.

Meredith made a groaning noise.

'You still aren't listening to me properly.'

'I am. I promise.'

All at once the idea of a ghost in her grandmother's house felt like a violation. The only magic Verity trusted was the benign sort. A ghost was another kind altogether and suggested something far more malevolent than fairies and woodland guardians.

She turned away from the window. 'And you think it's her – Angharad? In the house?'

Meredith nodded her head, making her tangled curls bounce like burnished dandelion clocks. 'I'm almost sure.' She paused. 'I'm pretty sure I can hear her, only what if it is my imagination and I'm as mad as they said Angharad was?' Meredith looked up. 'She was here before, I swear; this morning.'

Verity shivered. 'It is very cold in here, I'll give you that.'

'But you still don't want to believe me.'

I know when she's lying … this isn't one of those times…

Playing for time, Verity said, 'Meri, are you sure *you* believe you?'

'Don't be stupid. Anyway, I do. And so long as I don't fall asleep and it's dark, I can hear her.'

'Saying what?'

'Not saying exactly, whispering. I don't know. Sometimes I can hardly hear a thing. Then it's as clear a bell and she's saying how the house looked and how her brother was cruel and her father wouldn't let her go to school. She was afraid of the sea too – the way I am.'

Verity frowned. 'And you can hear her saying this?'

'She asked me if I was brave enough to hear her story and says she's telling me so she'll be remembered.'

'You're sure you aren't imagining it?'

'I'm dreaming some of it and I don't like those bits. She sounds different; angrier and I can't understand her.' Meredith hesitated. 'When I'm not asleep she makes more sense, so I pinch myself and try to stay awake.' She swallowed and rubbed her arm.

'You pinch yourself to stay awake?' Verity was appalled. 'Meri, that's awful.'

Taking hold of her sister's arm she pushed up the sleeve of her cardigan. There were small bruises on the inside of her forearm.

Verity stared at them. 'You did this to yourself?'

Meredith whimpered. 'Don't be cross.'

'You pinch yourself because the ghost of a girl who died a hundred years ago is trying to talk to you in your dreams and it scares you?'

Meredith tried to pull her arm away. 'It's not her fault. And I'm not scared.'

Verity held on to it, stroked the blemished skin. 'And I'm supposed to believe you? My God, Meri, look at your poor arm.'

You know when she's lying…

Meredith tugged her arm again and Verity let go.

'I'm not asking you to believe me,' she cried. 'If you can't then I'm asking you to pretend. Because if you don't, Verity; I won't be able to speak to you ever again.'

It wasn't the first time Meredith had made such a threat, only this time her manner struck Verity with a deeper intensity. She shivered and the curtains did too. She closed the window. A gull flew across her vision and as it disappeared she took a deep breath. 'Well, we can't have that, can we?'

Meredith stared at her and her eyes shone; the lights in them brilliant with hope. 'So, are you saying you do believe me?'

'I might be.' Verity moved away from the window and knelt in front of Meredith. 'You could be right and maybe it's a ghost.'

I'm not saying it is – and I can always take it back…

Without questioning her sister's apparent change of heart, Meredith's body relaxed and her face became grave. She took hold of Verity's hands. 'I can feel her sadness. It's inside me, only worse, I'm sad and it's her sad. In my dreams I'm furious and then it's her fury too.'

'What do you mean?'

'It's like her anger's boiling over and one way or another she's determined to make me understand.'

'It sounds like bullying to me.'

It sounds dangerous.

The hairs on Verity's arm stood on end. 'Maybe you ought to tell her to go away. Stand up to her.'

'I don't want her to go away.' Meredith let go of her sister's hands. 'What would be the point of that? She's chosen me, so why wouldn't I listen to her? And in any case, I want to know what happened.'

Drowning the silence, the sounds of evening filled the garden: an owl's hoot: the wind through the trees.

And the thudding of Verity's heart.

She hadn't meant to come outside. Nain had been on the telephone wanting to talk to Allegra who was nowhere to be found.

'Look for her, *cariad* and ask her to call me back,' Mared said.

'Check the house,' Verity told Meredith. 'I'll do the garden.'

Five minutes later she heard Meredith calling from the kitchen. Allegra had been on the beach and now she was back.

Verity stayed where she was, by the half-open gate on the edge of her grandmother's dusky walled garden, still shaken by what Meredith had told her. A brittle moon skittered between the trees.

Am I the crazy one, believing her nonsense?

It has to be made up; Meredith must be lying.

I know when she is and this isn't...

Caught in her thoughts, all at once she felt certain she wasn't alone. Fear crawled up her spine. She knew that unless she made herself invisible she ran the risk of being observed. It was a gift she didn't have. She stood as still as a stone, clinging to the half open gate.

Please don't let anything see me.

She closed her eyes and immediately opened them, as wide as she could, staring through the fading light into the shadowy garden.

What is it I believe I'm seeing?

The moon disappeared behind a bank of cloud.

Verity didn't know what a ghost was supposed to look like. She had a vague idea it would be pale with blank eyes perhaps – beyond dead. There was nothing to see and yet she couldn't shake the feeling someone else was in the garden.

As the non-colour of the gathering night flowed around her, she peered round the gate and for a second saw a shape, imprecise and barely discernible.

It can't be real. There's no such thing as ghosts.

The hairs on the back of Verity's neck stood on end and for a single unrealistic second she thought how melodramatic this was; the kind of thing you read about in books.

Or what your idiot sister insisted was true.

It takes a special person to see a ghost, Verity...

Every sense in her body told her someone was there.

Some ... *thing* ...

In spite of her unease, Verity wanted to see whatever or whoever it was, try to make sense of it. Part of her was furious. If it really was a ghost, how dare a dead thing invade her grandmother's perfect garden?

Ahead of her, the shape hovered. Determined to prove it must be a quirk of darkness interfering with her sight she blinked, expecting it to dissolve. When it didn't she stopped breathing for a second.

It's only shadows and your imagination.

And yet there it was: a figure impossible to age with alabaster skin and eyes as black and old as the world, a sense of utter loneliness surrounding it.

The temperature plummeted.

Verity blinked and whatever had been there was gone.

Shaking uncontrollably, she stared into the gloom. There was only the familiarity of trees and plants, and the ever-decreasing visibility.

Straining to hear, her ears were no more use than her eyes. There was nothing, save for a residue of her own shocked apprehension, and the earlier recollection of the look on her sister's face.

Her sadness is inside me ... she's real....

Still trembling, Verity looked around, searching for what she knew she'd seen. In the gloom, the garden's tranquillity was stained by a feeling of tragedy made of sorrow and threads of mist.

And now I believe it, too.

Present

As quickly as it came the rain has disappeared.

I try the caretaker's number again; wave my phone in the air, summoning a signal.

Gull House is a dead spot.

Behind me, the wood is as hushed as a graveyard where only ghosts come to mourn. The tree shadows are alien and filled with sadness.

I am not tempted by the wood. It was always more my sister's place than mine. After the events of 1979 and our move to London she rarely spoke of it and when she did, it was with a wistful longing.

Her grief at leaving was always deeper than mine. Gull House was the only home I'd ever known; it represented comfortable familiarity and heritage. It was different for Meredith. She loved the house for itself, as if it was part of her, and you could almost imagine it loving her back. Even as a small girl she said the idea of leaving made holes in her heart and no matter what happened she never would. The house was more than a home to Meredith; it was a haven and perfect and always the same: the stone walls solid and safe, the drifting gulls loyal and the sun always shining.

In front of me the garden runs downhill, a slope of overgrown lawn. The ground is thick with leaf mould. Averting my gaze from the trees, I step out, one foot in front of the other concentrating on my sturdy sandals, on the blades of coarse grass giving way under the leather soles. And beneath my feet, the dark earth uncurls as if a lay-line runs there.

My foot strikes a rock poking out of the ground. It is part of a low, moss-covered retaining wall surrounding a stone water feature: part bird-bath, part fountain, silted with algae and silent. A cloud of insects hover above my head and I flap my hand at them. The three blank-eyed stone cherubs holding up the dish still strike me as freakish and I'm reminded how maudlin the Victorians had been.

The sky is now a heart-stopping blue. As a solitary cloud dissolves, a mesmerising sunlight makes sunspots behind my eyes, momentarily blinding me and I miss my sister so badly it hurts.

You mistrusted strangers because we hardly ever met anyone and yet, eventually you ran away to be with people.

I'm listening for an answer, an argument; anything as long as it's her voice.

Where are you, sweet thing? Still in Spain, in Africa perhaps, or Japan? Are you floating in a perfect foreign sea, your moth shadow holding you up?

At the thought of it I'm undone.

I step away from the dead fountain.

The thread connecting me to my sister may be slender – yet it still exists and I can touch my hand to a point on my chest and the knot of it, the faint tug.

Twenty

'Have you taken my necklace?'

Verity stopped brushing Meredith's hair. 'What necklace?'

'The coral one Nain gave me for my birthday. I can't find it.'

'I haven't got it. When did you last see it?'

'Oh, I don't know. It's just gone.'

'Well, you know what you're like; you've probably left it somewhere.'

Meredith jerked her head away from the hairbrush. 'That hurts!'

'Don't fuss; your hair's a nightmare.'

Meredith heaved her shoulders and settled into the chair. 'So, what are we going to do?'

'Do?' She pulled the hairbrush through Meredith's tangled hair, dragging on her scalp.

'One of these days, Verity Pryce, you'll answer one of my questions properly.'

'I know you, Meredith. Nothing's ever simple with you. Why does my opinion matter so much anyway? It doesn't usually.'

'That's not true.'

If you're distracted, or scared, it can make you unkind. Verity yanked on the hairbrush.

'Ouch!' Meredith pulled away again. 'I only want to know what you think.'

Verity tugged harder. 'I wish you'd never found that stupid sewing box.'

'I did though.' Meredith wriggled in the seat. 'you're as curious as me; I know you are.' She clutched her hands to the back of her head. 'Ouch again, that hurts! What's the matter with you?'

'Sorry.' Verity stroked her sister's hair, remembering the bleak face from the night before, how alien the garden had appeared, as if her grandmother had never set foot in it, never created a place of gentle sanctuary. 'If you brushed it properly in the first place or let me plait it, it wouldn't tangle.'

Meredith's eyes narrowed. 'When was the last time you saw anyone over the age of three with plaits? In any case, they make my head hurt.' She turned and stared at her sister. 'What? You've gone all weird.'

Verity took hold of her sister's head. 'Don't be soft. Sit still.'

Meredith's hair reached past her shoulders. Verity caught it up in a single heavy bunch, divided it into three. 'Hang on and let me try before you say you hate it.'

'All right, only don't pull and don't do it tight. And don't do two or I'll look a right idiot.'

Verity braided the thick red ringlets into a loose plait. When she was done, she ran her hands over the criss-crossed braid. It reminded her of a fox's tail. 'There you go.'

'I don't want an elastic band.'

'Ribbon?'

'Go on then.'

From a heap lying coiled on the table, Verity chose a green ribbon, tied it at the bottom of the plait leaving the ends trailing. 'It looks pretty.'

Meredith reached over her shoulder, grabbed her hair and smiled. 'No bow. Well done.'

'Madam is most welcome.' Verity gave a mock curtsy. She looked towards the back door. 'Where's Allegra? Five minutes, she said and that was an hour ago. I need to get going before the library closes.'

'Can I come with you?'

'You'll only get bored.'

Meredith made a snorting noise. 'It's going to snow.'

'No it isn't.'

110

'It is – I heard you telling Allegra. And you can smell weather. You're like a witch girl!' Her face broke out in a grin and she pointed to the window. 'Look, it's started already.'

'No it hasn't. I'm going anyway, Meri so get over it.'

'It'll rain then! Hailstones, as big as bullets!' Meredith began dancing round the room. 'It's raining, it's pouring; the old man's snoring!'

'Stop it, you pest.'

'You best not go, Verity. There's going to be thunder and you'll be struck down by lightning and you'll drown in a deluge of hail.'

'That's enough,' Verity snapped. 'Stop it. You're fourteen for goodness sake, start acting your age.'

Meredith continued capering around the room. 'You'll be sorry. You'll see.'

'What on earth's going on in here?' Allegra came through the back door, a basket of roses in her hand. 'I can hear you two from the bottom of the garden.'

Verity looked up. 'There you are. Thank goodness. Can I go now?'

Allegra placed the basket on the table. 'Go where?'

'To the library; I told you, my books are due back. And you said—'

'She won't let me go with her.'

'Well, that's Verity all over isn't it?' Allegra stroked the top of Meredith's head. 'And what on earth have you done to your hair?'

'Verity did it.'

'You won't make her less pretty by spoiling her hair.' Allegra pulled at the green ribbon and began unravelling the braid. 'Here, let's make you beautiful again. And let Verity go to her stuffy old library. Stay with me and help with the flowers.'

Meredith pulled away from her mother's hands, clutching the ruined plait. 'Why did you do that? I liked it.'

Before Allegra could answer, Verity said, 'It doesn't matter, Meri; she's right, you look better with it loose.'

Meredith scowled. 'So why did you want to make me look awful then? And why can't I come with you?'

They looked at one another and Verity caught her finger under her sister's chin.

'I'll bring you something nice, okay?'

Behind her she sensed her mother frowning.

'Chocolate?' Meredith let her lip tremble. 'Will you be back by tea time?'

'Ages before then and I'll bring you chocolate and a book as well.'

'Make sure it's something suitable this time,' Allegra snapped. 'None of that Enid Blyton rubbish.

'I happen to like Enid Blyton.' Meredith said. 'And in any case, I don't care what it is, or if she doesn't bring me a book at all. We've got loads of books and Verity will read to me if I ask her. Or she'll make up a story.' There was a dash of defiance in her voice making Verity angry. Not with her sister, with her mother and her manipulation.

'Yes, darling,' Allegra went on, oblivious to Meredith's benign challenge. 'I know that, but you're much too clever for such childish stuff. You were a free reader when you were no more than a baby. Really, darling, you're capable of far more grown-up books than Enid Blyton.' Allegra turned to Verity. 'Find something age-appropriate. Oh, and while you're in town, drop by Mrs Thing for my usual.'

'Do I have to?'

'For goodness sake, what's your problem? It's only some gin.'

'It's embarrassing.'

'Don't be difficult, Verity. It's boring.'

'Money?'

'Tell her to put it on my account.'

On account of we've got no money?

'Haven't you paid her? I told you, she asked me the last time, said could you go and settle the bill.'

112

Allegra made a face. 'I don't think my finances are any of your business, do you?' She turned to Meredith. 'Now, you – go and get me a vase and let's arrange these roses.'

You have no idea how this makes me feel, do you.

Verity held her tongue, pulled on her hat and waited.

'Well, go on then, if you're going.'

Verity was dismissed.

By the glory hole, Meredith caught hold of her sister's arm and whispered, 'I don't mind what book you get me and another *Famous Five* would actually be fantastic.'

Verity grinned. 'I'll try, I promise. Now you have to promise too.' She lowered her voice. 'Be good and no more talk about a ghost, okay?'

'I promise. And thank you for my hair.'

'It's okay.' Verity gave her sister a hug.

Meredith followed her outside to where Verity's bicycle stood propped against the wall. 'She doesn't mean to be horrible.'

Verity sighed. 'I don't care, Meri, honestly, I don't.' She straddled the bicycle, her foot poised on the pedal. 'You two have a nice time.'

Meredith crossed her fingers and held them up in front of Verity's face. 'I've made a deal with myself. If I behave, you won't be cross with me.'

'I told you, I'm not cross.'

'Well, you still don't believe me about the ghost. Not deep down. I can tell.'

'You're very sure about it, aren't you?'

'Yes. And one way or another, I'm going to find a way to make you believe me.'

As she freewheeled down the drive towards the lane, Verity wondered if she ought to tell her sister she did believe her.

Twenty-one

'No Mr Tallis?'

'Still poorly.' Miss Jenkins peered over her spectacles. 'Says it's influenza but you know what men are like.'

Verity didn't. She smiled anyway.

'It's been utter bedlam.'

Verity eyed the almost empty library and thought, if this was bedlam, she'd take it.

It wasn't uncommon to send them to asylums…

'Did you enjoy it?' Miss Jenkins checked the date in the Mary Stewart book.

'I did, thank you, although I may have had my fill of Arthurian myths for a while. I'm going to look for something different.'

Miss Jenkins nodded. 'Widen your choices. Good girl. Off you go then, have fun.'

Searching along the shelves Verity came across an anthology about the supernatural. Flicking through it, she found herself wondering about Meredith again and how she had to be making things up.

It's what she does.

In her heart of hearts she knew this was wishful thinking.

Verity tucked the book under her arm, wandered along the rows looking for something to test her brain. In the children's department she found two Famous Five books she knew Meredith hadn't read and something called *Silver on the Tree* which she hoped would satisfy her mother's literary ambitions for her youngest daughter.

As Miss Jenkins approached with a pile of books in her arms Verity watched her taking note of the titles, smoothing the spines before she put each one on the shelf. As unobtrusively as she could, she followed, watched as the librarian double-checked each book before replacing it. Verity knew she would enjoy doing the same thing, cataloguing and bringing order out of chaos. Being a librarian looked to her like an ambition worth pursuing.

Miss Jenkins slotted the final book into place: a copy of *I Capture the Castle* – a gift from Nain to Verity on her last birthday. As Miss Jenkins walked back to the desk, Verity took it down and flicked it open – recalling being captivated by the first line and wanting to sit in a sink and write her own story.

Miss Jenkins reappeared, balancing yet more books.

'Ah, yes,' she said. 'Marvellous choice; splendid book.' She smiled at Verity. 'You have excellent taste, my dear.'

Ridiculously pleased, Verity hesitated, reluctant to admit she already owned a copy.

'I've decided I want to read everything.' She blushed, feeling foolish. 'What I mean is…'

'I know exactly what you mean. I'm the same. Reading is learning and learning is knowledge.'

'If I don't get to go to school, how will I learn anything?' Verity couldn't believe she'd said the words out loud. Although Miss Jenkins knew she didn't go to school it wasn't anything they had ever talked about.

'I thought you didn't mind.'

'I say I don't mind. I can't bear the arguments.'

And I can't let Meredith down.

'Sometimes, my dear, we have to fight for what we want.' Miss Jenkins paused. 'I wonder.' She narrowed her eyes. 'Remind me, how old are you now?'

'I'll be sixteen in September.'

Miss Jenkins tapped her finger against her nose. 'Hang on a moment.' She disappeared down the rows, into a room behind the desk, returned a few moments later holding a book aloft, a smile on her face.

'I may be overstepping the mark dear – you are grown up for your age and this book…' She gave a deep sigh. 'It isn't all about fiction, and this book … well, in my view every girl ought to read it. Not least one in search of learning.'

She handed the book to Verity. 'They're poems, only so much more. A friend sent it to me from America; I've been carrying it around ever since.'

Verity's hand ran across the title.

The Dream of a Common Language.

'Goodness, what a lovely idea.'

Miss Jenkins smiled. 'I shouldn't say this, although I'm going to. It isn't about being given an education, Verity; you have to believe you have the right to claim one. I'm where I am in my own life because good women shared their dreams with me.'

Wherever Miss Jenkins was, Verity decided, was a place she'd like to be.

The librarian laid her hand on Verity's arm. 'Maybe, if you like the poems, I'll lend you some of her other books. Her name is Adrienne Rich.' Miss Jenkins said the name as if it mattered.

'Thank you, Miss Jenkins, you're so kind and…'

'I'm a woman on a mission. In my view, no girl should be denied a proper education and a bit of subversion never hurt anyone.' Miss Jenkins was brisk efficiency again. 'Make sure you take care of it.'

Verity checked out the other books, tucked the mystery one in between them and made her way into the cold.

Outside Mrs Trahaearn's shop, she waited until the coast was clear before collecting a bottle of gin for her mother.

Mrs Trahaearn said, one more time, there was a limit to her patience. 'Don't fret, *cariad* – I'll give her a ring.'

Verity tried not to imagine the kind of conversation Mrs Trahaearn might have with Allegra.

If only she would say no and refuse to serve me.

Stuffing the bottle of gin under the books, she told herself it would only make things worse. Allegra would find a way to make it Verity's fault and the fuss she was then bound to cause in the shop would reverberate through town. Everyone would know. And Allegra would find another shop, move on and run up another bill.

'Did you get some books for your sister?'

The girls were in the sitting room curled on a sofa.

'Yes.'

'What's this?' Allegra tapped the copy of *I Capture the Castle* lying on the sofa

The conversation with Miss Jenkins had distracted Verity. She'd left the library with only Meredith's books, a novel she already owned and the ghost anthology. 'A library book?'

'I can see it's a library book, you already have it.'

'Yes, I know. Miss Jenkins didn't realise and she was being nice. I didn't...'

Allegra gave a pinched smile. 'Oh Verity, you have to learn to be assertive. Miss Jenkins doesn't have a clue. Librarians don't understand books. They're just glorified filing clerks.'

'That's not true. She—'

'Oh, it is, trust me. Librarians don't know a thing about literature or art. Let's face it; I can't see Miss Jenkins at the National.'

'You've barely ever spoken to her so how—'

Allegra voice was edged with its customary mockery. 'Good grief, Verity, don't take everything so seriously. We're teasing, aren't we, Meredith?'

'Are we?' Meredith made a rude noise. 'I didn't say a word. And in any case, when was the last time you went to an art gallery?' She turned the page of her own book.

'It's not about going to galleries, it's about appreciation. Unlike Verity, who is apparently an expert, Miss Jenkins doesn't know her Gauguin from her Rossetti.'

117

'She doesn't need to,' Verity said.

'Of course she does! If I go into a library and ask for a book about the Pre-Raphaelites, I don't expect to be asked who they are.'

'Were.' Verity couldn't resist. 'And Gauguin was an Impressionist.'

Allegra tutted. 'You know what I mean; stop trying to be clever.'

'She's a librarian, Mam, which is the whole point; she knows where the right books are, if you ask for them. And she knows about loads of things, she's always helping me with stuff.'

She thought about the mystery book, lying in the space under the window seat in her bedroom. Before hiding it, she'd sneaked a look.

No one has imagined us....

Verity wasn't sure she understood quite what the poet meant. It sounded grown up in a way she thought she wanted to discover.

'The point is, Verity, Miss bloody Jenkins doesn't think art counts.' Allegra's voice battered Verity's thoughts. 'Good Lord, the one time I asked her for a book on Millais, she hadn't heard of him.'

'Who has?'

And I bet she did. You've probably made it up to make yourself look smart.

Allegra marched out of the room. 'I'll show you, you pair of Philistines.'

'Why does she always have to be such a pain?' Verity slammed shut her book.

'Humour her,' Meredith said. 'Otherwise she won't stop.'

Allegra returned with a large book open at a page which she shoved under Verity's nose. 'Now then, tell me this doesn't matter!'

Meredith leaned over her sister's shoulder and peered at the page. It was a picture of a red-haired woman in a green gown holding a pomegranate. She looked sad.

She looked like Allegra.

'It's lovely,' Verity said. 'And no one's saying it doesn't matter but other than hanging it on a wall and looking at it, what's it for?'

A look of genuine pain crossed Allegra's face. 'It's Rossetti! Dear God, it isn't *for* anything. Art just is. It doesn't have to have a purpose, it *is* the purpose.'

Verity suspected her mother was quoting someone. She knew better than to suggest it.

'If someone bought one of your paintings,' Meredith said, 'then it would have a purpose. We could have some new clothes.'

'You have the frocks your grandmother made for you. And the house is full of clothes.' Allegra turned her eye on her eldest daughter again. 'You don't need Miss Jenkins, is what I'm saying. And neither does Meredith. You're both far cleverer than she is.'

No, she's cleverer than you can imagine, and you can't stand the competition.

Allegra picked up her shawl and wrapped it round her shoulders. 'Well, I can't hang around here all day. I want to finish the sea thing before the light goes.' She turned to Meredith. 'And for your information, baby brat, three of my paintings sold last month, so there.'

Pleased her mother had regained her temper, Meredith said, 'That's great, Mam, and the new one's looking lovely.'

'Thank you darling. You're sweet. If it sells, maybe we can run to another new frock. From a shop this time and not homemade. And perhaps when I've finished it, we can invite the redoubtable Miss Jenkins to take a look and see what she has to say.'

Not wanting the argument resurrected, Meredith asked why Allegra didn't paint a picture of them. 'Like the one you did when we were little.'

'You mean the one in my bedroom?'

'Yes. You said you painted it for my birthday.'

'I did. You were two and Verity was three. You were so tiny, both of you, like little animals.' A fleeting shadow crossed her face and in a second was gone, replaced by her sharp smile.

Allegra's smile could cut diamonds.

'I suppose I could try another one. Now you've grown so pretty.' She blew Meredith a kiss. 'We'll see.'

Meredith followed her mother to the door. 'Verity's prettier than me. She's beautiful.'

Allegra's smile flattened. 'Yes, of course she is.' She pulled her shawl tighter. 'Bloody hell, it's cold.'

'Cold enough for snow.' Meredith gazed out of the window.

'It won't snow, Meredith – your sister doesn't know what she's talking about.' Allegra opened the door. 'Now don't bother me, either of you.'

'She's doesn't get it, does she?' Meredith leaned on the windowsill. 'Why do you love snow, Verity?'

'It's like friendly rain; softer and kinder.'

'Good answer.'

'Why do you love it?'

The light from the window turned Meredith's hair to coral candyfloss. 'Snow makes me brave. When it snows, the sad part of me goes away.'

Twenty-two

Meredith went to bed early, hungry for more of Angharad's story.

I wonder what she thought about snow.

Would a girl who wasn't supposed to go anywhere without a chaperone be allowed to play in the snow?

She noticed her slippers on the window seat, wondered if Verity had put them there.

Why would she? It made no sense. And she still hadn't found her necklace.

Because it upset Verity, Meredith had stopped pinching herself. She didn't think it would make any difference. Angharad's voice hovered on the periphery of her mind, waiting.

The words have been inside me for a hundred years…

Meredith clutched the red heart to her chest.

He saw my terror … it left him cold…

Curling up she held Nelly tight and closed her eyes, drifted into sleep. The shadow of whispered words spread around her like the wings of a dark bird. The dream came back and Angharad inhabited it.

It wasn't hard to anger him…

Meredith woke with a start. Her heart raced under her ribs.

I knew he could hurt me…

The words were a breath of broken sentence.

Meredith scanned the room, less sure than before whether what she heard was her imagination or a ghost.

You're always making stuff up…

And yet in the dark, with nothing to distract her or insist she was imagining things, Angharad was as real as if she were in the room, her unfolding story as authentic as Meredith's drumming heart. In spite of a layer of fear prickling her skin like needles, she refused to let it overcome her. Angharad had chosen her and Meredith wasn't about to let her down.

Through a gap in the curtain the sky loomed and the room grew colder and gloomier.

Vermin must be destroyed…

The words hung on the air, throaty and harsh and frightening. Angharad sounded angry, her voice heavy with acrimony.

She sounds furious, she sounds terrified too…

In the early hours of the following morning, Meredith woke up and looking in the mirror, saw dark circles under her eyes. The eyes themselves were as bright as raindrops. She tried to recall what the ghost had said. The detail evaded her and this time she didn't bother trying to write anything down.

The best I can do is to listen.

She found Verity in the kitchen.

'Is it catching? Waking early?'

'I finished my book,' Verity said, 'and I'm hungry.'

'Me too.'

As they nibbled toast by the range, Meredith said, 'I don't know if it's my dreams or not.'

She looked so solemn; Verity learned over and gave her a hug. 'Silly old sausage; it probably is.'

'Yes, only they're not like ordinary ones any more. I don't like them and maybe madness is catching.'

'Now you're being soft. Of course it isn't.'

'It's too cold in my room. And things move about.'

'I do that all the time. Put things in one place and they turn up somewhere else.'

'This is different.' She pointed to her feet. 'My slippers were on the window seat and I still can't find my necklace. It's her, I know it is.'

Verity didn't say anything.

'I'm freezing.' Meredith scooped some coal from the scuttle onto the fire.

'Well, I still think it's going to snow,' Verity said. 'It's not just me; it was on the weather forecast.'

The door opened and Allegra came in, dishevelled, half asleep. 'Still going on about snow?' She rubbed her eyes. 'Has the kettle boiled? God, I need coffee. What on earth time is it?'

'Half past seven.'

Allegra groaned. 'It's all right for you, you're a lark.'

'I'll make you a cup of coffee.' Verity switched on the electric kettle.

'What are you doing up, Meredith; you're usually like me, a proper little night person.'

'No I'm not, I'm a snow person.'

Allegra ruffled Meredith's hair. 'I almost hope it does snow, anything to shut you up.' She took the mug of coffee from Verity. 'Thanks. I'm going back to bed.'

Meredith poked a log with the toe of her slipper, snatched it back as a shower of hot ash broke free. She watched the new flames leap up. 'She's frightened.'

'Of what? Snow?'

'Not Mam, you idiot; Angharad.'

'Sorry.'

'We have to help her, Verity. I know it. I knew it when I found the sewing box and saw her name; when I touched the red hearts for the first time.' Meredith narrowed her eyes. 'And you do believe me, I know you do.'

'Even if I did, I don't see what we can do. Or what she could possibly want.'

Meredith shivered and this time it wasn't from the cold. 'She's afraid, Verity, really afraid.'

It was so cold Meredith developed chilblains and for once didn't make a fuss about wearing socks.

They were supposed to be doing maths and she was wasting time, questioning why anyone would want to do sums made of letters.

'It's algebra, you idiot.'

'I know what it is, Verity; I want to know what it's for.'

'It isn't *for* anything. It's like *art*, darling.' Verity pulled a face. 'It just is!'

Meredith giggled. 'Well I can't do it so I'm not going to.' She pushed the book away, dropped her pencil in the muddle on the table. 'And Allegra won't check so botheration to it.'

Verity gazed out of the window. 'I honestly think it's going to snow.'

'You could be right. It's spooky weather.'

'Everything's spooky to you.'

'She's still telling me things.'

'Like what?' Verity wasn't sure she wanted to know but she couldn't resist asking.

'I'm not sure.'

'Do you think she's always been here?'

Verity refused to believe her grandmother wouldn't have known if a ghost had lived in Gull House. And if she had, that she wouldn't have given it short shrift.

'I don't know,' Meredith said. 'What if she's been stuck here and I've woken her up?'

'That's crazy.'

'No it isn't. Not if you think about it.' Meredith leaned forward. 'You know that book you brought from the library. It says ghosts who haven't found peace can wake up if something triggers them.'

'Such as?'

'Such as finding a personal possession?'

'Like a sewing box.'

'Exactly.'

'I don't believe you.' Verity had to say this because otherwise she would be buying into the beginning of something she didn't understand and didn't want to.

Meredith was having none of it. 'You do, Verity. I know you do.'

Outside, Meredith stamped her feet.

She wasn't sure at what point she'd become convinced she'd woken up Angharad's ghost. It made perfect sense to her and whatever Verity said, Meredith knew her sister believed it too. What mattered now was making sure Allegra didn't find out about it.

Trusting her mother was a doubled-edged sword.

She wouldn't only want the sewing box; she'd want my ghost too.

The garden wore a pelt of frost. In the chilly morning light, Meredith crunched across the grass, the cold making her skin burn. She imagined herself as Jadis, ordering the snow, never allowing it to melt.

'Please, please let it snow.'

She screwed up her eyes and said the words out loud like a spell.

Stars, books, Gull House, magic and snow: these were the things that made sense to Meredith.

Her breath made a cloud in front of her face. A solitary snowflake floated onto her eyelash and Meredith's heart leapt in her chest.

Verity's right. It is going to snow.

Twenty-three

'Nain?'

'Hello, *cariad*. What a lovely surprise.'

The sound of her grandmother's voice almost made Verity cry.

'Is everything okay?'

'Everything's fine. I felt like a chat.' The telephone receiver was sticky in her hand. 'How's Gethin?'

'Gethin's as good as it gets. Now then, my lovely, what's up with you?'

How does she manage to do that?

'Nain, can I ask you something?'

'Anything you like; you know you can.'

'It's about Angharad Lewis.'

There was a small pause, as if the line had gone dead.

'Nain?'

'I'm still here, *cariad*. You took me by surprise, that's all. What about Angharad Lewis?'

'Do you remember her? You told us about her ages ago.'

'Of course I remember her. Why do you want to know about her now? I was expecting you to be complaining about your mother.'

'I can; if you want me to.'

Mared laughed and immediately Verity felt better. Her grandmother's laugh sounded as comforting as hot chocolate or the softest quilt.

'What reminded you about Angharad Lewis?'

Verity swallowed. 'Oh, some gossip Meredith heard.'

'Go on.'

'We got talking about her, and we wondered, was she a real person or was she made up.'

'Oh, she was real all right. It's a very sad story.'

'Why?'

'Well, for one thing, they said she was mad and if you ask me that's a very unkind thing to say about any child. My mother knew all about her. She showed me a book written by some local historian. Oh, I don't know – Victorian houses and asylums or something. Gull House was mentioned, and poor Angharad.'

'Do you know what happened to her?'

'Not really. She was supposed to have had some sort of breakdown and they committed her to that old asylum and then she died.'

'She died in the asylum?'

'I'm pretty sure that's what happened. There was some talk of her running away. It wasn't in the book mind; my mother told me that part, and about her committing suicide, but who knows? Your great grandmother wasn't the full ticket either, bless her.'

'So is Angharad buried in the chapel down by us?'

'I wouldn't think so, *cariad*. Suicides weren't allowed to be buried in hallowed ground.'

'That's awful,' Verity said.

Her grandmother went on. 'And not something you or your sister ought to be dwelling on. I should never have told you.'

Verity hesitated. 'Nain, did you ever get a sense of her? In the house?'

'What? Like a ghost? Good grief no, whatever made you think that?'

'Oh, nothing, just some silliness of Meri's. You know what she's like.'

'Indeed I do, *cariad*.'

'How old would Angharad have been, when she died?'

'About seventeen or eighteen? She would have been sheltered and probably young for her age; living there in those days, isolated and most likely not going to school. Girls didn't, not the gentry at any rate. A lot of poor girls were locked up in those days for all sorts of things. Older ones too; they were dreadful times for women.'

'Why would her parents do that?'

Nain said she couldn't say; things were different a hundred years ago. 'There was a brother if I remember rightly; it was only a small mention in that book. The rest of it was mostly gossip and rumour and honestly I can't remember. Maybe my mam told me that bit too – about her having a brother, so it could be a lot of nonsense.' Mared laughed. 'She loved the old tales and the gossip, Dilys did. Those stories might not go away, they do get exaggerated.'

'Have you still got it?' Verity realised she was holding the telephone receiver so tightly the plastic in her hand was hot enough to melt. 'The book.'

'Well, yes, I expect so; it'll be there, in the house. I wouldn't have brought a book like that all the way to London.'

Verity took a deep breath, tried to sound a lot more casual than she felt. 'So, do you know where it might be?'

'Goodness, you are keen to find out about her, aren't you?'

'You know what Meredith's like when she's got a bee in her bonnet.'

'No change there then.' Mared laughed again and said, 'It'll keep her occupied I suppose. Local history – maybe you can call it a proper lesson, instead of the rubbish your mother pretends to teach you.'

'Oh, Nain, you are funny. We miss you ever so much.'

'I've only been back home five minutes!'

It may as well be five years.

'I miss you too, more than I can say.' Mared paused again. 'Now then, if I were you, I'd try the bookcase in the tower room, the one with the glass front and the encyclopaedias and your grandfather's war books. If that old book's anywhere, it'll be there.'

'That's brilliant, Nain, thanks.'

'His name was Emlyn Trahaearn, the chap who wrote it.' Mared gave a small hoot. 'There, I remember it now – same as Mari Trahaearn from the shop. You know who I mean.'

Verity did. 'She's still there.'

'No, no. You're thinking of her daughter, Llinos. I'm talking about the old lady.'

'Right.'

'Llinos still giving your mam credit is she?'

Verity didn't answer.

'You don't have to do it, Verity. I know she won't like it but you are allowed to say no. I should have had a word last time…'

'Please don't, Nain. It's all right and she hardly ever…'

'If you say so, *cariad*. Now then, come on, I want to hear your real news. Are you eating properly and how are my chickens? And apart from chasing ghosts, what else have you and your sister been up to?'

Seeing them?

Verity made up some stuff about the beach and the woods, they talked about the chickens until Mared said she had to go and see to Gethin.

'Give your mother my love, *cariad*, and tell her to keep in touch.'

They rarely ventured into the tower room. Allegra kept her unsold paintings in there. Otherwise she avoided it. It had once been their grandfather's study. After he died, Mared had quietly tidied her husband away leaving only the space and some dull furniture.

Verity opened the door and peered inside. Shadows swallowed the inside of the room. She crossed the wooden floor towards a padded seat curving in front of three tall windows. Parchment blinds screened the view of the driveway. She pulled the cord on one of the blinds and it snapped up, the sound loud in the dusty silence. A pale light landed on a large desk taking up most of the floor space, and against a wall, a glass-fronted bookcase.

Above the high ceiling line was the attic where Meredith had found the sewing box. It was accessed by a mahogany ladder. The hatch was open. It would have been too heavy for Meredith to close.

Verity opened the doors of the bookcase and dug around amongst the books. Sure enough, there it was, a dusty old thing called, *A Brief History of the Victorian House in Wales* by Emlyn Trahaearn.

It was large and thin, the pages stiff and shiny. The text was small, the photographs tiny. Verity turned to the index hoping for a clue. To her surprise, under 'G' she found Gull House. Turning to the relevant page she discovered a grainy photograph accompanying a short piece of text. The house looked huge, perhaps because posed by the front door stood the slight figures of two people. One, a woman, wore a plain, elegant gown; the other – a thin young man – was clad in riding clothes.

'A house of peculiar and unusual interest is Gull House designed in 1860 by Sir Gilbert Wynstanley and built for Caradog Lewis, a prominent local businessman. Overlooking the sea, it was a building whose simple and elegant façade was somewhat spoiled by a small tower more suited to a house of larger proportions. Remote and accessed from the road by a narrow drive it was virtually hidden from view. Lewis was a banker and a magistrate, married with two children and the family were well respected in the district. Sadly, in 1879 tragedy struck when the youngest child, a daughter, was declared 'morally insane' and confined to a local lunatic asylum. She committed suicide and the family left the area although it is not recorded where they went. It was rumoured the mother and the son died soon after, the former also by her own hand, the latter in a hunting accident.'

Verity sat for a while, bemused and shocked. She tried to imagine the terror of a young girl, who was sent away for being "morally insane".

What did that even mean? Shuddering, she closed the book. Whatever had occurred in this house one hundred years ago remained a mystery although it was looking as if Meredith was right: something terrible had happened to Angharad Elin Lewis.

And for whatever reason, her ghost has woken up determined to tell my sister her story.

She found her sister in her bedroom, rummaging in a drawer.

'Hi,' Meredith said. 'What's up? You look like you lost a five pound note and found a penny.' She tipped a pile of underwear onto the already clothes-strewn floor. 'I still can't find my necklace. Are you sure you haven't seen it?'

'No, I found something though.' Verity waved the book at Meredith. 'You were right. Here, I've marked the page.'

Meredith turned and stared at the book. 'Where did you get this? How did you…?'

Verity explained. 'Nain knew all about it. Well, not everything. She remembered quite a lot though and she remembered this. And don't worry, I didn't mention the sewing box or the ghost.'

Snatching the book from Verity, Meredith frowned as she read; stopping once to comment: 'Bloody cheek! Our tower's perfect.'

Verity sat on her sister's bed. 'You have to stop now, Meri. Stop trying to find out the story, stop thinking about it too. It's horrible and sad and I don't…'

'Are you kidding? Verity, this is gold dust. It means I'm right and it's her. Why would we stop now?

Because it's scary…

'It makes me uncomfortable. It's private. It's her life and it's like prying.'

'Speak for yourself – I'm helping her.' Meredith's eyes glittered as she scanned the page again. 'Looks like the evil brother got what was coming to him.'

'Don't say that.'

'Why not? Sounds like rough justice to me.'

'Whatever he did—'

'Verity, don't be naïve. He did something vile.'

'What do you think 'morally insane' means?'

'I'm not sure, but whatever it is, it sounds disgusting. Moral is like being good and not sinning, isn't it? All that Bible stuff.'

Verity felt sick. 'Yes, and it's horrible. I think we ought to forget all about it.'

'No way, and in any case, it's too late and I couldn't stop her if I wanted to.'

'You could try.' Verity didn't like where this ghost was taking them.

Meredith's face held the mutinous look. 'I don't want to try. I keep telling you, Angharad's made her choice and I'm not going to let her down.'

'But why is she telling *you*, Meri? And why now, after a hundred years?'

'Because I woke her up and because you're right and it's horrible. And because the story isn't for me, Verity, it's for her.'

Present

I'm staring at the cracked and pitted fountain.

It looks unsteady and an odd thing happens: it's as if I shrink and instead of looking into the bowl the birds drank from, I'm reaching up to the lip and I'm a little girl again barely able to see over the edge. The hairs on my arms rise, gold against my pale skin and the air changes and I have a vivid recollection of somebody calling out a warning.

'Be careful!'

It's Nain's voice and I turn, half-expecting to see her.

The moment is gone and I'm me again, grown up and alone, standing next to a dried-up old stone fountain surrounded by the half-glimpsed past and too many imagined ghosts.

I reach for my jacket again – whether or not it's my imagination is immaterial. I'm unsettled and a chill runs through me.

That April, the last one before we left, it snowed.

Lilac and snow; an impossible combination Allegra said, only she was wrong. The snow was ephemeral and magical, there and gone in less than a week; a phenomenon, people said later, an anomaly and a quirk of nature, but snow it did, and it was deliriously beautiful.

I look up at the sky. There's no sign of snow.

About to step across the broken wall, I see it.

Another cigarette butt.

This one is smoked almost to the tip. It's crushed in the dried-out stone bowl. Bits of tobacco splay from the stub, the end of the filter stained with nicotine. It smells like the other one – pungent with an edge of recent burning.

One night as I went to bed, snow began falling.

Unable to sleep, I watched from my window as it swirled like spinning moths. The house slept and there was no one else to see how it stopped for a short time, began again, falling slow and straight, adding to the previous layer until the garden became a shroud.

Dawn cast a translucent light turning the garden and the view beyond it spectral. I leaned out of my window again, transfixed by the spiralling flakes, whiter than the moon. Silent as a shadow, I crept downstairs and in the scullery, pulled on my heavy cloak and a pair of boots. I made my way through the conservatory and stood at the door.

A heavy coating of snow rendered the garden timeless. Looking up I could see how snow had reshaped the roof, and icicles under the eaves as sharp as daggers.

Snow in April was as rare as a comet.

I took a few steps and my feet plunged into deep snow almost covering my boots. The edge of my cloak and the hem of my nightgown were instantly soaked. Fearing my mother's wrath, knowing it would be wiser to wait for permission, I returned indoors.

Passing the parlour I saw him, in front of the fireplace, dressed for riding, slapping a crop against the palm of his hand. It was new – a gift from Papa to mark my brother's acceptance into the hunt.

Snow drifted across the tall windows.

'Where have you been, at this time of the morning?'

'Outside, to look at the snow.'

'Half dressed?' He scowled and ordered me into the room. 'Close the door.'

The dull click isolated me. I tried not to look as nervous as I felt.

'I am perfectly decent, brother.' My cloak more than covered me, but this seemingly innocent remark was my undoing. As the words left my mouth I already heard the edge of his criticism.

'Decent.' He licked his lips and a shudder ran through me. 'You are dripping filthy snow all over the floor. Have a care, sister; you treat this house with disrespect at your peril.' The crop swished, the sharp sound of it menacing the air.

Some demon in me refused to be quiet. 'Better to disrespect a house than fail to respect an innocent animal.'

His eyes narrowed, his mouth twisted and he took a step forward. 'What did you say?'

'Killing animals for sport; it disgusts me.'

'Foxes are disgusting, they're vermin and vermin must be destroyed.'

'And you are a bully; no wonder girls dislike you.'

Inwardly cursing myself for a fool, I made to leave the room.

'Stop right there. How dare you! Bullies are weak and I am no weakling, miss.'

I stayed silent, afraid of his vile temper and fouler tongue and yet beneath my cold skin my blood boiled and I was contemptuous of my weakness. I said no more, knowing how he could hurt me.

'Apologise at once!'

I shook my head and before he could do or say anything further, I turned on my heel, wrenched open the door and fled.

Twenty-four

Across the bay a bone-coloured sky receded into the night.

Snow began drifting in from the far side of the mountains. By morning it had stopped, the ground was icy and a puddle by the kitchen door had frozen solid.

Verity opened her eyes with a start. Slipping out of bed she opened the curtains on an unblemished landscape, a vast unbroken expanse of brilliant white. On the other side of the glass the sky split open like a pillow, white feathers falling through the air; an unexpected interlude as April played her most audacious trick. The branches of the trees were heavy with snow. Everything appeared twice its normal size. A pale sun washed the garden in a silent light.

She opened the window, dislodged the snow on the sill and watched as it thudded to the ground. A snowflake landed on her open palm. As it dissolved she imagined it under her skin: starlight in her veins.

Downstairs she rattled the embers in the range, placed some wood and coal on top of them and moved the big kettle onto the hot plate.

The silence in the kitchen hovered.

Through the window the sky now held a tinge of pink. Verity watched as new flakes began blowing against the windowpane.

Hearing her mother, she turned.

'I suppose you're feeling pleased with yourself,' Allegra said.

'Not particularly.'

'At this rate we'll be snowed in.'

'No we won't. It'll be gone in a day or two.'

'I daresay. In the meantime, we'll have to lump it.' Allegra came into the room, watched the steam beginning to curl from the kettle. 'Have you seen Meredith?'

'Still in bed I reckon.'

'No she isn't. I looked. I knew she'd be excited about the snow.'

'Let me guess. She's gone outside already.'

They peered out of the window together. The snow was beginning to obliterate the familiarity of the garden. The new fall had already covered any footprints Meredith might have left and the ground glittered like sugar.

'Do you think we ought to look for her?'

Allegra began rolling a cigarette. 'She won't have gone far. I daresay she'll show up in a minute, no point in both of us freezing to death.'

'Meaning, if anyone's going to look, it'll be me.'

'What's the betting she'll come in looking like a little snowman? Or she's out there making one.' Allegra lit the cigarette, coughed hard, her hand held to her mouth.

'Your cough's getting worse. You need to stop smoking.'

'It's a frog in my throat. Don't fuss.' Allegra rummaged in the dresser. 'We ought to dig the camera out.'

'Do we still have one?'

'Here,' Allegra said. 'And good gracious, it's even got film in it.'

Meredith was incapable of standing still long enough to have her photograph taken and Allegra refused to pose. As the heroine of her own rose-coloured narrative she expected people to catch her unawares and immortalise her.

No one did.

No one came to Gull House, with or without a camera.

Meredith hurled herself through the door, snow flying around her. 'It's like Narnia! It's so cold out there, I have frostbite! Look at my fingers. They're purple! Verity, come on! We have to make snow angels.' Turning on her heel she ran off.

Verity and her mother watched the snowflakes as big as silver moths. This was no ordinary snowfall. It lay like a great white cushion muffling the sound of the sea.

Snow in April: rare and without reason.

They could hear Meredith plodding round to the terrace, laughing as she fell, picking herself up and carrying on.

'Verity,' Allegra said, 'you better get out there before your sister drowns.'

'I'm going.' Verity pulled on her coat and a pair of mittens, stood in the doorway pushing her feet into her boots. 'You should come too, Mam, it's beautiful.'

Apart from Meredith's footprints the garden was becalmed in unbroken, glittering drifts. In the centre of the lawn the fountain stood like a snow ghost. Verity stepped into the holes made by Meredith's feet, following them round the corner of the house to where the stones steps lay buried.

Meredith lay on the ground, arms and legs akimbo, moving them up and down. 'Help me up, Verity; I want to see my angel.'

Verity grabbed her sister's hands and hauled her to her feet.

'Look! Watch me!' She fell back again, delirious with joy, flapping her arms and legs, climbing out by herself this time, making half a dozen more angels before she collapsed, panting and exhausted.

'You have to make some now.'

Within no time the entire lawn was covered in snow angels. The two girls raced about in the pure blue-white, calling to one another, their voices lost in the echoing vastness of it.

Verity remembered the camera. She pulled it from the pocket of her coat.

'Lie in one of the angels, Meredith – I'll take your picture.' She took off her mittens and pointed the camera.

Meredith's teeth were chattering. 'Did you take it?'

'Yes, don't worry, it going to look great.' Verity had a keen awareness of a memory being made. 'Come on now, that's enough

— we're soaked to the skin – we have to go in and dry off before we die of cold.' She began pulling her sister toward the steps. Meredith grabbed her hand and stopped her.

'Be careful,' she said. 'We mustn't disturb the angels. I want Angharad to see them.'

Verity stopped. 'Do you think she comes out here?'

'I think she's everywhere. It's her home. Or at least it was. She loved it here once, like we do. What happened to her might have made her hate it though.'

'Meri, you can't know that.'

'No, but I can guess. In my dream last night I heard crying and I saw the shadow of a bad man. It was her dream too and then I woke up and I was crying as well.'

'Oh, Meri, you poor thing, that's awful.' Verity put her arm around her sister's shoulder.

'No it isn't. It's just sad. Hearing her is what I'm supposed to do.'

'Aren't you even a bit scared?'

'Of what? A sad ghost? Why would I be? I told you, she needs me. And I'm not frightened of the dark.'

It was true. Meredith was like her grandmother: she wasn't scared of anything.

'But a ghost? I'd be terrified.'

Meredith touched her sister's cold hand. 'Verity, you're trembling. And I thought you were the one who never feels the cold.'

Verity thought about the night in the garden and the shadow in the trees.

It wasn't the cold making her shiver.

Twenty-five

The following morning the world woke again to an unfamiliar light.

In the silent white there was no sky or garden, only snow suspended on the air, icing the windowpanes, erasing the edges, hushing the land.

As much as she loved it, snow in April seemed to Verity like a spell gone awry. She didn't mind the cold but something about the intensity of the snow made her unsure, as if it was trying to hide something. Around the house, icy puddles reflected a soft grey sky; frozen spikes of grass stood like spears and icicles hung from the eaves.

'Snow in April is so cool,' Meredith said.

Verity found her digging out the chickens. They stood in an indignant huddle, fluffed up to twice their normal size.

'Poor chickies, it won't last and you'll be fine.' Meredith gave them extra grain, swept the roof of the hen house free of snow, found some old blankets in the glory hole to spread over it.

The snow fell and fell in fat calm flakes lying across the garden in dense stretches of silent white, rising and falling in solemn, blue-tinged waves.

Verity and Meredith made so many snow angels there was barely a space left without wings.

Allegra decided it was too much. The wet clothes draped everywhere were steaming the house up. 'And it's giving me a headache. It's so white. How am I supposed to paint white.'

She went to bed and asked for tea. Meredith refused to come

indoors, and when Verity took a tray up, Allegra looked taken aback.

'How nice of you,' she said. 'Biscuits too.'

'I do my best.'

'Yes,' Allegra said. 'I know you do.'

Deciding not to try and unpack any meaning in her mother's unexpected words, Verity left the room, went in search of Meredith. If she stayed outside any longer she would turn to ice or catch a chill and then there would be trouble.

And it was bound to be her fault.

She found her sister at the lookout tree next to the outline of a single angel. Meredith had written something in the snow.

'What does it say?'

'It's for Angharad.'

'Only you, Meri.'

'I don't suppose the poor thing would have been allowed to play in the snow.'

By late afternoon the sky turned to the colour of ash, heavy with the promise of more snow and it was so cold Allegra panicked, thinking the pipes would freeze.

'That's all I need. Oh God, how I hate this house.'

'No you don't,' Meredith said. 'Don't say that.'

'Oh darling, I didn't mean anything.'

You so did.

She watched Verity cutting bread and Allegra whisking eggs for an omelette.

'Well don't joke about it, please.' She warmed her toes in front of the range. 'Everything's fine and dandy and you aren't allowed to spoil it.'

'Oh, my little snow goose, I'm sorry. I won't ever say it again.'

Later, when darkness fell and Meredith had gone to bed, exhausted and happier than she had been for weeks, Verity slipped outside. Something wasn't right and she found herself thinking about the ghost again. She was still afraid, though she didn't know why.

There was something odd about this snow-filled night. The garden lay eerily still, transformed and peculiarly beautiful.

It's like I'm the last person alive in the whole world.

The only sound was the light crunching of her feet in the snow. The power of the silence overwhelmed her. Having seen her sister's face unexpectedly glowing with colour, all notions of dreams and terror banished, at least for a while, Verity had been overcome by a desire to make things normal again.

Fine and dandy…

She couldn't get the idea of a weird spell out of her head. A girl with her feet on the ground, Verity normally had no truck with spells. Spells were her grandmother's domain – or silly games her sister played.

It's her … I can hear her … what if it's my imagination … what if I'm as mad as Angharad…

'And what if I try and find out.'

Verity found a spade in the shed and at the entrance to the blue garden, shovelled snow from in front of the gate. She pressed down on the latch and stood as still as could be, holding her breath, willing something to happen. It was time to face her. If Angharad's ghost was real then Verity wanted to be sure. She wanted to stand up to her, or stop her and make her go away.

If you're real, then show yourself. Stop bullying my sister and get out of my grandmother's garden.

Still holding her breath, she heaved open the gate, breathed out and the air billowed in front of her face in a cloud.

Deep in drifts of snow, the garden appeared unearthly. Imagining icy breath on her face she swept her hand across her cheek. From the corner of her eye, Verity caught a movement, a distorted shape as though someone tried to paint on the air and the melting snow made it run and blur.

The night listened.

I don't believe in ghosts.

Each atom of Verity's being didn't want to call what she wasn't sure she was seeing, a ghost.

'I don't believe in ghosts,' she said into the dark garden. 'So stop haunting us.'

For a moment she thought it was going to be all right. The vague shape was no longer there and she let out a tight sigh of relief. She closed her eyes for a second and when she opened them, knew she had been mistaken.

It wasn't a dream. She wasn't asleep; she was outside in the dark with the cold on her face and the figure was real.

It turned and Verity felt its gaze as if a real person stood in front of her and not a ghost.

Because, oh my life, it's what you are ... a ghost...

Something cold slid down her back and she wanted to blink again because in stories that's what happened, you blinked and the thing disappeared; only her eyes were stuck open and the apparition was still there.

Are you really Angharad? Are you who my sister keeps hearing?

A whirling mass of snow flew at her, caught the side of her head and for a second she saw a face, white with fury, eyes blazing and as she fell to the ground the world turned black.

She came to, covered in snow, shaky, unsure how much time had passed.

Did I faint?

Getting to her feet she looked around. There was nothing to see, only the shape of the dark night and a smattering of snow caught in the ends of her hair.

He came to my room that night.

Outside the snow lay thick as clouds. In spite of the cold, I had already settled into sleep. The creak of the doorknob woke me, and peering from beneath my bedcovers, I saw him in the dimness of the open doorway. Save for my shallow breathing, the room was silent. I didn't dare sit up or turn my head.

'You.'

His voice unnerved me and needing to be on my feet, I slipped out of bed. My robe lay across a chair. I caught his cold eye and found myself rooted to the spot, afraid to move.

I could smell whisky and knew he had been at Papa's decanter.

'Look at you, standing there, half naked as a harlot.'

'What am I meant to wear in bed?' Shaking, I pointed to where my robe lay.

He took a step forward and I faltered, my nightgown fluttering around me making me more like a ghost than a girl.

'You have no right to come in here uninvited. What do you want?'

'I have every right.' He took a step toward me. 'And you chose to get out of your bed. Why did you do that?'

'Why wouldn't I?' Puzzled, and in spite of my nervousness, I couldn't stop myself even though I knew I was probably making things worse.

Like a magician, he summoned my words and turned them on me. 'Why wouldn't you?' He licked his fleshy lips. 'Of course you would, you are wanton, like all women.'

Only half aware of what he meant, I nevertheless bridled.

'You are foul, brother, and worse; you are disgusting for thinking such a thing of your own sister.'

He gave no answer, only stared his fish stare, looking at me with such contempt, fear coiled in my stomach. And there was something else; behind his eyes, something I didn't understand, yet still recognised as a thread of madness.

My voice faltered. 'It's not attractive: bullying.'

'I am no bully! Don't say that! And it's your own fault.' He edged

144

closer and whispered at me, his voice sibilant with menace. 'Little wanton.'

The whisky on his breath stank. His eyes were dull with drink and he gave a grunt.

'How am I responsible for this ... this hateful behaviour?'

He lurched across the room and to my horror I saw him fumble with his clothing.

The force of his assault paralysed me. It was brutal and in a state of terror I was too small to fend him off.

Afterwards, he laughed although it was more snarl than mirth and my fear turned to abject dread. His eyes narrowed and in them I saw pure evil.

When he spoke, his words struck me like a hissing cat. 'Don't imagine this is over. Or that anyone will believe you.'

In an instant, I saw with blinding clarity a probable future.

However naïve I was, however sheltered my life, I wasn't a total ignoramus. Maids gossiped, even my governess allowed herself the occasional salacious disclosure if only as a warning against any fall from grace I might contemplate.

My mother had told me nothing of sexual matters. She even left the business of my monthly courses to an embarrassed maid. What little I knew about it I'd gleaned from whispers and cautionary tales overheard at doors left ajar: servants gossip concerning girls no better than they ought to be; women of ill-repute, and references to women 'in trouble'.

If my understanding of bodily functions was rudimentary, I knew enough to understand I was in terrible danger. Innocence would not save me. I knew there were rules and that a terrible fate befell girls who were perceived to have broken them. The kind of rules my parents shaped their life by.

Somehow, with a single, shocking act, without asking for or inviting it, I had become one of those girls.

Above all I recognised that by stepping over the boundary of verbal bullying into the foulness of his assault, my brother now relied on another set of rules, unwritten and yet as ingrained in our society as the evil in his heart.

Sick with disgust and in pain, I watched him adjust his clothing and leave the room.

My arms were drained of strength, I held onto myself as if the act of doing so was the only thing stopping my body from disintegrating.

Before that night, I hadn't been afraid of the dark. This was a different kind of darkness and it stole my hope. Everything about my life, my room, the house, was tainted.

I smelled my own blood and knew I was tainted.

My hair was a weight threatening to topple me, I wanted to unpeel my skin and step out of it.

Too numb to cry, I crawled under the covers.

I must have slept. When I woke I had no way of knowing what time it was. I listened for the familiar sounds of the house to give me a clue. Save for the ticking of a clock somewhere, it was utterly quiet. Crawling from my bed I drew the drapes and looked out on an altered landscape. More snow surrounded the house. Snow and silence, the austere lines of the garden softened.

My heart beat sharp as a blade. Gazing down at the terrace below my window, I saw a line of animal paw prints in the powdery snow, a fox perhaps or one of the cats and I longed to follow them, to disappear.

You cannot walk away from such a degree of horror.

There was a danger to the day; only the light behind the heavy curtains holding it in check. Elsewhere throughout the house, the rattle and clatter of morning began: a door opening, a clock chiming; my father's voice.

The echo of my brother's…

Don't imagine this is over…

The sense of an ordinary day made abominable. A day like no other I had known or expected to ever know.

The maid brought a jug of hot water. Ignoring her greeting, I waited until she left the room. Shaking, I rose from my bed, washed my wounded body as best I could and dressed, still stunned, and with no clear idea of what I ought to do.

Tell someone? Who would I tell? Who would believe me? My mother was a woman wrapped in self-interest; vain and brought up to please men, to be subservient. She would never challenge or gainsay either my father or my brother. Even so, I still harboured a faint notion that she might take pity and help me.

I met her on the dark, unlit landing. She stared and asked, was I sick? Mute with shock my words choked me. My mother's eyes raked mine, scanned my body and it was as if my shame seeped through my pores, soiling my clothes. I saw her falter before she swallowed whatever words had formed in her head. Her face was unreadable and yet every line on it spoke a hideous truth.

There was no doubt in my mind; the lie would be mine.

I made my escape, grateful for only one thing; for a day at least, as if by some unspoken agreement, she set me no tasks.

My father had always treated me as if I were a nonentity. My mother I believe had a fear of how alive I was; she would do everything she could to supress this.

As for him – my depraved brother – he had always been a stranger to me, now he became the coldest kind of threat. My sly, unclever brother who at school I believe must have been bullied, at home turned into the worst kind of abuser. A boy who pulled the wings off butterflies had grown into a man who tore mine from my body.

I am a ghost and I am not mad. I am a thing made from grief, treachery and a terrible secret.

Ask the birds, child... The birds know everything.

Twenty-six

Although the temperature began to rise slightly, it still felt like winter.

Small birds protested. The chickens refused to lay a single egg, at night the sky turned black and stars hovered like diamonds. Before the end of the week however, a thaw set in. Drip by drip the snow melted; the sound of it relentless.

Meredith slept late, her dreams turned to nightmares. She woke in the night and Verity heard her crying.

'Hush now, I'm here.' Verity shook her sister out of whatever dream was troubling her, and afraid she might wake Allegra, took her into her own bed.

'Everything's going to be all right.'

'He hurt her…' Meredith sobbed and trembled. 'She said the birds know… What do the birds know?'

Meredith lay on her back, exhausted now and sleeping deeply.

Beyond the weeping garden Verity could see flat waves sighing up the beach, relentless thin white creases. Further out, the sea was dark and threatening. She went downstairs, poured a glass of milk and was about to go back to bed when she noticed a light under the door of the sitting-room.

Her mother lay on the window seat, lolling back against the frame, a half-smoked cigarette in her fingers. The skirt of her heavy silk kimono fell away, exposing her slender legs.

Allegra looked up, the cigarette singeing the skin of her fingers. Shreds of cloud slid across the moon.

'You should get some proper sleep,' Verity said.

'I never sleep. You know I don't.'

Only the tick of a clock disturbed the silence.

'I know you do your best, Verity.'

Verity eyed her mother warily. Faint praise made her suspicious and this was twice in as many days.

'Don't look so serious. I'm not saying it to be nice. I know you mean well.'

Together they gazed out to the horizon, listened to the sea, darkly deep and roaring in from Ireland.

Verity noticed her mother's pale bony knees under her nightdress, the thinness of her fingers as she pulled the edges of her kimono close again. She saw how narrow her arms were. How angular her face. There were no curves to her.

Verity wanted her mother to know she was paying attention. 'You don't eat enough.'

'Nonsense.' Allegra's eyes remained fixed on the view. The wind shifted, took a patch of cloud with it, revealing a luminous slice of moon the colour of ice.

'A lover's moon,' Allegra said. She reached for her tarot cards, scattered on a round table at her side, scooped them up and dropped them into the space between her and Verity, carelessly as if for once she didn't care how they landed. Most of them slid sideways, falling to the floor leaving two, face-down on the seat, like a challenge.

'Go on then,' she said.

As usual, it sounded like an order.

'Do I have to?'

'Why not?' Allegra's look was one of amusement. 'Indulge me.'

Verity paused. Her mother's smile felt like a trick.

It's a load of rubbish, what do I care?

She turned over one of the cards. The Two of Swords: a seated, blindfolded woman holding two swords crossed over her chest: above her, a crescent moon and behind her the sea.

Allegra started.

'What?' Verity was unwilling to give the image credence. 'What's she supposed to stand for?'

Allegra gave a sliver of a shrug. Her voice sounded distant. 'Stalemate? Some sort of impasse.'

Verity touched her finger to the woman's bound face. It was a picture on a piece of card. It meant nothing. She tapped the second one. 'Your turn now.'

Without looking, Allegra turned the card over. 'What is it?'

'Another sword. The Knight.'

'Did you swap it?' Allegra's voice sounded choked.

'Of course I didn't. Why would I do that? I don't believe in this stuff anyway. And you only do when it suits you.'

Allegra grabbed the cards, scrabbled for the ones on the floor and crammed them into the velvet bag.

'You haven't said what it means.'

'It doesn't matter,' her mother muttered. 'If you can't take it seriously, what's the point? Go back to bed.'

The sky darkened, clouds thickened, obliterating the moon. For a moment Verity thought it might have started snowing again.

Distracted, Allegra turned to the window, spotted now with a mosaic of rain. 'That's all I need. I suppose it's going to pour with rain until August now.'

'There's supposed to be a village near here where it rains every day in August.'

Allegra made a snorting sound. 'Now who's being gullible? I suppose that's more of your grandmother's nonsense.' She ran her hands along her arms. 'God, how I loathe this place.' The words came out as thin as she was. 'Why are you still here? Well, I'm going to bed even if you aren't.'

As the door closed behind her mother, Verity watched the clouds wrestling for prominence and the rain as it began to fall in earnest. What was left of the snow would be gone by morning.

On the floor by the window seat she spotted a small book. Her mother's tarot bible. Verity opened it, knowing she would find the text underlined, the margins annotated in her mother's spidery hand, notes she made and yet barely took notice of. She turned the pages until she found the Knight of Swords and read the description.

The word that stood out was 'ruthless'.

Twenty-seven

The snow was almost gone and spring was making an effort.

Outside the weather became more seasonal, indoors the house still felt bleak and upstairs it smelled of damp.

'It's as if nature's got it in for me.' Allegra huddled in front of the range drinking cup after cup of hot coffee.

'Miss Jenkins says it's to do with the climate.' Verity was trying to work out some sums in a book the education board had supplied. Meredith was nowhere to be seen.

'Miss Jenkins would,' Allegra said. The scorn in her voice was muted, as if she could barely be bothered to argue.

'She's ahead of her time according to Mr Tallis. They were talking about it – about a climate change conference last February and…'

'They're as mad as bats those two. The weather's fine now.'

'It's not the same thing … weather and climate…'

'Oh for God's sake, Verity, stop trying to be clever.'

'I'm not. I'm saying what I believe. You can't erase my thoughts because you don't agree with them. It's what men do.'

'Good grief, Verity, you sound like a women's libber. Wherever did you get an idea like that?

We stayed mute and disloyal because we were afraid…

The poems were beginning to make sense.

'It isn't an idea, it's a fact.' Verity took a breath. 'Have you heard of a writer called Adrienne Rich?'

'No, I haven't, who's she when she's at home.'

'She's an American poet…'

'Ah, more Miss Jenkins I suppose. I wouldn't be surprised if she was into all that women's rights stuff.'

'What's wrong with it?'

'Oh, Verity, it's so graceless, so strident.'

'It makes a lot of sense.'

Allegra brushed off feminism as if it were a stray hair on her shawl. 'Oh, it's nonsense, the bloody climate too for that matter. Between you, you and your precious librarian are driving me crazy. Bloody feminists – thinking they have all the answers.'

Verity met her mother's eyes and she saw an emotion behind them, impossible to hide.

'Are you okay?'

Allegra twisted the little pearl ring.

'You never take it off, do you?'

'Why would I? He gave it to me. In spite of his faults, he was very gallant, your father. You know?'

'I thought you hated him.'

He was a poet...

Not, she suspected, like Adrienne Rich...

'You can still despise someone you love.' Allegra sighed and the sound was expansive. 'I've lost so much, Verity. Your father, my friends; any life I might have had. Buried here like Miss bloody Havisham. Look at this place; it's a wreck, a mausoleum.'

'Don't exaggerate. It's a bit shabby, but that's because we don't do proper housework.' Verity moved across to the fire, next to her mother. 'We're lucky to live here, Mam. Nain could have sold it and then where would we have gone?'

'There's no future here, not for you girls.'

It was the first time Verity remembered hearing her mother consider them or their future.

'What do you mean?

'Nothing, I don't mean anything.'

'You aren't thinking of leaving are you?'

'Would it be so awful?' Allegra knew a difficult question was best answered by another. Her voice wobbled. She rubbed her temple. A frown appeared, marring her otherwise perfect brow.

She kept her eyes shut, her fists clenched. 'Bloody Dickens would have had a field day in this dump.' She scowled. 'And what the hell has feminism ever done for me?'

Allegra habitually spoke her thoughts out loud and Verity was used to it; accustomed to ignoring her. After a second's hesitation, she touched her mother's hand and for a moment thought Allegra was going to allow her to take it. Instead it was snatched it away and she made a barrier of both her hands and the moment was over.

'I don't want to talk about it. Any of it. It doesn't matter. Get on with your work and stop bothering me.'

Verity gathered her books. 'Whatever. Sorry to be such a pain. I'll finish this in my room then shall I?'

The door didn't slam behind her. Verity was too contained for that kind of petulance, a trait Allegra found vaguely irritating.

Why does she have to be so passive?

She fingered an unopened letter from the bank lying on the table like a summons. Poking the fire she watched as a shower of sparks exploded onto the hearth. The envelope was brown with one of those cellophane windows that always struck her as lazy, as if the sender couldn't be bothered to write a simple name and address.

Her name was wrong in any case. It was always wrong: Mrs Allegra Dilys Kingdom – official looking, entirely incorrect. It was a borrowed name, which in spite of her legal claim, hadn't ever felt as if it belonged to her.

Allegra's heart was fashioned from hope and impetuous wishes; his had been made from declarations written in sand. When Idris Kingdom left and took her dreams with him, she became plain Allegra Pryce once more. By then, the forms had been filled in, the façade erected, the illusion set in place. Everyone assumed Mrs Allegra Dilys Kingdom was like any married woman whose husband had upped and left.

All you had to do was look behind her ash-coloured eyes to know this wasn't true.

Present

At this rate, I'll have a collection.

Allegra's chain-smoking habit put Meredith and me off cigarettes for life. I still find the smell disgusting. I wrinkle my nose, add the second stub to the first; stuff the tissue into my pocket. My phone still shows no signal. Calling the caretaker will have to wait.

In my bag there's a bottle of water and some apples, and a packet of cheese and tomato sandwiches Carla insisted on making for me.

Realising I'm hungry I pull them out and start eating as I watch the ragwort, tall as flags, waving in the breeze. A few sparrows gather, unafraid and bold. I tear at the crusts of my sandwich, break them into small pieces and fling them into the grass.

In the undergrowth the breeze shifts, the wild flowers rustle and whisper.

The sandwiches are soggy. I told her they would be, even though I don't mind. Carla's care for me is more than I know I deserve. She is utterly selfless and there are times when I find it hard to understand why she would want to be with someone like me.

I'm not selfish; I have simply become circumspect. I don't like to show my feelings. Over the past few years, they have taken too much of a battering.

The sparrows fly up, regroup and land again. I look towards the dark side of the garden, overgrown and silent, and it isn't a ghost I'm concerned with.

The sense someone has been here is acute.

I tear at the remains of my sandwich. Out of sight I hear the gulls – supreme opportunists – and half expect an invasion. For now they leave the sparrows to their feast. High on the thermals, their cry becomes a scream.

I drain the water and wander across the garden. There's a shed behind the kitchen. We kept our bicycles in it; it was filled with tools: hoes and spades, an old lawn mower belching petrol. The door is open and I wonder again about the man Nain has been paying to keep an eye on the house, and if his caretaking is meant to include the grounds. If it is, he isn't earning his money. I shall have to get hold of him somehow. I don't look forward to questioning someone I don't know, trying to find out if my grandmother has been cheated.

I ask myself what Carla would do and try to be kind. Maybe he's heard about Mared's death and doesn't know what to do either.

Meredith's bicycle leans against the shed, up to its saddle in nettles and weeds.

Don't forget to put your bike away; if it rains, it'll go rusty...

Meredith never put her bicycle away.

Looking down I notice the grass is flattened, as if someone has recently been standing on it. A tremor runs down my back and I turn away, walk back to the fountain, quickly, in search of the sky, away from shadows. The birds have disappeared, the crumbs finished and for a moment I'm ridiculously alone.

We were always alone. And Meredith is still travelling, wandering wherever the wind takes her. I don't know for sure where she is and here, with memories crowding me, I miss her more than I ever have.

I sent a letter to the last known address, telling her about Mared's death. After three months and no response, I fear the worst.

Carla says, if I want to, we can go and look for her. I know this would be a bad idea. I may not have seen my sister for over twenty years but I know her and understand how she would hate to be followed.

Meredith is more like Allegra than she knows.

Once was not enough and he sought me out again.

I locked my door. Mama wanted to know why and when I had no answer, she took the key.

Sitting at my dressing table a few nights later, I felt his dark, demanding shadow at my back. My protest was smothered by brutish hands; he told me if I made a noise, he would kill me. Rigid with dread, I almost hoped I would die. Survival is an instinct though and had my mouth not been dry from terror, I might have screamed. But then, recalling my mother's impenetrable face, I froze.

He took my muteness for acquiescence. This time he didn't bother with the bed. It was over in minutes and his rank, whisky-laden breath on my neck as he snarled his warning not to tell sickened me almost as much as the hideousness of his assault.

A week later, while my father was away on the business men conduct, my brother risked a daytime assault. I was making my way to the conservatory, instructed by my mother to check for frost damage amongst her delicate orchids. Behind the wet splashing of the thawing snow, I didn't hear him.

He grabbed me from behind, pinned me against the wall. This time some inner fury lent me a power I didn't know I possessed. I fought like a cat, bit and scratched his face and shrieked my refusal. He tore at the bodice of my gown, but alarmed and taken aback by my resistance and cries, his fear of being discovered overrode his foul intention.

Raising his hand, he hit me hard across the side of my head. Stunned, I almost fell. At the same moment, we both heard the tap of my mother's boots, her voice calling, demanding to know what the commotion was.

My brother, the coward, ran for his life.

Part two

Part two

Twenty-eight

He came out of nowhere.

There's no such thing as nothing … no such place as nowhere…

It wasn't the first time she'd seen him. It was the first time he'd spoken to her.

'May I see?'

Pale and light-saturated, that morning the sea was tinged with milky blue, making itself up as it went along. Allegra was attempting to capture the horizon. It shifted: a line of purple and black, one second as clear as if some invisible hand had drawn it with a ruler, the next, merged with the sky and turning to mist.

She feigned surprise. 'God, you made me jump.'

'Really?'

Allegra didn't like being found out. As he laughed it sounded contrite enough and she relented. The sun was behind him. Tall and gauntly handsome, he merged into the cliff.

'I was drawn by the glint in your hair. Like diamonds.'

She touched a finger to the clip.

'Am I forgiven?' His smile was a question too.

'Forgive is a theory, but yes, if you like.'

'That sounds cynical.'

'Perhaps it's because I'm a cynic?'

'You're far too lovely for cynicism. And any woman who can paint like this has to be acquainted with certainty.' He paused. 'With idealism and passion maybe?'

'You have no idea what you're talking about.' She laughed with him because she wasn't going to allow anyone, let alone a stranger, to see her heart.

Hers was an old love story, its trail gone cold although Allegra hadn't completely lost sight of it. She may not have forgiven her feckless husband his desertion, yet he still had his place, albeit as a stubborn stain on her heart. Allegra's heart was broken and impossible to mend. Too many of the pieces were lost.

She dropped her brush into a jar of water poised on a rock; searched in her bag for her tobacco pouch.

'Here,' he said, offering a pack of tailor-mades, 'have one of these.'

'No thanks, I prefer to roll my own.'

'I've seen you before.' He stared at her with careless eyes and she touched her hair again.

'Is that so?'

'Do you live nearby?'

She nodded and raised a hand, the cigarette paper pointing. 'Up there.'

He followed her gaze. From the beach the house appeared blurred; only the roof was visible. It looked like a house from another landscape, a wash of watercolour through the trees.

A lone gull sailed across the sky, ragged wings tilted.

He turned back to her. 'Can I see you again?'

She carried on rolling her cigarette. 'It's a free country.'

Allegra had disappeared to paint.

'Let's watch telly,' Meredith said.

They made French toast and baked beans and settled in front of the television, plates perched on their laps. A cartoon wound to an end. Verity set her plate on the floor, then wandered over to the window. She pressed her head against the glass, and watched her mother strolling up the garden lost in thought, her bag looped by its strap over her shoulder, the easel under her arm.

'She's back.'

'Who cares,' Meredith said. 'Come on, *Grange Hill* is starting.'

As her mother came closer, she looked up, saw Verity, and

shaking her head rearranged her face into a smile holding no greeting. Verity understood she was somehow guilty of spying; of witnessing a private moment.

She concentrated on the television.

When Allegra came into the room it was as if she brought a secret with her, the scent of sweat and sea and flames. The skin on her normally pale face was flushed; as she breathed in her nostrils flared and Verity sensed something wild and agitated about her.

Flinging her shawl onto a chair, Allegra advanced across the room and turned off the television.

Meredith let out a wail. 'Mam! What are you doing?'

'Have you really got nothing better to do than watch that rubbish?' Allegra glared. 'Television will rot your brain.'

'It's *Grange Hill*, Mam,' Verity said, 'not—'

'I despise television.'

'Everyone watches television.'

'Well, I'm not everyone.'

You can say that again.

'Verity's right,' Meredith said. 'Normal children watch television. You do too, you just pretend you don't.'

Allegra regularly stayed up late watching films and arts programmes. Now and then they caught her out, glued to some second-rate movie. She would always have an excuse, although neither of them thought she needed one. They knew there were times their mother couldn't bear her own company or to be alone at night, and that she would rarely admit it.

'Meredith, that's very cheeky!' Allegra was laughing now, her sooty, kohl-rimmed eyes glittering. She was wearing a velvet waistcoat over her frock and a glittery clip in her hair. She rolled a cigarette, ran the tip of her tongue along the gummed edge of the paper. Her tongue was pink and it looked to Verity like a newborn kitten.

Allegra raised her head and her look was challenging. 'And you can take that disapproving look off your face.'

163

There it was again: a hint of mockery in her voice and Verity reacted. 'Why do you always think I'm having a go?'

Meredith turned on the television. 'Shut up Verity. Both of you, can I please watch my programme?'

'Good grief, Verity, chill out. We were just teasing, weren't we Meredith?'

Verity waited for Meredith to say something, even if, in her current mood she probably wouldn't.

The look on her mother's face was almost triumphant. Verity felt a knot in her stomach. She bit down on her lip, on the words she refused to say and made sure she didn't slam the door behind her.

It wasn't only because of what Allegra had said; there was something else behind her mother's look and she had brought it with her, from the beach.

Whenever they hid from their mother, Meredith tried not to feel guilty.

Allegra would call out for them and search all over the place. She rarely came into the blue garden. It was as if an invisible barrier made it impossible for her to go further than the gate. When the girls returned to the house with forget-me-nots and bluebells, and the ends of conspiracy tangled in their hair, she would accuse Verity of some vague defiance, of leading her sister astray.

Angry with her mother and with herself for not sticking up for Verity, Meredith found her in the blue garden, under the wisteria tree. Patches of snow still clung in gaps between overgrown plants.

'I'm sorry I didn't say anything. She makes me—'

'It's all right.'

When Verity said Allegra was a drama queen, it wasn't about them, and wasn't Meredith's fault, Meredith's heart tripped over itself with love for her sister.

'Does she know where we are?'

'No.' Meredith picked a dandelion clock and blew on it sending tiny parachutes of time into the air. 'I told her you'd probably gone to the beach and I was going to find you.'

'You don't have to lie for me.'

'That's not a lie, Verity, it's an alibi.'

Verity laughed. 'You're impossible.' She turned to her sister and made her voice serious. 'You don't have to be like her, you know.' It was dim beneath the wisteria and the only thing they could see was each other's faces. 'You can be you and in the end it will make you happier.'

Twenty-nine

Meredith's dreams darkened.

Chilled to the bone, surrounded by shadows, she sought the warmth of her sister.

'Can I get into bed with you?' She climbed in beside Verity anyway. 'My dreams have changed. I don't have the words.'

'Try.'

'Doors open and close, it's dark and she's crying. Sobbing, it's awful.'

'Did you see her?' Verity almost hoped Meredith had.

'No. I told you, you don't see ghosts.'

I think maybe you do...

'It's more a sensation; that she wants me.'

'What for?'

'I don't know. She says she's made from treachery – and a secret.'

Verity didn't say how the word treachery bothered her.

'I don't mind when I'm awake – or half-wake and dreamy,' Meredith went on. 'Her voice is ... I don't know – normal? When I go to sleep though, it follows me into my dreams. Not the actual words – it's like when all sorts of sounds get mixed up.'

'A cacophony?'

'Yes.' Meredith managed a small smile. 'I'm going to steal that one.'

'It sounds dreadful.'

'It was, for her. Not for me though – it's what she needs to do.'

'And you definitely can't see her?'

Meredith hesitated. 'Tricks of the light don't count. And I told you; it's not like that. She doesn't want to hurt me. It's not like a haunting – it's not like being watched or anything.'

Oh yes it is…

'Meri, you're scaring me.'

'No. We can't be scared.' She turned in the bed, propped her chin on her hand. 'Did you know they called them the "mad-doctors" – the ones who looked after the poor people in the asylums?'

'That's creepy.'

'I read it in your library book.'

In spite of her earlier agitation, Meredith looked elated. Verity was the one who was frightened. Her heart beat faster and her skin was clammy with goose bumps.

Meredith patted her arm. 'Don't worry, Verity. She trusts me.'

Air drifted in through the window, fragrant with the scent of lilac and bluebells.

Verity drew in a long breath. 'But can you trust her?'

Upstairs, the house remained cold.

'It'll be the heating system.' Verity said. 'It's always playing up. I'll ask Allegra to phone the man who came before.'

It's not the heating, it's the ghost.

'You can't use logic to explain away everything, Verity.'

When did Meredith get to be so eloquent? Or were these even Meredith's words? Was this the ghost too, real or imagined, speaking through her? Maybe the cold was down to the heating system after all and she was over-reacting… It wasn't and she knew it. Perhaps she was the one going mad.

'I don't see why not,' she said, not quite trusting her voice.

Meredith shrugged. 'If it makes you uncomfortable, you don't have to be involved anymore. I can do it by myself.'

'Do what?'

'Carry on listening? Try and find out what happened to Angharad and help her?'

167

'Have you thought about where she goes, when she isn't talking to you? Or where she comes from?'

'No. I never met a ghost before. I suppose it's in a space between the worlds. Nain said it's a veil.'

Verity thought that if there was a veil between the worlds, someone must have torn it.

It was twilight, the moon had barely begun to rise and behind a bank of loose cloud it was visible only in fragments. It was damp from a recent fall of rain.

Drawn to the garden again, Verity stood by the half-open gate adjusting her eyes to the dimness. On the other side, the blue garden was still; not a mouse stirred. It appeared uncharacteristically dreary and lifeless. Breathing quietly she hesitated. Taking a deep breath, she took a few steps and aware of a sensation to her left, turned, her heart pounding under her ribs.

This time, as if summoned, the ghost came from the direction of the rain-drenched, melancholy trees. The wall faded and through a haze of mist Verity could see the wood, smell ancient layers of leaf mould and the sorrowful scent of long-dead animal bones.

The figure floated through the space where the wall ought to have been, and for a second it appeared incongruous, like something out of a bad horror film. Verity blinked, looked harder and as she did the ghost turned and Verity found herself looking at Angharad.

Who else could it be?

It was like seeing from a distance. The ghost was surrounded by a tunnel of grey, a hole in reality, undefined and faint.

Is she looking at me?

Something was happening that in the usual way was impossible. Terrified, she wanted to run back to the house. It looked a million miles away and she was blinded by the whiteness of the moon which now broke from behind the cloud. Rooted to the spot Verity stared at the ghost's face. As the clouds snatched up the moon again it disappeared, everything turned black and this time it was a different kind of blindness.

If she didn't get away from the garden she was sure she wouldn't be able to see again.

Verity held her breath. In the silence, the ghost's mouth moved. There was no sound and Verity saw her eyes, blank and sunken; her hair with bits of twigs and leaves caught in it.

Whatever she was trying to say, Verity couldn't hear a word.

Who are you?

Unable to speak herself, she watched the wretched creature. She appeared bereft, and in spite of the fear making her scalp tingle and her legs shake, it was the saddest thing Verity had ever known. And then the figure turned and looked up. And Verity, who, until that moment had been scared and curious, now felt deeply afraid.

As the feeling flooded her body, cold crawled from her feet to her scalp. The ghost's eyes bored into her; beseeching, impossible eyes. Fainter now she dissolved into the wall and a trick of vision meant her image repeated like a fog-laden hall of mirrors.

Verity's throat had dried to dust, fear jolted through her until finally she was able to let out a strangled cry. She felt a sweep of wind and the tunnel into the wood closed.

Angharad's ghost was gone.

Thirty

'Can we please go now?'

Allegra was concentrating on her painting and made a noise that might have had a criticism attached to it.

The clean afternoon light which, as the day proceeded, had become more perfect, clearly delighted her. Second by second the aspect changed; a fluid movement of current and waves, cloud drift and distant mist. She blinked and the sea shifted, her eyes took it in: a swell of green, an echo of silver in perpetual motion.

'Look', she said. 'How lovely it is.'

On her canvas Allegra had captured washes of pale colour with dashes of black and red indicating the oystercatchers at the edge of the water, a curve of creamy white for the ever-present gulls.

Tired and still unsettled by the encounter with the ghost, Verity couldn't summon any enthusiasm for the beach. The memory of it lodged like a stone in the middle of her chest. Sweat ran into her eyes. Wretched in the heat she wished she hadn't agreed to come.

'It's boiling, Mam,' she said. 'Please, can I go back?'

The weather had changed overnight, inexplicably and completely, as if summer had found its rhythm and was now edging out the cold, unreasonable spring. Within days it became so hot the birds wilted and throughout the garden wild flowers grew as tall as trees. The heat was impossible and when Allegra went round the house opening windows, the sun struck the glass with such intensity they almost caught fire.

'Stop fussing, child. Do what you like, you usually do.'

Oblivious to anything the girls were doing, or the change in Verity's mood, Allegra had planned today's outing.

'We'll do something together,' she'd announced at breakfast – brightly, as if they were a normal family. 'I'll make a picnic and we can go to the beach!'

'You always say you don't like us being on the beach with you when you're painting,' Verity said.

'Nonsense, I've never said any such thing. Wherever do you get these ideas?'

A truth, if it's contradicted with enough determination, can easily turn into a fiction.

Verity knew better than to defend herself. She had other things on her mind and she hadn't forgotten what Allegra had said the other night.

There's no future here, not for you girls…

By the time they made it to the beach the morning was already half gone. The sun hung high and hot in the sky. The picnic was a disaster. Brown banana sandwiches drawing flies, everything assembled with haste and no thought given to essentials. The sun – and a forgotten hat – meant Verity was overheated and cross.

'Wear my shawl on your head,' Allegra said from under a flower-strewn straw hat. She threw the poppy silk across the sand. 'It can only enhance your current look.'

Verity eyed her faded shorts with a frown. They looked all right to her. Worn and washed out perhaps, still clean and suitable. She hadn't wanted to risk spoiling the lovely new frock her grandmother had made. It was the colour of cornflowers and had pockets in the skirt.

And anyway, why do you always look as if you're wearing the contents of the dressing-up box?

Allegra's eyes darted everywhere but at her painting.

'Who are you looking for?'

'I'm not looking for anyone; I'm looking at what I'm painting.'

No you aren't, you're twitchy.

'Go and see what Meredith's up to.' Allegra peered hard at her canvas.

You don't fool me.

Meredith had wandered away, down to the shoreline to talk to the birds. Verity could see her in the distance, a flash of flowered green, picking her way through the rocks, a floppy hat protecting her head. She wrapped the shawl round her hair, angry enough to imagine her mother might have deliberately chosen not to remind her about a sunhat.

Allegra looked up. 'I suppose you get points for trying.'

How can she think I'm doing it wrong? It's a shawl wrapped round my head. How many ways can there be?

The sky was luminous, a flat sheet of blue as perfect as a bolt of silk, patterned with a gauze of cloud. The idea they might live anywhere else struck Verity as too outlandish for words.

Would it be so awful…?

Could she have meant it? Was Allegra really thinking about leaving Gull House? Verity made her way across the sand towards where her sister crouched by a rock pool. Behind her, her feet left indentations in the wet sand and closer to the shoreline they filled with water. The tide was on the turn, and soon it would be running up the beach and her footprints would be gone.

Could we be gone too, like sandy footprints, and would it be as if we'd never been here?

A sudden need to be nearer to Meredith sent Verity running across the last stretch of sand. Allegra's shawl unwound from her head, floating in her wake like exotic wings. At the edge of the sea the waves shushed on the flat sand. Meredith had discarded her hat; she was filling it with shells and pieces of white quartz sparkling with crystals.

'Look, Verity,' she said, 'Underwaterland.'

Verity leaned over her sister's shoulder into the rock pool, watched trails of seaweed, violet and green, pink and gold, waving

172

under the shallow water; barnacles attached to the shiny rocks and thin fish shimmering in the ripples. Sunlight skimmed the surface: an alchemy of water and light. It caught in her sister's tangled hair turning it to fire.

'Yes,' she said, 'Underwaterland.'

Meredith looked up and smiled. 'I could be persuaded to love the beach almost as much as I love the wood.'

'Well, in that case, I better make an effort to like the wood a bit more.'

'Either way, we're the luckiest girls in the world.'

Verity's heart skipped a beat. 'Nothing lasts forever, Meri.'

'Some things do.'

'Like what?'

Meredith's face was lit up by the sun. 'Like us. Like Gull House.' She flicked the surface of the rock pool, launching tiny sprays of water into the air. 'Don't look so worried, Verity. I'm going to help Angharad and make it all right. And you and me – even Mam – we're going to be fine too.'

Drops of water rose and hovered, and for a moment Verity saw them in slow motion, before they landed on her sister's face like tiny rainbow tears.

My mother let me know I could not say it.

Her invisible finger lay on my wretched lips. She could not acknowledge such a monstrous thing, least of all to herself. For a second she dared to make eye contact with me and I saw the loss of my innocence clearly mirrored there. The rest of her denied me. It was easier for her to concoct depravity in me than any weakness in her son.

Watching her eyes turn to the colour of steel, I saw behind them to her turmoil. And for the first time, how like him she was, an edge of cruelty disguising her own vulnerability. If she took my side, her own fate was surely sealed. In her own way my mother was as much a victim as me.

As my brother disappeared, and in spite of my distraught state, my mother offered no assistance, only bade me make myself presentable.

Had she really made the choice to abandon me?

For weeks, other than the niceties of civilised discourse, she barely spoke to me. By the time I began to suspect the consequences of my brother's assault, I knew she did too and there would be no comfort.

As the shocking truth of my condition slowly dawned on me, deprived of pride, beset by despair and revulsion, I had nothing to lose.

I sought him out and told him.

For a second, I felt a frisson of power. I saw shock on his face and genuine fear, but in a moment he recovered, resorting to his usual arrogance.

He warned me if I disclosed the truth no one would believe me. He would bribe some idiot village boy to say I had lain with him willingly.

Present

There were, I believed, only two kinds of sky: a town one fighting for space with rooftops and false light, and a wider one that only fitted in the countryside.

Outside Gull House, this sky is an elemental wonder, like nothing I remember. It's vast and constantly shifting, the colours swirl like Allegra's paint water. The air is filled with more unshed Welsh rain. (It's a cliché I cleave to – the idea Welsh rain isn't like any other kind.)

I step over molehills, past tall thistles and the ubiquitous ragwort. The shrill call of the gulls sounds edgier and agitated. The sight of the flattened grass, like the cigarettes stubs, has unsettled me. Allegra worried about intruders although the worst I recall was the occasional tramp looking for a free sandwich or a bowl of soup before tipping his hat and taking his leave. When we were little, Nain never turned anyone away. Allegra was less trusting, and she didn't like her privacy being invaded.

In the stillness, I wonder about vagrants. Would a tramp smoke filter-tip cigarettes? Possibly – these days' people are poor in a different way. Necessity has made them more opportunist, too, and less respectful.

I don't like myself for thinking this way.

Wondering about intruders my eyes scan the wood behind me. For a moment, political correctness deserts me and I imagine a gang of modern-day travellers crashing through the trees; dismissing soup, demanding money.

There is nothing to be afraid of. I'm quite alone.

The sun comes out again and if it does rain there'll be a

rainbow and I realise how much I want this. I can hear waves shushing in the distance. Although I'm tempted by the sound of the sea, it feels too soon.

Whenever we went to the beach, Meredith insisted we took buckets and spades and fishing nets. The first time we went fishing for shrimps by ourselves, I was seven and she was nearly six. We filled the bucket with the tiny transparent creatures and back at the house Nain said she wasn't sure they were shrimps. When we looked it up in a book, we discovered we'd caught prawns.

Ever after that we went 'prawning'.

It was one of our secrets – a small one, like most of them were. Until an act of curiosity and my sister's kindness woke the ghost of Angharad Elin Lewis and she began revealing her huge, forbidding secret.

Thirty-one

Some days you had to listen hard to hear the songs of the small birds.

The gulls ruled their fine rooftop roost, quarrelling and strutting with the certainty of possession. Their cries clung to the air; rooks joined in, hurling sharp words with an equally determined arrogance at trios of crows. The voices of less vocal birds existed in the spaces in between.

After the heat of the day, Verity breathed in the cooling air, listening as the sweet birds made the most of it. She wandered across the lawn, the impulse to go into the blue garden hard to resist. Despite her fear, and an underlying resentment towards the intrusive nature of the ghost, Verity needed to see it again. That way she could believe her sister without prejudice.

As if stilled by an invisible baton, the birdsong ceased. In the shadows, although there was no wind, the trees rippled. Underneath her cardigan, goose bumps slid along her skin like a rash.

'Come on, you thing – whatever you are – show yourself.' Her voice trembled and faded into the dimness. The quiet spread around her like water in a lake. Everything stilled, even the sky.

Ragged in the evening light the ghost's pale eyes were a blur; the silent mouth once again mime-speaking words Verity couldn't hear. The look of desolation on her face was heart-breaking.

Don't faint, don't fall.

Verity looked up again and the figure and the unheard words had vanished, there was no one in the garden apart from her and the dew on the grass.

'What's up, Verity, you look like you've seen a ghost.'

Verity thought she might be sick.

'It's okay, I'm joking.' Meredith was playing solitaire at the kitchen table. The glass marbles clicked against one another, in and out of the wooden holes. 'If you can see it, it isn't a ghost.'

You have no idea what you are talking about.

Allegra, wandering into the kitchen, let out a sharp laugh. 'Honestly, Meredith, you do say the most extraordinary things.'

'It's true.' Meredith's calmness and apparent absence of fear was almost more unnerving to Verity than if she had been in a flat panic. 'The ghosts people believe they see are mostly a figment of their imagination.'

You have to tell her.

Allegra said she needed to talk to Mared and would they please not disturb her.

As the door closed behind her, Verity stared at her sister. 'What was that about?'

Meredith held her gaze. 'We can't give her so much as a hint. I said it to put her off.' Bright spots of excited colour touched her pale face. 'I know what she's up to.'

'Who? Mam?'

'Don't be dull.'

Verity said nothing.

'Real ghosts, Verity; they do things differently. They play tricks.'

'What?'

'I saw something, behind me in the mirror the other day. It might have been the ghost.'

The sick sensation came back.

'Please stop, Meredith. I can't bear this anymore. It doesn't make sense.'

'Even though you know it's true and I'm not making any of it up?'

'It's dangerous.'

Meredith's eyes narrowed. 'Why would you keep saying a thing like that?'

'It just is.' Verity recalled the silent, moving mouth and shuddered. She closed her eyes, tried to blot out the image. 'I don't know.'

She was in the garden again, with the ghost's blank, hopeless eyes on her. 'If you've changed your mind, it means you're saying I'm a liar.'

'No it doesn't.'

Meredith's shoulders drooped. 'You don't get it do you? I have to look out for her; she chose me. We know the truth now, or at least we're getting close. If you could only hear her, you'd understand what I mean.'

I don't need to hear her; I've seen her.

The other night Verity had been scared witless, and earlier, moved beyond words. She shut both feelings away. Nothing on earth would persuade her to make it any more real by telling her sister. Meredith already believed the house was alive. During the day she was wild and erratic, at night, black-eyed with exhaustion.

If we add a ghost, goodness knows where it will lead. And even though Meredith doesn't want Allegra to know about Angharad, sooner or later, even Mam's going to notice something's up and then all hell's going to break loose.

'Verity?'

'Whatever, Meri; I believe you, okay? I just don't want to talk about it.'

Thirty-two

The only room in the house no longer affected by the heat was Meredith's.

She woke up night after night, shivering, knowing she had been dreaming, still with only fragments of the ghost's voice in her head. Any thoughts of a story-writing competition had been abandoned and she no longer wrote anything down.

Instead, she willed herself to memorise as many of Angharad's words as she could.

My mother let me know I could not say it…

She burrowed under the bedclothes, goose-bumped with cold and into another dark dream.

Do not trust the mothers … mothers are deceitful and treacherous…

Verity's dream was visited by a tall dark man in a black coat. He had her by the arm and no matter how she fought, refused to let her go.

She woke before the birds, faint with the heat. Her hair stuck to her scalp and her skin itched. The air was thick and oppressive and made everything smell of cinders and smoke.

Meredith crashed through the door, her morning hair a riot of red. She had two books under her arm: Emlyn Trahaearn's and another one Verity didn't recognise.

'It *was* him. It was her brother.'

Verity groaned and rubbed her eyes. 'What are you on about now?'

'I told you it was a terrible thing. Her own mother didn't believe her. Except I think she did.'

'Meri, slow down.' Verity threw open the bedclothes to make space. 'Did Angharad tell you this?'

'Yes. He did it – her brother.'

The skin under Meredith's eyes was contused; she looked as if she'd been punched.

'Her brother?'

'Yes. Stop repeating everything I say.' Meredith was almost hyperventilating. 'He took her against her will.' As she said the words, her face flushed. 'Don't look so mortified, Verity, I'm not a baby. I'm fifteen, I know what rape is. I know as much as you do about the facts of life, even if they do sound disgusting.'

'Yes, of course you do. But, her *brother*?'

'Oh, Verity, it's worse than we thought.' Meredith's hand shook as she opened one of the books. 'See? It's about the Victorians. I found out some more about why they sent girls to those places; the asylums. It would explain why Angharad's parents got rid of her.'

'Where did you get it?'

'Verity, there's loads of books in Rapunzel's room.' She flipped through the pages. 'Taid was a very well-read man.'

Verity shifted to get a better look.

'It says here,' Meredith said, 'one of the reasons a girl might be diagnosed as mad, was if she had a baby out of wedlock.' She paused. 'That means, not married. Now, listen to this. "*Young women were often diagnosed with melancholy and hysteria and those unfortunate enough to find themselves with child were accused of moral depravity.*"'

Meredith pushed the book across her sister's lap. 'There you go – there it is again.'

The hairs on Verity's arms stood on end.

Melancholia and hysteria … moral depravity…

'If it's true…'

'Oh, it's true,' Meredith said. 'I know it is.'

'Okay, let's say you're right. We still don't know what actually happened. If she did get sent to an asylum, it could have been for all sorts of reasons.'

'We do though, Verity. He raped her, made her pregnant, they had her locked up and she had a baby.' Meredith closed the book. 'It's what happened, she told me and I know it is and eventually she'll tell me the rest.'

If Verity hadn't imagined seeing a ghost, then Meredith probably hadn't imagined hearing one. If she told her sister she thought it was real, would it make things better or worse?

And what if I told her Allegra might want to leave Gull House?

Both scenarios were impossible and equally irrational.

Was it better to tell Meredith she believed her and accept the fact she had seen a real ghost?

If my sister's crazy, then so am I.

Other than her grandmother, Verity couldn't think of anyone more sensible than herself.

'If I tell you something, will you promise not to over-react?'

'Is it about the ghost?'

Verity nodded. 'Yes.'

'I knew it. You do know something don't you?'

'I've seen her. Or at least I might have.' She swallowed. 'No, I have. I've seen her.'

Instead of squealing or leaping up and down, Meredith simply smiled. 'Oh, Verity, that's sweet of you, only I told you, you can't see ghosts. I probably imagined what I saw. It was the light…'

'I think you can see them.'

A frown crossed Meredith's face and her mouth fell open. 'You're serious, aren't you?'

Verity nodded again. 'You know I wouldn't lie to you, Meri, and unfortunately, I'm far too sensible to either make this up or imagine it. I wasn't sure and I'm sorry I didn't tell you before now. I've seen Angharad's ghost in the blue garden.'

'Well, there's a thing.' Meredith pushed her hair off her face. 'I don't usually like it when I'm wrong; in this case, I'm prepared to make an exception. If there's one thing I know about you, Verity Pryce, it's that you couldn't tell a lie to save your life.'

Verity laughed. She couldn't help it.

'And you reckon this revelation is going to make me over-react?' The smile split Meredith's face. 'You're saying you believe me?'

If Verity nodded any harder, her head would fall off.

'I can't believe you didn't tell me.'

'I had to be sure.'

I'm sorry I didn't trust you...

'Oh my god, Verity, what does she look like? Fancy that, I did see her! What was she wearing? Is she—'

'Slow down.' Verity tucked her arms round her knees. 'Yes, I believe you. I've seen her a several times now. I wasn't sure at first only who else would it be?'

'One ghost is enough. Of course it's her.' Meredith held her hands to her face, grinning behind them. 'Well done, Verity.'

Meredith's acceptance of Verity's *volte-face* was touching and utterly naïve. If Verity had told her she believed in Pin and Stinky Minky, her sister couldn't have been more delighted. She explained what had happened, how she'd first seen a shadow, how the cold had surrounded her. She left out how terrified she'd felt.

Meredith's face was glowing. 'Oh, wow, Verity, I wasn't imagining it.' She hesitated. 'I wonder why she lets you see her and I don't?'

Verity said she didn't know, and it didn't matter.

'You're right,' Meredith said. 'What matters is we both believe in her now and it means we can help her.'

At some point my father was informed.

He stared at me for an age, contempt masking his face.

Summoning what little courage still remained to me, I stammered my brother's name.

'He…'

My father silenced me with a thundering denial. 'Do not add to your depravity with despicable accusations. Your brother has already informed me of his suspicions, how he has noted your behaviour around delivery boys and riff-raff from the village.'

I wept and pleaded but he was adamant and when I tried to say more, slapped me hard across my face.

'Your wickedness shames the family. Leave my sight.'

I was confined to my room, watched, almost every second of every hour. Mama timed any absences to the second.

My brother went away, to the army I overheard a servant say, and I never saw him again. This confirmed, if nothing else did, that my parents suspected the truth. Appalled they could cleave so determinedly to their perceived version of respectability, with no regard for me, I first thought to kill myself. Starve myself to death or fling myself from a window. I lacked the courage for either and with no friends, who would I run to? I could only weep like a scared child, dreading what fate my father surely had in store for me.

On one occasion, creeping past the parlour I overheard my parents talking. I recognised my mother's plaintive tone, could almost see her wringing her hands.

And Papa's interrupting growl, as if he was as angry with her as he was with me.

'How could you allow this to happen … my mother warned me: your sister went the same way … bad blood will out and isn't from my side of the family. I have my position to think of, my reputation … I will not have it, the girl will have to go…'

Eavesdroppers, so my mother insisted – rarely hear any good of themselves.

If I was bad blood, it begged the question, what kind flowed through my brother's veins? And was my mother's somehow tainted too? I knew nothing of a sister; she was never spoken of.

A few days later, unable to sleep I woke at first light. Hearing a carriage scrape its way up our narrow driveway, I peered from my window. A man alighted, severe and dark with purpose. Some premonition caused me to risk discovery, make my way to the terrace; listen at the open French window.

The words I heard drew horror into my heart.

My father and the strange man he addressed as 'doctor' spoke in lowered tones of moral depravity, hysteria and melancholia.

'Where, Sir, do I sign?'

That was all it took. My life, signed away with the scratch of a pen by my own father.

I fled, horrified and unwilling to hear more. There was no need. I knew my fate was sealed and soon after they came, two tall men and a woman with red hands and the coldest eyes I had ever seen. At my parent's behest I was taken away. Because what else could they do with my disgrace, my soon-to-be bloated body announcing my shame to the world? A woman is her reputation and mine would be destroyed.

My father left the final wickedness for Mama to oversee. Before they took me, I tried one last time; pleaded with her, and as she turned her unblinking eyes on me, the last shreds of hope died. I fought then, for the second time, to no avail. It was my last protest and I determined my mother's final sight of me would be my defiance.

'This is wrong; you know it is! You know the truth.'

The only clue to her real thoughts was a small intake of breath and the way it shuddered in her mouth before she swallowed it. Nodding to the two tall men and the woman with red hands, she watched as they overpowered me, turned away, closing the eggshell-blue door behind her.

As the carriage drew away, dusk fell. All the dusks in the world descended on the catastrophe now besetting me. Inside my gown, a single red flannel heart lay next to my thudding one. It was the only thing I had left to console me and convince me I was still alive.

185

The wheels rattled and through the back window I glimpsed a limpid wash of sky, gulls taking off for the sea. I could smell the ocean and longed for it to take me too.

What they did wasn't called a crime. The commissioning of it had the sanction of law.

My clearest memory is how short was the journey before we stopped. On arrival I was taken to a small room and left in the care of a nurse whose sharp unmoving features terrified me more than the woman with the red hands. When I told her a mistake had been made she laughed, gripped my arm, steered me from the room, and made me march, faster and faster until I was almost running down endless corridors with high ceilings and into a cell-like room. There was too little light, only a square squeezed through a barred window.

Another doctor asked me questions; spoke to the stern nurse as if I wasn't there, about how my condition didn't begin with my shame. According to my notes, I had always been a difficult, contrary child prone to hysteria.

What notes?

Having always equated hysteria with tantrums and tears, the notion confused me. As a child I had learned to keep my tears to myself. My temper, such as it was, I had always hidden, for fear of chastisement.

The following days were shaped by tasks more meaningless than anything my mother ever devised; repeated rituals which at least had the virtue of holding the pieces of me together. The loss of my familiar life, for all its trials, weighed on my heart. I cried for my mother even though, months later, they told me she had died of a broken heart. I chose to believe them because accepting she wouldn't change her mind and leave me in that desolate, unforgiving place was beyond my comprehension. I never found out if what they told me about her death was true, or what became of my father. For all I know he lived a long life. I can only hope the evil he did haunted him to his grave.

My brother I prayed went to Hell where he belonged.

Thirty-three

Morning, for Allegra, was the worst time: the muddled moment of waking, half-aware, her unsought dreams cut off as the day claimed her.

Her bedroom, a cave as draped and extravagantly dressed as her, was full of faded finery. Clothes hung from picture rails like shapeless sketches. Drawers stood open, an explosion of scarves, slips and stockings. Shoes tripped each other up, some lay single, at a loss.

From her chaotic, ragged bed she eyed the day as it slid through washed-out lace curtains.

And any woman who can paint like this has to be acquainted with passion...

She couldn't remember what his eyes looked like. She leaned back on her pillows, reached for her tobacco. Her heart fluttered in her chest and she closed her eyes, let the pouch fall onto the bedspread.

Allegra believed herself in mourning – not for the man who had fathered her children and abandoned her (and in any case, as far as she knew, he wasn't dead). She grieved for the state of being in love.

When her father died, Allegra had been distraught. She was only seventeen and too young to deal with the death of a parent. She saw no difference between that loss and Idris abandoning her. Unhinged by grief, she hurled abuse at anyone who crossed her. And her relationship with the language of apology was dependent on what was in it for her.

She wasn't made for responsibility. She had expected to grow old with a husband, to remain touched by love, in possession of a shared future. Instead, her heart was worn and empty, the responsibility of mothering onerous.

I am alone and lonely – and even Meredith's stopped being nice to me.

Both girls had become more secretive than usual. If Allegra could summon the energy, she'd try and find out what they were up to. It would be some silliness of Verity's.

She can go shopping – it'll keep her away from her sister. I shall spend the day painting and Meredith can come with me.

His face hovered and her eyes fluttered open.

Do you live nearby?

Her mother caught up with Verity on the landing.

'I need you to do some shopping.' Her gaze fell like a shaft of sunlight and Verity knew there was no escape.

'We weren't planning on going to town.'

'Oh don't make a fuss. It'll do you good. You could do with some fresh air; you're both looking very pale.'

We're always pale. We're the palest family in Wales.

Allegra thrust a piece of paper at Verity. 'Here's a list.' She pulled a note from her pocket. 'And money, for Mrs Thing.'

Verity couldn't help herself. 'I'm not your slave, Mam. I'm your daughter.'

'Why do you always have to make such a drama out of a simple request? It's like you deliberately look for ways to annoy me. You nag me about paying the bloody woman and when I do, it's still not good enough.'

Verity snatched the list and the money and went downstairs.

Her mother ran after her. 'Don't you walk away from me, Verity Pryce, I won't have it; do you hear me?'

At the kitchen door, Verity turned. 'It's not like I have a choice, is it? And I expect the people in Swansea can hear you.'

Allegra swept past her, banged around, making coffee, making a mess. 'Where the hell is Meredith?'

'She's waiting outside for me.'

'I want her to stay here.'

Verity unhooked a shopping bag from behind the door. 'Well, she's coming with me. We've planned it and she wants to.' She paused, her hand on the doorknob.

'What are you looking at?'

'You.' Verity frowned. 'What do you actually do, Allegra? Apart from lie in bed all morning and then fling paint around.' Before her mother could answer, Verity strode through the door, shutting it firmly behind her.

Meredith was waiting, her bicycle propped against a wall. 'Both my tyres are flat.'

'So pump them up.' Verity flung the shopping bag into the basket of her own bicycle. 'Or are you waiting for your servant to show up, too?'

'Blimey. Who got out the wrong side of the bed?' Meredith waved the bicycle pump in the air. 'It's not my fault. I can't get the stupid bendy thing to screw onto the stupid valve. I've been waiting for you for ages.'

'You've been waiting for me for ten minutes.' Verity snatched the hose from her sister. 'Here. I'll do it.'

'What was she yelling about this time?'

'The usual, you know.' Verity started pumping up the tyre. 'She's the drama queen, only apparently, I'm the one making a fuss.'

'Yes, well, let's forget about the parent. We have a plan, remember?'

It wasn't much of plan – more a whim Meredith had conjured the night before.

'We need to find out everything we can,' she'd said. 'I bet you there are people round here who still remember the Lewis family.'

'Such as?'

'Old Mrs Trahaearn at the shop.'

'I haven't seen her for ages.'

'I have, in the garden round the side. She sits there when it's sunny, getting more and more wrinkled. She must be at least a hundred years old, so she might have known Angharad or about her at least.'

'Even so...'

'Verity, stop putting obstacles in the way, I thought you were into this.'

'But—'

Meredith played her trump card. 'I thought you said you believed me.'

Reluctantly, Verity had said she did and agreed to what looked to her like a fool's errand.

Above them, the sky was light and luminous. By the time they arrived at the shop, the sweat was pouring off both of them and Verity spent some of Allegra's money on ice lollies.

'How's your mother, Mrs Trahaearn?' Meredith smiled her most winning smile.

'Well, it's kind of you to ask, Meredith Pryce, I'm sure. She's fine, if you can call doolally as a fish, fine.' Mrs Trahaearn lowered her voice. 'Not a lot going on up top anymore, poor old thing. She's happy enough in her own way. Bit like your uncle Gethin.'

'It must be a terrible thing to lose your mind.'

'She's not ready for the funny farm, dear, if that's what you mean.'

Sensing an opportunity, Meredith pounced. 'Oh, no, I didn't mean anything. I didn't mean any offence.' She lowered her voice. 'It's not like in the olden days, is it, when they locked people up for nothing.' She paused. 'Like Angharad Lewis, who lived in our house?'

Verity grabbed her arm and pinched her.

'That hurts, Verity.'

Mrs Trahaearn narrowed her eyes. 'What have you heard about Angharad Lewis?'

'Oh, our grandmother told us about her.'

'Did she indeed? Well, Mared Pryce isn't one to mince her words.'

Meredith lowered her voice. 'She told us about Angharad's brother as well.'

'Well, now that was a thing.' Mrs Trahaearn made a tutting noise. 'Although why two young girls like you would want to know about anything as nasty as that I can't imagine.'

'Was she really mad?'

'My mother always reckoned it was the brother needed locking up, not the daughter.'

'Did she know her then?'

'*Duw*, no, she's not that old. Her best friend's mother did mind. Sian knew one of the maids who worked there. The local girls said he was sly as a slug and this maid said he'd... Well...' Mrs Trahaearn gave a nervous cough. 'Goodness me, I'm not sure this is a suitable conversation for children!'

'We aren't exactly children, Mrs Trahaearn. I'm nearly fifteen and Verity's sixteen.'

You little liar.

'Well, these days, you girls know everything. And if Mared's already told you that much, it's no skin off my nose.' Mrs Trahaearn cleared her throat. 'After they locked the sister up, the brother was sent away and no one saw him again. He died when he was quite young apparently, although I wouldn't know about that, or the reason.' She looked over her shoulder. The shop was empty. 'The mother is supposed to have committed suicide.'

If Meredith's eyes grew any bigger, Verity swore they would pop out of her head.

'Oh, my grandmother knows about that too, thanks all the same.'

'Well, I daresay she does.' Mrs Trahaearn patted her hair. 'How is Mared by the way? It can't be easy. I miss seeing her. You remember me to her won't you?'

191

'She's fine, thank you Mrs Trahaearn.' Meredith's smile was making her face hurt. 'And of course I will. You can count on it.'

Outside, Verity pressed her hand to her mouth to stifle her laughter.

'You're impossible,' she hissed.

'I'm good though.' Meredith winked and peered through the hedge into the garden at the side of the shop.

There was no sign of the old lady.

'It doesn't matter though does it?' she said. 'We've everything we need.'

Thirty-four

Ghosts linger in the seams and cracks in time; the still places between human breath.

In Meredith's dreams there was now no ambiguity. She woke with them intact, each detail imprinted. She didn't know what to do with the weight of Angharad's sadness. In the darkness, she made her way to Verity's room, curled in beside her sister, and for once, Verity didn't complain.

'I wish she'd stop crying,' Meredith said. 'It's the saddest thing in the world.'

Verity gazed into her sister's face. Her skin was as thin as a soap bubble.

'A bad thing really did happen to her, Verity.'

'Yes, I think it did.'

'Even though it's hard for her, she doesn't want to leave anything out.'

'You mustn't leave any of it out either, Meri – tell me everything you can remember. I can't bear for you to be sad too.'

'Are we in this together then?'

Verity recalled the desolate look on the ghost's face, how she disappeared through the wall; she felt the snowball against her skin and the sensation of fainting. The idea she had imagined any of it now seemed improbable. Whatever purpose or plan the ghost had, Verity wasn't going to leave her sister to deal with it alone.

And if I deny Angharad, Meri won't. She won't stop, whatever I decide.

'I promise.'

Meredith nodded. Beneath her eyes the skin was still blemished with fatigue.

'Have you had any sleep?'

'I must have or I wouldn't dream.'

Verity stroked Meredith's hair away from her forehead. 'It doesn't count. You need proper sleep without dreaming. Why don't you stay here? I'll read you a story, see if that helps.'

Meredith eyes brightened.

'Will you go and get Nelly?'

'Yes, then a story and we'll both try and sleep a bit more.'

In Meredith's room the air was damp. As Verity collected Nelly she wondered if she was grown up enough to deal with what was happening. She thought about telling her grandmother and knew she wouldn't. She wouldn't go back on her word. But thinking about Meredith's bruised eyes, her determination to help a ghost neither of them could prove existed, she wasn't sure how long she could keep her promise.

They slept curled like animals.

Verity had watched as Meredith fell asleep, her head filled with the remnants of Narnia.

When she closed her own eyes and fell into a dream, the ghost of Angharad Elin Lewis came to meet her. Her arms outstretched, she drifted through mist, the bones of her fingers showing through thin skin; her hands spread in supplication.

I am waiting for someone to come for me...

Each syllable was a whisper.

Do not trust the mothers...

Verity jolted awake. It was still dark and Meredith lay on her back, her eyes wide open, dried tears on her face.

'It didn't work, did it?'

Meredith couldn't speak, only point.

As Verity looked up, a chill swept through her. In front of the window, shifting in the moonlit cotton curtains, the ghost of Angharad held out her arms and as they watched, fell back and floated out into the nothing of the night.

When Meredith described her dream, it was the same as Verity's.

Thirty-five

Verity heard the sound of wisteria scraping the stone outside the window.

Next to her, Meredith slept so deeply her chest barely moved. Verity leaned over her, listening for her breath.

Satisfied, she slipped from her bed, crept from the house and ran down the field to the lookout. In spite of a chill in the air, the sun was shining and she could smell summer. Leaning against the old dead tree she watched the tide running up the beach filling the rock pools as it went.

Verity pulled her mother's tarot book from under her cardigan. If Allegra left her belongings lying around, picking them up wasn't stealing and in any case, if Verity had a pound for each time her mother tried to get her to read the book, she'd be worth a fortune.

It was, like her mother's cards, worn and creased. Flicking it open, she noticed how the edges of the pages were brown with age; a few showing a trace of fine trails where a worm had eaten through the paper. It was an old book and full of secrets.

Full of nonsense more like.

Turning to the section about swords, she read how they symbolised air: sky and clouds and birds, the colour blue. She turned to the picture of the knight. He was armoured, mounted on a fast moving horse, his sword raised above his head, a sense of action surrounding him. When she looked closer, beneath the visor Verity could see how narrow and cunning the knight's eyes were.

I don't like you one little bit.

As a metaphor, the book said, although he had a magnetic

personality he represented grand ideas that could quickly become chaotic. He was selfish and pursued his own ends. Above all, he was not to be trusted.

I'm not sure I trust anything.

The dream hovered and she pushed it away.

Although Verity imagined a person who knew what they were about might make sense of the tarot symbols, the way her mother read them was arrant nonsense. And trying to second guess Allegra through a pack of raggedy old cards all at once struck her as a pointless exercise.

Snapping the book shut and shoving it in her pocket, she was about to go down to the stile and onto the beach when she spotted a figure, close to the cliff near the stone dragon. No one came to this end of the beach. It was a dead end and didn't lead anywhere.

The tide surged across the sand, closing in; leaving only a narrow strip of shingle to walk on. Ducking low, Verity scrambled down to the stile, peeked over the ledge and saw him. Tall and dark-haired, wearing a jacket with the collar turned up, his hands thrust into deep pockets.

A tall man in a dark coat…

He stopped, steadied himself on the rocks, shaded his eyes.

Verity ducked down afraid of being spotted as a spy. He hadn't seen her; he was too busy staring up at the house, intently, as if he recognised it.

The Knight of Swords…

Verity's bones chilled; it was as if they had turned to glass and, were she to fall over, she would shatter.

He has a ruthless quality … pursues his own ends… he cannot be trusted…

As my body grew I wanted to hate it. Sensing the life inside me, I was unable to summon such a base emotion.

There had been too much hatred; the child I carried may have been conceived in violence, in the absence of family, I could love it while I waited for someone to come for me.

No one came.

The sense of abandonment grew in tandem with my belly. I do not choose to record the physical indignities I was initially subjected to – suffice it to say, they were almost as vile as my brother's assaults. As my pregnancy progressed, I was eventually left alone and because I was with child, escaped the worst excesses of asylum life. It was, nevertheless, harsh and demeaning.

I forced myself not to cry, sensing it would be seen as weakness. Other poor souls fared worse. Women named degenerate, wailing and crazed; others silent and mute, driven to madness by a wickedness it was hard to describe. In spite of what was in plain sight, I could summon no pity for them, offer no help or succour to anyone else. I covered my ears to the dreadful sounds, turned from the sights and closed my heart from everyone knowing my survival depended on acquiescence and my good behaviour.

I turned my heart from my family too.

Present

It is barely three months since my grandmother died – years since either of us have been here.

In my hand, the keys are hot. I walk up the stone steps, stand in front of the egg-shell blue door. For a ridiculous moment I feel as if I ought to knock. The vertical brass letterbox is dull and pitted. There are two locks, one each above and below an iron door-handle and I fumble until I work out the correct keys. Expecting the door to be stiff, it takes me by surprise when it glides open, as if it's in charge, inviting me in.

Inside it isn't as gloomy as I expect. I stare into the hallway, at my grandmother's long-case clock still stopped at tea-time. I can see my mother winding it; hear Nain objecting.

'Leave the clock to me, Allegra, you always overwind it.'

The frog telephone sits on the half-moon table, solitary and black. Everything is coated with the dust of too many silent years. The air is thick with must and damp. The walls are patched with faded spaces where the mirrors Nain took to London once hung. Mirrors were another of her passions. Like clocks and pretty chickens, kindness and the colour blue.

Behind me the front door closes with a familiar, slow click. It always did, as if some invisible maid waited until we were safely inside before shutting it behind us.

I notice a dustsheet, fallen to the floor beneath the one remaining mirror. I see my grandmother, pausing and patting her hair, the gesture automatic and entirely lacking in vanity, the mirror privy to a thousand fleeting moments of unconscious ritual.

It is smeared with neglect.

And finger marks.

They run down the glass, the shape of them fresh and clear. My throat is dry. My reflection peers at me through the ghostly, glassy finger-marks and I am disturbingly visible – to what or whom I cannot imagine.

The silence is acute.

I don't want strangers to have been here, with or without my grandmother's permission or a spare key.

I want the scent of Pride furniture polish; the sound of Mared's laughter and the only other presence an unexpected cat; the touch of fur on my bare legs.

I want roses, forget-me-nots and bluebells from the garden, unarranged and perfect.

Thirty-six

'Who are you and what are you doing here?'

He lingered on the path by the back door, a cigarette between his lips, and it annoyed her.

'I'm looking for Allegra? Allegra Pryce?'

Said like a question, in an English accent, her mother's name sounded odd. Verity leaned into the door, meaning to go back inside, heard it click as it closed behind her.

He reminded her of the kestrels circling their prey above the field, hovering, searching until they spotted something, and dropping like arrows.

'What do you want with my mother?' She glared at him, at his unkempt hair and unruly clothes.

He offered a hint of a frown. His look was sardonic and she didn't like it. He held out a scrap of paper. Verity recognised it. It was the same kind of paper her mother used to sketch ideas for paintings. Close up he smelled of cigarettes and something she recognised and which at the same time eluded her. She leaned away to let him know he was standing too close, felt the hardness of the door at her back like a barrier. He stayed where he was and her discomfort grew.

Glancing down at the paper she saw her mother's name, the name of the house and their scribbled telephone number. 'Why didn't you call first instead of creeping up, like…'

'Like what?' His smile barely skimmed his eyes. 'Like a burglar?' He grinned then and his teeth filled the space. 'It's broad daylight.'

Verity's unease increased and she knew he was trouble; her vague irritation turned to doubt. She couldn't look at him for fear he would notice. Her gaze dropped to the ground, fixed on her feet, the weeds, anywhere so long as she could ignore the warning vibrations running through her.

'Yes,' she said, forcing herself to look at him. 'Like a burglar.' She sidestepped, furious now. He made her feel like a child and his arrogance grated. Something about him suggested he was used to getting his own way.

Like Allegra.

An instant of resentment struck her. He was intruding and yet here he was, at her mother's invitation, his shadow predatory and unwelcome. All her senses were alert to the fact and she felt an unexpected need to protect her mother.

Above all, he cannot be trusted...

'I'll come back,' the man said. 'Be sure to tell Allegra I called.'

Quiet people possess an innate sense of other people's drama.

It was late and unable to sleep, the memory of the strange man still bothering her, Verity went in search of a drink. The moment she walked through the door she felt the shimmer of Allegra's restlessness. She was reading her tarot cards by candlelight. It made her face paler than ever, the circles under her eyes dark as soot.

Everyone in this house needs a decent night's sleep.

'Mam?'

As her mother looked up, Verity saw how wild her eyes were. A few cards lay across the table.

'You need the Knight of Cups.'

'What?'

'If you're looking for a tall, dark, allegedly handsome man; surely you need the stupid questing knight? Or maybe you think you'd be safer with the sword chap – the chaotic one.' Verity shrugged and sat down. 'At least he'd be more honest.'

Allegra scowled. 'Oh shut up, Verity. You don't know what you're talking about.'

'That's the point, Mam, I do. And those cards won't tell you anything you don't already know.'

'If you despise the cards, why do you care so much?'

'I don't despise them; you have to know what they mean before you can interpret them. And if you shuffle them enough, as well as Mr Sword Man, eventually, you're bound to get the Lovers.' She leaned across her mother and turned over one of the cards. 'Oh, look – there he is. What a surprise.' As she gazed at the man flying through the wind on his horse, she swallowed, knowing what was coming.

Her mother's eyes brightened and Verity saw they were made of ice. 'I don't have to listen to this.'

'True, but I'm here so you may as well. I'm not stupid, Mam.' She nodded her head at the cards. 'You can make them say whatever you like and you do.'

'I do not! How dare you, you stupid girl.'

'I'm not stupid. In fact, I'm smart and so is Meredith. Just because you've refused to educate us doesn't mean we haven't learned things.'

'Oh, and I suppose you've learned about the occult too and the next thing is, you'll cast a spell on me?' Allegra laughed now, a harsh unkind sound.

'No. It means I've been reading your tarot book.' She pulled it from her dressing gown pocket and threw it on the table. 'It's a tool, not a crutch. You can't tell the future with the cards, Mam. You may as well check the entrails of a chicken.'

'And you think that makes you smart? That answering me back and trashing my beliefs makes you clever?' Allegra snatched up the book. 'Since when did you become so sickeningly vain? Is this all the thanks I get—'

'Yes! This is all the thanks you get! Less in fact; you get no thanks because you haven't done anything worthy of them.' Trembling now, Verity shouted. 'It's *not* listening to you makes me clever. And the sooner I can stop Meredith listening, the better.'

Allegra's voice became a snarl. 'Typical. This is how you always operate isn't it. Trying to turn your sister against me any chance you get.'

Verity ignored this. 'So, come on then, who is he? A new daddy?'

'What do you mean?'

'He was here, looking for you. I told him to go away.'

'You had no right. You know nothing about him, you—'

'I know he's horrible and rude and I already hate him.' Verity managed to lower her voice. 'We're your daughters not your toys. We're not here for your amusement.'

'Why would you say a thing like that?'

'Why would you invite a creepy stranger into our house?'

'You don't know him and you obviously have no intention of trying.' Allegra grabbed the cards, stuffed them roughly into the bag. 'He came all the way to see me, at my invitation and you turned him away. It was you who was rude.'

'He scared me.'

'Don't be dramatic. I know you, Verity; I know what's going on. And don't you dare accuse me of not caring about your welfare.'

'So, finally, you're making our well-being your business?'

'I'm your mother, I—'

'You no longer have the right.' Verity's revulsion overwhelmed her.

Allegra made a mewing noise and flung her head into her hands. 'Stop saying this stuff. What's got into you?'

'If you start crying,' Verity said, 'instead of despising you, I'll hate you. You disgust me.

Thirty-seven

'I've invited a friend to have supper with us.'

Meredith and her mother sat together at the kitchen table, matching socks, rolling them into little bundles.

Verity felt a curl of dread in her stomach.

'It will give you a chance to get to know him.' Allegra smiled her unreadable smile.

'Why would we want to do that?' Verity couldn't believe her ears. 'Didn't you hear what I said earlier? I don't like him, he's creepy.'

'Nonsense. I'm not having this discussion with you, Verity.' Allegra spoke over her. 'You don't mind, do you, Meredith?'

It was a strategy that no longer worked.

'Actually, I do.' Meredith pushed the socks to one side. 'I hate visitors. And if Verity doesn't like him, whoever he is, then I won't. Who is he anyway?'

'Someone I met on the beach,' Allegra said. 'Don't be silly, Meredith, he's into art and he's really very nice. As Verity was extremely rude to him the least we can do is be hospitable.'

'Verity isn't rude to anyone.'

'Well, she was very rude to me! I've invited him and he's coming, so that's an end to it.' Allegra scooped up the folded laundry. 'I expect you both to be on your best behaviour. Meredith, you'll like him, honestly, he's charming.'

Verity winced. Had she really not noticed? Was Allegra so thick-skinned she couldn't see how much they both minded?

'Is he her new boyfriend?' Meredith sat by the hen house with a chicken on her lap. 'You don't want any stupid old visitors do you, Miss O'Hara?'

The chicken dipped her head, submitted to Meredith's petting.

'Who knows? She must be about due for one. I saw him on the beach looking up at the house the other day, and then he just showed up here.'

Meredith said there was no way she would share a meal with a creepy man Verity didn't like. 'And in any case, I don't like meeting new people.'

'I know. Neither do I, not people like him at any rate. Don't worry, we can hide.'

'Good plan.' Meredith stroked the chicken's feathery head. 'And good luck to him, whatever she makes, it won't be edible. What do you suppose it'll be?

'Spaghetti Bolognaise?'

'You took the words right out of my mouth.'

As good as their word, the girls refused to eat supper with the man. Watching him wandering up the drive, they took off for the wood and stayed in the ruin until darkness drove them home.

Initially furious, as the days passed Allegra paid them no mind. She became manic and overexcited, dragging clothes out of drawers, changing her hairstyle, ignoring her painting. She didn't notice how quiet her daughters had become or how Meredith had almost stopped eating.

The house was more of a mess than usual; Allegra cooked crazy meals and in spite of her daughters' protests, invited the man to join them again and again. They continued to ignore him. When he came into a room, they left. In the event they were forced to spend time with him, they did whatever they could to annoy him.

'I can fix that.' The latch on the kitchen window had come loose.

'Wonderful.' Allegra beamed.

'No problem.' He looked around. 'It'll take a while; if you want a decent job.'

'I'll fix lunch.'

The next day he brought a toolkit with him, set it on a bench under the window. Allegra hovered, watching him work, as if she hadn't seen anything quite so wonderful in her entire life.

Wandering up from the beach, Verity and Meredith paused.

'Darlings!' Allegra waved her arms. 'Look! Soon be fixed and good as new! No more horrid draughts! Isn't that marvellous?'

As Meredith sidled past, she nudged the toolbox, sent it crashing to the ground.

'Accidents will happen.' Although he addressed his words to Allegra – and with a smile – his snake eyes landed on Meredith.

Instinctively, Verity stepped between them.

'All the time,' she said. In spite of the fluttering in her chest she kept her voice level. 'But I'll never let anything bad happen to my sister.'

Her coming into the world was shaped by pain and the smell of blood.

In front of them, I cried only once – the moment they took her – and it was more a wail which at first I failed to realise came from me. That kind of howling comes from a raw place, and is as much a feeling as a sound.

Her head was turned away and I couldn't see her face. A tiny arm waved free of the catching blanket, I reached for her, my lips brushed a finger and the sensation seared my skin. A life and death kiss before I heard someone whisper she was a girl. I felt the flicker of a pulse against my hand, a thread from her heart as I tried to take hold of her, and then she was gone.

They said she died.

'It's for the best.'

In the stillness, I recognised the sound of consciences being appeased.

They took her like they would a dead kitten, snatched her away and refused my entreaties to be told where she had been buried. My cries turned to rage but however I begged and pleaded, they turned their faces from me, hard and unfeeling, saying it was no longer my business.

How could it be that my dead child's last resting place was not my business? What cruelty contrived this final wickedness?

One nurse, kinder than the rest, returned the blanket. The scent of her caught on it, the sweet breath of her ... my tiny lost child, laid in a cold, dark, unnamed grave with no one to mourn her.

I held the blanket to my face, inhaled her, felt the thread of my baby's heart...

And shattered into a million pieces.

Thirty-eight

The man changed everything.

At first, Meredith thought he was little more than an inconvenience.

'If we ignore him,' she said, 'maybe he'll go away.'

'Don't count on it,' Verity replied.

'Well, I have far more important things to worry about.'

No longer caring if her dreams were disturbed, needing to be near Angharad, she had returned to her own room to sleep.

One morning, she prodded her sister awake.

'We have to make a baby for her.'

Verity rubbed sleep from her eyes. 'What?'

'She had a baby and they took it away.'

Lost for words, Verity stared at her sister's animated face.

'It's true, she told me. She did have a baby, just like I said. They took it away and her heart broke.'

Sleep-deprived and manic, Meredith's words were wild and scattered. A shiver of fear slid down Verity's spine.

'I'm going to make her one,' Meredith said. 'Not an actual baby – more like a doll baby and made of flowers and stuff from the garden. The sewing box was in my dream too – we have to use *her* things.'

'You're saying you want to make a baby?'

'I have to.'

Meredith's face was no longer mutinous; it was open and traced with something Verity couldn't translate.

'Just tell me why, Meredith. Why does it matter so much?'

'I *love* her, Verity, I can't stop now. She trusts me so it doesn't matter why. And you won't regret helping me; what we're doing is a good thing.'

If Verity was unconvinced, she knew there was no point in saying so. She may as well agree. That way she could keep an eye on her sister.

Keep her safe.

'What did she actually say? Can you remember?'

'The baby died. And they stole it.'

They were sitting in the blue garden, under the wisteria, surrounded by twigs and leaves and flowers.

'She doesn't know where they buried it. It's about laying the baby to rest.'

Meredith had brought the sewing box with her, hidden under a cardigan in case Allegra saw them.

'Don't worry about her,' Verity said, 'she's at the gallery today.'

'Good. We have to get this done.' Meredith concentrated on her task. She was fashioning a body from sticks and thin strips of bark.

Verity handed her sister what she asked for. Meredith was adamant. They had to use Angharad's things – her scissors and needles and bits of thread.

'They're a link to her, do you see?'

Verity was starting to. The box had been the beginning of it. She recalled Meredith opening it, laying out the faded flannel hearts.

They made me go shivery…

Verity unfolded pieces of lace. 'Why do you say they stole the baby?'

'They did. The people at the asylum took it off her when it was born and buried it somewhere.'

'It's not exactly stealing though, is it? If it was dead, they'd have to bury it.'

'What if they didn't?'

'Oh, Meredith, of course they did.'

'No, I mean what if they didn't tell her where?'

In the garden, surrounded by the old magic her grandmother had once conjured, Verity wondered what Mared would make of what they were doing.

'Do you think Nain would understand about a ghost?'

'Probably,' Meredith said. 'I still don't want to tell her though. We can't risk Allegra finding out.'

Verity agreed. 'What I meant was, would she understand about us making a twig baby for a ghost.'

'Of course she would,' Meredith said. 'She's a witch.'

'Oh, Meri, that's a game.'

'You reckon?' Meredith raised her head from her work. 'This is a magical place – we've always known it. Nothing's ever died in here, not even after Nain went away. Allegra's never lifted a finger to look after any part of the garden and neither have we, not really. The chickens don't count.' She waved her arm. 'Look around, Verity, where are the weeds?'

It was true. Since Mared left the blue garden may have become wild and overgrown – still the weeds hadn't entirely taken over.

'Nain's always said it's protected, hasn't she?'

Meredith snipped a bit of thread with the tiny pearl-handled scissors. 'Yes. It's like the wood. She told me, if I wanted to see the Others, I just had to look properly.'

'Like the fairies, in here.'

Meredith sighed. 'Not *fairies*, Verity. How many times, they're called the Fae.'

'Sorry.'

'Yes, it's the same in here; it's why you were able to see Angharad's ghost. It's Nain's magic.'

'If Nain's a witch, what does that make Allegra?'

'An idiot? She wouldn't know a spell if it bit her on her bum.'

For the first time in days, they fell about laughing, uncontrollable, joyous laughter making the birds sit up and listen.

'Do you suppose we're witches too?'

'I don't know, I certainly hope so,' Meredith said. 'We have a special spell to make.'

Verity fashioned a face for the twig baby from a small round piece of wood and Meredith produced one of her mother's paint boxes.

'Are you sure she didn't see you take it?'

'She won't miss it,' Meredith said. 'This one's been in the glory hole for ages.'

Carefully, she licked the brush, painted closed eyes and a tiny rosebud mouth.

'You're very sure it was a girl,' Verity said.

'I know it was. Angharad said so.'

Now she had allowed herself to become so irrevocably involved, Verity no longer questioned any of it. In some part of her she sensed her sister knew exactly what she was doing. She watched as Meredith played with different grasses, with scraps of thistledown and old man's beard until she'd created a cloud of hair.

'Find me some feathers,' she ordered.

Verity wandered off, found some tiny ones the colour of mist and Meredith wove them into the thistledown.

The little head was fragile; Verity fastened it to the body with silk thread and a few thin roots, weaving them in a neat spiral, making a neck. It was basic and rough but so delicate and slender it looked right. Meredith fiddled with the hair, told Verity to sort out some bits from the sewing box to make clothes.

With scraps of lace and one of the lawn handkerchiefs, they made a trailing gown to cover the stick arms and legs. Meredith sewed stitchwort to the waist so it fell down the skirt. Once she was satisfied, she played with the arms and legs, twisted more tiny bits of twig into slender hands and feet.

She wanted it to be pretty, she said, like a real child.

Verity thought it looked more like one of her sister's Fae people.

Meredith tied a narrow length of pale pink ribbon at the twig baby's waist and wound sprigs of speedwell into the hair.

'There,' she said. 'It's done.'

Verity said it was perfect. 'What now?'

'We'll leave it here for tonight.' She placed the twig baby in the cleft of a low branch of the wisteria.

'What if it rains?'

'It won't.' Meredith smiled. 'It'll be fine. The moon's dark tomorrow so we'll come back then. No one will see us. She'll be safe there and if Angharad comes, she'll find her and she'll let us know if we've done it properly. That's the test. Then later, we can bury her.'

Verity rolled up a piece of lace. 'I keep wondering why it was only me who saw her, at first.'

'Maybe it's because you struggled to believe she was real and she was trying to prove herself to you?'

Verity decided this made sense. 'We do have to be careful though, Meri. I know you're not scared, but I still am. A bit.'

'Oh, don't be silly. Angharad won't hurt you.' She began packing away the contents of the sewing box. 'The thing now is, Allegra mustn't find out. We have to tread on eggshells and you have to be nice to her.'

'I'll do my best.' Verity handed the lace to Meredith. 'Don't you wonder what she'd have to say about it though?'

'No.' Meredith's pale face became defiant again. 'I'm not interested in what she thinks. All I know is I'm not letting her or anyone else stop me.'

Thirty-nine

Early the next morning, they crept past Allegra's silent bedroom.

'We have to go while she's asleep,' Meredith insisted.

At this time of the day, the house looked different. The stairs appeared endless, the hall cavernous. A thin trail of dawn light bled through the window, pooling on the floor like spilled cream.

Invisible as ghost children themselves, the Pryce Sisters left the house.

The blue garden looked different too. Verity shivered, unsure if she wanted to be there.

Meredith had been persuasive. 'We have to take care of it; like it's a real baby. And get things ready for tonight.'

Verity knew she ought to say no. Put a stop to the venture. Meredith was elated and focused and Verity kept thinking back to how she had looked when Mrs Trahaearn said it was the brother needing locking up and not the daughter.

It doesn't matter ... I've everything I need...

They found the doll exactly where they'd left her.

Meredith had brought one of the red flannel hearts with her. She lifted up the twig baby. 'Verity, look.' Trailing through the thistledown hair were more flowers; yellow ones like tiny suns, and more feathers attached to the skirt. 'She must have done it – Angharad. It's a sign. I told you she'd let us know.'

'That's impossible. How could she?'

'Ghosts can do anything.'

Laying aside a sense of disbelief comes easier to a child who once convinced herself she could grow flowers out of her fingers.

Meredith stroked the feathers. 'We can't start questioning this stuff now, Verity. If we can't accept it, then it means we don't believe it's real.' She stroked the twig baby's hair, touched her silent, sleeping face.

Verity watched as her sister tidied the folds of lace and lawn, retied the pink ribbon.

She's making it a certainty...

It was one thing to close your eyes and pretend to believe in fairies; to leave acorns and biscuits for imaginary beings from a make-believe otherworld. This ghost story was beginning to look as if was happening, right here in their grandmother's garden.

Perhaps it was her own fault for telling Meredith what she wanted to hear.

But I saw her ... we both saw her...

'Angharad approves,' Meredith said. 'She must do, she wouldn't have added these extra bits if she didn't like what we've done.' She smoothed the flimsy lawn skirt. 'You're Angharad's baby now. You belong to her.'

'I'm still worried about rain.'

Meredith tucked the red heart into the crook of the arm. 'Don't be. Nothing's going to touch her – only Angharad.' She adjusted the position of the twig baby until she was satisfied. 'Because you're the one who sees her best, I think she'll let you know when it's time to bury the baby.'

'What?'

'Don't look so freaked.' Meredith placed a hand on her sister's arm. 'It'll be all right. Angharad won't hurt you. Tonight though, you have to try and see her.'

To Verity's dismay, tears appeared in Meredith's eyes.

'Don't cry, Meri. Please don't get upset.'

'You have to do it, Verity. You have to try and see her again. Not for me, for her. So she can tell us it's right.' Meredith's hand hovered on the twig baby.

Its tangible presence made Verity more nervous. In the face of Meredith's tears she gave in.

'Okay, I'll try,' she said. 'I promise.'

'And I'm coming with you.'

'Are you? Why?'

'Because you're still scared and I'm proud of you.' Meredith's eyes still shone with tears. She smiled and took Verity's hand in hers. 'And perhaps this time, we'll both see her again.'

'It's dark, Verity,' Meredith whispered. 'It's time to go.'

Verity struggled to wakefulness. 'I'm not sure...'

Meredith hadn't bothered to dress; she wore a cardigan over her nightgown and thick socks.

'Come on,' she said. 'And be quiet. I heard her go to bed about an hour ago, but she might still be awake.'

Verity didn't need any urging. The last thing she wanted was for Allegra to find out what they were up to. She swung her legs over the edge of her bed, pulled on her dressing gown and followed Meredith downstairs. Once again they slipped from the house like a couple of wraiths.

The night was radiant with stars, brilliant trails of them scattered across the sky. With the door to the blue garden ajar, Meredith hovered on the threshold, urging her sister ahead.

'I'll wait here; you have to promise to tell me the moment she comes.'

It was colder than either of them expected and it had rained earlier. Verity felt a damp chill on her legs. It wasn't quite dark; slivers of rainlight shifted in the shadows. She fastened her hands across her chest, clasped her arms and waited.

I must be mad.

It was as if she had fallen into one of Meredith's dreams.

And then, in front of her she saw how the little patch of grass in the centre of the garden was flattened out, as if a foot trod on it. The air shifted and the indentation became a dark shadow.

She gulped and blew out a long, low breath. 'Are you there?' Her voice caught and she stared at the shape on the grass, watched it move and spring back into place. An opaque swirl moved towards the wisteria tree.

'Meri?' It was barely a whisper and the best she could do.

Verity knew her sister hadn't heard her.

It's mist ... only mist...

The shadow stopped, drawn to the tree; still wavering as if it unravelled, separated into skeins of grey then refolded itself. As Verity watched, it became more solid, a thin creature, one arm stretched out towards the tree, pale fingers searching.

Verity couldn't move. She couldn't breathe and inside her chest something threatened to choke her. It was a moment so intimate and desolate, that if she had been able to move she wouldn't have wanted to.

The garden ceased to move too: grass, stones, insects; flowers and birds: each one stopped, witnessing the ghost of a vanished girl reaching for her lost, dead child.

'Verity?'

Meredith stood at her side and unable to speak, Verity pointed.

As she did, the ghost turned, her eyes beseeching and Meredith fastened her hand into her sister's.

Take her ... make it right...

Meredith shook so hard her breath came out in a series of jerks.

The ghost unravelled into the darkness. The twig baby slipped to one side in the cleft of the tree. Meredith squeezed Verity's hand so hard the nails dug into her palms before letting go.

'It's okay,' she said, 'I'll get her.'

In spite of the rain the twig baby was still perfectly dry. Meredith wrapped her in her cardigan, cradled her in her arms.

'I promise,' she whispered and walked back to her sister.

'Come on, Verity, we can go now. I know what we have to do.'

Forty

The moths in Meredith's bed were dead or dying.

'They know something.'

Verity helped her get rid of the crushed bodies.

'It's him, isn't it?' Meredith cradled a still fluttering moth in her hands. 'I was wrong; he's part of a very bad spell.'

Verity said she didn't believe spells had anything to do with it. 'He's far too real.'

Another week passed and although he wasn't there all the time, the man hung around, like a dealer in desire, tempting Allegra – already addicted – with her downfall.

Determined to make herself as visible as she could, whenever he was in the house Meredith shadowed them both, making no effort to conceal the fact she was listening to their conversations. Each time she saw him she stared straight at his face, infecting him with her light-littered eyes so he couldn't doubt he was being watched; that he was an intruder and superfluous.

From the sitting-room window, she observed the two of them together; saw her mother, stretched out and languorous on the lawn, her elbow bent; her head in her hand, leaning back to get his attention. The man didn't look at her; he sat with his own elbows on his knees, answering something she said, shifting position, turning to the window and then away as if he hadn't seen Meredith.

She knew he had.

Good.

It wasn't until Allegra's conversation became peppered with his name they spotted the real danger. She became more distracted, her attention more erratic than usual. Meredith still tried to convince herself he was a passing fancy, like the others. He wasn't good enough for her mother and Allegra would surely see this.

It made no difference. He was there: in the house and almost part of the furniture.

Meredith became alarmed.

'I don't trust him, creeping around like he owns the place. We can't risk burying the baby yet in case he sees us.'

She sent her sister to collect the twig baby and they hid it in the space under the window seat in Verity's room.

'I've made an invisibility spell,' she said, 'so no one will find it.'

He found some things: the paintings that hadn't sold, stacked in the tower room, faces to the wall. Without asking, he turned several round, stared at the light and the loveliness of them.

'They're remarkable.'

As he reached for a larger canvas, Allegra took a step forward, her hand poised to stop him.

'No,' she said, 'not that one.'

'Why not?' He turned it round anyway and was met by a startling, extravagant swathe of brilliant colour. 'Well, well, what do have we here?' He stood back, narrowed his eyes. 'This is more like it.'

'I'm not much of an abstract painter. It's not my thing ... more of an experiment.'

'Oh, I think you are,' he said, 'but unless you show this stuff – any of it – have an exhibition, who's going to know how good you are?'

Meredith watched her mother blush and appear flustered.

'Like that's going to happen,' Allegra said, 'round here. It's the back of beyond.'

She had already explained about the gallery, which was little more than a craft shop, the stretch of wall space she rented, how she was lucky if she sold half a dozen decent sized paintings throughout the entire summer.

'You said it. You're talking about here, not London.'

He raised his eyebrows and although he managed to make Allegra return his smile, Meredith wasn't fooled. She knew what she was seeing and her heart beat faster.

'And landscapes? Really?' He emphasised the question, stroked his hair back from his forehead. 'No offence, sweetheart, they're lovely, but landscapes?'

Allegra said she wasn't at all offended.

Meredith was. His hair reminded her of an animal's pelt; a wolf's.

'My mother's landscapes are phenomenal.'

The man turned, as if surprised to see her although Meredith knew he was perfectly aware of her presence.

'And I suppose you're an expert.'

'As a matter of fact, I am. My mother's paintings are renowned.'

Allegra laughed. 'Oh, darling, you're so sweet; he does have a point though. They don't sell well.'

'Yes, they do. They do all right. And everyone who buys one says how beautiful they are.'

The man moved between them, blocking Meredith's view of her mother, his head moving from side to side, taking in both of them.

'You paint landscapes because it's what people think they want,' he said. 'You're conforming to an ideal instead of painting what *you* want. You have to stop being a painter and become an artist.' He winked his wolf eye. 'Make some real money?'

He moved closer to Allegra.

Meredith watched his narrow lips move, his Adam's apple as he swallowed.

A hungry, dangerous wolf.

'I thought the point about art,' she said, refusing to back down from his stare, 'was it matters for its own sake.'

Allegra went to town, came back with new paints and a roll of canvas; she ordered frames and overnight, changed her style and began painting abstracts.

She stopped going to the beach and worked solely in the conservatory, focused on paintings which to the girls looked like unconnected daubs of colour. She worked for hours at a time, oblivious to their criticism, surrounded by paints and palettes and over-flowing ashtrays.

The man came and went.

'He has contacts in London,' Allegra said to the girls, when they asked if he had left for good. 'He knows people on the lookout for this kind of art.'

It was no longer her kind of art. Gone were the subtle splashes of luminescence, the wistful, iconic views of the house and ocean. Birds no longer flew up from her brush, no skies swept across her canvases.

Behind her back, the girls called these new paintings, 'distracts' and Meredith refused to hide her scorn.

'They're horrible,' she said. 'He doesn't know what he's talking about.' She asked her mother what the man did in London. 'What kind of connections does he have?'

'He knows important people, darling. In the art world, it's about who you know...'

Meredith interrupted and said she thought it was more likely to be about how good you were and her mother's new paintings weren't a patch on her landscapes.

'Landscapes are so old-fashioned. It's about reinventing oneself, it's about—'

'Good luck with that then.'

'What?'

'Nothing.'

Allegra gave an exasperated sigh. 'Now I've forgotten what I was going to say. It's rude to interrupt, Meredith. Just because Verity—'

'Oh, I expect you'll remember. Or you'll think of something equally uninteresting to say.'

'Meredith!' Allegra's hands – the little pearl ring glinting – fluttered like birds.

'You're acting like a teenager.'

Allegra played her cards the way she thought they would work.

'Darling, I know you don't mean that,' she said. 'You don't mean any of it and you know me best. You've always known how much my work means to me. And he understands too. No one's ever understood my work before. He can make my name for me; you, my sweetling – you know my heart!'

Meredith stared at her mother and she looked like an enchantment. Her eyes were the colour of smoke and her hair looked as if it might catch fire. The air in Meredith's chest stuttered and it hurt to breathe. She wanted to believe in her mother's enthusiasm and her fly-away compliments, only this time they sounded like another spell gone wrong.

She turned on her heel and ran from the room

He came in through the French windows so quietly he really might have been a burglar.

Curled in an armchair, reading, Verity nearly jumped out of her skin.

'Creeping up on people is weird,' she said. 'And this isn't your house. You ought to at least knock.'

He said he was sorry, and how was he to know she was hiding in the corner.

She watched him as he spoke, his eyes as they darted round the room, taking everything in as if he was taking an inventory. She noticed how his words formed on his lips, distorted by his English accent.

'I'm not hiding,' she said. 'I live here.'

She asked him if he planned on staying around.

He said it depended on Allegra. 'What do you think?'

'We shan't get far if you keep on answering my questions with questions.'

'How far do you suppose we might go?'

Disarmed and old enough to sense the threat, too young to deal with it, Verity blushed.

Allegra appeared behind him – a floating, flaunting shadow. She ran her hand down his arm and her smile was a cat's.

'Verity,' she said. 'Everywhere we go, here you are.'

Eventually the sexual tension drove them both out: Verity, as a result of embarrassment, Meredith because she was furious that her dislike of the man was being ignored.

'How can she? He's … repugnant.'

Verity agreed. 'Good word. And she pretty much threw me out of the sitting room.'

Meredith lolled against the back door, picking the peeling paint. 'Why doesn't she like you?'

Startled by the change of topic, Verity said, 'It's a game, Meri.'

No it isn't. I don't know why…

'I'm not so sure. I sometimes think she's nice to me to make you look bad, and that's about as mean as it gets.' Meredith sighed. 'Not that she's particularly nice to me these days. Good job I don't care.'

'Let's go for a walk.' Verity wanted to get as far away from the house and her mother as possible.

'Beach?'

'Do you mind?'

The dark silhouette of the lookout filled the sky. Below, as they approached the edge of the field they could see shallow waves, curves of foam dragging across the sand, back and forth, shushing and rhythmic on the shingle. Further out, the sea was black as ink. At the shoreline the oystercatchers were agitated, crying and strutting. Above them, gulls wheeled and shrieked warnings across the sky.

'A storm's coming,' Meredith said.

'It already came.'

Present

For a moment, until my eyes adjust to the gloom, the sitting room appears empty.

Shrouded furniture recedes into shadow. Through the double doors, I begin to see more clearly: more lifeless dustsheets covering pieces Nain believed we would one day come back to: sofas, tables, armchairs and sideboards. Bookcases still filled to bursting.

The carpet on the floor is faded to a pattern of ghost roses.

In the silence, I imagine flipping a dustsheet away, exposing a spellbound sleeping princess. An acorn on one of the old blind cords taps against the windowpane. I release the cords and one by one the blinds snap up.

Light pours through the room as if it has been waiting. It's dim and I realise it's because the windows are filthy. On the other side of the French window, above the terrace, the sky spreads, catches the endless cry of the gulls. Beyond the shallow stone steps I can see the fountain. How small it looks from here.

The chandelier is wrapped in cloth, an ugly grey teardrop; the heavy rope securing it hangs like a noose. I reach up and release it. It slides away like a girl letting her frock fall to the ground. The crystals are dull although one or two lustres catch the light.

Shivering, I run my hands over my upper arms.

Here are the real ghosts, slumped, grey shapes, too inert to be frightening, others hanging like stage curtains from the tops of bookcases; stillness and dust and not even the skittering of a mouse to scare anyone.

In spite of my best endeavour, I picture Allegra again, her too-bright eyes, her mad hair and the ever-present cigarette.

I've had enough of the house. I need a break. As with the front door, I half expect the French window doors to be stiff. They aren't and when I unlock them, they open easily and the room is filled with the scent of the sea.

Forty-one

Verity and Meredith weren't normally the kind of children who listened at keyholes.

They left that to their mother who couldn't bear to be left out and, after a while, bored by what they heard, gave up. Maybe if they hadn't, they might not have been surprised when they learned it was true: they were leaving Gull House.

'My mind is made up, Mam.'

Verity, at the top of the stairs, stopped in her tracks.

Allegra held the telephone receiver to her ear and with her other hand marked extravagant arcs in the air. 'You cannot rule my life like this. I need you to understand. I need you to be my mother for God's sake, and on my side. It's only for a few weeks until we find somewhere suitable.'

There was a fractured silence and Verity knew her grandmother was talking.

'Of course I know what I'm doing. Why are you being like this? You've never believed in me.' Allegra gripped the edge of the table. 'He knows more about it than you do! He's knows what he's doing and so do I.'

Verity held her breath.

'Can't you do this one thing for me, Mam? For the girls? It won't be for long, I promise…' She came to a halt, made a sound of exasperation and went on, 'That isn't true! Oh, I can't talk to you when you're like this. I'll call you later, when you've calmed down.'

Verity ran down the stairs. As her mother slammed down the receiver, Verity grabbed her arm, forcing Allegra to look at her.

'You cannot be doing what that sounded like.'

Allegra's voice was shrill. 'It's none of your business.'

Verity watched the querulous movements of her mother's mouth. 'If you're planning on making me move; making Meredith move, then how is it not our business?'

Allegra tried to shake her daughter off.

Verity tightened her grip. 'If you make us leave I will never speak to you again and I'll make sure Meredith doesn't either.'

Shaken, wrenching her arm away, Allegra swallowed and Verity saw she had touched a nerve.

'I shan't give up, Allegra. You can't do this. I swear I'll make him hate you and he'll leave you and when you end up alone, it'll be no more than you deserve.'

'You're hiding something.'

'No I'm not.' Verity was still shaking after her encounter with her mother.

'I know you, Verity Pryce. Don't … prevaricate.' Meredith had followed her outside, down the steps to the fountain. 'When you lie, your cheeks go red.'

Verity flopped down on the grass, her back to the retaining wall. 'There's nothing to tell.'

Unconvinced, Meredith said, 'I don't believe you but I'm going to pretend I do and wait for you to let whatever it is slip. You will; you always do.'

Verity chewed her lip. Lying made her feel awful. She wanted to tell Meredith the truth, couldn't bear for her to be unhappy.

'If you won't tell me your secret, then tell me what else you're thinking about.' Meredith crossed her legs and started making a daisy chain. Verity could see how grubby her bare feet were.

'Angharad's baby?' She made it a question because it wasn't the truth. Verity wasn't sure she cared what happened to the twig baby. Life was making her worry, not dead ghost babies.

'Don't fret about her,' Meredith said. 'When it's the right time,

227

we'll bury her and it'll be okay. I told you, I want to wait until *he's* not around.'

She picked some more daisies, sliding her fingers down the stems making sure they were long enough for a chain. 'Everything will be all right, Verity. He'll go soon, you see if he doesn't.'

Verity shrugged. 'I guess.'

'If we believe, it'll be all right.'

Meredith sounded so certain.

Say it and mean it…

They weren't living in Neverland and Meredith wasn't Tinkerbell.

'Meri…'

'There's nothing to it.' Meredith jabbed the stem of a daisy with her thumbnail. 'You refuse to believe the bad things can hurt you, and they don't.'

Verity knew happiness was fragile and as fleeting as apple blossom – in the moment and best grasped with both hands.

She managed a smile.

Opening her bedroom window in the middle of the night, Verity discovered the world enveloped in mist. The house settled around her and outside, the still of evening: layer upon layer of quiet, the air saturated with the scent of disaster.

Her fury kept her from sleeping. It was blind and raging and it shocked her. Verity wasn't used to this level of turmoil. The merest hint of a showdown with her mother made her blood run cold.

Questions filled her head.

Why had that awful man come here? What did he want? Was it his idea they should leave Gull House? And if it was, how could her mother allow it to happen?

Allegra's intention hovered like a horrible hint; a despicable secret Verity knew and couldn't bring herself to believe. It was a nasty taste at the back of the tongue, a glimpse of something fearful caught in the corner of an eye.

She knocked on her mother's bedroom door, knowing better than to go in unasked. There was no answer and she gave the door a push.

Allegra sat at her dressing table, brushing her hair.

The room was overlaid in its usual chaos. It stank of smoke and sex.

'If you've come to scream at me again, you can leave. I won't be spoken to like that. You're worse than my mother! It was outrageous.' Allegra coughed and covered her mouth.

'It was true, Mam. Only you needn't worry, I'm not going to argue with you.'

I'm going to tell you… Make you tell me…

'Well, so I should think.' Allegra dabbed her lips with a handkerchief, turned again to her mirror, tilted her head for a better view as if the harsh words from earlier hadn't been spoken.

She let out a long sigh. 'I can't bear for people to know how poor we are, Verity. Can't you understand?'

If Verity was surprised by this admission she gave no indication.

'No prospects.' Allegra said. 'No chance. I never had a chance.' She looked over her shoulder, and Verity could see her mother wanted to make eye contact and couldn't quite manage it. 'Your father saw to that.'

'I don't want to talk about him. And in any case, we had Nain. You had Nain.'

'And where is she now, pray? When I need her?'

'Gethin needs her more. You know he does.'

'Oh, him. Let's all feel sorry for mad Gethin. I'm her *daughter*. I should come first. But no, she dropped everything and abandoned me.'

Verity wasn't sure she'd ever heard her mother criticise Nain outright. The fierceness of the accusation startled her. Her callous disregard for Gethin's wellbeing was new too, and shocked her.

Allegra's voice became plaintive and Verity saw the anger drain away.

'What's the point, it's up to me now anyway.'

She heard something unfamiliar, as if Allegra revealed an older hurt, and she knew a moment of guilt. When she finally caught her mother's eye she saw only confrontation.

'You may as well accept the situation, Verity. It's no use, I have to go. Which means you and your sister have to come with me. It's for the best.'

'Go?' Quiet as a ghost, Meredith came into the room. 'Go where?'

There is more than one kind of silence. Some are a pause for breath, others hostile and indifferent, artificial or laden with mischief. The one that met Verity and her sister was weighted with prevarication. For a woman who liked the sound of her own voice, Allegra had the art of silence tamed and as biddable as a kitten in an instant.

'Say something!'

'Don't shout, Verity,' Meredith said. 'She doesn't mean it. She can't.'

'Yes she does. She's already admitted it. Stop making excuses for her.' Verity glared at her mother. 'Go on, tell her! Tell her what you just told me.'

Allegra exhaled through her nose, as if she was smoking. Her hands flew up and she held them at the side of her face, framing it, the better to be seen.

'I know,' she said, 'how hard this is for you both to understand—'

Meredith cut her off. 'It isn't hard at all. It's simple. If you're thinking of taking us away, then say so.' She paused and the silence held them again. 'You are; you're making us move aren't you? Because it's what you want, what that vile man wants, and you don't care what I want or what Verity wants.'

'Oh for Christ's sake, not this again.' Allegra's hands landed on her thighs with a slap. 'How can you be so selfish? So ungrateful? Meredith, what's got into you? All I've ever done is my best and now, when I have a chance, the only thing you can do is to try and wreck it. You're as bad as her!'

A look of such devastation crossed Meredith's face that Verity could have burst into tears.

'We may as well be some other woman's daughters.'

'What?' Allegra rose from her chair, flapped her hands in front of her face.

Meredith was shaking. 'I don't know who you are anymore.'

'Don't talk nonsense. I'm your mother! And you'll do as I say!'

Meredith's eyes grew pale and cold, as if the light drained from them. 'And what's worse, I don't know what it means to be me.'

Verity knew it was more than this. Her sister was on the verge of falling apart and Allegra couldn't care less.

If her mother made them leave, Verity didn't dare imagine what would happen next. Everything Meredith knew existed in Gull House. The air she breathed, the dust motes and the moths; the whispering walls and secret spaces. Her sister could only deal with what was happening now: the ghost of Angharad, and her belief that she had to lay the twig baby to rest in the sanctuary of Mared's garden. If Allegra took her away, it would destroy her.

It will destroy me too...

'Mam, why are you being so cruel?' Verity pulled Meredith to her and felt shudders running through her sister's body. 'Look at her! Look at what you're doing. To both of us. You don't need him. You could be anything...'

'It's you, isn't it?' Allegra turned from Verity and addressed Meredith. 'It's her. She put you up to this, didn't she?'

'Why is it always Verity's fault?' Consumed by fear and disgust, Meredith fought the tears welling up again. 'Why are you so hateful to her?'

Allegra's face closed in. 'And why are you taking her side?'

'There aren't any sides,' Meredith shouted. 'Since when have there been sides?' She shifted against Verity's body and her voice dropped to a whimper. 'There's no point is there? She's gone mad. Really mad, and no one's making her. She's doing it all by herself.'

Unaware of any hidden meaning behind her daughter's words, Allegra snarled. 'Oh, don't be so melodramatic.'

There are more ways than one to go mad, reasons beyond imagining.

Her face darkened. 'Why don't you listen and let me explain? London isn't the end of the world.'

Meredith fixed her grey eyes on her mother. They looked so much like Allegra's it was as if she stared into a mirror.

'This is your story, and you can have it. I don't want to be in it anymore. I don't want to be your daughter.'

Allegra took a step forward and Verity felt her sister flinched. For a moment, she thought Allegra might lash out. She placed a protective arm round Meredith's head.

'I don't care what you say,' Meredith lowered her voice. 'I'm never leaving here. Never.'

'You can't do this, Mam.' Verity's words faltered in the air, falling like the dead moths in Meredith's bedroom. 'You can't.'

Allegra looked at both her daughters as if she no longer recognised them. Her eyes raked Verity's face. 'This is betrayal and it's on your shoulders. Get out of my sight and take that wretched child with you.'

Forty-two

The air in the house lay as heavy as old ashes.

Meredith wanted to be somebody else, an ordinary girl with a normal mother. When her sister asked her how she was feeling, she didn't have an answer. Her emotions swallowed her whole. She was inside herself barely able to speak and when she did her words came out cracked.

'When did she tell you?'

'She didn't,' Verity said. 'I heard her talking to Nain, on the telephone.'

'You should have told me straight away. It's impossible. She can't mean it.'

'I wanted to see if I could make her change her mind first. You came in on us. I'm so sorry.'

Meredith gave a spasm of a smile. 'Why are you sorry? It's not as if it's your idea.'

Verity moved to hug her and Meredith shook her off.

'No,' she said. 'Don't.' Her bones shook with the force of her fear. All she could think was, she couldn't think. Right then she wouldn't have cared if Verity had shouted at her or ignored her for the rest of her life, so long as the nightmare wasn't true and they weren't leaving Gull House.

She didn't move. She knew if she tried she would fall over. Her breath hovered in her chest and she looked around and there was nothing, only her mother's voice.

Take that wretched child with you…

There is a language to loss. Verity sensed it murmuring at the margins of her sister's days.

Meredith was a crushed thing, a butterfly or a bird at the mercy of a cat.

'I'm not going, she can't make me.'

Verity made hot chocolate, sat in the kitchen with her sister in front of the range, watching showers of fire stars dance against the sooty back-plate.

'Maybe I ought to apologise,' she said.

'Apologise for what? She's the one in the wrong.' Meredith's voice sounded old.

'I don't have to mean it.'

Their mother's face hovered between them like a spectre, pronouncing her decision non-negotiable.

'I mean it,' Meredith whispered. 'I'll run away.'

Verity's heart sank. Although she knew her sister would hate London with its vastness and din and clatter, she wasn't about to become her accomplice in some hare-brained scheme.

'Even if we could, where would we go?'

Meredith's lip wobbled. 'I don't know.'

They both knew there was nowhere to run to.

Verity had never had a real adventure, she now realised. She hadn't taken any proper risks or been particularly brave.

It isn't the end of the world...

Her mother's voice seared itself on her brain, like a burn. Verity understood perfectly well what it was. It wasn't the end; it was an unknown beginning. She also knew there were times when the only thing it took to change a person's life forever was a single word.

Betrayal...

For a second, she would have agreed to anything, however hopeless; however crazy.

As if she sensed this, Meredith said, 'Okay, not proper running away but we have to do something. She's madder than poor

Angharad ever was and no one's trying to stop her. Even Nain's acting as if this is normal by the sound of things.' She trembled with rage. 'It's the opposite of normal, so why aren't we trying to make her stop?' With each word her agitation grew. 'I thought she loved me – sometimes, I imagined she loved me better than she loves you, but it's not true. She hates us both.'

'Oh, Meri...'

'You know it. You've always known it.'

'If she knew how you felt...'

'She does know, of course she knows, she doesn't care.' Meredith's thin shoulders shifted as if she were stiffening them. 'All she cares about is that disgusting man. What can she possibly see in him?'

Verity didn't know.

'And you know what the really awful part is? It's going to go horribly wrong and we're going to be miles away from here and there won't be anyone to save us.'

'Nain will look after us, Meri. She will; she always does. It'll be all right. I promise.'

Meredith gave her a look and her words scattered to the ground like little bits of gravel. 'Don't make promises you know you can't keep, Verity. It'll make you like her. You said I didn't have to be, so why would you want to? And don't kid yourself. Nain can't save us; we have to do it for ourselves.'

Forty-three

Meredith stopped crying.

She swallowed her misery and dried her eyes. She said crying meant Allegra had won and they really would be leaving Gull House. Grief encroached in other ways. She didn't eat and lost weight so quickly that she shrank before Verity's eyes. She stopped speaking too, unless it was absolutely necessary. Stubborn, her face a mask of misery, she hung onto the last vestiges of her courage.

'We could go on a proper hunger strike.'

'Meri, you're hardly eating as it is and she hasn't noticed.'

'If we go, we won't come back.'

'No, don't say that.'

'I know it, Verity, the way I know the touch of snow on my face.'

Any love Verity still had for her mother lay under her ribs, hard as a stone and as obdurate.

Verity put her anger somewhere safe. She made a last attempt at persuading her mother to give up on her foolish plan.

'Please, can't we at least discuss it?'

Allegra's mouth was set and wry; not quite a smile, impossible to decipher. She was on the terrace, sitting at the iron table drinking coffee.

Verity stood so still she was barely breathing.

Allegra tilted her cup and Verity risked a glance, caught her mother's eye over the rim and looked away.

'Will there ever be a time when you put me first, Verity? I can have exhibitions in London. You have to understand: he knows people. Why would you want to deny me or sabotage my future?'

Idris adored my work ... he wanted me to show in London...

And here she was, trading one man's futile daydream for another. Verity swallowed the thought and said to her mother, 'What about our future? How does that figure in your grand plan?'

'You can go to school! It's what you've always wanted. Don't pretend it isn't.'

Verity was horrified.

Be careful what you ask for.

'You *cannot* make Meredith go to school.'

'Meredith will be fine. She'll blossom at school.'

'So much for your principles.'

'People change. You're older; school will be good for both of you. And in any case, I'm your mother; I can do as I please.'

'Meredith's right. You really do hate us don't you?'

Don't use that word, Verity, only evil people hate...

Allegra started rolling a cigarette. 'If you say that one more time...'

'So, when are we going?'

'When I say we are.'

The house, black-eyed and brooding, closed in as if it already suspected its fate and must chide them.

It's our home. It knows us.

For the first time, Verity thought she understood what her sister meant when she insisted the house was alive. A girl who rarely concerned herself with other people's business, she sharpened her senses and began paying attention; to unlocked drawers in her mother's desk and carelessly scattered correspondence. Unsure of what she was looking for she poked and pried, searching for clues she could use to thwart her mother's plans.

And if I find anything, what difference will it make?

She eavesdropped on half-understood conversations between her mother and the man. Like leaves on the wind their words blew away, the snatches she managed to decipher meaningless.

Eventually, snooping made her uncomfortable and in any case she didn't discover a thing.

Meredith moved into Verity's room. Exhausted and distraught, for several nights she slept too deeply for dreams, curled into her sister's bed as if it were a nest.

The twig baby lay in the dark, wrapped in Meredith's cardigan.

'Have you seen how the flowers in her hair haven't wilted?'

Verity didn't need to look; she knew Meredith was telling the truth.

Waking one night needing the lavatory, as she padded back along the landing, Verity found her thoughts drawn to the blue garden. Making her way across the grass in the thinning light, she realised she was no longer afraid. Angharad's ghost was now too tragic to be a threat. Each night as she closed her eyes, Verity saw her, reaching out for her dead baby in the still silence, her face turned in supplication. Rather than fear, it was a sense of helplessness she now felt. She wasn't sure she trusted Meredith's blind faith that if they buried the twig baby it would somehow make everything all right.

The air stirred around her. Like a reflection in a fly-spotted mirror it was as if only the edges of her eyes worked, distorting what came into view. Something moved and half expecting it to stay where it was, when the image flew at her, Verity was rooted to the spot. She didn't scream; she was too startled to be scared. Her toe caught against something hard. Looking down at the foot of the wisteria, she saw tiny pieces of stone: parts of one of the cherubs, what looked like pieces of curly hair and a stubby fragment of a baby's finger, its little stone nail still intact. They had been gathered together, deliberately placed.

You cannot go ... not yet ... make her safe...

The words weren't in her head; they had entered Verity's blood, seeped into her pores and occupied her. She picked up a scrap of the stone cherub and it cut her skin. Her glass bones trembled and she hugged her arms to her chest. A wind whipped through the garden, shaking the trees, rising to a scream and Verity turned toward the house, afraid for it.

Stumbling, wrenching open the gate, she ran, and when she reached her bedroom, slammed the door behind her not caring who she woke.

In the silence the only thing she heard was her ragged breath and her heart as it shook against her ribs.

When she finally gave in to sleep it was dreamless.

In the morning, when her sister woke up, Verity told her what she had seen.

'She's a restless soul.' Meredith said. 'And she knows Allegra wants us to leave.'

Verity shuddered. Her finger still stung where the stone had nicked it. She sucked at the cut.

'I thought I'd lost her. Thank you for seeing her again.' Meredith sighed. 'I heard a baby last night, in my dream. It breaks my heart; like they broke hers.'

'And not all broken things can be mended.'

'Don't. If she's been broken into a million pieces, I won't give up on her. If you had a baby and people stole it, first your heart would shrivel and then you'd die.'

Verity said their childhood was being stolen and it was more far-reaching than a ghost's baby who might not even be real.

'You know it's exactly the same. And you know it's real.'

Verity sighed. Meredith was right. It was as if she was growing up in front of her eyes.

A tear traced Meredith's cheek. 'It's why I can't leave. Not just because I can't leave Gull House, I can't abandon her. Angharad.'

'We can't win, Meri.'

'We have to.' She paused. 'I don't want my life to be about any future she's got planned. These are my memories: being here right now. And now Angharad's part of them too. I'm not going to let Allegra wreck everything or steal my life.'

With the sun drifting through the trees, Meredith went to her grandmother's garden. She told Verity she needed to be alone for a while and not to worry. Angharad wouldn't hurt her. She tried to be aware of nothing, only the fluttering in her chest as if the moths were inside her. Lying down amongst the bluebells she asked the Fae to steal her, keep her here forever, even though she knew she was probably too old to be swapped for a changeling.

She remembered believing she could make flowers grow from her fingers. Sunbeams made patterns on her hands. She curled them into fists, made her body as small as possible. No one came for her, and the otherworld she had always believed was as close as a sigh felt as far away as the sun.

I cannot pinpoint the moment I lost hope.

At first I was too traumatised and frightened to protest. There was no question of me leaving, that much was made clear. Still no one came for me.

I had nothing save for the memory of my finger brushing hers, a last sweet kiss and a blanket. The world vanished; a cut appeared, an opening between the world I knew and the one into which I fell. I became invisible and although I passed unseen, I saw. Hidden in my darkness, the ease with which I slipped into this parallel world made me wonder how many other worlds existed, side-by-side, resembling the one we thought we knew.

The world I came from had become a fearful place, the one I was forced into turned equally menacing. Even supposing I'd been accorded a choice, it would have been no choice at all. I imagined myself dead or dying because I couldn't bear to be alive. Without my child I became weightless, as if we had both died.

And still no one came for me.

Hope became an ephemeral thing made of memory, of soft wind and the delicate scent of bluebells.

The thread of her heart ... her touch.

Time died too – withering like frostbitten flowers.

Passing ... pausing ... gone...

My grief for that half-glimpsed tiny bundle overwhelmed me. I knew she was gone, but I couldn't let her go. I wasn't ready for that parting. In spite of my continued pleas, they refused to tell me where she was buried. Once I realised no gain would come from making a scene, I hid myself away until they made me dress and return to work. It was easier to comply; soon they thought me passive and biddable again.

Inside I began to rage and when I regained my strength a hitherto unknown determination to escape rose in me.

If I searched until my dying day, I would find my child's resting place.

Forty-four

'I hope I didn't disturb you.' There was a hint of insolence in his voice, as if concern for her was the last thing on his mind.

Verity loathed the fact he was coming out of her mother's bedroom, that she was in her dressing gown. She vowed she wouldn't leave her room again unless she was fully clothed.

For a big man he walked silently.

Like a wolf.

Verity made her look sharp; the pause calculated. 'Why would you think you had?'

'You tell me.'

She could have ignored him; slipped downstairs. The space they occupied felt like a cocoon. Her glass bones trembled.

He watched her, eyes narrowed, as if he still waited for some kind of disclosure from her.

'Did Meredith wake up too? I thought I heard her. Did she have a bad night?'

Verity swallowed and said Meredith was fine. 'She's asleep in my room; it has nothing to do with you.'

For a moment she thought he might challenge her.

'I was worried.'

'Don't be, there's no need. I take care of my sister.'

'So everything's all right then?'

To lend her voice conviction, she took an exaggerated breath. 'Perfectly, thank you.'

She didn't care what he believed, or if he thought she was lying. She had heard the undercurrent of disdain in his voice. She was on to him.

Verity tried again to talk to her mother.

'I don't trust him. He asks questions about us – personal things. It makes me uncomfortable. Why is he still here?'

'You're imagining things.' Allegra dismissed Verity with a wave of her hand.

When he tried to befriend Meredith, Verity became more concerned. She didn't need to be. Meredith's dislike of him was evident; she let him know at every opportunity. His refusal to be intimidated simply made Verity worry all the more.

He didn't give the impression he was afraid of anything.

'Angharad doesn't trust him either,' Meredith said. 'He's one of the bad men.' She told Verity she could make him leave. 'I know how and if it doesn't work, maybe Angharad will help.'

'Meri, don't. We have enough on our plate. Don't start making stupid spells.'

'They aren't stupid.'

Verity made her promise not to do anything.

'Okay, I promise.' Meredith chewed her lip. 'It doesn't mean I shan't stop willing him to leave.'

'Why can't you give him a chance?' Allegra looked pained, unused to Meredith gainsaying her. 'It's not only about you, is it? Think about it for a moment; about what it's like for me.' She sat at the iron table, twisting the ends of her poppy-strewn scarf into knots.

Out on the terrace with the sun shining on the bricks, it was possible to believe nothing could be wrong.

'This isn't like you, darling' Allegra said. 'Why are you being difficult all of a sudden?' Her voice took on a plaintive tone. 'It's your bloody sister, isn't it, stirring the pot.'

Meredith was astounded. Had she been asked to say one way or the other, in that moment she might have said she hated Allegra. Since the night of the big row, a shift in Meredith's perception had taken place; a painful recognition that Allegra wasn't who she thought she was, and what she saw disturbed her.

She stared at her mother, shaking her head

'What?' Allegra said. 'What is it, Meredith?'

'You; it's you.' She dug out a sneer. 'To accuse Verity of lying is outrageous and totally unjust.'

'Oh, that's unfair; I'm just saying…'

'You're saying my sister is a liar and she isn't. You are. You're a monster.'

Expecting a more violent reaction, when her mother simply shrugged and raised her palms, Meredith's words deserted her.

'Even though that's a dreadful thing to say, I'll let it go,' Allegra said 'I know you're being influenced by Verity. She's wrong, baby, and once we're settled you'll be happy. I promise.'

I'll never be happy again.

Meredith saw how her mother's hand hovered over a book on Miró the man had given her, how her attention had drifted. She knew she had disappeared from Allegra's thoughts like a leaf on the wind.

Present

At the lookout I stop, inhale the clear air.

I want where I'm standing stand to be where I always stood, although I'm no longer sure where that is. The oak has sunk deeper into the ground. Tall grass and nettles sprout along its length, parts of the wood are decomposing.

Leaning against it, I scan the horizon.

Where does the sea end...?

The sun is in my eyes and I can't see properly and in any case, it's the wrong direction.

Go east young woman...

My unease returns. Jabbing at my phone I try the caretaker again. There's still no connection and I'm more isolated than ever. I tell myself I'm being an idiot.

Moving away from the tree, this time I shade my eyes. And there it is – a sheet of silver as familiar as it's always been. The bay is full of sky, the tide out and the sea smaller than I recall.

Imagine if it went on forever...

I scramble over the stile and down the ledge to the narrow strip of shingle. Slipping off my sandals, I pick my way to where the sand begins; walk slowly, letting it run between my toes. Salty air catches in my hair, I can see a group of oystercatchers at the lip of the sea and as I watch, they twirl into the air and I want to believe it is to welcome me.

Where the dry sand meets the wet, I stop. A gentle breeze fans the beach and the waves near the shoreline are capped with foam. Crouching down beside a rock pool I see the prawns we swore were shrimps and I can hear her laughing, collecting nets and buckets.

Let's go prawning, Verity.

I cast around for treasure, and almost immediately find a stone with a hole in it. I am absurdly pleased, seized by a moment of joy so acute it sends a shiver through my entire body.

Peering through the hole, I recall the endless hours I spent here by myself or with only Meredith for company and how, for the past two decades, unless I was studying, I've rarely been completely alone.

A slew of gulls career above my head and I shade my eyes again against the sun and its glittering reflection as it catches on the water. The sea is no longer small – it's vast and lonely and the horizon looks so far away it could be America.

Where does it end…?

I don't want to think about it – about how far away she is.

The day closes in on me like a spell. An old one I don't want anything to do with.

Forty-five

The voice of Angharad's ghost was like an infection, persistent and each night louder, as if she knew time was running out.

You cannot trust the mothers...

In Verity's bed, Meredith's woke from a vivid dream. Beside her, her sister trembled like a leaf.

'You heard her too, didn't you?'

Verity could barely speak. She drew Meredith close. 'I'm trying not to be scared, Meri.'

'Don't be, it's all right, I promise.'

The sense of Angharad's presence was intense. Neither of them could see anything although they could both hear her, her voice low and clearer than it had ever been inside Meredith's head.

You cannot leave ... stay with me and be my little girl...

'I don't want to go,' Meredith tried to make her voice convincing. 'I'm doing my...'

The voice interrupted, sounding harsh.

She will make you ... mothers cannot be trusted ... it wasn't my time to die... what happened to my baby...?

'Did you hear that?' Meredith's voice trembled.

'Yes.' Verity leaned out of the bed, turned on the bedside lamp and as the pool of light spread, the voice disappeared.

'She wasn't ready to die,' Meredith said. 'And they didn't even allow her to bury her own baby.' She sat up. 'Every mother deserves to know her child's last resting place. We have to do it tonight, Verity. It's time.'

In the garden, with the moon shedding a sliver of light, they stood hand in hand, as still as statues. The twig baby lay on the ground close to the wisteria. Drifts of poppies were beginning to replace the bluebells. Meredith could see them, a different shade of blue; the petals transparent, folding into the night. She thought her heart would break, certain she would never see any of the blue flowers again.

Holding back her tears she whispered. 'What do you do to make her come?'

'Nothing,' Verity said. 'She just appears.'

Her hands shaking, Meredith struck a match and lit a candle next to the twig baby. Verity's hand touched her shoulder and Meredith stared, her mouth open, watching a figure slide through the poppies. 'Is it her?' A hint of rags hovered in the gloom. 'I'm not sure, it's a shadow. Perhaps I'm imagining it.'

'No, you aren't. Oh look, I can see her too. Look, Verity, she's kneeling down.'

Verity drew in a long breath. 'Yes.'

As they watched, at the foot of the wisteria the figure stooped as if in prayer. Her hands hovered and she touched the twig baby, stroked her cobweb hair. Her head turned, her face wretched with sorrow, and her mouth, for a shred of a second, smiled.

Meredith let out a small gasp and Verity grabbed her hand. Tears rolled down her face, she blinked and the ghost began to disintegrate until the only thing left were feathered shreds. Then they too were gone and she was nothing more than a trace of mist vanished into the night.

'Has she gone?'

Verity shivered. 'I think so.'

Meredith let go of her sister's hand and wiped her eyes on her sleeve. 'Come on, we have to dig a grave.'

'Here?'

'No, in the middle on the grass, where Nain reads to us.'

They had brought a shovel from the shed. Meredith pushed the tip of it into the earth. Softened by the rain, it yielded and the hole was soon made. She pulled a long cotton scarf from her bag – turquoise blue and scattered with silver stars. Unfolding it she laid it on the ground, placed the twig baby on it; tucked a red heart into the folds of the dress close to where the baby's heart would have been. She rummaged in her bag for a pair of scissors and reaching for a piece of her own hair, snipped off a lock, made Verity do the same.

'There ought to be something of Nain's too,' she said, placing the curls of hair on top of the heart.

'This is her garden, remember?' Verity smiled. 'Her place, it'll be enough.'

'Do you think so? If Nain knew about Angharad, I think she'd want to be part of this.'

Verity slipped her hand into the pocket of her jeans. 'Here,' she said, 'will this do?'

In the moonlight, the stone with the hole in the centre was as pale as milk.

'Nain gave it to me. She found it in here. She said the hole was made by a star. I've been saving it for a special occasion.'

'It's perfect. Oh, Verity, are you sure?'

'Of course I am.'

Taking her best care, Meredith wrapped the twig baby in the scarf. 'It's going to be so cold for her. The way it was for Angharad's real baby – buried alone, with no one to say a prayer for her.'

'You don't know that's what happened.'

'I do. You're doing it again.'

'Sorry, it's …'

'I know, but Angharad didn't get to say goodbye to her baby, she didn't know where she was buried and it was cruel. People like that wouldn't bother with prayers. That's what was missing and makes it so much worse. And why we have to make it right.'

Verity put her arm around her sister's shoulder. 'We'll say a prayer for her. You're right; it's what she'd want us to do.'

At the edge of the garden, they heard a rustle.

Their eyes met.

'Do you think she's still here?

Verity nodded.

As Meredith folded the ends of the scarf to tidy them, she said, 'I wonder where they buried the real baby.'

'Maybe she didn't die. Maybe they lied and gave her to a family to adopt.'

Meredith said, no, Angharad's baby had died. 'I know she did.' Scooping some of the fresh earth into her hands she stared at it. 'And a mother would know that kind of thing. Angharad did.' It was almost dark now and deep shadows filled the space. Soil fell through her fingers, caught in the folds of the scarf where the outline of the twig hands tried to poke through. A few grains marked the place shrouding her face. 'I can't look, Verity. Will you do it?'

Verity filled in the rest of the tiny grave, scooping the soil into the hole, smoothing and patting the ground flat. They covered it with small stones and leaves and flowers. Meredith said she didn't want the place marked; she wanted the grass to grow over it so no one but them would know it was there.

'I hope you approve, Angharad.'

The garden was silent. Inside her head it was as quiet as if she had never had a dream or heard the voice of a sad ghost girl asking her if she was brave enough.

They stood facing one another, fingers linked, lost in the moment. A white moth, drawn to the candlelight, hovered at Meredith's shoulder. Tears welled in her eyes and she watched as it fluttered across the garden toward the wisteria.

'We've done our best,' she said. 'The poppies will hide her and next year the bluebells will come back. The garden will protect her – the birds and the animals too.' She lifted her head, glanced into the shadows. 'Our grandmother's magic will keep your baby safe, Angharad.'

Verity tightened her hold on her sister's hand. 'You are the kindest person in the world, Meri.'

Pulling another one of the red hearts from her bag, Meredith laid it on the earth. 'Wherever your soul is, baby girl, it's loved by us and the ghost of your mother will watch over you.' She looked over her shoulder again. 'She knows where you are now.'

Her hands shook, tears ran down her cheeks and she gazed up at Verity. 'Amen?'

Verity pressed her lips together. 'Amen.'

A fretful gust of wind whirled through the grass, between the sleeping poppies and the fading bluebells. It rustled in the leaves of the wisteria and both girls felt it catching in their hair, stroking the skin on their faces like invisible fingers. It sighed and died to nothing and the garden settled.

The candle blew out.

'Was it her?' Meredith whispered.

'I'm not sure.'

'If it was, she's gone now, hasn't she?' Meredith let out a little cry. 'I can't bear it. What if I never hear her again?'

'It means she's at rest. Now her baby is, she can rest too.'

'I don't want her to go.' Meredith clutched at her sister's sleeve.

Verity felt tears on her own face. 'It's okay Meri, we did it; we did what she asked.'

'But don't you see? If Angharad's gone then it means we'll be going too. And Allegra will have won.'

'What do you mean?'

'Now the baby's been buried, Angharad won't need me. She won't care if we leave.'

'No, that's not true. She'll be grateful. You've done what she asked…'

'Verity, she's a ghost. They don't think the way living people do.'

'Perhaps.'

'Definitely. In any case, Angharad hates mothers. And she's right.'

You cannot trust the mothers…

She could almost see what her sister was thinking.

'Don't try and comfort me, Verity,' she said. 'You can't. Angharad isn't going to stop Allegra. Nothing will. And if we leave, it's over. I'll never find out what happened to her.'

Forty-six

Allegra sat at her dressing table unravelling her hair, and a curious despair overtook her.

In an attempt to placate Meredith she had resolved to paint a last picture of the house. It wasn't working. She had failed to capture the light, and once it was gone there was no reclaiming it. That was the trouble with light; it was like cloud reflected in water, constantly on the move and you had to be quick, so quick. Once she was in London she would concentrate on the new paintings – it was a departure and he was right – the new style suited her personality. And in any case, Meredith was as ungrateful as her sister.

'I don't care about your stupid painting,' she'd said. 'I don't need a picture to remember it.'

In which case, why should I bother?

It was time for new beginnings, and she would start this one by clearing her dressing table in preparation for the move. Dropping the hairpins into a glass dish, she pulled open the bottom drawer, began dragging things out, surrounding herself with a pile of belongings she had half-forgotten she owned.

She rolled a cigarette, found a match and lit it, inhaled and coughed, hard and too long.

Jeez, I need to give up these things. Maybe I will, in London.

Leaving the cigarette to burn in the ashtray, she watched the smoke curl into the gloom, turned her attention back to the drawer. Her fingers grazed a small leather box – empty, the bits of jewellery Idris had bought her gone, given away, removed.

You left me … you said you loved me and you lied.

Outside her window the gulls were settling into their night-time places, bickering and vying for space on the roof.

I won't miss you lot and your hideous noise.

What would she miss?

You're a monster…

'I am not a monster!' She hurled the words into the silent room.

She wouldn't miss a damn thing. And the girls could like it or lump it. It was ridiculous to imagine they wouldn't cope. Verity would fit right in at school – too clever for her own good – and so would Meredith, now she was older.

The night before last, before he left for London, he had told her she was beautiful, that she had stolen his heart.

If you have been told often enough you are a beauty it either turns your head or you become bored by the notion. And if you have been an artist's model, you become blasé about your body.

I'm not as vain as people imagine I am.

'It's irrelevant,' she told him. 'I want your approval, not your compliments.'

Opinions mattered to Allegra, as much as appearances.

And her capacity for kidding herself was endless.

She wanted him devoted, a little bit besotted. Above all, she wanted to be loved. Lifting her head, she glanced at her reflection and then away. Her eyes reminded her of her father and she blinked away a tear.

You would have understood, Pa, wouldn't you?

At the edge of her thoughts, her mother's voice intruded.

Selfish … you can't control everything … what about the girls…

She wasn't trying to control anyone – only make sure she did her best for her family. And what did her mother know about anything anyway?

She doesn't care about me. And why isn't she happier at the thought of seeing more of her only daughter? Why isn't she pleased I've found someone to love me? If anyone's selfish, it's her.

While she still lived at Gull House, Mared may have been a tangible comfort; now she was a thorn in Allegra's flesh.

She's difficult and obstructive; always trying to force her views on me.

Allegra didn't do irony.

Somewhere in the house, Meredith's voice called out and Verity answered. Allegra didn't like the idea they might be planning more defiance, to sabotage her dream.

What's so bad about wanting the best for us?

Her lover, with his cool eyes and hot hands, had changed everything. His desire consumed her. He was dynamic and full of ideas too; he made her feel alive. She shuddered and it felt delicious.

They'll come round. In any case, they don't have any choice.

It was the only way and for the best. Her mother had to take responsibility. If she hadn't upped and left in the first place, Allegra reasoned, the girls wouldn't be in this position now.

She left me to cope when she knew I wouldn't be able to. What kind of a mother does that?

She stubbed out the cigarette, ran her fingers through her hair, and imagined his hands in it. Looking up at her reflection in the mirror, light caught the silvering and this time, her face, with a hint of a blush, almost embarrassed her. Her foot caught the edge of the open drawer of the dressing table.

She kicked it shut.

Another flutter ran through her body; this time it was less sensual and more a moment of bewilderment.

You can't control everything...

Dropping her head, she leaned on her forearms and began to cry.

My mind played tricks.

I dreamed of my mother's garden as a wilderness, her plants gone to seed, a sea of weeds, brambles, nettles and ivy as thick as rope, strangling the precious formality. It belonged to the beetles and bats, the foxes and mice.

Ghost owls and crows claimed it.

I wandered between towering plants the colour of heartbreak and old sky, past black roses with thorns like daggers.

At the gate, my mother appeared, her mouth moving in silent agitation. When I reached for her, she turned and was gone.

Forty-seven

Each day they imagined Allegra might have changed her mind, only to have their hope dashed.

Verity lay on her bed, eyes scanning the room she had known all her life. It had become ephemeral, a stage set that might be dismantled in moments: her future unwritten and uncertain. Books and posters, stones, feathers and sea-washed glass, her shoes and clothes, her records – everything could vanish on her mother's whim. She knew herself here – anywhere else and she wouldn't fit. She would overlap or worse, shrink. This was her life and it suited her. Any other life would belong to some other girl.

You could go to school and become a librarian.

She pushed the thought away, telling herself if she was determined enough she could make that dream come true anyway.

It's Meri's dreams that matter.

Her sister's dreams were slowly being taken apart. The ghost dreams and the one she'd conjured as a tiny girl, made of stars and certainty and a future in which she never left Gull House. Meredith, she knew, was capable of imagining herself as an old woman, older than her grandmother, talking to birds, her hair turned as white as the moon with moths and ladybirds living in it.

Verity wished she could cry, although she knew it would only exacerbate the sense of emptiness. She couldn't think about the rest of the house, the garden, her beach or Meredith's wood. Could she contemplate fighting her mother again? She feared Allegra's reaction to the slightest act of rebellion. And she was terrified of the consequences, especially if Meredith made a stand.

They were poised on the edge of the biggest drama of their lives, with Allegra excelling herself, the star of the show, centre stage. It looked as if Meredith too was becoming a scapegoat. Allegra no longer had need of allies; she wanted accomplices.

Or victims: we'll be casualties; collateral damage.

Meredith still insisted, whatever Allegra said, that if she tried to make them go she would refuse. She would live in the ruin, rebuild the walls, and if she couldn't manage then she would live in a tent.

Verity didn't put anything past her angry sister.

The air was expectant with rain, the garden layered in mist. Meredith gazed up at the house, considered the walls and the stone, the roots of it like a tree reaching under the earth, the worms and small animals that made their home there. If she went away, who would be left to make sure it was looked after.

If they left, the house would know. The walls and the windows, every nook and cranny.

Crooks and nannies…

Meredith's belief that, like them, the house had a heart, was absolute. Each breeze that lifted a curtain was its breath, every creak of the floorboards its old bones protesting. When rain rattled against the windows she imagined the house muttering and answering back, repelling intruders.

It loves me because I love it back. The house knows me. I'm supposed to stay here forever.

What bothered her almost as much was the idea she would have to leave Angharad behind. Although the ghost appeared to have gone and Meredith no longer dreamed of her or heard her, leaving still felt like another betrayal.

And this time it will be mine. If she comes back and I'm not here…

Meredith guessed there was more to the story of the girl who had lived here one hundred years ago. It didn't end with the dead baby and although part of her dreaded the outcome, she was a witness who was supposed to see the story through to the end. Like the house, she felt her love for Angharad so deeply she knew few people would understand it.

She wandered across the lawn, past the fountain, considering her options. She could go to the lookout and watch for the tide, collect shells for Verity; she could play with the chickens, head into the wood and the hut, leave treats for the Fae and ask for their best spells.

What's the point? I don't think I believe in it anymore. If magic was real, it would have saved Angharad.

She knew how foolish she sounded; like a child.

I want to stay one.

If you weren't careful, when you grew up, you could lose the magic.

At the edge of the blue garden, she stood by the wall and broke off a spray of orange blossom. The scent was heady and she inhaled it as if she might hold the memory forever.

I could sit and watch for dragonflies, watch over the baby's grave. I could make daisy chains, and dream-catchers from hazel sticks.

None of these things would be available to her in London. In London she knew she would be too afraid to go outside. It would be noisy and dirty and terrifying. She wasn't sure they had flowers in London. Turning her hand over, she looked at her fingertips from which no flowers had ever really grown.

It was a kid's stupid fantasy.

Shading her eyes she looked behind her, to the edge of the wood. She could walk through it blindfold. Her mouth tightened and she spread her fingers.

I mustn't stop believing in magic just because Allegra's lost the plot or because it's over for us. This place doesn't need me. Wherever I am, the wood and the garden and the beach won't stop being magical.

Looking at it from a distance, she saw how deliciously menacing the wood still appeared, how alive and how, if she listened hard enough she'd hear music meant to entice the unwary.

She couldn't imagine there would be anything as remotely beautiful or mysterious in London. Here she knew she would never be afraid to step off the path because however scary it might appear to a person who wasn't familiar with it, the wood was the safest place on earth.

I can walk round the house blindfold too, and know if a mouse creeps along the wainscot or a cobweb falls.

In spite of her threats to Verity, Meredith didn't have anything left to fight with. She knew she wouldn't run away. The idea was almost as scary as going to London.

The orange blossom trembled in her hand; a few petals twirled in mid-air and they looked to Meredith like moths.

The next morning, she woke to a change in the weather. Clouds had heaved themselves into place, obliterating the light, and rain fell, caught in a rising wind. The sound of it against the window was the saddest thing Meredith had ever heard.

Next to her, Verity lay on her back, her eyelashes fluttering in her morning dream and Meredith swallowed, on the edge of tears.

Sister love matters … you're the kindest person in the world…

'I'm so glad I have you.' The whisper hovered on the pillow.

A sound broke the spell. The man's heavy tread on the landing; and how he paused outside Verity's bedroom as if he listened.

You cannot know how much I hate you.

She hugged Nelly so close that the rabbit bent backwards. Meredith clutched the red heart which rarely left her person, imagined spells and the kind of magic she knew her grandmother would disapprove of.

I don't care. He has to go.

Forty-eight

Meredith's nights continued undisturbed, the loss of the ghost like a bereavement.

Or a trick.

With an air of defiance, she told Verity she could still sense Angharad, as if she mocked her, as if she knew they were leaving and was angry.

'It's like when people have their leg cut off,' she said. 'A phantom leg.'

Who would have thought it – a phantom ghost?

She couldn't stand to be inside the house.

They sat on the steps below the terrace, scattering toast crusts, watching the starlings squabble.

'I made it so she'd want to go,' Meredith said, 'and now I can't bear it. Once we're gone, all this it will turn to dust.'

'No it won't. Don't be silly. Remember what Nain said, about the house being made of stern stuff?'

Meredith was adamant. 'Nothing lasts forever, you said that. And I'm not being silly. I needed to say a proper goodbye to Angharad. She didn't give me the chance and now I'll never get another one. Allegra's making us leave and whatever she says – or Nain – I don't think we'll ever come back.'

'You can't know—'

'I can.' Meredith pulled the petals off an innocent daisy. 'And you do too. Stop pretending you don't, Verity. She'll send me to school, she'll send both of us; we'll never come back and it's *his* fault.'

Verity thought it took two to tango and pointed out at least he'd disappeared for a while.

'He's gone to sort things out at his scummy flat, that's all. You heard her. He'll be back and when he comes I've a good mind to make a really nasty spell and get rid of him forever.'

'Don't talk like that, Meredith.'

'I made Idris go.'

'No you didn't. You don't even remember him.'

Meredith threw the shredded daisy to the ground. 'He must have hated me, and that's what made Mam sad, and then he went away.'

'You were a baby, Meri. And he didn't hate either of us. It's not as simple as that.'

'So why did he leave?' Meredith's face closed up in the familiar mutiny and Verity could almost wish her tragic again. 'He can't have been very nice if his own child's birth made him leave. How can it not have been me ill-wished him and made him go?' Meredith's eyes filled up with hot tears of frustration.

'That's not how it was. He left when I was born and I'm not about to start making it my fault.'

'He came back and they had me and he went away again.'

'Yes, and it was because of her, not us. Nain told me. He loved us.'

'So where is he then?'

Verity said, 'I don't know Meri and I don't care.'

'Me neither.' Meredith started work on another daisy. 'If you ask me, men are the problem and if you say this one isn't…'

Oh, men are the problem all right… But then so is Allegra.

'I agree, he is, and I don't trust him, I just think—'

'Well, don't. These are … extenuating circumstances. Let's do something and get rid of him.'

'Meri, stop it.'

'Why should I, if he's so horrible? And in any case, it might be fun.' She kicked the grass and a clump flew up. 'I'm fed up with behaving myself. And it would serve her right if I made her go too. Then we could stay here by ourselves.'

'Oh, shut up, Meri, stop being childish. You don't know what you're talking about and you mustn't pretend you do.' Verity caught her sister's stare; she was no match for it.

'Not even in an emergency?' Meredith's voice was like hot silk and she said not to worry, she'd take care of everything. Before Verity could say another word her sister took off across the grass to the side of the house and into the wood.

Two days later, there was still no sign of the man.

Triumphant, Meredith appeared in the kitchen, showed her sister a pile of burnt feathers in a saucer, a roughly folded piece of cloth with a pin sticking out of it. 'I told you I could make him go.'

Furious, Verity snatched the saucer and flung the contents into the grate. 'And I told you not to meddle, you stupid girl. What on earth did you think you were playing at?'

'I wasn't playing.'

'Oh, Meredith, stop it. Okay, maybe he's gone, and soon we'll be gone as well. It's too late, she won't change her mind now. And even if he isn't here, he'll be in London when we get there.'

'You cannot give up, Verity Pryce. How can you be so defeatist?'

'Accept it, Meri, there's nothing we can do. In any case, I'm sick of it. I want a normal life.'

'Normal? You think London will be normal?'

The evening sky hunched over the house.

Verity found Meredith in her own bedroom, curled on the window seat.

'I'm sorry for shouting at you,' she said. 'I don't want to go either, I promise you.'

'I know.' Meredith hugged Nelly to her chest. 'It doesn't matter and I know we can't stop her. I was being stupid. I don't believe in magic anymore.'

'Yes you do. Kind magic is always good. And the bad magic doesn't count. It isn't proper magic so it wouldn't work anyway.'

'I suppose Nain told you that.'

'Yes. She told you too. You're just choosing not to remember.'

Because you're terrified and clutching at straws...

They sat together until the dark bled through the curtains and the stars began to come out.

'My moths have gone.'

Verity didn't know what to say. Meredith was still sharing her bed but even though she opened the window in her room as wide as it would go, no moths came to find her sister.

Meredith said she needed to go to the blue garden. 'One last time; in case she's changed her mind.'

As they padded across the landing they could hear Allegra in her bedroom, dragging things around, singing tunelessly and occasionally coughing.

'I wish she'd stop smoking,' Verity whispered.

'Who cares? She can die for all I care.'

Verity was shocked. 'Don't say that, Meri, not even if you don't mean it.'

In the garden they settled down on the grass by the twig baby's grave. Save for the skittering of night creatures and a lone owl on her way to her hunting ground, it was suitably silent.

'We did the right thing,' Meredith whispered. 'Burying the baby, but Verity, I miss Angharad so much and I don't know the end of her story. It isn't only about the baby. I don't know how *she* died or where *she's* buried. And if I can't hear her and I go to London, I'll never find out.'

All at once she was inconsolable and her sorrow was such it made Verity's heart hurt. She slipped her arm through Meredith's.

'If we're leaving, I have to find a way to tell her, so she knows I'm not abandoning her.'

'We don't know for sure she's gone. Maybe she needs to grieve. Perhaps we need to give her some space.'

Meredith's face lit up. 'That's it. Oh, Verity, you're so clever. Of course, she needs some time. Maybe it isn't over and if we wait, she will come back, only maybe not quite yet. And if she's still here, the garden will let us know.'

'Just don't get your hopes up, okay?' Verity couldn't resist being sensible.

'It'll be fine. Maybe the birds will tell me. She said they knew. I have to be patient and wait. It'll be fine.'

It soon became apparent what little judgement Allegra still had was being annihilated. The euphoria surrounding her conviction a big break was round the corner now drove her. She gave in her notice at the art shop and to Meredith it seemed like another strand in the bad spell.

She thought of her grandmother, about living with her and great uncle Gethin and what Verity called a normal life. She thought about routine and food in the cupboards, about cinemas and parks and found no comfort in any of it. Each morning and evening, she went to the blue garden, listened for the ghost and to the birds and wondered again about the ones in London. Would she be able to hear the birds above the traffic and the shouting? Meredith knew she would hate it. She couldn't imagine liking anything about London.

Folding her hands in her lap, she waited each night for the moths, and for a sign that her ghost hadn't gone.

Forty-nine

The future remained hidden, a monster in the shadows.

By contrast, the blue garden began to feel like a shrine. There was no further sign of the ghost and Meredith stopped dreaming altogether. Clinging to hope she continued to insist Angharad hadn't gone.

'She hasn't, Verity. I know she hasn't. She's tired, like you said.'

The days passed and they walked on the beach and in the wood because they would do anything to get away from the house and where else would they go?

Allegra stayed in her room or spent hours on the telephone, talking to the man or arguing with Mared.

When they were weary of wandering, the girls baked cakes and read books. They painted their nails, Verity cut her hair and Meredith caught a chill. She dug out a space in Verity's bed, like a puppy, and made it hers. During those last weeks she was an animal, fearful and functioning by instinct, fierce too, snarling whenever Allegra came near her.

Meredith had never contemplated a future away from Gull House. She hadn't needed to and with time running out, it carried her like a relentless wave and as the days passed, Verity saw her determination falter.

Another week flew by and one morning, Allegra told them.

'It's settled. We're leaving at the end of the month. You're going to stay with Mared for a while. Won't that be amazing?'

If her grandmother had capitulated and agreed to the collusion, Verity knew the last of her own hope had died.

When Meredith finally burst into the tears she'd been holding onto, Allegra became angry, screaming and ranting, banging doors, coughing so hard she held her heart and gasped for breath, and Verity feared she would have some kind of seizure.

'Please, Meredith, stop crying,' she begged. 'Don't make it worse.'

'How can it get any worse?'

'We're children. There's nothing we can do.'

'We can run away.'

'Stop saying that! Run away where?'

'Anywhere, it doesn't matter!'

Meredith was like a withering flower; one by one her petals dropped until the only thing left was a shrivelled stamen. Her hair grew dull, her skin erupted in spots. Both girls stopped eating. Bread turned to cardboard in their mouths and when Allegra made a chocolate cake as a half-hearted peace offering, it tasted of bitterness and duplicity. They left it on the dresser where it went hard and when Meredith threw it out for the birds, they flew away.

Even the gulls ignored it.

Verity looked toward the sea only vaguely registering the view. Logically, she knew the water was moving, frilling back and forth against the sand; the sky layered in silver mackerel stripes and flecked with gulls. She saw none of this detail because if she did then she would weep. Inside her head was in turmoil, a slab of whirling horror. She forced herself to focus on inconsequential and random things: her fingernails were too long and needed cutting; the hens' eggs hadn't been collected. And it was time they ate a proper meal. No one had cooked, and then she thought how no one ever really cooked and this was a different kind of not cooking – as if to do so would be like saying they were having a last supper.

The condemned girls ate a hearty meal.

They mounted one last campaign, born of desperation.

Allegra's voice took on a borrowed authority and as she planned and packed, she glittered and glowed and was interested only in her own future. There was no stopping her.

In Rapunzel's room they found her picking through canvases.

'If you'd only talk it over with us,' Verity said, choosing her words with care. 'Listen to us?'

Meredith threw caution out with the ashes from the fire and wept, no longer caring if Allegra thought she'd won. 'Mam, please don't do this to us. How can you? How can you be so heartless?'

Allegra simply looked pained and carried on, flicking through her paintings, setting one or two aside. 'Meredith, you aren't being rational. I told you, it'll be good for us.'

'For you! It will be good for you! Except it won't and you're too stupid to see it. He's got you exactly where he wants you, mostly in bed!'

Taken aback, Allegra took in a long, hissing breath. It was Meredith who had spoken, but when she drew her next battle lines it wasn't her youngest daughter she had in her sights.

Eyes narrowed, she fixed her attention on Verity. 'So, that's what this is about. Ha! You're jealous!' She moved her head and her long neck stretched even further. 'What nastiness have you been filling your sister's head with?'

'How many times…? I haven't said anything. And Meri's not blind. She's right. You're disgusting.'

Meredith wailed and said it was true; Verity didn't need to say anything and they weren't stupid. They knew exactly what was going on. She hovered in the doorway, shaking with rage. 'You stink of him.'

If Allegra was shocked she didn't show it. Instead, she kept her eye firmly on Verity. 'Why do you hate me so much?'

'Oh, for God's sake, not this again,' Verity said. 'I don't. It's like *you* hate *us*, Mam. Our feelings obviously don't mean a thing to you but we're children, we can't fight you. It doesn't mean we have to like what you're doing.' She paused. 'Any of it.'

Meredith held her hands to her mouth. Allegra pushed past her, turned and paused, one hand raised. 'That's enough from both of you. I'm done with this. It's ridiculous. You'll adapt. It's what people do.' She glared at Meredith. 'And I can't believe you of all people would behave this way. What's happened to you, Meredith? We could be so happy – if you'd only open your mind.'

She smiled then and it cut through Verity like a blade. Her mother smiled this way when she wanted to impress people.

'Stop it!' Verity snarled and clenched her fists. 'It won't work. We don't want your pathetic, second-hand longings or your pointless promises.'

Allegra looked genuinely bemused and Verity realised, her mother had no idea what she was talking about.

'You're delusional,' she said. 'Besotted by a man who is so obviously going to leave you.'

Meredith was sobbing bitterly now.

Verity tried to pacify her and was thrown off.

'You're right. She does hate us.' Meredith whirled on her mother. 'You do, and if we leave here we won't come back; and I have to be here, at least until I know.'

'What do you mean? Know what?'

Verity saw her sister's pain and knew where it came from.

Ghost...

Meredith fled, and curled into one of the giant linen cupboards on the landing, the way she used to when she was a little girl.

It took her sister an hour to find her.

'Will you read to me?'

She could see Verity was oddly touched by the request.

'Of course, I will. Your wish is my command.'

Meredith thought about wishes and the only one she would ever make again, and how even her clever sister with her kind heart couldn't make it so they didn't have to leave Gull House. She smiled and said thank you, curled up beside Verity and put her wish into a corner of her heart; later she would place it in the fishing net and look for a shooting star.

'Meredith is in pieces. Her heart is breaking.'

'Now who's being dramatic?' Allegra wrapped random items of crockery in newspaper and threw them into a box. 'Meredith will be fine and of course we're coming back.'

They both knew this was a lie.

'Don't be so bloody obstructive. I told you, you're being ridiculous, both of you. I'm not going to discuss it anymore.'

'What does Nain say?'

'Mared doesn't care. She wants us to be happy.'

She wants us to be safe.

'It'll be an adventure.'

If she says it enough; she'll believe it.

When Verity telephoned, Mared tried her best to reassure her. 'It's a whim, lovely. You know what she's like. And it will be so good to have you here for a while. I know it'll be a squash and you girls will have to share but we'll manage.'

It wasn't a whim. Verity knew exactly what her mother was up to. Her grandmother knew it too.

'Why can't we stay here, Nain? We'd be all right.'

'Oh sweetheart, you know that's not possible. You're far too young.'

'I'm almost sixteen.' It was a forlorn hope and died as quickly as it was born. 'What will happen to the house?'

'The house will be fine. It'll be closed up for the time being. And when your mother's got this nonsense out of her system, then you'll go home.'

As it became apparent there would be no reprieve, the endeavour turned into a full-scale panic – a scramble to salvage the things they valued and desired.

Meredith refused to pack so much as a sock. Whereas before

270

she had been angry and vocal, now she was diminished. In her head what was happening wasn't possible. The plans Allegra made were for another family, a family with different names. They would wake up at some point in the same house; get on with their familiar lives, everything they knew in its rightful place. The other family with other names would be the ones to leave.

As if the horror of the last argument hadn't happened, Allegra became elated.

'It's an adventure and that's the only way to look at it,' she insisted. 'Look forward and wait and see what happens next!'

Verity and Meredith knew they would never be ready for what happened next.

'I know you're sad, Meri.'

'The word doesn't exist for how I am.'

It was late and, too wretched to read, they lay in Meredith's bed. She wanted to see if the moths would come back if she slept in her own room. She didn't want to sleep by herself unless they did and had persuaded Verity to move in with her. In her clenched fist she held the red flannel heart.

'All the words have gone,' she said. 'Like the birds and the ghost. And the moths.'

'Try and sleep.' Verity stroked her sister's arm, buried her face in the mass of her hair. It smelled of chamomile and bewilderment.

Meredith sighed and closed her eyes. Not expecting to dream, she did and the ghost's voice filled her mind again, this time with a mixture of hope and horror.

Shaking her sister awake, she whispered in her ear.

'She's back. She was braver than us,' Meredith said. 'She ran away.'

I inhabited my own world because why would I choose to be in theirs?

In order to draw as little attention to myself as possible, I learned to breathe quietly. I was practically mute and they thought me harmless. It isn't possible to become completely invisible; the trick is to fade, to think yourself unremarkable. After a while I was no longer considered a liability and they became complacent.

With each passing day the memory made from the brush of a finger and the faint beat of her heart imprinted on mine. My heartache became an anger stinging like a thousand wasps.

They thought I had forgotten. They were wrong. I remembered everything and although I had put my mother from my mind, I still occasionally dreamed of her, wondered what could have caused her to abandon me. Even knowing how making fallen women invisible was a social imperative, it still felt like a thin excuse and unworthy of any mother.

I hadn't fallen; I had been pushed aside and then discarded.

As plans go, mine was rudimentary. If I was patient, I believed an opportunity would present itself. I made no trouble and as the weeks turned into months, I became unremarkable. My watcher was a drunkard: brutalised and occasionally brutal but mostly lazy. When the time came it wasn't difficult to give her the slip.

One night a storm came in from the north. I knew these storms well and how this one was likely to play out. It was fierce, full of menace and although it didn't last long, while it did it was a blessing. Distracted by the thunder and lightning, afraid and taking to her bottle, my watcher took her eye off me long enough for me to see my chance and seize it.

A set of keys, a stolen cloak and like a ghost I was gone – through unlit night corridors, out through a side door.

I fled into the night, enclosed by the kindness of a storm.

Knowing unless I went to ground quickly, I would soon be found, I ran. I knew I couldn't go far and also that I wasn't far from Gull House. Over the course of two days, I walked by night and slept in the shadows during the day, until eventually I found myself in the familiar wood and at the old hut.

The sun shone through the trees making patterns on the woodland floor. Inside the hut the light changed, the shadows lengthened and I was finally safe.

It was colder even than the desolate chill of the asylum and at first I struggled to keep warm. Night sounds were different from day ones and frightened me. There was an intensity to the air at night; the wind bit deep and hurt my skin.

A few basic things remained: the tinder box, a cup, a dish and a knife. Tea leaves in a rusty canister. I risked a fire, boiled water I collected from a stream, and although it was stale the tea tasted delicious and warmed my shivering body.

The blankets were damp and mouldy. I hung them out and although they took days to dry out, they were enough.

What mattered was I was free. My old hurt mind squeezed closed and another new version of my psyche took hold.

Present

Returning to the house, I shiver, knowing I must finish what I've begun.

My sandals tap on the wooden floor. The stairs are bare, the carpet taken up and stored. I place one foot on the first step. On the bannister, my hand feels sweaty, sticks on the smooth wood.

I walk past Allegra's room. I have no interest in it. There was always something helpless about the chaos my mother surrounded herself with, as if she was waiting for someone else to bring order. When the man arrived, and she allowed him to stay, we heard them: the bed creaking, her small cries which we closed our ears to.

Taking a deep breath I open the door to my bedroom. It is almost more than I can bear. Memory floods my mind and I see myself, packing my things, choosing randomly because Allegra was screaming and there was no time.

A blanket of dust lies undisturbed: a layer of grief, like lost hope and once more I'm close to tears. My clothes are gone of course, and most of the books too, although not all of them. A line, slanted and tired, still sits on the windowsill. I fear they will be spoiled, and so it proves: all but one are curled and slightly swollen.

In the end, Gull House has been no match for twenty years of Welsh damp.

The exception is the Dodie Smith, my own copy; I took the other one back.

You have good taste ... good girl, no fines...

Would Miss Jenkins have been pleased with me? Would it have

made her happy that I had claimed my right to an education, read the books? (I have become quite an authority on feminist theory.)

My bed remains, still facing the window and the sea. It is a child's bed and looks small and lost. The silence is unnerving, I can't stand it and walk out. Hovering on the landing, I touch the solid wood of my sister's bedroom door. The grain looks deeper, the door smaller. In the central panel I can see the letter 'M' etched into the wood.

When had she done this, for it must surely be Meredith's handiwork?

Trembling, my hand hovers on the brass doorknob. Closing my eyes, for a moment I'm tempted to run. Back to London, to Carla, abandon Gull House and consign it to memory.

There was nothing for me ... I said there wouldn't be...

It would be easy to make her believe me – it wouldn't occur to Carla I would lie to her.

Hesitating, I understand why I'm so reluctant to go into her room. Once I take Meredith out of the house, the garden or the beach or the wood, I have to place her in London and spoil her happiness; remove the magic from both our lives. I'm not sure I can face having the sweetness of her cobwebbed by the passage of time.

Fifty

Allegra was high as a kite, the packing deranged and nothing made sense.

She was wilful in her unreasoning haste and they left in such a hurry, precious things were abandoned.

'Please, Mam, you have to let me.' Meredith wailed her despair at being told there was no time to dismantle Mared's doll house.

'There's no room in Gethin's flat,' Allegra said. 'Don't be selfish.'

The days were an endless succession of catastrophes. One day the chickens disappeared and Meredith's anguish when she discovered her mother had sold them to a neighbour boiled over into fury. She flew at Allegra, clawing her face and Verity had to drag her off.

The man appeared briefly, with a van, and although he was polite to them, Verity sensed his underlying hostility. She took to following them again; listening at doors for hints because her instinct told her that this man, unlike the others, had an agenda. On the terrace outside the sitting room she slid her body into the embrace of the wisteria's great trunk.

'It's better this way.' His voice was smooth. 'Why stay with your mother when she's clearly so set against us? The girls will be fine with her, until we find something more suitable. The place I've found for us is perfect. Wait until you see it.'

'You're sure?'

'I'm sure.'

'There's enough light?'

'As much light as you need. You're going to do your best work in London, I know it.' He lowered his voice and Verity held her breath.

'And about the other thing … it's not as if you're attached to this place … not as if you'll need it … once you make your name … imagine what you could do with the money…'

It was all Verity could do not to burst into the room and confront him.

He hung around, helped with the smaller pieces of furniture Allegra insisted on taking; sorted her painting things, took them – and the new canvases – away with him.

When he left he kissed her too lightly and when her mother clung to him, Verity thought she saw a look of irritation cross his face.

'Call me?'

He nodded, extracted himself and Verity felt her blood run cold.

'What makes you think you'll be allowed to sell my grandmother's house behind her back?'

'What are you talking about?'

Her mother dragged laundry off the wooden rack.

'I heard you.'

'Listening at doors again, Verity. You know what they say about eavesdroppers.' Allegra threw clothes and pillowslips and underwear onto one of the cane chairs; began folding things, randomly without noticing what she was doing, her back to Verity.

'It wasn't about me though, was it? It was about you.' Verity came closer. 'Can't you see? He's not interested in you. He wants the house, or the money he thinks it'll make.'

'Don't be ridiculous.'

'I'm not – you are. Nain will never sell Gull House. She promised us when we were little girls. I remember, she said it would be over her dead body.'

Her mother's face had paled to a ghost's pallor. 'Shut up.' Her voice was low, yet still with a shrill edge, and behind it Verity heard panic. 'I've warned you before, Verity, about undermining me. You will not wreck my life. I won't allow it.'

'No, but you're perfectly happy to wreck ours. And by the look of things, you're making a pretty good job of destroying your own.'

'Enough.' Allegra banged her hands on the back of the chair and the pile of clothes wobbled; a slip slid to the ground in slow motion, landing in a pool on the floor.

Allegra stared at it and without lifting her head, said, 'Pack the rest of your things today, and make sure your sister does the same.'

Verity saw nothing she wanted to take with her. Her things belonged here. Beaten by her mother's refusal to face the truth, she threw a few clothes into a suitcase.

It was different for Meredith.

In her indignation at what she saw as Verity's defection, she screamed at her. 'You're supposed to be on my side. Why are you packing?'

'There is no side, Meri. There's no choice either. We're children.'

'Stop saying that! As if being children makes us incapable…'

Verity shook her head. 'That's just it. It does. What is it you think we can do?'

'Stop her.'

'We've tried. You know we have. I don't know what else there is.'

Outside, the sky darkened, and fierce clouds swallowed the day.

Fifty-one

Meredith lay in bed with moonlight on her eyelids and moths haloed round her hair.

Convinced they didn't know where she was, determined to be brave, she'd started sleeping in her own bedroom by herself.

For a sweet second, their return delighted her.

Wrinkling her nose, she breathed in. The air gave off a sour smell. The cold struck her face and she snatched at it, thinking a web brushed against her skin. A draught crept from somewhere. This was a dependable, sturdy house with no gaps and no ill-fitting windows. Where did the draught come from?

The room had turned icy again, the way it had been a few weeks before.

As she climbed out of bed, the moths scattered. Crossing to the door she ran her hand round the frame feeling for a draught. She reached for the doorknob. It refused to turn. She tried it again, the door held fast and she noticed the key was missing.

Peering through the keyhole she caught a glimmer of light then a shadow across the gap, blocking it.

'Who's there? Is that you, Verity?'

No one answered.

She called out again. 'Verity, where are you? I'm locked in my room.'

When there was still no answer, she shouted, rattled the knob and peered through the keyhole again. This time the light was completely blocked as if someone stood there. 'It isn't funny, Verity.'

Badly frightened now, Meredith backed away from the door.

Her heart thudded in her chest and she bit her lip to stop herself from crying out. On the other side of the door she heard a noise, let out a sound that was half gasp and half scream.

'Meredith?'

'I'm here. I'm locked in. I can't find the key.'

'It's all right, I've got it. Be quiet, you'll wake Allegra.'

Meredith heard the rasp as the key turned in the lock. Verity stood in the doorway, the light from the moonlit window streaming down the landing behind her, real and substantial, the key in her hand.

'I found it on the floor. What's going on?'

Meredith flung herself into her sister's arms. 'I don't know. I woke up and the moths were back and then there was a smell and the horrible cold again.' She was shaking so hard her teeth were chattering. 'The key was there, I swear it was; it's always there, and then it wasn't and the door was locked from the outside.'

'Well, I'm here now and you're safe. Shush, it's okay. Quiet now.' Verity pulled her sister close. 'Come on, you're all right. I'm here.' She led Meredith to the bed, sat her down; stroked her hair. As the worst of Meredith's fear subsided, she told Verity what had happened.

'How weird, it doesn't make sense.'

'The door was *locked*, Verity. Don't pretend it wasn't.'

'I'm not. I unlocked it, remember?'

'It's her. It's Angharad. She must be back and she doesn't want us to leave.'

Verity stroked her sister's face. 'Why don't you sleep with me again tonight? If your dreams are getting bad again, I can wake you up.'

'It won't make any difference. I don't have to be asleep.'

'Do you actually believe she locked you in your room? That she's trying to stop you leaving?'

'She doesn't want me to go until she's finished telling her story. She isn't trying to be horrible, just make sure I hear her. It's getting harder for her, she's so tired.'

280

Verity gazed at the key.

'She's still here.' Meredith's face was defiant.

'Well, maybe. You can't be sure…'

'I was locked in my room,' Meredith said. 'So, no, she hasn't gone. And in any case, she would have told me.'

Verity sighed. She knew her sister had a point.

'Being locked up makes you go mad, you know.'

Verity gave a short involuntary cry and all at once, Meredith's mood changed.

'Oh Verity, don't get upset, I'm not talking about me,' she said. 'There's nothing to get upset over because in the end, Angharad escaped and for a short time she was as free as the moths.' Meredith managed a small smile. 'They've come back.'

As if to vindicate her, a single moth fluttered behind her head, aiming for the bedside light.

'I know what you're thinking, Verity but a moth doesn't know it isn't going to live for long.' She reached out her hand. The tiny creature skimmed her skin, dived into the shaded light and Meredith caught it and cupped it in her hands. 'And for a while at least, they couldn't stop Angharad being a moth either.' She crossed the room. 'Look.'

More moths were gathering at the window. Meredith opened it and let the captive go. Confused, caught up in the melee, for a moment it flew in frantic circles before taking off into the darkness. 'Let's leave another wish in the net. And I want to sleep in here. Stay with me?'

Curled into her sister's warmth, Meredith dreamed of the blue garden, the moths and the world between the veil, and that she was finally taken by the Fae. In her place they left a well-behaved changeling child for her mother to take to London.

When she woke, she pinched her arm and knew her wish hadn't worked.

The only thing remaining was the echoing angry voice of a sad girl driven mad.

Fifty-two

There were many ways a girl made of glass could break: storms and fierce winds, lightning strikes or simply tripping up and falling over.

Verity began to look where she was going. Meredith needed her more than ever. After the incident with the key and the brief interlude of hope when Meredith believed the ghost was back, Angharad vanished.

'I think she's gone again. I can't hear her.'

Meredith was disappearing too. Verity tried to hold onto her sister, enticing her with outings to safe places like the cinema or a walk along the promenade. She tempted her with new stories, the best books the library had to offer.

Meredith no longer cared about books or films, food or dreams. She spoke only if she was spoken to, and if it was her mother, not even then. When Allegra addressed her or asked a question, Meredith stared at her and flinched as if, instead of words, she had thrown stones at her.

'You can't ignore me forever.'

Verity knew her mother was wrong.

Meredith had stopped believing in love and happiness; only in the power of fate. She sat in her room, watching for moths, waiting for the voice of Angharad.

When Verity told her the red heart from the grave had gone, and said it must mean the ghost had come back, Meredith's shoulders sagged.

'No, Verity, it means a bird took it, or a fox.'

The man finally left, for the final time he said. He would see them in London.

Allegra disappeared for hours on end, and the girls didn't ask where she'd been because they were no longer interested. When she came back, she often appeared muddled and scattered, as if she no longer had the necessary faith in herself to accomplish the venture.

Verity found her in the conservatory, packing the last of her paints, her hands jittery, unable to choose between one bunch of brushes and another, between this or that tube of paint. It was humid and the steamed-up window panes made the place claustrophobic.

Watching her, Verity realised her mother was about to go on the run, and they would be expected to keep up.

'This isn't right,' she said. 'You know it isn't.'

'Don't start again, Verity. I don't have the energy for your craziness.'

'You don't have to go, Mam, is what I'm saying. And you don't want to, do you? It's him. The rest is a pipe dream.'

'You don't know what I want.' Allegra snatched up a bunch of brushes, folded them into a canvas holder. 'This place is a prison. I can't be confined; it's time to go, escape.'

'Escape from what? You won't have any of this in London! The views and the landscape.'

'I have nothing! Do you hear me? If I stay, I'll wither away and die. You could make it easy, and what do you do? Sneak behind my back, fill your sister's head with rubbish.'

Verity's heart pounded. She took a deep breath, afraid Allegra would hear the lie in her voice. 'I don't care what you say to me anymore. And it's not as if anything Meri or I say will make a difference. You've won. Take a bow.'

Allegra's eyes blazed with triumph, or maybe it was scorn: Verity no longer tried to decipher the difference. Her mother possessed a range of expressions an actor would have died for.

'What's the matter,' Allegra said. 'Can't get your own way so throwing a hissy fit?'

The staggering hubris of this struck Verity like a blow and she burst out laughing. Even to herself she sounded a bit hysterical. 'You still don't get it, do you? What this place means to us and what it stands for: security and happiness and reason.' She searched her mother's eyes.

Allegra looked down, fastened the ties on the paintbrush holder.

'Don't start in about Meredith again. Your sister will be fine. She'll do as I tell her because deep down she knows I only want what's best for her.'

'If you say that one more time, I swear…' Verity took a deep breath. 'We *all* do as you tell us. And when have you ever done what's best for anyone other than yourself? My way or the highway – that's your stupid, selfish mantra, isn't it? You don't see *us*, our needs or our pain. You don't see our loneliness, and you never, ever give us credit for accomplishing anything.'

'Now you're being pathetic.' Allegra grabbed a paint easel. 'Your sister doesn't know what she wants and I'll thank you not to fill her head with any more of your sentimental clap-trap and your lies! It's a house, Verity, just a house. We can live anywhere.'

That's things, Verity … that's not the house… This house is special…

'You are so wrong and if Meredith heard you saying so she'd tell you the same. It's never been just a house.'

'This jealousy is becoming a real thing, isn't it?' Allegra unscrewed the wingnuts on the easel. 'You think you know her, but your sister isn't a bit like you. She's sensitive and vulnerable. You've always had a hard edge and it's horribly unattractive.'

'Is that what he says?'

Allegra's face stilled, only her eyes giving anything away. Lying in the folds of her mother's spite Verity saw uncertainty and confusion. She could see her own eyes looking back at her and held Allegra's gaze, the meaning behind her mother's words becoming clearer.

'Unbelievable. No one else exists, do they? And don't pretend you care about Meredith. You've been vile to her these past weeks, and she can't bear to be near you.' A line of sweat ran down her back. 'Why do you do this, Allegra? And why do we let ourselves be manipulated? How can you not know what an evil, scheming bitch you are?'

'How clever-clever you sound.' Allegra said it slowly and Verity felt a quiver of unease.

She stood her ground. 'Maybe I am clever; have you ever considered I might be more intelligent than I seem? To you or to me? Maybe if I'd been allowed to find out we might both have been surprised.'

As soon as the words were out they became true.

The heat in the conservatory overwhelmed her.

'Whatever else happens,' she said. 'I swear this – I'll show you I can be somebody.'

Verity turned to leave. Allegra grabbed her arm and Verity's heart sank. It was like being in a falling lift shaft. She watched her mother's face as it gave the rest away. Like an actor attempting to convey wretchedness, she clung to Verity, her grip claw-like and desperate. Verity realised she was no longer intimidated by Allegra's drama.

'What?' Allegra's voice trembled and her grip on Verity's arm relaxed.

Verity shook her head. 'You're absurd. And there's more than one kind of prison, Mam.'

Was she speaking out loud? Her heart felt so high in her throat, if she swallowed, she knew she would choke on it. Although her mother's voice levelled, her eyes still glittered and it was only a lull. Verity guessed Allegra was gathering herself for the tipping point.

Be careful what you say now … so careful.

'What's the matter, Verity? Cat got your tongue?'

'Well, she sure as sugar hasn't got yours.' Glaring at her arm, at her mother's hand, Verity willed it away. 'Look at you, Mam, scrunched up in misery trying to control everything, floundering like a fool because in spite of you; in spite of this chaos and whatever you try and make us do, eventually *he'll leave you*. We'll end up happy and you'll be on your own.'

It was only half true. Whatever the future had in store for Verity, right then she knew her sister's heart really was breaking.

'What a prospect, eh, mother dear?'

Allegra faltered, as if she had run out of words.

From up in the roof, a bird neither of them had noticed flew down and Allegra ducked as if expecting an attack.

'It won't hurt you, Allegra, only don't imagine you can hide. The birds listen and see and they know everything.'

Of all my prisons, the old hut was the least confining.

Here I could come and go as I pleased. Even so, the wood and the sky marked the boundary of my world and I dared not venture further for fear of discovery. Each day I expected to be discovered. Thanks to a God I no longer believed in, no one found me.

I was too filled with hate to die – not then – and at first barely noticed my hunger. Once it began to gnaw at me, I wandered the woods looking for things to eat. Ashamed at first, I stole birds' eggs and stilled my conscience by taking only a single one from each nest I came across. I couldn't bring myself to kill an animal; I did find a dead rabbit and made a fair job of skinning and cooking it. I foraged for the rest of my food, for mushrooms, ransoms and nuts.

Somehow I survived.

Lacking possessions and with only the clothes I wore and the stolen cloak, I made do with impersonal, less tangible things: the scent of morning, the air on my face, birdsong and the half-glimpsed faces of otherworld creatures.

I became a thing of skin and bone and revenge grew in my shrivelled heart.

Slowly the last remnants of winter passed and I was marginally warmer, but the hut was barely habitable; it was a damp, desperate, exposed existence. Before long, gloom and mildew began to surround me. Outside the door, impossibly tall nettles and deadly nightshade loomed, when it rained the dripping woods filled me with despair.

Weeks passed – maybe months – I had no way of telling, no energy to try to work it out. And I could not forget my child or the cruelty done to me. I spent my days sleeping, my nights roaming, searching for my child's resting place.

Hunger still gnawed until after a while I became immune.

I had the blanket they caught her in. I feared the scent of her would fade, instead it grew stronger; the smell of her tiny finger and her heartbeat clung to it with the tenacity of love. It settled under my skin, made of the moment before they took her, before she could turn her face to me and I could commit it to memory.

287

I never saw her face…

Time slipped through the folds of my mind. I had space only for my child, for the brief, ephemeral warmth of her. The part of me still holding any meaning and which had had no chance to grow: a child conceived in hate; the best of her born in love. For I loved her more than I could say, the only human I ever had.

If I thought about my parents, it was with a heart turned to stone. I no longer cared or thought about what might have happened to them.

As for my brother – I wished him in Hell.

Present

In this room my sister encountered a ghost who at first I didn't believe in.

We were children and my sister's ability to draw me into her fantasies was a thing, however hard I tried, I was unable to resist. Whatever the truth, I'm now convinced Meredith felt accountable to Angharad. Somehow, by becoming privy to her story, she took on the mantle of responsibility.

I turn the doorknob and to my surprise, the door doesn't creak or shudder. Inside the silence belies any notions of a ghost. And yet I can't shake off the sense that what happened in nineteen seventy-nine was real, the London years made up and meaningless.

More dust, thick as blankets, covers everything. Like the ones in my room, the books she'd been forced to leave behind lie on a shelf at angles alongside a collection of *Bunty* annuals. Hanging on the wardrobe door is a solitary frock, a small, limp relic.

It strikes me as unutterably sad.

'Where are you?' My whispered question echoes in the silent, dust-laden air.

In the corner, the doll's house stands, lonely and deserted.

Moving round the room, I begin opening vacated drawers, peering inside empty cupboards, searching for something tangible that might take me back to the real past. This version has stopped in a slip of time, folded away between the pleats of our abandoned belongings and the nonsense of ghosts.

Because she always believed we would come back, our grandmother chose to leave some things as they were. Nothing moved or tidied. Our bedrooms with their abandoned belongings resemble shrines.

I sniff; there is an odd smell and it isn't damp. It's the scent of a cigarette and I wake from my reverie, furious at the idea that the caretaker has been inside the house after all.

'Is there anyone there?'

I sound like an extra from a B-movie. The cane table next to the bed is bare and dusty. I stare. There are fresh fingerprints in the dust.

My breath leaves my body so slowly I can hear it.

I sit heavily on the bed. Under my hand the slippery eiderdown is like water. Turning away from the fingerprints I place my hand on the pillow, still wearing a case traced with faded yellow roses.

My grandmother teased Meredith about the things she kept under her pillow – shells and feathers, wild flowers and books.

My hand slips underneath the sad flatness of the pillow, an act of unconscious connection and I'm surprised when my fingers find something. Not a book or a forgotten feather. Sliding my hand back and forth, I feel for the note Meredith wrote to the house before we left, a last act of love.

It isn't there.

The envelope is. It's ripped, the edge ragged as if someone has opened it in a hurry, or in anger. Something pale detaches itself from the pillowcase and settles on my hand. It's a moth and even in death it is perfect.

I remember believing my bones were made of glass, and I sit perfectly still, afraid I might break.

Fifty-three

A silken dawn broke over Gull House.

Inside the tension mounted, as if the fabric of the house was becoming agitated. Doors stuck, ceilings creaked, the boiler clanked and rattled. Outside, cunning winds shook windows, found gaps that before hadn't existed.

The fire was out, grey ash spilled onto the hearth. Allegra was cold and wanted a fire. Casting around for kindling, she discovered the box was empty. She grabbed it and yanked on the backdoor handle. It resisted her and close to tears, she kicked the door, screeched her fury as her toe hit the wood. 'You stupid fucking thing! For God's sake, what the hell is going on round here?'

'It's the house; it doesn't want us to leave.' Meredith, still mutinous around her mother, occasionally allowed herself to speak. 'You'll regret it.'

Allegra fixed her daughter with calculating eyes. 'Don't think that'll work, you silly girl.' She hit the door with the heel of her hand, tears of frustration spilling over. 'Stupid games, stupid door.'

As if it heard her and resented the accusation, the door flew open and Allegra almost lost her footing.

'The sooner we're away from this place the better.'

When she turned, Meredith was gone.

Verity slept late, dreamed of the ocean and as soon as her eyes opened she remembered the man and lost her dream.

Quickly she pulled on her clothes and came downstairs. In the kitchen she could hear her mother swearing. Meredith flew through the door, her face paler than chalk, her hair rust-coloured tumbleweed.

'What are you looking at?'

'Nothing. Are you okay?'

'Never better, thanks.' Meredith's voice was ragged with the effort it took to hold onto her tears. 'She's lighting a fire. I wouldn't be surprised if she's planning to set the entire house alight.'

Verity didn't know what to say.

'Don't look at me like that, Verity. I'm not *twp*. I'm not *demented*, even though she thinks I am, and given half a chance she'd have us both locked up, the way Angharad was.' She gripped the bannister. 'That way, she could be done with everything: the house and us. I wouldn't put anything past her.'

Before Verity could conjure an adequate response, her sister was running up the stairs her feet barely touching the carpet. Tiptoeing across the hall, determined to avoid her mother, Verity opened the front door and raced across the lawn to the lookout. Sitting with her back against the tree, she gazed across a vast sky to the clouds shifting like silver-blue scales.

Let's go sky-fishing…

She let her eyes move slowly, taking in each familiar point and landmark.

As she stared at the rocks, they quivered as if they were alive. Her arms were folded around her body, tight and taut, and she felt heavy: heavier than the rock and it was as if she had changed places with it.

She couldn't move and realised she didn't want to.

I'm saying goodbye from here, where I can see it all and make a memory.

Fifty-four

Meredith's fear was palpable.

She wandered through the house touching objects; talking to them as if to reassure them, even though she was convinced they wouldn't be coming back. If she caught sight of her face in a mirror, she didn't recognise herself. She dreamed silent dreams. Time and her weightless arms and legs moved through grey air touched with glimpses of silver like rips in cloth, and Meredith dreamed she saw Angharad. As she reached out to the slashed edges, they sealed up.

Two nights in a row she woke, certain the ghost was in her room. There was nothing – only a jumble of frantic whispers in her head. And then she felt a touch on her hand as if fingers stroked her skin.

Have you come back..?

Something brushed her hair and Meredith froze. And then it was gone and it was impossible for her to get back to sleep. She lay in a half-dreaming state until dawn.

Seeking her reflection in the mirror again, what she saw was paler than any ghost.

One night she went out to the blue garden and waited in the last place they had seen Angharad.

Above her and between the black leaves of the trees, stars burned holes in the sky. She thought she glimpsed a figure between the trees; it could just as well have been mist in the shadows. She lay down by the twig baby's grave and fell asleep amongst the forget-me-nots and speedwell already beginning to grow over it.

In the middle of the night, Verity woke and checking her sister's room found her gone. She ran out to her grandmother's garden and found Meredith covered in leaves with tiny double-winged insects like miniature dragonflies hovering above her.

Fairies...

'Wake up, Meri,' she whispered, 'come on, it's the middle of the night.'

'Don't leave me.'

'Whatever happens, I'll never leave you; never go anywhere you can't come too, or follow and find me.'

'Do you promise?'

'You know I do.'

Meredith's eyes brimmed with tears. Verity touched her cheek and they knew they were holding a moment they wouldn't ever relinquish.

Brushing leaves off her legs, Meredith said, 'They've started falling. It's too early. The magic is spoiled.'

Verity's glass bones shivered; her sister's hand was cold as ice. 'You're freezing. We'd better to go inside.'

'Do you mind if I stay by myself a bit longer?'

'Of course not, but don't be too long.' Verity pulled off her cardigan and wrapped it round her sister's shoulders. 'And sleep in my bed, yes?'

Meredith nodded and watched her sister walk away, running her palm down the frame of the gate, as if to make an imprint of the wood on her skin. She stared across her grandmother's garden, to the wisteria – in spite of knowing it was pointless because the ghost had gone. Her tears left salt tracks on her face. She thought she heard the sound of sobbing so raw, a piece of her heart died.

It was over.

'I want to write a note for the house,' Meredith said, flourishing a pencil.

Her hair was a red-gold halo against the window. Long fingers hovered over a page of thick paper.

'Did you nick that from Allegra?'

'What if I did? The least she can do is to provide some nice paper.'

Verity didn't ask her sister what she planned to write.

Meredith's head bent to her task. 'How about this?'

Her writing was pretty with the right amount of flourishes.

Dear house
We won't forget you and we promise to come back.
Look after Angharad Elin Lewis and her baby.
Signed Verity and Meredith Pryce (sisters)

'It's perfect.'

Meredith sealed the note in an envelope and as she slid it under her pillow, Verity touched her sister's hand. A small spasm shot through her.

'If we believe, Verity…'

'Yes, I know.'

Meredith's face was a mask made of desperate hope and resignation. She smelled of sorrow and dead roses and as Verity watched the tears fall down her face, the wish she whispered to herself settled on her heart like a brand.

We will come back, I promise.

Part Three

Part Three

Present

The letter has somehow found its way to her.

She is in a garden, under an agapanthus blue sky. It's hot, more yellow and red than green, what grass there is gilded and shining, tiny blades of gold. Her pale skin still recoils from the sun and she shelters in the shade of a lemon tree filled with tiny brilliant birds.

The birds are different here...

As they take off their wings sweep through the brittle air. She blinks and for a second she's in another garden, white and smooth as her grandmother's bed linen. Her bare toes scuff the sandy ground, her eyes drawn westward, to where this white-hot sun will slip below the horizon.

Your handwriting hasn't improved.

The paper is pristine and white.

White as snow.

Closing her eyes she falls.

Her sister waves and smiles, laughs when she says she can't wave back because she's making angels' wings. The golden shimmer turns to silver. They shimmer too – girls in snow drifting in fat flakes, deeper and deeper until they are gone.

Her eyes blink open. In spite of the heat, her skin is icy; the sweat on her chest runs cold.

It's too late, Verity...

The sun starts its slide, falling away into another sea: underworld and oystercatchers and a mackerel sky...

Looking at her hands, she floats in the heat. Blue flowers sprout from her fingers, trail across the snow white paper.

I knew one day I'd be gone too long to go back...

Fifty-five

Under a sky rendered unreal by sodium lights, Mared Pryce noticed how the light fell on the wet pavement making it look like glass.

She thought how her granddaughters would hate the non-silence and the rattling, the lines of parked cars and the raucousness of it: the buildings, row on mile and never being alone. Trying not to mind for them she wondered if, for once in her life, her wilful daughter might yet be persuaded to see sense.

Who am I kidding?

Mared rearranged her brother's home, and crossed her fingers.

The first floor apartment was old in an entirely different way to Gull House. Elegant in its Georgian simplicity, number twenty-three was a house to be quiet in. Tall windows looked out onto a grassed square edged with ornamental plants, surrounded by iron railings and mature trees. Ornate lamps cast false night-light. In the centre, a statue of a woman – her draped gown fixed in perpetual flight – gazed at passers-by with blank eyes.

Mared drew her granddaughters to her, doing her best to soothe their fears.

Meredith's fears woke the house up.

Clocks struck the wrong hour; dust spiralled into spiteful whirlwinds, landed on piano keys sabotaging the sound. When Mared sent for the piano tuner he said he couldn't find anything wrong. In the room she had made warm and welcoming, windows that normally didn't budge unless forced, began rattling; moths no one had ever seen before caught in the curtains. Busy with her brother, whose fragility meant he no longer knew who anyone was, Mared struggled with this new chaos.

Meredith rescued the moths and told Verity it was proof Angharad wasn't done with them. When she found her coral necklace, tucked inside a pair of socks, her conviction overrode Verity's insistence it must have been there all the time.

Meredith threw her a look like knives.

'You wait,' was the only thing she said.

Both girls became unhappier versions of themselves but when they went to London, Meredith broke. She became fearful of the smallest things. You would never believe a girl who would happily sleep in a wood under the moon could be so terrified of traffic and trains or tramps in doorways. Meredith, who, before she left Gull House hadn't been afraid of anything, in London became a hostage to irrational fear.

One night she fled the house, convinced the bedroom was full of spiders. The noise of the front door slamming woke Verity and she ran downstairs. She caught up with her sister and held her as she sobbed her terror.

'I want to go home.'

'I know you do. So do I.'

'I'm not afraid of anything in Wales.'

They walked back to the house, two grey shadows with no direction.

It was a devastating time. There was nowhere for Meredith to be happy. Her yearning for home was so deeply embedded she stopped eating again. Meredith tried to forget about gulls and trees, cried herself to sleep and listened for the voice of a ghost.

'Where is she, Verity?'

Verity said she didn't know.

'Because you don't care.'

It would have made sense to assume that when they were forced to leave Gull House it would bring them closer. The opposite happened. Meredith blamed Verity for not standing up to Allegra the way she had tried to.

301

Meredith's fears had been confirmed. London was every bit as daunting as she had expected and worse – her mother really did intend sending her to school. Helpless, she improvised her way through the days in a state of shock and if Allegra didn't notice it was because she was rarely around to see anything. Busy settling into the flat the man had found for them, she had no time for what she called tantrums.

And once again it became Verity's fault, only this time her sister blamed her too.

When Verity began attending the local comprehensive school Meredith said that if her mother tried to make her go, she would run away.

'And don't expect me to tell you where I go.'

Meredith's fear of London meant there was nowhere to run to; she was too young and frightened to take off on her own.

She wondered if Angharad was disappointed in her, and that was the reason her ghost had vanished.

Are you brave enough…

Not brave enough to run away, the way Angharad had.

Forced to join her sister at school and paralysed by fear, Meredith was finally confronted by the kind of girls she had always dreaded: critical, condescending in their taunts and without mercy. Clever too, in comparison, because school learning came down to the kind of knowledge Allegra had eschewed as pointless. Meredith knew what time the moon rose without opening her eyes but she had no idea how far away from the earth it was.

And it wasn't only her clothes that were wrong; she didn't understand these terrifying girls or their culture, their music or their gangs. From the first day, she played truant vowing as soon as she was old enough, she would run so far no one would ever find her.

'It's not a threat,' she told anyone who would listen. 'It's my best promise.'

It was easy to dismiss it as another of her obsessions, even her grandmother made the mistake of brushing aside the warnings.

Her teachers reported her as a truant.

Mared muttered, '*Déja vu*,' and, 'Talk about history repeating itself.'

Verity, to her surprise, found school easy. Her natural love of learning exerted itself and she was too ordinary to become the butt of anyone's negative attention. When she tried to protect her sister from the inevitable bullying, Meredith turned on her, declaring Verity's willingness to go to school collusion.

'Stop pretending you care,' she yelled. 'And you don't have to worry about me; I'll cast spells on them all.'

She insisted Angharad would come back and save her.

'Her story isn't finished and when she finds me, those bitches will regret saying so much as a single word to me.'

At night in bed she was too scared not to allow her sister to comfort her. When Verity asked her how she felt, Meredith said the word was too long; too hard to spell or remember.

Even Mared ran out of ways to make her feel better.

'Leave her be, *cariad*,' she said to Verity. 'She'll work it out for herself.'

And eventually, she did.

Fifty-six

Meredith left each morning in a version of her school uniform, fooling no one.

It was anyone's guess whether she showed up and Verity, seventeen months ahead of her, stopped checking.

Distracted by other responsibilities, Mared shrugged her shoulders. 'She has to work out her own demons.'

'Is there nothing you can do, Nain, to keep her safe?'

'How do you know I haven't?'

If Mared said this to reassure Verity, if she cast a small spell to keep her other granddaughter from harm, it was no one's business but hers.

Meredith grew taller and thinner, lost in a world she didn't share, opening the bedroom window each night to let in the moths. She tossed and turned in her sleep, called Angharad's name.

'Are you having dreams again?' Verity asked.

'Like you care?'

Verity tried to reassure her sister she could trust her with her dreams.

'I'm not the enemy.'

The strength of Meredith's love for the ghost knew no bounds. Somehow the voice of Angharad Elin Lewis had followed her to London, and Verity knew it.

'She knows what we did,' was all Meredith said. 'I told you there was more.'

London broke Allegra too. In another part of the city, she tried to make the best of things. It soon became clear her best wasn't working.

Mared insisted they spend their weekends together and that Allegra saw the girls alone. 'He's nothing to do with them,' she said. 'They come first. It's the least you can do.'

Allegra, already sensing the precariousness of her situation, on the edge of denial, reluctantly agreed.

'If you got to know him,' she said to Verity, 'you'd—'

'Don't.' School made Verity braver. 'What's he up to anyway? Organising your first exhibition?'

The man was a presence casting another kind of spell. Until he turned up, Allegra's life had been driven by the shade of her vanished husband. In an effort to recapture the past, she'd embarked on an endless search for perfect love into which she fell, time and again, like a puppy down a well. Each time she reinvented love, she created another version of her life. This time it was different. In thrall to her lover, she embraced his ideas; and yet her yearning for a metropolitan life in London made no sense. Allegra may have been artistic and eccentric, but she wasn't sophisticated. And of course, she never listened.

On principle, Mared said, in case she heard the truth.

Mared had suspected the truth from the beginning. When Allegra asked her again about selling Gull House, her fury exploded.

'I knew he was a wrong 'un. Now will you see sense?'

'I don't see what the problem is. We won't be going back and I need money...'

'Who says you won't go back? And what do you need money for? I thought he was going to see to things? Introduce you to his fancy friends; watch you dazzle them with your talent.'

'It's not as simple as—'

'Oh, I think it is. He has no contacts, Allegra, he never did. Not the right ones at any rate, just a few wannabe wasters and conmen. He's a cheapskate looking for easy money and he saw you coming.'

It was true. And Allegra knew it.

She'd met them – his contacts – with their imitation leather jackets and coarse language. They filled the flat with their maleness and innuendo, and bottles of placatory gin. No one owned a gallery; they hung around the fringes of an art world they saw as an opportunity, uninterested in art for art's sake.

They were interested in making money and getting wasted.

When their snake eyes ignored her paintings, and she looked to him for validation, the man changed the subject. When they told jokes at her expense, he laughed and told her she was imagining things.

'Don't stress, baby, these things take time,' he said. 'And nothing works without money. Talk to your mother again about the house. Or a loan, she owns two properties for fuck's sake.'

She wasn't comfortable with the kind of language he was beginning to use. And when she tried to explain there was no money – Gethin owned the London apartment and Mared couldn't be persuaded to sell Gull House – she watched the passion in his eyes change colour.

It was the mistake too many of Allegra's casual lovers had made – the assumption of wealth. Gull House played its outwardly grand role well. Old things made with attention to detail give off an air of prosperity and greedy people are the easiest to hoodwink.

Love, or what passed for it, had followed Allegra all her adult life, the way the smoke from her liquorice cigarettes did. She moved like a murmuration, first this way then that, pausing, forging ahead, never properly still. And in her wake they came, seduced by her and then by what they imagined she might own.

He left her to paint, he said, and went about his business.

Most people only saw what was obvious. When it came to painting, in Wales Allegra had seen beyond the normal colours of water and sky and stone; she'd seen the loveliness beneath the surface, hints and tints, gold-flecked and luminous as butterfly wings. In London, it wasn't there. When she tried to paint, the new, garish colours looked wrong. Bird droppings smeared the skylight making the room dark.

'What am I supposed to paint,' she asked him, 'if I can't see the sky?'

Allegra talked a lot about being in control of the events in her life when in fact she was imprisoned by them. Sitting in a dingy flat she hadn't bargained for she thought about the nature of a bargain. It was, she had assumed, an agreement, a thing one person did for the other. Surrounded by paintings she was beginning to despise, she feared she was in control of nothing. The empty room closed in on her and her fear.

Being abandoned had always been Allegra's greatest terror.

And it was happening again.

The season changed, the way seasons do.

Through the trees a keen wind blew the first hint of snow. I soon realised nature was not the friend I thought and because there was no one to talk to, forgot how to speak. I had no strength left, no will. Weak and starving I succumbed to a fever. I cried pitifully at first; then with such a depth of anger it washed away the fever, and any kindness from my heart until the only thing left was a desire to survive until I found her.

Months of foul food in the asylum had trained my stomach and although I was accustomed to hunger, eventually, I became too weak to move.

And always, the longing for her, an ache that refused to leave me.

Death took my baby's breath; the scent of it was in the air and the soil, and in the scrap of blanket. It wrapped itself into me and I embraced it. The wretched part of me gave in; floated up, found the spaces and places to cling to and wait in.

Your heart, child, is as big as the moon.

I have not abandoned you… I followed you because you are brave enough…

Present

The early bluebells make patches of the grass look as if they've turned to water.

Mared's garden will soon be filled with them. I hesitate and change my mind. In front of me the wood looks denser than I remember, as if, like the garden, it has drawn itself in, become less visible. It is lovely and forlorn, thick with wild-branched trees, dark and whispering.

Follow me...

In my hand, the ripped envelope crackles like a dead leaf. Not wanting to damage the moth, I fold the envelope and slide it into my bag. Stepping toward the trees, I sense the wood waiting to gather me in. The silence is muted and overlaying it I hear the sound of the sea.

Next time I go to the wood, I'll listen for it...

My foot catches in a root and I place my hand on the trunk of a tree to steady myself. There is still no apparent path and I hesitate.

Second stone on the right...

I can't see it, can't see a thing I recognise. It is wilderness woodland with no directions. Only the green makes sense, the intensity of it catches in my throat.

And then I do see something – a tree with a cleft where Meredith left offerings for the Fae, and caught on a twig, a scrap of torn cloth. It reminds me of summer leaves and I loosen it, clutch it in my hand.

I walk in a little further, my footsteps vanishing behind me.

Fifty-seven

Verity hadn't asked to be part of Angharad's story.

Her sister had other ideas. Meredith's imagination possessed wings; it could sweep you up like an unexpected midsummer wind. Certain the ghost of Angharad wasn't done with her, Meredith said she'd begun to hear her voice again, and Verity was once again drawn into her sister's obsession.

The bedroom they shared was barely big enough for both of them. If Verity missed the privacy of her old room, and the sound of the sea, she consoled herself with the thought that for Meredith it was probably far worse.

'Meri, it's over, you know it is. I'm not being horrible; I don't think Angharad's here anymore, that's all. We did our best.'

They were getting ready for school.

Meredith stamped round the room.

'You've broken your promise,' she said. 'You told me we were in this together.'

Verity, with homework to contend with, refused to bite.

'I still believe you, Meri. You're the one being stroppy and giving me a hard time.'

'That's not fair.'

It wasn't and Verity swallowed her irritation. 'Okay, but it's over, and you have to accept it.'

'You're a hypocrite; you're only saying it to shut me up. You can go to hell.'

'You don't mean that.'

'I mean everything I say. How can you not hate it here? Even the birds are different. I don't understand their songs.'

Outside the window, Verity could see the trees in the square, brown birds littering the branches.

'You just have to listen harder.'

'Oh shut up, Verity, you aren't helping.' She snatched up a pair of patterned leggings from the floor.

Meredith no longer pretended to wear school uniform. She threw on an oversized jumper so many sizes too big it reached her knees, and the green Dr Martens boots she'd persuaded her mother to buy in return for a trip to the cinema. Rings Verity hadn't seen before littered her fingers.

'You look quite cool,' Verity said, attempting to make things right, ignoring Meredith's bitten nails.

How do I make it the way it was?

Meredith rammed a rose-coloured beret over her wild hair and sneered. 'I look unapproachable, which is the idea.'

Verity pulled on her school skirt and blouse, began brushing her hair and although she missed Meredith so much it made her heart ache, she knew she couldn't afford to allow her to make a bad situation worse. She knew when your old life disappeared the only thing to do was make a new one.

'If you aren't going to school – and I know you aren't – I've got a free period this afternoon. Why don't we go somewhere?'

Without expecting to, Verity had begun to find London fascinating. Walking or travelling by bus, at first she found herself excitingly lost, jumping off wherever the fancy took her, discovering bookshops and parks, libraries, cafes and alleyways leading to broad streets full of the sort of shops she had never imagined. Through their doors came the kind of music that made her blood sing.

'Come with me, Meri,' she said. 'Bits of London are wonderful and not in the least bit frightening.'

'Who says I'm scared? And you have no idea what I do or where I go.'

'So why don't we swap notes then?'

'Because I don't trust you.'

If she meant her words to be brutal she was successful.

Verity tried not to look as shocked as she felt.

'If you really cared about me, Verity, you'd listen to me instead of trying to create some fake friendship that ended the day you agreed to go to school.'

'I wanted to go to school. I always did.'

'Which makes you a liar as well as a traitor.'

'White lies, Meri, the kind you're always saying are fibs, so I wouldn't upset you.'

'I'm not upset, Verity, I told you, there isn't a word for the way I feel.'

'You know we have to go to school.'

Meredith glared. 'But not like this. Not here!'

'No. I didn't plan it like this either, but…'

'Fuck but.'

'Meredith!'

'Sorry, I didn't mean to swear at you. I'm not the one lying though. Not this time.'

'So you admit you sometimes do?'

'Maybe.'

Verity smiled and sighed. 'I don't know what to say.'

'I don't want you to say anything!'

'All right, I'll listen then. Tell me.'

'There's nothing to tell, except she's back.' A tear bloomed in Meredith's eye. 'I can hear her. She told me death took her baby's breath, and she gave up. I think it means she died.'

Verity pressed her hand to her chest, her voice dropped to a whisper. 'You heard her say that?'

'She found a place to wait – for me – she says she hasn't left.'

Verity's heart skipped too many beats. She wanted to tell her sister she believed her. All she said was, 'I'm sorry.'

Meredith shrugged. 'It doesn't matter. I've been in this by myself from the beginning. You've never cared about Angharad, not the way I do. And now you have your precious school…'

'How dare you say I didn't care? I saw her remember! I saw her first!' Verity snatched back her apology. 'If you weren't so busy being a brat maybe I'd be more inclined to listen to you.'

Meredith's face drained of what little colour it had and she burst into tears. 'I can't bear it, Verity. I don't know who I am anymore. It's like you've left me behind, she hates me, Nain is always with Gethin and if I don't have Angharad, who am I supposed to believe in? I've lost everyone.'

'You haven't lost me, Meri. I'm trying to make sense of things too. We do this stuff differently,'

'You promise?'

'Always. I believe you – if you say Angharad's here, then I believe you. And you can tell me anything.'

Meredith gulped and sniffed.

'And though I know it doesn't look that way,' Verity went on, 'Allegra does love you – she loves us both. She just loves him more right now. It won't last, Meri, we'll get her back.'

Meredith crossed the road to the square. The leaves on the birch trees were turning to gold, spiralling in the light air, looking for a place to be.

She wondered if, when winter came, it would snow. Sweeping leaves off the bench she wrapped herself in her misery. This kind of being alone stung, as cold as icicles, sharp enough to hurt her. She watched the London birds, listened to their songs and her heart longed for the sound of gulls and the smell of snow.

Fifty-eight

Although she was one of her earliest obsessions, Meredith dropped her mother as if she were nothing more than a redundant bus ticket.

She found Allegra out, and it was as if the proverbial light bulb lit up.

They were expected to spend weekends with their mother, ostensibly to give Mared a break. In reality, it was to make Allegra look like a responsible parent and, Verity suspected, to keep her company.

She persuaded Meredith to go. 'It won't hurt you and she's—'

'She's in the process of being dumped.'

The man periodically absented himself.

'He has things to do,' Allegra said waving away their enquiries. She chain-smoked now and her cough was worse.

They both hated the flat. Situated over a junk shop, in spite of a large skylight, it struck them as depressingly sleazy: two pokey rooms furnished with what the owner of the shop couldn't sell, plus a tiny kitchen and bathroom. A destitute smell of stale milk, cigarettes and sex permeated the place.

After only a few visits, Meredith refused to go again.

'She can't make me.' She refused to use her mother's name.

Allegra tried everything, from bribes to entreaties.

Meredith missed the way things once were too much to allow her mother to make amends.

She accepted the Dr Martens boots with a shrug.

(*More fool you.*)

'Please, darling, can't you see how much I miss you?'

Meredith remembered the way her mother had looked when the man came into a room at Gull House, how her attention had snapped away like an elastic band.

'You're pathetic. I will never forgive you.'

Concerned about how much her mother was drinking, Verity confided in Mared.

'Is it him? Is he making her drink more?'

'Maybe, to be honest, *cariad*, it's an old addiction.'

'You mean because of Idris.'

Mared sighed. 'Yes.'

'Do I need to worry about it?'

'They always drank a lot. It was him got her into it but she didn't take much encouraging. And when have you known her not to drink?'

'I guess.'

'Don't overthink it, Verity. It gives her courage.'

It's making her ill.

Verity didn't say this and her grandmother didn't say what was on her mind either.

'Do you think she still loves Idris?'

'Addiction's a hard thing to shake.'

'She never takes the pearl ring off does she?'

'Pearls are for tears, lovely,' Mared said. 'What did she expect? She tells the world she won't forgive him, yet she can't let go.'

'You always manage to make me feel sorry for her.'

'Good. She's your mother, and however it looks, she loves you.'

To Verity her mother's kind of love was incidental and conditional.

'It's a waste to love someone who doesn't love you back.'

'That's as maybe, *cariad*, the trouble is, Allegra's heart is her weakness; it's where she keeps her truth.'

Verity thought about her mother's imperfect heart, locked into an impossible version of reality.

'Love makes mischief, Verity. You keep your eye open for its tricks.'

For a moment, Verity felt her own heart speed up.

'I told you before,' Mared said. 'I was always a bit scared of your mam.'

'You aren't scared of anyone!'

Mared laughed and her spectacles wobbled on her nose. 'She was a holy terror when she was little, and as for discipline, well… Forget it. In Allegra's world, she was always right and from the start my instinct was never to cross her.'

'Even though you're sometimes quite strict with us?'

'Am I?'

'A bit.'

Mared laughed again and said it was different with grandchildren. 'You get a second chance to get it right.' She stroked Verity's hair, told her she was a good girl and it was easy to be kind to her and her sister. 'Your mother took over – I can't explain it – not in a way that makes any sense.'

Verity didn't need an explanation; she had the evidence of her own eyes.

'Allegra's problem is she didn't fall out of love enough with Idris to fall in love with anyone else.'

'She seems pretty loved up with this one.'

Her grandmother made a rude noise. 'It's something, *bach*, I promise you, it isn't love.'

Verity did her best to persuade Allegra to come to the apartment in the square.

'Nain misses you.'

'We both know that isn't true.'

From time to time Allegra acquiesced; it was the only way she was able to see Meredith. Her daughter had other ideas and all too often, even if no one mentioned her mother was coming, Meredith wouldn't be there.

316

'You reap what you sow,' Mared said.

'And you can't wait for it to go wrong, can you? Still trying to ill-wish me, Mam?'

Allegra raged and most of the time Mared fielded the verbal blows as if they were thistledown.

It wasn't always easy.

One evening, after Allegra brought her back to the apartment, Verity overheard an argument. Hovering in the hallway, she listened to her mother's plaintive whine.

'It's a pile of stone no one cares about.'

'It's a pile of stone *you* don't care about. Shame on you, Allegra for asking me again. Your children love Gull House, it's their inheritance. My physical body may be here, my heart's still in my home.'

When Allegra stormed out of the house, Mared turned to Verity as if she had known all the time she was there.

Her voice was alive with passion. 'Remember this day, *cariad*. And my promise: under no circumstances will I ever sell your inheritance.'

Fifty-nine

After only one term, Verity decided to leave school.

It was 1980; she was sixteen. Her life may have changed, her ambition hadn't and she had a plan.

You should consider librarianship … you could do a lot worse.

Encouraged by her grandmother, she signed up for college. It was the first step on the road to university. She didn't tell Meredith, suppressed the guilt and told herself it made no difference.

She's hardly ever at school anyway.

Verity finally turned into who she was. She bought her own copy of the book Miss Jenkins had introduced her too, and more besides.

'Old before your time, that's what you are,' Mared said, peering over her shoulder. 'Goodness me, you're getting serious.'

'I've always been serious and you're never too young to find things out, Nain.'

Mared flipped through the books, let her eyes dwell. 'If you ask me, feminism is another version of kindness.'

'Does it mean you're a feminist then?'

'Women died so I could vote, and I do vote, so yes, if that makes me a feminist, I guess I must be.'

'Allegra isn't. She says women's libbers are man-haters.'

'Allegra says a lot of things that don't bear scrutiny.'

'Could Meredith ever be one?'

'Your sister has to work out who she is before she can work out what she is.'

'I think perhaps they're the same.'

Mared smiled. 'See? I told you, old before your time.'

She looked like any other girl on a bus on her way to college. An ordinary girl reading a novel; perhaps looking up now and then, staring out of the window before returning her gaze to the page. In her jeans and neat blouses, her hair tied back with an Alice band, you would take Verity Pryce for a shop girl or a typist.

Or a trainee librarian.

Her carefully arranged face disguised whatever delight or disaster lay beneath. Verity Pryce learned to make the best of things. College opened doors and she marched through them, light on her feet, wearing the green boots Meredith decided she no longer wanted to wear.

'After the fuss you made?'

'I didn't make a fuss, I made her feel guilty and it worked.'

'But you love them.'

'I don't want anything from her.'

From an open book Meredith changed into one as closed as a locked diary. She couldn't bear for people to see who she really was – a lost girl with a hole where her heart once was – so she let them see a made-up version, a weirdo no one wanted to get close to.

A million words stuck in her throat and she wrote herself in invisible ink hiding anything that might give her away. She began wearing the kind of clothes that drew attention to her defiance.

With Mared's permission, she rooted in her grandmother's wardrobe; borrowed Mared's sewing machine, cut up old tea dresses, dyed them black and remade them into floating extravaganzas which, if she had seen them, Allegra would have envied. She twisted her hair into dreadlocks, bought a pair of granny boots and played *Rumours* until Verity threatened to throw the record out.

The change to Meredith's life had happened in a moment. Or that was how it seemed to her. She'd had no time to prepare. One day she was in Gull House, the next an alternate, dismal narrative sidled in, took the place of the other one, and what went before became a memory.

She continued running away from school, and eventually kept her promise and ran as far as her granny heels could carry her.

With her own life falling apart, Allegra had nothing to spare for her traumatised daughter. And the education authorities didn't appear to care about Meredith's absences. Warnings about prosecutions washed over Allegra's head like rain, and Meredith fell between the bureaucratic cracks. Already in danger of disappearing, she went unnoticed, as if she had finally learned how to make a spell that worked. She drifted in and out of the house, dressed in black, barely speaking.

One day, Verity followed her and discovered her sister hanging out in a local park with a group of people bedecked like troubadours, swathed in a sweet scent Verity suspected might be marijuana.

Meredith didn't mind her sister discovering her.

'Hey, sis,' she said, 'how's it going?' and Verity realised Meredith hadn't called her 'sis' before or used any kind of language reminiscent of a world she'd thought neither of them knew much about.

Somehow, Meredith had found it; fallen in with a group of people who expected nothing of her and at the same time, in the event she had anything to say, were willing to listen.

If I want to I can make flowers grow from my fingertips…

Because they were kind, they pretended to believe her. Then they saw how deeply her sorrow was etched, how her tears turned to seeds and then to flowers an impossible shade of blue, so beautiful no one knew the name of them.

It didn't matter if it was true or not. Imaginary flowers would do nicely.

They introduced Meredith to the animal rights movement and she joined *PETA*; joined in protests against animal farms.

'Animal suffering isn't new, Verity. It isn't only women who need liberating.'

She celebrated her sixteenth birthday by turning up at school in an anti-vivisection t-shirt, to inform her teacher she wouldn't be coming back.

'That'll show her I'm not the rude, stupid person she says I am. I could have just as well have not bothered.'

She moved out of her grandmother's house and into a squat, and at first her new friends fed her. When Mared, deciding to side with the devil she knew, made her granddaughter a small allowance, she bought food to share and made her room so beautiful that people came from miles around to admire it. Her originality drew the sort of friends who liked her for her own sake, for her gentleness and generosity, and she became a true bohemian, the kind Allegra could only aspire to be.

She promised Verity she wasn't smoking drugs and Verity decided it didn't matter if her sister was lying.

I tell fibs to keep you safe...

Meredith was far more addicted to the past than she would ever be to drugs; she didn't want to forget anything.

'Just because the pieces of me look like they're holding together,' she told Verity, 'it doesn't mean bits of me aren't broken.'

'Are you going to be all right?'

'Of course I am. I'm always all right.' She didn't look at Verity when she said this. 'I have Angharad.'

'I thought...'

'You thought because I'd stopped talking about her, I'd forgotten her? Oh, Verity, you mustn't worry about Angharad.'

Verity hadn't thought about her for months.

'I told you before, she hasn't left me. She'll follow me wherever I go, until she gets to the end of it.'

'Have you told your new friends about her?'

'No. Why would I? She's my secret. And they're the same as her; they don't expect anything, they just want someone to listen.

321

And they don't ask questions. They live in a world they've chosen because the real one doesn't have room for them. When I'm with them I can lose myself. I forget the bad stuff.'

'Like Angharad?'

'You know that isn't what I mean.'

'Sorry. I—'

'Verity, I don't mind.' Meredith smiled her grave smile. 'About her.' Her refusal to use their mother's name had become a habit. Her eyes still looked like lights but it was as if a dimmer switch had turned them down. 'It doesn't matter. About Angharad either. I can do it by myself.'

'Do what?'

'Listen? She's still telling me, and it's still sad. So sad sometimes it's hard to hear because her voice is getting fainter.'

'Can you tell me?'

'Do you still want me too?'

She'll follow me wherever I go…

Verity's glass bones clinked together and she held her breath.

Tell me everything, because I don't think you're going to stay…

I survived neither the grief nor the elements.

In the end, it wasn't only the cold or starvation that brought me to my end. My heart withered and once winter came, I lasted only a short time and one night I died.

Slowly, with the dying back of the season, my heart curled in on itself and turned to dust. Too weak to search for her, I gave in, tucked the tiny flannel heart under my worn-out gown and drifted into my final sleep.

If the God I no longer believed in proved to be real, then perhaps my child and I would be reunited. Maybe I would discover angels were real. If not, I had the remnants of my hurt and prayed that unlike my mortal self, my unquiet spirit wouldn't give up.

I became as light as a feathered wing, as heavy as death's sleep, a thing made of vapour and dead bones.

The creature I became still searched for her resting place, for her lost child...

When they found me, they declared me a suicide and disposed of my remains in a place where no one would know I had existed. They put me in the ground but although they stripped me of my tattered, gown, they didn't care enough to remove my chemise.

They left the little red heart still attached to my silent one.

In my cold, unmarked grave I was not found. Like an animal no trace of me remained. My flesh became a feast for the worms, my bones turned to dust and the earth took them.

Only my bloodless ghost heart beat on.

When the snow came, it fell like a final shroud, softening the ground and hiding all trace of me. It weighed down the trees where only the birds bore witness.

I will write my words into your dreams ... because you are brave...

Present

The hut is hard to find, the markers gone, consumed by the wood.

I wonder if it's been pulled down. The path, such as it is, is largely hidden and I use my forearms to fight my way through ferns and branches alive with liquid green.

It never stopped being her favourite colour. I open my hand, realise I've dropped the scrap of green cloth and I search fruitlessly for it. The woodland green is a disguise and I give up.

Something brushes my hand and I start back, half expecting… What? A fairy?

They aren't the kind in our storybooks, Verity … they're Other…

Looking down I see a spider web lying against my skin and brush it off.

The trees thin, open out and here it is, in a patchy clearing dotted with clumps of tall grass: the hut, a huddle of partially visible lichen-covered stone. What is left grows out of the ground, the past reclaimed by nature. Vines and brambles wind over what remains, knotting and concealing. Beneath the ivy, I still recognise the shape of it, the short run of wall, the corner where we sat and I allow myself a brief smile because like so much I'm discovering today it strikes me as smaller, the way things are when we grow up and go looking for the past.

I'm standing in a memory.

She'll follow me wherever I go…

For a while, in London, Meredith hovered on the edge of insanity. In the end, she took herself off, saved herself by leaving, wandering with the wind. Allegra threw her hands in the air and said she supposed her daughter was trying to find herself. It was the opposite. What had been sacred to Meredith was lost and the only thing she could do was keep moving, taking this or that fork in the road, not caring enough to find out if she had a place in the world.

The air is alive with the smell of wild garlic and old fungi.

A place where ghosts come to mourn...

Sixty

To no one's surprise, the promises and assurances Allegra had relied on turned to ashes.

One day the man upped and left and only Allegra found the fact impossible to grasp.

'It's not like we didn't try to tell you,' Meredith said, not caring if she sounded cruel. 'You should have listened.'

'And look at you,' Allegra said, 'turning up to mock.'

It wasn't altogether untrue. Meredith hadn't seen her mother for months. Nagged by her sister, she'd agreed to pay a visit.

She watched Verity emptying ashtrays.

'He must have said something to one of you. Did he?' Allegra's voice was tight with disbelief.

'Mam, you know he didn't.' Verity laid the poppy shawl round her mother's shoulders.

'Well someone must know something.'

'He told you what you wanted to hear, until he realised there was no money.'

'Meredith, that's enough.' Verity pushed her sister out of the room. 'Go away, you aren't helping.'

'I didn't come to gloat. I came to please you.'

'I know, even so, you aren't helping.'

Meredith shrugged, took her bruised heart outside into the echoing grey of a London sky.

'She hates me,' Allegra said.

'No, Mam,' Verity said, 'you broke her heart – you can't expect her to care about yours.'

Her mother's grief was immeasurable. Allegra had burnt her

rotting boat and nothing would ever be the same again. Verity tried to work out when the despair began but it was before she was born, when her mother was a favoured child, carried everywhere by a father who'd adored her. And then he died and it was the first loss, the first desertion.

Allegra wasn't made to be left behind.

Dumbfounded, Allegra slunk like a beaten dog, began drinking on her own in a nearby pub and once or twice became so intoxicated one of the barmaids had to bring her home, find her keys and see her up to the flat.

Verity did what she could. The flat became more chaotic. Her mother smelled of something other than sweat and gin. A trace caught in Verity's nostrils.

If despair had a smell this would be it.

She cleaned the flat, threw out the empty gin bottles; took the bed linen to the launderette. She found her mother's tarot cards, abandoned under a pile of clothes.

'We could do a reading if you like.'

'You despise my cards and in any case, I don't trust them with the truth.'

A pessimist at heart, Allegra was too deeply wounded to any longer believe in anything.

'Humour me.' Verity shuffled the cards and spread them face down on the floor. 'Go on, pick one. Please?'

Allegra shrugged, snatched a card and turned it over.

Silver stars decorated a blue sky; a solitary golden one hovered above a naked woman kneeling at a pool. She poured water from two pitchers.

'What does it mean?'

'Nothing.' Allegra flipped the card onto the floor.

'Are you sure? You always used to say the cards explained everything.'

Allegra looked as if she was watching from a distance.

'I can't be explained,' she said, her voice shaky and unsure. 'Because I'm not me, don't you see? Not anymore.'

That makes two of you.

Later, remaking the bed, Verity found the book about the tarot underneath it, read the page about the star card and how, without the inspiration of the star, a person's life could become drab and without purpose.

Perhaps the tarot cards knew more than she thought.

Bereft of hope, her wild illusions shattered, Allegra drifted into a state of melancholy.

'Please go away,' she said to Verity.

Given time, both Verity and her grandmother thought Allegra would come round. They were wrong; the man's leaving was a desertion too far and Allegra's mind changed course. As the weeks passed, they realised the grief wasn't temporary. With the unkind parts of her diminished, Allegra no longer had the energy to be mean to anyone.

My mother is fading.

Verity's fear crept in and she visited her mother whether she liked it or not.

'You again,' was all Allegra said, pouring herself a gin, fingering her dull curls, the neck of an unwashed frock.

Verity plucked up the courage to ask her mother why she drank so much.

Allegra looked so pained she wished she hadn't.

'It isn't to forget, if that's what you think.' Allegra sighed, as if she was weary of breathing. 'I'm tired of old clichés, Verity.'

The glass trembled in her hand.

If before she had drunk to forget, now, she said, it made her brave enough to remember.

'I was an artists' model, did you know that?'

'Nain said.'

'You should have seen me those days, I was a beauty; they all wanted to paint me. Before Idris, I had so many admirers. He wasn't that special.'

A tear bloomed on the edge of her eye. She tipped her glass, drank down the dregs.

Don't overthink it … it gives her courage.

'It's only anger keeps me going, Verity. Keeps me in touch with who I really am.'

Verity watched her mother and knew it wasn't anger.

Her mother was scared, fearful of forgetting and terrified of disappearing.

Sixty-one

A year passed: it was 1982 and John Lennon was still asking people to imagine a perfect world.

The Pryce sisters still dreamed of deep snow. In London snow flew sideways, as if it was in too much of a hurry to land.

Verity and Meredith sat in a café drinking hot chocolate, watching. It was a dusting, barely an inch.

'I've seen thicker snow on a Christmas cake,' Meredith said.

She still lived in the squat and had a part-time job at an animal shelter.

'You wouldn't believe how many dogs get abandoned.'

Verity thought her sister looked abandoned. She was thinner than she'd ever been, edgier, and the skin on her face looked as if it might shred if you touched it. Steam from the hot chocolate began fogging the window and outside the snowflakes turned blurry and blue.

'Are you eating properly?'

Meredith laughed and it sounded like bells. 'Of course I am! Verity, have you seen the food parcels Nain makes me take away every weekend?'

The thin snow drifted against doorways, making little white heaps. Wherever they looked, Londoners lapsed into complaint, grabbed shovels and attacked.

'It's like they see snow as the enemy,' Meredith said. 'Why can't they let it alone? Let it be white for at least a day. People in London are ridiculous.'

Neither of them said a word about Welsh snow and how they missed it – the cleanness and taste of it. How, when it snowed in Wales you couldn't hear the birds, as if they too were in awe. In

London buses still rumbled and doors slammed, agitated voices rang out. In the country when it snowed, the world fell silent.

'How's college?'

Verity smiled. 'You don't have to pretend to be interested.'

'I am interested! I love knowing how you're getting on.'

'Well … I passed my exams. I'm going to university.'

'Oh my days, Verity, that's amazing! You clever thing, you're actually going to be a librarian.'

'I actually am.'

'And you won't have to get married!'

'No.'

'When you're famous and working in the best library in the world, I shall tell everyone you're my sister and how lucky they are to have you.'

'And what do you think you'll be doing?' Verity crossed her fingers and made her best wish.

'One thing's for sure, I won't be here.' Meredith rubbed a space in the steamy window. 'Look at it. Imagine having to live here all your life.'

The snow was already turning to slush, discoloured and grey.

Verity kept her eyes on her sister, tried not to look as if she was noticing how Meredith's hair was red as molten copper and the dreadlocks coiled like magical snakes, how the edges of her eyes were lit up with sparks.

Don't leave…

Over her black clothes, Meredith was wearing a coat one of her friends had given her. It was meant for a soldier and looked as if it might drown her. She didn't care – in London no one noticed what she wore and the coat kept out the cold.

I have to remember her…

Verity changed the subject.

'Do you still hear…?'

'The ghost?'

Verity noticed how Meredith no longer said Angharad's name.

'Sometimes. A while back, she told me they buried her in unhallowed ground.' Meredith chewed her lip the way she used to when she was little. 'She said she would write her words into my dreams.'

'Oh, Meri, that's beautiful.'

'She was beautiful. And the bravest person I've ever known. She was ... audacious.'

The way you are... Don't go...

Another smattering of snow slipped past the window.

'Will it settle? It did last year.'

Meredith shook her head and her hair moved like coiled rope. 'I don't remember.'

Verity knew this was a lie. Meredith had simply dismissed the snowstorm that hit the city just before Christmas.

'It's not like the Welsh kind,' was all she'd said.

The air in the café was warm and heavy. The mirrors and glasses, even the sugar shaker, reflected Meredith's hair making them sparkle like fireflies.

'Go on then,' she said, 'I know why we're here. I know you want to talk about her. I can read your mind. It won't make any difference; you can't make me care about her.'

Verity tried not to feel hurt for her mother. She wanted to be on her sister's side, only if taking sides hadn't worked in the past, why would it now?

'Don't tell her anything about me, Verity.'

Hurt for herself now, Verity snapped. 'I never tell your secrets.'

'All right, I'm sorry, so tell me. What's worrying you this time?'

Verity heard the edge of indifference, how pointless an argument would be.

'Sometimes,' she said, 'I look at her and she's like snow: impossibly beautiful only underneath it's the same old crazy, the same old darkness.'

Meredith drained her mug. 'We're all like snowflakes – we're unique.'

'Allegra isn't unique, not any more. I'm worried about her, Meri.'

'She'll be fine, and if she isn't, there isn't a thing you can do about it. People make their own lives. Their own luck.'

'I know but…'

'She's unique, we all are. Snowflakes may look the same when they're falling, they aren't – and people *en masse* look the same too.' She nodded to herself. 'The trick, Verity, is to see your own singularity and be a snowflake.'

A hundred years have passed and this garden has become as blue as longing, beautiful and darkly protecting.

The ghost of me waited through a hundred winters under the weight of snow and the secret it concealed.

Because of you, I was finally able to wander in my forever night into the places where I'm safe – in the wood and this wild garden hoping, always hoping to find her.

You knew me … and I knew you … I knew you … I knew you…

I am a ghost and I have written my story into your dreams in ink made from my blood and the tears of birds.

You heard me.

You are brave enough for both of us.

Sixty-two

Meredith left soon after.

Verity almost missed her going. When her friends decided they'd had enough of the cold, it was time for an adventure, and asked Meredith if she would go with them, she smiled and said, why not.

She told her sister she'd thought about not saying goodbye because she didn't want Verity to try and stop her.

'Then I decided you wouldn't let go of me until you knew there was no point in holding on.'

'What am I supposed to do, if you go?'

They sat on the bench in the square, watching the sky, still hoping for snow.

'Write me down in your address book and I'll seal it with a kiss.'

'What do I write?'

'My name for now, I'll let you know the rest when I find it.'

Verity found a pen and Meredith dug a deep red lipstick out of her bag, made a lipstick kiss on the page.

'There you are. Now you won't ever lose me.'

'Can't you at least stay until Christmas?' Verity, bareheaded, wearing a long, navy-blue coat, held her gloveless hands in her lap.

She still didn't feel the cold.

The trees were bare and against the pale sky they looked like a scribbled drawing. Verity watched how their shadows ran away from them across the gravel and onto the grass on the other side of the path.

'Nain will be so disappointed if she doesn't see you over the holiday. Without Gethin the house is empty…'

(Mared had finally been persuaded her beloved brother would be happier in a home. 'This is his home,' she had said to Verity. 'Yes, Nain, but you can't manage. Neither of us can.')

'… and I'm out all day now,' Verity went on. 'Can't you please stay, until Christmas Day?'

Meredith blew into the wool of her mittens to warm her hands. 'I'm sorry for Nain, really I am.' She paused. 'I don't want to see *her*, Verity.'

Verity nodded. 'Aren't you nervous, going off like this?'

'Not particularly.'

'I would be.'

'No you wouldn't.' Meredith said, 'You're far braver than I've ever been.'

'You've always done what you wanted.'

'That's not bravery, Verity, it's self-preservation.' Her voice softened. 'You stuck to your guns and followed your dream. And look at you now. You're practically a librarian.'

For a moment neither of them said a word. Then they grinned and each of them made a face and said, 'A lib*rar*ian!' extending the middle syllable in an almost perfect imitation of their mother. They burst out laughing and the sound of it sent a group of starlings into the air.

Meredith watched them fly away. 'Don't call me brave, sis. I'm not. I'm a fraud, like her. Maybe if I go away I'll work my real self out.'

Verity turned to face her sister, laid an arm across the back of the bench. Meredith was wearing the rose-coloured beret and although most of her hair was caught inside it, a few red dreadlocks escaped and Verity touched one. 'I love your hair that way.'

Meredith stroked her sister's bare hand and said nothing.

'Why do you have to go?' Verity maintained her gaze.

'You know why.'

Verity did.

'Not really,' she said.

Meredith carried on stroking Verity's hand. 'Spain isn't so far. It's warm there and maybe I'll finally learn how to swim.'

'I want you to stay.'

'I know.'

Meredith leaned back, still holding Verity's hand, and swung her crossed feet sideways catching her heels on the gravel, the movement creating its own momentum.

'You'll ruin your boots,' Verity said.

Meredith said they were only boots and things could be replaced.

It's only things, Verity … not a house…

'She'll miss you.'

'No she won't.'

'She's not as bad as you think and she's our mother…'

'We don't have parents, we have escape artists.'

'And that's why you're going.'

'Not entirely.' Meredith shuffled down the bench, leaned against her sister's shoulder. 'I'm no one here, Verity, and when you aren't anybody you have to make yourself up. I've been doing it ever since we came here and I'm tired of it.'

A chill ran through Verity and it had nothing to do with the weather. Before she could speak, Meredith put her hand in her pocket and brought out a little box. She fumbled: the woolly mittens made her clumsy.

She opened it and inside lay one the red hearts.

Tears sprang into Verity's eyes. 'You kept them.'

'Of course I did. I'll keep them forever; the sewing-box too. I want you to have this one. Keep it close and so long as you do we'll never be parted.' She pressed the heart into Verity's hand. 'We'll be inseparable. Indivisible.'

'You and your words.'

'You and your rationality.'

Verity drew in a breath and blew it out, slowly, through pursed lips. 'You're going soon, aren't you?'

'Today.'

'You can't go today!' Verity sat bolt upright, put the flannel heart down on the bench between them. She waited, not trusting herself to say anything else.

'Yes I can,' Meredith said picking up the heart and thrusting back into Verity's hand. 'And you have to take this and keep it and you know why. It'll be all right, sis, I promise. We'll be all right.'

Don't make promises you know you can't keep…

Verity brushed the heel of her hand across one of her eyes and didn't look up. 'I hate it when you call me sis.'

'All right, Ver-it-y,' Meredith said and laughed. 'Verity, my best beloved sister, you have to promise too – you won't come looking for me.'

'I can't promise that.'

Verity said she hated her, because she didn't know what else to say and because she wanted Meredith to cry, to be upset enough to change her mind.

Meredith didn't cry; she smiled and said, 'No you don't, you love me. Now swear on this, that you won't look for me.' She pulled her battered copy of *The Lion, the Witch and the Wardrobe* from a deep pocket in her soldier's coat. 'And never say you hate me, only evil people say that.'

'Idiot.' Verity placed her hand on the book. 'I swear and I'm sorry; I don't know what I'm saying. Of course I love you. It's why—'

Meredith pulled her sister to her feet, took off her mittens and held Verity's face in her hands, the way Nain did. 'How about we make a deal? If I promise to keep in touch, you're allowed to come and find me, but only when you've found the magic. I'll come back for that.'

Verity only half understood what Meredith meant; she knew it was the best she could hope for. 'And you'll always let me know where you are?'

'Always. My name's already in your silly old address book, remember?'

'You promise?'

'On Angharad's life.'

It was the first time in ages Meredith had said the ghost girl's name. She fished in her pocket again. 'Here, it's your day for being given things.'

In her hand lay a silver pendant shaped like a snowflake. Meredith opened the top of her coat, pulled out an identical one on a chain.

'To remind us we're unique.' She placed the pendant in Verity's palm, drew her into a hug.

Verity closed her eyes, soaked up the scent of her sister's hair, her old grief, her impossible optimism and it spread through her like medicine.

'Like a spell,' Meredith whispered. 'And you aren't allowed to worry about me either.'

Their faces touched. Verity was on the brink of tears. She breathed deeply, inhaled Meredith some more, the scent and the inside out of her.

'I'll always worry about you.'

She kissed her sister and let her go.

Sixty-three

Allegra stopped painting.

It wasn't a question of talent. She no longer drew any pleasure from her work and saw no point in it. For a while after Meredith left, she painted images of her daughter in emeralds and greens as pale as new leaves. She painted her lost daughter with green eyes and hair, dozens of pictures, each one poignant with her loss and missing until she could bear it no longer and gave up altogether.

There was no longer any ego to Allegra and Verity found it unbearably sad. The shadow of a perpetual hangover clung to her mother as if the only thing she wanted was to exist in a state of withdrawal from the world.

Because she was taller and still gauche, Verity remained in her mother's sights. But Allegra had used up all her insults.

'What am I doing in this dreary place?' she asked, as if this daughter must surely have the answer.

She patted tobacco into liquorice paper. The scent filled the room. Verity watched as Allegra twisted excess fibres from the end, dropped them into the pouch. She lit up and immediately began coughing, harsh paroxysms causing her to hold the heel of her hand against her heart.

'Mam?'

'I'm fine. You never give up do you?'

The idea Verity might not know her sister forever only occurred to her once Meredith was gone.

Now it was her turn to be broken. Although Meredith stayed

in touch she was always reticent about her whereabouts. The only clue would be a stamp and a smattering of foreign words in amongst the English ones. In her neat, pretty hand she told Verity about bazaars and souks, heat and oceans as clear as glass. Although she insisted she loved the freedom, Verity knew that when a person took off with no directions it was usually because they were trying to get away from themselves.

For years, what saddened her most was the absence, the whirlwind of Meredith's obsessions, the cadence of her voice; the brilliant lights in her eyes foreshadowing her various moods.

Verity knew her sister wouldn't want to be found.

On the few rare and precious occasions she telephoned, her voice always sounded as if it was a million miles away.

'Where are you?'

'It doesn't matter where I am, so long as I'm somewhere.'

If it wasn't enough it would have to do. Verity pieced together her sister's tattered life as best she could, made her promise to stay safe.

Meredith continued to send cards and occasional letters, from Spain then France and Italy, until she moved further away and they tailed off. Verity added each new address and tried to understand.

One night Meredith telephoned, sounding so far away she might as well have been on the moon. For an entire minute lasting an hour, she didn't say a word and then told Verity not to worry, she was fine and the line went dead.

On Verity's eighteenth birthday, a parcel arrived, postmarked Morocco, and inside was a pair of soft leather gloves, dark blue, lined with grey fur, inlaid with the most exquisitely embroidered silver stars.

"*Wear them at night under the moon,*" she wrote on a card, in her delicate writing.

Star gloves from Morocco.

It sounded like the name of a song.

Sixty-four

Verity met Carla in her first week at university and it began with a random act of kindness.

Carla was lost, outside the wrong lecture room and Verity pointed the way.

Later, this time in the right place, they met in the café. They were drawn to one another from the beginning and if other people viewed their relationship with a raised eyebrow, they took no notice.

Verity, who had long suspected when her prince turned up she might be a princess, noticed how Carla moved between other people as if they were merely tall grasses in a breeze. She placed her tray on the table at precisely the same moment Verity put down hers.

'Hello, again.'

Neither of them gave their meeting more than a passing thought, until one day they did and it was perfect. Around them, people played the field, fell in love, broke up, broke down. Verity and Carla made friends and made it last.

'You are my still point,' Carla said.

She had huge brown eyes and spiky hair the colour of toast. She was studying English Literature, loved The Smiths and that first day had roared with laughter when Verity said she preferred The Clash.

'Who's a dark horse? I wouldn't have had you down as a punk.'

'I'm on a mission to erase the relentless sound of a Fleetwood Mac earworm.'

'*Pourquoi?*'

Carla had a way with words too.

'My sister was addicted to Stevie Nicks. Still can't get it out of my head.'

'And punk's the antidote?'

'Do I look like a punk?'

Carla said no, Verity looked like she meant business, as if she knew more than she let on and she had dreams.

'I have a dream of a common language.'

'Adrienne Rich?'

'You've heard of her?'

'She's my shero.'

In the centre of Carla's dark eyes, paths opened and Verity held her breath, held herself back.

'And your sister?'

'My sister is mine.'

Within weeks Verity had told Carla so much about Meredith it felt like a betrayal. They wandered along the banks of a stream, watched the sun glittering on the water, shivery shadows of willow trees caught in the ripples. Carla brought a paper bag full of stale bread. She threw the bread out across the water and dozens of ducks appeared.

'Disappearing and going away aren't the same,' she said. 'Whichever way you view it though, the person isn't there. Telling me is safe, Verity.'

'My mother thinks she's never coming back.'

If willing a person back had any power, Mared and Verity would have succeeded.

'My grandmother said my father left because he needed to be anywhere my mother wasn't.'

'Is she so bad?' Carla emptied the last of the crumbs onto the grass.

'Worse.'

'Do you reckon she's right? About Meredith?'

Verity said she didn't know. 'Allegra's fragile. She's forgotten how to be optimistic, or happy.'

Her heart is her weakness…

'My sister is another one of my mother's disappeared dreams.'

Verity watched a crow fly across the sky.

'I'm not going anywhere,' Carla said. The paths in her eyes opened, welcoming Verity in.

'I know.'

Allegra had been nineteen when she met Idris, the love of her life who lasted only a few years. At the same age, Verity already knew some kinds of love could last forever.

Saved by work, Verity fell into it with a diligence she hadn't known herself capable of. Discovering she was right about her small ambition, she remained forever grateful to Miss Jenkins for her trust.

Over the years Meredith's absence stretched.

Verity stopped missing her as a presence; she missed the person she feared she might no longer recognise. So long as she had the snowflake pendant and the red flannel heart, she had to believe her sister's face wouldn't fade.

'I'm sharing too little of my adult life with her,' she said to Carla. 'There ought to be two of us noticing, being affected by what's happening to Allegra.'

'I notice.'

'You're amazing.'

She showed Carla some photographs of Meredith.

'She's gorgeous. Like your mother. You can see it. They're both so quick and stylish.'

Impractical and volatile was what Verity saw. 'They're a couple of absurd show-offs.'

'Beautiful though.'

It was undeniable.

'You're definitely my favourite. You must admit, though, they're both pretty stunning.'

Verity thought about her mother, lost and heartbroken (and

now, she feared, unwell). As children, Verity and Meredith had accepted Allegra's loveliness – they were used to it.

She showed Carla the photo of Meredith making snow angels.

'Oh my goodness, that's a classic,' Carla said. 'And that's real snow.'

'Wales is good at snow. It's our magic.'

'No wonder you miss her.'

'Every year on my birthday she sends me a gift. Nothing grand – a stone or a feather, a necklace once that broke, and most of the beads fell between the floorboards.'

'You're always in her heart then.'

Verity explained how each gift came with a note; lines from songs, random words Verity guessed were aimed at keeping the past alive.

Underworld and a shell the colour of rock pools. *The songbirds keep singing like they know the score,* accompanying a little blue bird made from glass.

'She's never sent my mother a single thing. I stopped showing Allegra; she still can't bear to be left out. If life isn't about my mother, it doesn't exist. And Mam and Meredith are more alike than just looks. Their obsessions were like babies or chickens to them, until they began to cry or peck.'

Carla laughed. 'Did you have chickens?'

'Cream Legbars, my grandmother's favourite. Meredith adored them. It broke her heart when … you know. Leaving and everything, and the chickens had to go. And Mam didn't give a damn for Meredith's feelings.'

'And now she's shut herself away.'

'When we were kids she was everywhere – only she wasn't – if it makes sense. Like an indignant ghost.'

'The best kind, I love a good ghost story.'

Verity hadn't told Carla about Angharad. If her ghost was still around, Verity no longer sensed her.

'Do you ever consider going back?'

'To Gull House?'

'Why not?'

Verity scraped the soles of her boots on the path. The sun shifted in the silver-blue sky and she imagined the same sky in another place, and Meredith, a moth on the wind.

'Maybe, one day. Allegra won't go back and I can't abandon her. And in any case, my life's here now.' She paused. 'Meredith said she'd come back when I found the magic.'

Carla didn't say anything. It was her speciality.

'She said she'd come back when I found it, the magic we knew when we were kids.' She frowned. 'I wonder if she looks the same, if I'd know her.'

'You make it sound like ages. It's only been a few years. And do people change so much we stop recognising them?'

The idea Meredith might have changed beyond recognition, that her radiance might have dimmed, was too much.

'I can't be bothered with it,' Verity said emphatically. 'I have to look after my mother, and my grandmother. She's feeling guilty about Gethin being in a home, even though he's perfectly okay.'

'You have to think about you as well, about getting your degree.'

'Yes, that too.'

'You can't save everyone, Verity.'

'No, but I can try.'

Sixty-five

It gave Carla no pleasure to be proved right.

Allegra's health began to cause real concern, her dependence on cigarettes and gin finally exacerbating a childhood heart condition.

Her heart is her weakness ... it's where she keeps her truth...

As her light dimmed, Carla did her best to get Verity to face things.

'Your mother's very ill,' she said.

With Meredith between nomadic destinations, it had been comforting to have someone to lean on when Allegra refused to take the doctor's warnings seriously. Whether this was out of fear or her life-long talent for dismissing anything inconvenient – or simply against her better judgement – was anybody's guess.

Alarmed by her daughter's deterioration but short on patience, Mared almost gave up. And when it came, the force of her grief at Allegra's death was devastating.

Mothers aren't supposed to bury their children.

And Mared watched her daughter die. She was there, at her hospital bedside when Allegra's poor, beaten, shattered heart stopped.

The depth of her own wretchedness overwhelmed Verity.

Allegra died from heart failure. She was fifty-nine and it was too young. It didn't matter what the doctors said about an old defect, Verity listened and nodded and pretended to agree. She knew the truth; it was possible to die of a broken heart.

The funeral was a quiet affair lacking the flamboyance Allegra would no doubt have chosen. No one spoke about the fact Meredith wasn't there. The space next to Verity, a seat left vacant for the missing daughter, loomed like a reproach.

The letter Verity sent might have gone astray. She told herself Meredith could have moved on again.

Maybe it's because she doesn't know…

She didn't believe this for a moment.

At the funeral, Verity didn't cry. She sat in the crematorium, listening to a stranger talk about her mother, the artist, and tried to understand her better.

She was an artist – a brilliant one – it was her talent and her tragedy.

'We didn't hate her,' she said to Carla. 'She was just too much, too certain and larger than all our lives. Is it terrible that I'm still struggling to forgive her for Meredith leaving?'

'You'll find a way,' Carla said. 'You aren't as unkind as you think you are.'

Verity knew better. 'I'm not sure I can excuse her.'

'Allegra didn't accept she was responsible. She was too narcissistic to realise it.' Carla stopped. 'Sorry, that's unforgiveable, it's not my place.'

'No, you're right.' Verity allowed herself a smile. 'I knew there was a word for what my mother was. Now I know, maybe I can learn to be kinder.' A tear came into Verity's eye and it was the first time in her life she cried for her mother.

Mared's sadness was unbearable. She shrank before Verity's eyes and though she picked up what pieces were left, some of them didn't quite fit. In the weeks after Allegra died, Verity sat with her grandmother watching her watch her tea go cold. Mared's hand stroked the wild silk poppies of Allegra's shawl, sliding it through her fingers like a rosary until Verity wondered how the colours didn't rub right away.

Carla did her best and it was good enough. She made chicken soup and washed clothes, visited Gethin even though he didn't know who she was. And when he died and Mared was too stunned to cope, it was Carla who helped organise the second funeral.

The years passed and Mared's silver hair thinned and yellowed. Her skin shrank on her bones. She stared out of the window, watching the street, searching for a flash of colour unfurling under the grey London day. She was so still she could have been dead, yet behind the stillness she was as alert as she'd ever been. She noticed what she could be bothered with and never failed to hear Verity's quiet tread across the carpet, the cat padding into the room.

Her death was a different kind of dying, another version of a breaking heart, as if she had no more use for life.

One day she was gone and there was another funeral to organise. With the arrangements made, a kindly man at the funeral parlour sympathised, asked if there was anything else he could do.

'Thank you, no,' Verity said. 'I come from a family of mourners.'

It was a bright day better suited to a wedding.

Verity and Carla, older, still making love work, stood beneath a flowering cherry tree in the crematorium grounds, watching the petals fall like pink snow.

'I can't believe she didn't come.'

There are certain things that even if they don't appear to have changed, are never going to be what they once were. Like moths or gardens made of blue flowers, or girls who have to run away in order to find out if the dreams they once trusted still exist.

Present

Gulls wheel on the thermals, calling and seeing the things birds see.

The view is timeless. I'm reminded of how it was when we were children.

This is our castle and no one can scale the ramparts...

A vast cloak of ivy and bramble smothers most of what remains of the ruin. There's no longer an obvious way inside. I drag a swathe of ivy to one side, clear a space, sit in the crook of two walls on the exposed remains, lean against crumbling stone and close my eyes.

It was always more her place than mine.

There is a sound from the trees, a rustling movement and my eyes flick open. I turn, look around.

Nothing.

For a moment I worry about the invisible caretaker, a tramp...

A bird calls and I don't recognise it.

Even the birds are different ...

In my bag the empty water bottle emphasizes how thirsty I am. And the torn envelope reminds me of the moths in Meredith's old bedroom. I can't get the dusty fingerprints out of my head, the smeared handprint on the mirror. The cigarette ends. Telling myself to get a grip, I take a deep breath and behind me, in the folds and shades of green, something definitely moves. A branch snaps and a deep shiver runs through me.

I'm not alone and I don't know if I'm afraid.

'Who's there?' My voice is pathetic, it trips me and I'm overcome by an intensity of knowing.

My fingers reach for the dip below my throat, find the snowflake pendant. Around me, dozens of paths reveal themselves – the green is illuminated and the old trees watch me. Letting the pendant drop against my skin I close my eyes and when I open them again everything is where it's supposed to be.

Uncertain still, I stare into the dark trees, through the creepers, thoroughly unsettled and I don't know what to do. Ferns wave and the trees are making faces and hers is everywhere, made of leaves, a pagan green woman with ivy trailing from between her lips and her hair wild as green dandelion clocks.

She steps from between the crowded trees, and I see her hair is red.

I am dumbfounded, until I look into her eyes…

… and they are hers.

The colour and shape of my sister's eyes stare at me from this pagan woman's face.

'Meredith.'

I do not make it a question because I know it's her.

She stays where she is. She's wearing a trailing green scarf with snowflakes on it.

'Verity.'

My name on her lips sounds odd to me, as if I'm hearing it for the first time.

She is smoking a cigarette. The smell of it unfurls away from her.

'You don't smoke.'

She regards the cigarette as if it's nothing to do with her. 'Apparently I do now.'

I swallow; my mouth is as dry as sandpaper. 'How did you know I'd be here?'

'Where else would I look for you?'

'Why would you look for me at all; after so long?'

'I never stopped.'

'You didn't come back when she died.'

A shadow crosses my sister's face.

'Nain's dead, too.' I'm deliberately cruel and I know it. I'm fighting a mixture of fury and another emotion threatening to wash me away. What does she expect? I hold my ground, dare her to cross it. My fingers holding the envelope are hot and I may set it on fire.

'Oh, Verity, please don't hate me.'

My heart lurches, unkindness takes wing and is gone.

Pulling the envelope from my bag, I say, 'I found this, in your room.'

My sister holds out the note. 'Yes, it's a clue.'

I take it; gaze at her message, the pencil faded to a palimpsest, still legible to Meredith because her heart has held its meaning and kept it alive.

'It's all been you? The finger-marks on the mirror, the fag ends…?'

'All me.' She flicks the cigarette away, pulls a key from her pocket and holds it on her palm. It's the one from the conservatory.

'No tramps?'

She grins. 'Is that what you thought? Oh, Verity, tell me you aren't still as cautious as a cat.'

The note drops from my hand and she is in my arms.

'Meri, oh, Meri.' My voice shakes and it sounds like it belongs to a girl made of glass. 'It's really you.'

'It's really me.'

'I don't hate you.'

'I know.'

'You stopped writing.'

'I'm sorry.'

'It's been so long.'

'Twenty-one years, eleven months and six days.'

I pull away, grip my sister's hands and gaze into her perfect silver-grey eyes, touch the torn edge of a green scarf dotted with snowflakes draped carelessly round her neck.

'You don't do maths.'

She flicks her hair over her shoulder. The dreadlocks are gone. It looks the way it did when she was a girl, wild as mutant dandelion clocks, a conflagration of reds.

'That's not maths, Verity, it's counting.'

I have been waiting for so long, I've lost count. Meredith hasn't. She's stepped from a green wood, from across the blue sea; she has smoke curled in her hair, like our mother, and she can keep count. And I realise my memory is intact. She's still part of me, my wild sister and I know the shape of her heart. She's under my skin, threaded into my heartbeat, her shadow is stitched to my edges.

My glass bones shimmer, reflecting every dream I've ever had in the past twenty-one years, eleven months and six days.

Come back, Meredith, bring me stories from the other side of wherever you are, from other seas and other sands; tell me about mountains and castles and fields of magical flowers.

My body is light as a feather, the glass is gone and I know if I fall I won't break.

'You're here.'

'I'm definitely here; I didn't leave. I made a spell story for us before I went, so we'd never be apart.' She puts her head on one side and for a second the lights in her eyes flash like Catherine wheels. 'It was my best one too, I made it from snow and prawns and dragon's tears, stars and a twig baby's smile.'

It blows through me, my sister's spell story; I hold my breath and catch it. I can hear a bird and I know it's a thrush.

If love went away for too long, I always thought it might not come back. I was wrong.

'What happened to Angharad?'

'I'll tell you later, it's your turn now, Verity. Tell me your story.'

The sunset on the sea turns it to wine, impossibly shot with gold from a sky layered with pale cloud.

353

Gulls, their flung wingtips hovering, bank away and from the edge of the wood we watch them fly out over the garden toward the ocean.

I won't allow her to apologise. 'We've both done what we needed to. None of it was our fault.'

My sister nods. 'We thought we'd grow up stupid and have to get married.'

'Did you?'

'No way! My legion of lovers is a story for another day.'

She winks and I am overwhelmed with love for her.

'When did you decide to come back?' I say. 'Was it because you thought I'd found the magic, like you said I'd have to?'

Meredith is fiddling with her hair. 'Did I say that?'

'You know you did.'

'I wasn't ready to grow up.'

'You've always been grown up.'

'Not as grown up as you.'

We stare at one another and we're young again, two little girls hiding in their grandmother's garden, determined not to be found.

Meredith shades her eyes. 'Would you believe I can swim under water now and hold my breath for ages?'

'Like a pearl diver?'

Pearls are for tears ... what did she expect...?

Our grandmother's voice fills the air and emerging from the trees we make our way to her garden. Pausing at the gate I push down on the latch. When the gate sticks in the ruts I bend down, clear knots of grass. I tug the gate forward, enough to make a space we can slide through.

In the dim shade of the wisteria, grown vast in our absence, bluebells stray through the garden, the scent of them making us giddy with delight. I listen for the birds. It's silent and I imagine them pausing, wondering who we are. Untouched for two decades the garden has a secret loveliness and what we can see is also what it still hides.

We have to bury her...

The garden is full of seeds and worms and snails; vast ferns and a myriad flowers, and in the corner, the graceful elongated branches of the wisteria dripping with lush blue lanterns.

Wistful wisteria ... sad, but a lot prettier...

The memories I have spent the day resisting flood in.

'Can you still smell snow?'

'I don't know,' I say, 'it's not the same in London.'

'Allegra never believed you.'

'She hated snow.'

'I haven't seen snow for so long, I've forgotten what it looks like.'

'Make a wish, then, you never know. It's still April.'

Meredith grins. 'You wish.'

'Am I allowed to talk about Allegra?'

'Of course you are. I gave up hating Mam years ago, you know. It was me I had to work out, not her.'

I ask her if she thought Nain knew Allegra wouldn't ever be happy.

'I expect so. She was the cleverest of us all.' Meredith picks a bluebell, pokes it into her hair. 'Allegra just wanted to be loved.'

Her heart is where she keeps her truth...

In this moment I know my mother better.

Something still niggles.

'She made you go,' I say.

'No, Verity, I made me go.'

She is making it easy, making it make sense.

'You know I would have come back if I could.'

'Yes. It's all right.'

It will be, she's here and I can forgive her anything.

I hesitate. 'Tell me about the ghost.'

'She didn't leave, I told you. She's still here.'

So is Allegra.

Meredith strides ahead, parts tall grass and waist-high nettles, steps over roots and doesn't trip up.

She belongs here.

'Come on, sis.'

She disappears; the unrestrained garden gathers her in and I stumble after her. In the centre of the blue garden where we buried the twig baby, she stands, arms at her side, hair hovering as if it might lift her off the ground.

'Look.' Her voice is so normal, I feel foolish.

Here the weeds have been respectful, kept their distance. Tiny blue flowers gather, a sweet carpet: speedwell, violets and harebells. Meredith kneels down and I join her.

From the soft grass where the twig baby's heart would have been a small tree has taken root.

It's about four feet high, a wild lilac in fragile bloom and gently scented. Shaped like a girl, the upper branches reach in a dance of arms and twiggy fingers; lower down, blue-tinged flowers flutter like a gown. Meredith reaches for my hand. My vision blurs and I can't see anything. A dusting of chilly air as light and thin as spider web curls round us.

I smell snow.

Meredith lays her other hand on the ground, feeling the earth.

We have a special spell to make… We'll have to make it up…

I can see my sister surrounded by her makings, turning twigs into limbs and flowers into hair.

Flowers grow out of my fingers…

I see her painting the twig baby's face and how gentle she was as she wrapped it in the scarf she stole from our mother.

How she handed me the shovel…

'Oh, Meredith.' My voice is a whisper. 'We did it.'

My sister leans into me, I can smell the ocean and old stars; I can smell snow.

The light is fading and a mist is beginning to float through the garden. There is a clatter of wings, a cloud of birds rise and call before settling back into the wisteria disguised as brown flowers.

The birds saw everything.

Taking the envelope from my pocket, I open it; slide the moth onto the palm of my hand.

Meredith reaches out a finger, touches the dusty membrane and shudders. It isn't the unexpected cold; she's crying.

'I loved her so much.'

I hold her shaking body to me, my lost sister who never really left.

'She loved you too, because you were brave,' I say, 'and believed in her.'

'She was the brave one.'

'We're the Pryce sisters, we were born brave.'

Meredith snuggles into me. 'Can you hear her?'

I can't. It doesn't matter, because Meredith always will.

Somewhere a bird begins to sing, the notes trembling in the air and my sister takes my hand. Her skin is softer than I remember; it's like the sea and I think I shall ask her to teach me to swim.

Other birds join and I can hear their grace notes.

'She told us,' Meredith whispers. 'The birds miss nothing.'

The moment melts a hole in the sky and snow begins falling.

Whatever you may have heard, child; I didn't take my own life.

It was they who killed me.

And it was never that I was mad. What they did to me made me that way…

The birds gave this garden their blessing. I exist in the spaces between their songs and the rustling of leaves, in slivers of light between dusk and darkness, in folds of night and drifts of snow.

Leaving the world you see more clearly; you choose which pieces to remember. My story is told, and I move through a light that no longer exists.

My child is laid to rest.

Each lost thing is found.

My name is Angharad and I am not mad.

ACKNOWLEDGEMENTS

My sincere gratitude goes to Caroline Oakley, for her thoughtful, forensic editorial eye and for finding the superb cover image. Love and thanks to my wonderful mentor, Janet Thomas, for untangling the early muddle and showing me the story beneath. To the team at Honno, my continued appreciation for your hard work and dedication. Thank you to my sister authors at Honno for being the best gang ever.

My beloveds and cheerleaders remain faithful, kind and generous. Love and thanks, you know who you are.

Thanks and gratitude to the writers and readers I've met through Book Connectors, the brilliant brainchild of Anne Cater. Huge thanks go to the book blogging community and those of you who agreed to be included on the tour for this book. In particular, I want to thank Anne Williams for her continued invaluable support. And a special smiley thank you to Louise Beech and Amanda Jennings for insisting I can write.

Love to Janey Stevens, writing sister and co-conspiritor in the smallest writing group in Wales, who, from the moment she heard the first outline of this story, said it would be published. And for making me look good in photos.

To two of the kindest women in my world, boundless love. My niece, Sally, for her courage and loyalty. And my beloved daughter, Natalie, whose generosity of heart brought back the joy to mine.